# The Siren, the Song, and the Spy

# The Siren, the Song, and the Spy

### MAGGIE TOKUDA-HALL

CANDLEWICK PRESS

This is a work of fiction. Names, characters, places, and incidents are either products of the author's imagination or, if real, are used fictitiously.

Copyright © 2023 by Maggie Tokuda-Hall
Map and wave illustration copyright © 2020 by Rita Csizmadia

All rights reserved. No part of this book may be reproduced, transmitted, or stored in an information retrieval system in any form or by any means, graphic, electronic, or mechanical, including photocopying, taping, and recording, without prior written permission from the publisher.

First edition 2023

Library of Congress Catalog Card Number 2022923583
ISBN 978-1-5362-1805-3

23 24 25 26 27 28 APS 10 9 8 7 6 5 4 3 2 1

Printed in Humen, Dongguan, China

This book was typeset in Warnock Pro.

Candlewick Press
99 Dover Street
Somerville, Massachusetts 02144

www.candlewick.com

*This is still for Clare,
and the adult you've become.*

PART ONE

# The Siren

• PROLOGUE •

# Genevieve

Genevieve was not dead.

Thanks to the Emperor, she was alive. She was aware of her body, which lay on the sand, aware of the sun that cracked her skin. But she could not open her eyes.

Time had gone in all directions, and Genevieve did not know where in its vast landscape she had fallen. Sometimes she was at her mother's dinner table. Then she was back aboard the *Dove*. She had heard the *whumph* of a submerged explosion breaking the surface of the sea. The Lady Ayer called to her and bade she braid her hair. A boy her age held out his hand, his name lost in the blare of cannons and pistols firing.

The wind carried a name: Thistle.

She had not heard it aloud in years. She tried to move her chapped lips around the sound, but all that arose was a hiss. She coughed, her throat dry and aching.

She was alive.

Her survival was not the only impossible thing that had happened. The Imperials had lost. The Emperor's ships capsized and crushed. The Pirate Supreme had escaped the Emperor once again. The Lady Ayer was dead.

The Lady Ayer was dead.

Genevieve had watched it happen, had seen her lady fall. It was the slowest and fastest thing she had ever witnessed: the sudden and terrible explosion of blood at her lady's neck, the inexorable crumple of her body. The great Lady Ayer. The Emperor's greatest spy. She watched it happen again and again, but she could never stop it from happening. Her mentor's blood hung in the air, a fine mist.

Genevieve pushed her fingers into the wet sand. She made a fist. She could hear the Lady's voice in her mind, willing her to move. To open her eyes. She blinked against the blazing sun.

*Sit up*, said the Lady.

Genevieve obeyed her orders, just as she always had. It did not matter if she was dead or alive, real or only in her mind; the Lady Ayer would always be her master, her mentor. Her voice was a comfort and a compass, and Genevieve dearly needed both. Her body screamed in dissent as she sat up, but Genevieve did not listen to it, not even as the world spun around her.

*You need water. All the seawater you swallowed is making you sick. You need fresh water or else you'll die.*

At this, Genevieve let out a mirthless laugh. There was no fresh water here. There was only the stinging seawater and the burning red sand. The laugh turned into another round of racking coughs.

*Where is your pistol?* Genevieve felt down her leg. Still in its holster about her ankle. *Where is your dagger?* She felt her thigh and found the handle of her dagger.

The effort of sitting up, of moving, of coughing had been too much. She lay back down.

*Get up,* said the Lady's voice, but Genevieve could not. Tears did not fall, but she was crying all the same, ashamed of her disobedience. Lady Ayer had taught her better than that.

She saw Rake's face, the face of her countryman, the face of her captor, saw it alight with triumph after he pulled the trigger on the gun that would kill her lady. She could feel her hate like something corporeal, something literally in her belly, heavy and pointed and hot.

Distantly, she could hear laughter, high-pitched and echoing over the dunes. It was Rake, she knew, the Pirate Supreme's man. Rake laughing at the demise of the Emperor's men. Rake laughing at her pain.

"Hey," said a voice. He did not speak the Common Tongue, but Genevieve understood him even if she could not recall which language he spoke. "Hello?"

That accursed laughing, the giggling was closer now, so close she could feel hot gusts of breath against her burning skin. All around her was the stench of blood, of meat gone to rot. She flinched away from the reek of that breath, tried to blink open her eyes once more.

*Your pistol.*

She was in danger. The Lady had taught her to defend herself, and her voice was insistent now, urging her to grab her weapon. Genevieve was no damsel in distress. She had been molded by the Lady Ayer; she was her right hand.

She could see the man only as a shadow that loomed enormous over her, backlit by the cruel sun, which added to her confusion.

There was a man there, but his voice was absent, and the

Lady's voice was there, but she was absent. The world had become nothing but a flurry of noises and shapes and pain, and Genevieve could hardly parse it.

The figure nudged her with his foot, not hard but enough to bring what little remained of her last meal—eaten when? days ago maybe—in Genevieve's belly up and burning through her throat. She retched, and she was distantly aware of his sounds of consternation and disgust. It was, if uncomfortable, also a perfect cover. She curled into herself on one side and let her hand drift to her ankle.

She saw the animal before she saw the man, its great square head too close to her own, sniffing at her with interest. It let out a high giggle, chittering and chilling. She startled away from it, and the animal startled away from her, but not far enough. It bared its teeth at her, and she knew at once where the stench of blood had come from.

*Hyena.* The familiars of Wariuta warriors, the keepers of the Red Shore.

Genevieve remembered. She had seen etchings and paintings of the hyenas: vicious, horrible animals with blood dripping from their maws, their gnashing teeth that could take off a man's leg. When the warriors came of age, they found their familiar, and from then on, the two would be inseparable, and deadly. The warriors of the Red Shore had killed many Imperial men, even if their means were crude. But they did not have pistols. Genevieve's pistol was there, on her ankle. She let her fingers wrap around it.

*It's him or you.*

If this man was a warrior, then he would kill her.

"Are you OK?" he asked. He was easily twice as big as she was. If it came to hand-to-hand, she would lose unless she was extraordinarily lucky or he was extraordinarily stupid. She could not take that chance.

*Shoot.*

With what little strength she had, she turned on the man and pointed her pistol at him. He held his hands up. Genevieve squeezed the trigger.

• CHAPTER 1 •

*Thistle*

For nearly as long as she could remember, it had been Thistle and Dai. Dai and Thistle.

Dai Phan had been Thistle Vo's best friend since their first day of school. Dai had tried to push Thistle into the mud for the crime of being a girl, and, refusing to go down without a fight, Thistle had wrestled him so they both landed in a puddle, leaving them drenched and already in trouble by the time they arrived for class. Sensing that they had met their equals, the two became fast friends after that.

And now, all these years later, they were nearly grown, and often the adults around Gia Dinh wondered when they'd be wed. They were only thirteen, but marriages could be agreed upon around that age, and their close friendship did give rise to the question not *if* their parents would have a conversation about terms but *what* those terms would be. This was the way of things in Quark.

Thistle didn't find the idea of marriage all that appealing, but if she had to be married to anyone, she'd rather it be Dai. That would be fun, at least. And anyway, her mother had made it abundantly clear that she would not let her daughter marry poorly. Dai was a good match and Thistle would be grateful one day for the fine work her mother had done by her when she had a big expensive house full of healthy children and probably even a servant to do some of the cleaning like Dai's mother had.

Thistle did not like this idea, but she knew better than to argue when her mother took that tone, so she tried to push the reluctance deep into her belly, where she stored all her inconvenient thoughts and desires. She liked Dai. There was that. Not like *that*, but a *complete* lack of romantic desire didn't seem to matter when making life choices in Gia Dinh.

Though currently Dai was hard at work being as annoying a husband-to-be as husbands seemed universally to be. He'd promised a big surprise for her that morning and had yet to arrive. It was midday already.

Thistle watched from the kitchen window as the Imperial soldiers marched by. They did this each day at noon, the changing of the guard at the Consulate, and whenever she could, Thistle would wait by the window when the time came. She liked the orderly way their legs moved in unison, the way the golden lion epaulets on their uniforms glinted in the sun.

A new guest would arrive at their house that night. Thistle's mother was off at the market to purchase better-quality ingredients—fresh fish from the rivers, water spinach, and amaranth—than they would ever eat themselves. The stone guesthouse they called home was larger than many other native Quark homes; most of the largest estates had been taken over by Imperial ownership after Quark was colonized. But all the best rooms were reserved for paying guests. Thistle had busted her back this morning getting all the rooms clean as fast as she could so that she'd be ready for Dai's surprise, and now she regretted it. Of course he was late. He was always late.

Finally there was a knock at the door. Thistle ran to it, and there was Dai. But he looked . . . different. His hair, which was always a mess, was neatly combed to one side. And his clothes, which were usually stained with mud or food from the restaurant or Thistle didn't want to know what, were clean. Suspiciously clean.

"What's your deal?" Thistle asked. "You look like a ding-dong."

Dai ran a hand through his hair, mussing it a little. He looked fractionally more like himself. "Whatever. My mom made me do it." He heaved a heavy sigh, then held out one hand to Thistle. Like she was a girl. Like she was a girl he was asking to marry him. "Thistle Vo." His voice dripped with dreary obligation. "Our parents have begun the sacred discussion of terms, and it is upon me, your future husband and keeper, to tell you how glad I am that you will be my . . ." He trailed off. The rest of the script was nauseating, both of them knew that, knew that it was best unsaid. "Anyway, you get it."

Thistle curtsied as she was supposed to, but as soon as she looked up, both she and Dai broke into body-racking laughter. Relief.

"Was this the big surprise? Because I'm not really surprised." Her mother had been in talks casually with Dai's parents for ages and wasn't particularly coy about it. She thought getting married was the best thing Thistle could do with her life. Thistle wanted to disagree, but she also couldn't think of any realistic alternatives.

Anyway, it would have been a lousy surprise.

Dai grinned. "No. It's just why I'm late—Mom made me, like . . ." He motioned to his hair in a dismissive way. "But. I found something," he said. "By the river."

"What?"

Dai didn't answer. He looked over both his shoulders as though someone might be trying to listen in, as though anyone in all the city of Gia Dinh would possibly care what these two thirteen-year-olds were up to, let alone saying. Thistle rolled her eyes. Dai may have been her best friend, but he was certainly prone to theatrics.

"Come on," he said.

He took her hand.

A jolt ran through Thistle. They had never held hands before. In her shock, she did not pull away but rather let herself be led down the cobblestone streets out of town, downhill—past the rice paddies and the farms—to the river. His hand was hot, and he did not let go until they'd arrived. Where his hand had been, a sheen of sweat remained, cold with the sudden exposure to air. The sky had opened into a drizzle, and Thistle could feel her hair flattening against her neck.

"I was down here digging, you know?" Dai's parents owned a small restaurant favored by Imperial officers. The only discernible help Dai ever was to the enterprise was digging up wild root vegetables. Thistle nodded. He led her to a pile of recently overturned dirt. "And. Well. Look."

He started digging with his hands, and Thistle hustled to help him, her curiosity piqued. It was loose and damp, and soon they'd unearthed a plain crate. It was the kind in which goatskins were imported from the Floating Islands. Stacks of them were found all over Gia Dinh. It was hardly newsworthy.

Thistle glared at Dai. "It's a box," she said coolly.

"Open it."

Thistle could see that the crate had been locked—a broken bolt hung from it. She assumed Dai was responsible. Dubiously, she lifted the lid.

Inside, pistols gleamed among boxes of bullets.

Thistle slammed the crate shut, her heart racing.

Guns were not permitted in Quark. They hadn't been since the Colonization. Only Imperial soldiers could carry pistols, and Imperial soldiers did not keep secret weapons caches stowed by rivers—they kept them in the many official military outposts all over the country.

Whoever owned these guns owned them illegally.

"Whose are these?"

He could barely keep the grin from his face. "I think the Resistance is coming back," Dai whispered.

But Thistle did not smile.

◆ CHAPTER 2 ◆

## *Koa*

Koa should have been at the oasis, standing guard. But he couldn't bear to see Kaia squander the current peace. And so he had followed her. Or tried to.

The thing was, Kaia was a better scout than he was. Not just because she was smaller but because she was quicker, too, and silent. She and her familiar, Chima, moved in concert so easily. Not at all like Koa and his hyena, Tupac. The Wariuta said that familiars reflected the souls of their warriors, and maybe that was true. Koa and Tupac were both a little soft around the corners—all goofy and light and nervous giggles. There was nothing severe about either of them, no edge. They both made for poor warriors, a reality Koa had long since made peace with.

Kaia, on the other hand, was born to handle an ax. And Chima, at her side, was born to skulk and stalk and strike. And so his sister and her familiar had easily lost Koa and Tupac within the first hour of his attempt to track them.

Kaia had said she was hunting for weakness to leverage against the Colonizers—not exactly a tall order in her mind, but a dangerous one. And Koa suspected that was only a partial truth.

Still, he had gone where he assumed Kaia had gone: to the shore.

The Wariuta had lost dominion over the shore to the Colonizers. Many long and drawn-out months of battles had led to that, and though no Wariuta liked the arrangement, it was still a relief not to mourn, daily, the warriors and fishermen who'd been killed. And so the Wariuta were not supposed to be on the shore, Kaia especially. As the daughter of and heir to Ica—Koa and Kaia's mother and the leader of the Wariuta warriors—Kaia was too recognizable, too important. If she was spotted by a Colonizer, the tenuous peace that had settled would be destroyed. She knew that! And still she could not help herself ranging down to the shore.

Kaia hated the Colonizers and wanted them gone; that was genuine. No one wanted to fight them as ardently as Kaia did. But Koa knew his sister well, could see the dark corners of doubt behind her bravado. As long as they were at war, Ica would lead. And if Ica led? Kaia would not have to. Despite all her competence and her talent, Kaia was scared by nothing more than the weight of the leadership they all knew she'd carry—of that, Koa was sure. Neither sibling spoke this truth aloud, and neither needed to.

But Koa did not find Kaia on the shore.

Instead, he'd found a foreigner. She'd washed up on the beach like a piece of driftwood, her black hair seeping into the red sand, her pink skin so burnt it looked as if it had been flayed. She was like a gift from the sea. And a gift from the sea, Ica always said, was not to be trusted. Her arms stretched out as if in supplication to a god he did not know, her face turned to the sun.

She lay in the sand, letting the tide roll over her feet and her legs. Around her, jagged pieces of wood stuck out of the ground, remnants of whatever boat she'd been on. All thoughts of finding Kaia evaporated, and Koa rushed to the girl. She would die from exposure if she wasn't dead already. She needed water. She needed shelter. She needed care, and she needed it as soon as possible.

At his side, Tupac giggled in the way all familiars did when they were excited or nervous. They had only just been paired and were both in their youth. Tupac could sense Koa's worry, and Koa reached down and rubbed him behind the ears, feeling the prickle of his coarse fur beneath his fingernails. Tupac's coat had come in with more black spots than those of his siblings, but Koa could still see the likeness. Maybe someday he'd grow into something better than he was. Maybe Koa would, too.

"Come on," Koa said to Tupac. "She needs help."

Stilled by Koa's purpose, Tupac quieted, and the two made their way down the winding, rocky cliffs that abutted the shore.

As he got closer, Koa could see a few things about the girl: For one, she was about the same age as he was, maybe a year or two younger. She was dressed as a Colonizer, but she did not have the complexion of those from Nipran. Her yukata was in tatters, but even so, Koa could tell it had once been expensive.

Most important, he could see that she was still alive. Her chest rose and fell out of cadence with the waves. He ran to her.

He needed to be careful, he knew. Koa wasn't just tall but fat, too. Like his father before him, Koa was one of the largest of the Wariuta. He was easily twice the weight of this girl, and he did not know her. She'd be scared of him. He needed to counter that, needed to be gentle. He'd learned long ago that his big voice could scare those who didn't know him. And so it was in his nicest, most friendly voice that Koa greeted the girl.

She did not stir.

Was she asleep? He nudged her with his foot as delicately as he possibly could. Her body rocked to one side violently, as though he'd punted her, and she vomited onto the sand.

*Cool,* Koa thought. *Great job.*

What would Ica do? His mother had an uncanny sense for how to best handle people, to meet them where they were so she could navigate their needs and the needs of the Wariuta with equal respect. He needed to get this girl to Yunka, where she could be tended to by healers. But it was a long walk to Yunka, and as strong as Koa was, he didn't think he could carry her the whole way. He would if he had to, though. He had enough water on him to make it through the night, and he knew well how to put together makeshift temporary shelters from the cold and the wind. He just needed to get through to this girl!

Lost in his pondering and planning, Koa had not noticed Tupac as he snuffled up to the girl. She let out a yelp of terror and tried her best to scuttle away from him. Thinking she'd just started a fun new game, Tupac smiled his toothy grin and tried to get closer.

This, Koa knew, did nothing to help the girl feel more at ease, and so he called Tupac back. Tupac listened and, with resentful eyes, returned to Koa's side.

"It's OK. He's just curious. He wants to be your friend." Koa tried to comfort the girl, but he could tell his efforts were insufficient. "Are you OK?"

The words were barely out of his mouth before Koa was staring down the barrel of a pistol. Instinctively, Koa took a step back and put his hands up, and in that moment, the girl squeezed the trigger.

Nothing happened.

She squeezed it again and again and then let out a cry of despair. The powder, Koa realized. The gunpowder in the pistol had gotten too wet to ignite. He kept his hands up but took a step closer to the girl.

"I'm not here to hurt you," he said. "But you gotta stop—"

Whatever dignity or reconciliation he had hoped to garner did not come to pass.

He should have heard them coming. Chima's laugh was higher, sharper than Tupac's. But his mind had been on the girl and the pistol, not on the sounds that heralded his sister's approach. Chima charged the girl, snarling and baring her long yellow teeth.

The girl's scream was terrible and piercing even over the roar of the sea.

• CHAPTER 3 •

## *Kaia*

Kaia was only a little surprised when her brother threw his body in Chima's way, forcing the familiar to slam her forepaws into the sand so she wouldn't collide with him. Koa was a trained warrior, as was Kaia. They had not learned to fight for nothing, especially with Colonizers all around them. But he seemed determined to ignore his training, even if it meant shunting the responsibility of keeping him alive onto Kaia's shoulders. Which, of course, she would do, whether it meant sullying her conscience or not. Sometimes loving her brother felt like a curse.

She had watched from her spot in the cliffs as her brother meandered up to the Colonizer, trusting. Despite everything they had done! She would have stopped him then if she'd not been so sure the girl was a corpse. Or maybe it was her anger; he *had* followed her. As if she needed his supervision. But as soon as the girl vomited, Kaia had started moving toward them.

It did not matter how close to death a Colonizer was, they could still spring forth with deadly intent. And Kaia had been right. Koa was just lucky that her pistol was either out of bullets or broken. Kaia had her ax at the ready. She had sharpened it only that morning.

"Kaia!" Koa shouted. "Stop!"

It was no secret among the Wariuta that despite his size, his lineage, and the painstaking training Ica had seen to herself, Koa was a terrible warrior. He had all the wrong instincts. Sometimes the injustice of it rankled Kaia, and she resented her brother for things that were not his fault. He had not decided to be born big and strong. Nor had he decided that her left arm should end below her elbow. But here they were. And somehow she was still the better warrior of the two. She would hate him if she didn't love him so much.

Chima circled the girl, her laugh rising above them, mingling with the violent crash of the sea on the shore. And, giving Chima a wide and reverential berth, Tupac circled, too, his smaller form like a shadow of Chima's. Once the girl was dead, Chima would get first pass at what was left of her. And even if both animals ate well in Yunka, there was no substitute for fresh meat.

It did not take long for Kaia to reach the girl, who crouched, huddled and pathetic, on the sand. Up close, she was so small, so weak—her eyes full of tears, her lips cracked. If Kaia was not mistaken, the girl had pissed herself. It would be a mercy to kill her. Kaia lifted her ax.

But before she could bring it down, Koa caught her by the wrist. Kaia turned on him, her eyes wide with fury. He knew better than to interfere with her. But his jaw was set, his grip firm.

"Don't," he said quietly.

Kaia made to pull her arm from his grip, but Koa would not let go. In all their lives, he had never once stood up to Kaia. If she weren't so angry at him, she would have been proud. Had she not been telling him do to exactly this for years? In his eyes, finally, she could see the fire that forged warriors. Annoyance flickered in Kaia's chest. Why was this the moment he chose to ignite?

"Fine," she spat. She let her arm fall to her side. "But we tie her up. She can't be trusted."

"Fine," he replied.

His voice was tart, and he didn't have to say that this was all Kaia's fault for Kaia to know that was exactly what he thought. And anyway, it wasn't her fault that this was now complicated; they could have executed her and been done with it, and there'd be no reason to lie about where they'd been, where they'd found the girl. So, really, his mercy was the problem.

Kaia stood still as Koa undid the leather straps that crisscrossed her back.

Kaia pointed her ax at the girl. "You're lucky," she said. And even though they did not speak the same language, Kaia could see that the girl understood. She did not try to run again and instead kept a wary eye on the familiars. Chima did a good job looking intimidating, snapping now and again in the girl's direction. Tupac, on the other hand, lolled behind her and stopped, briefly, to lick himself.

"What are we going to tell Mom?" Koa asked.

What he meant was *Are you going to tell her you explicitly disobeyed her command? Again?* Kaia frowned.

"This wouldn't have happened if you hadn't followed me," she muttered.

She yanked the girl to her feet, and Koa, with an apologetic look on his face, bound the girl's wrists.

And, no, she wasn't going to tell Ica the exact truth.

The truth was, Kaia had a lot more at stake than Koa did. If Koa got in trouble, well, who cared? Everyone knew him, everyone loved him. Everyone knew he was a poor excuse for a warrior, knew that Koa's father, Chimu, would have been ashamed to see who his son had turned out to be. And everyone also knew that Ica loved Koa more, even if she had named Kaia her heir. In fact, everyone loved Koa more. Even Kaia. He was lovable. Just. Also really annoying.

"If you promise not to kill her—*or* advocate for her execution—I'll take the fall," Koa said.

His eyes were still on the girl, and Kaia wanted to shake the shit out of him, to yell at him. Colonizers were not friends! But Koa thought everyone was a pal just waiting to happen. If she hadn't known her brother so well, she might have thought he was nurturing a crush. But Koa wasn't like that. His immunity to desire was his greatest strength. That or, perhaps, his negotiation skills.

The girl was getting better than she deserved. For Koa's negotiation on her behalf. That Kaia could not afford to lose face in front of the other warriors again. The last dressing-down Ica had given her had echoed through the ranks for months, it felt like—no one listening to her because she had not listened to her mother. Kaia sighed.

"Here." Kaia thrust her waterskin at the girl. "I'm not hauling your corpse back to Yunka."

The girl drank greedily. Koa watched, smiling. Of course he hadn't thought to bring water with him. Koa was no tactician. But even through her irritation, Kaia was glad he was glad. His happiness was like that. Contagious.

The Colonizer presence had disrupted the relative peace not only of the Wariuta but of their family, too. Ica was forever occupied and defensive. When she did speak to her daughter, she was prone to lectures and admonishment. Kaia could not remember the last time her mother had simply listened. And the normal placid playfulness that rested between Koa and Kaia was constantly strained; Koa, true to Koa's form, thought a live-and-let-live arrangement was perfectly viable.

Kaia did not agree.

She looked at the Colonizer girl. She would need healers' attention for her skin, which was ruined. It'd take at least a few days of constant salve application. Pathetic. How was it possible that a people so ill-equipped for the world had managed to conquer it?

She stood before her and waited until the girl's eyes met hers. It did not take long. The girl had a steel spine, at least. She looked into Kaia's eyes without blinking, and Kaia could see fire there.

"If you try anything," Kaia said, "I will kill you without hesitation." Behind her, Chima giggled high and loud, and the girl swallowed but did not break eye contact. "Do you understand me?"

And though the girl did not respond, Kaia knew she had understood.

Kaia, none too gently, pushed the girl forward with the tip of her ax.

• CHAPTER 4 •

*Florian*

Florian let his fingers entwine with Evelyn's hair. He tried to let his mind rest. Above them, the moon's silver light filtered through the constant motion of the Sea. If he focused his eyes, if he really tried, he could see the cold pricks of starlight. But why would he?

Curled in his arms, Evelyn traced shapes Florian did not recognize on his chest. He had not known life could be like this: safe, calm. Quiet, not as in silence, or as in stealth, but as in quiescent. As in peace. As in contentedness.

They lay nestled in a soft bank of sand at the base of a great kelp forest. It was a spot Evelyn had quickly come to favor, since so many otters fed there. Together, they watched the otters as they dove and hunted and played, their little faces alight with mischief and mirth. They made Evelyn laugh, which made Florian laugh, and so they returned often.

"Do you remember day?" Florian asked. "The sun, that heat."

"I do," Evelyn replied. She pulled herself up, and Florian immediately regretted asking, for they were no longer touching. But he did not pull her down to his side. Evelyn smiled at him, and he smiled back. How could he explain to her that she was like the sun now? The thing that burned bright and beautiful and necessary and warm in his life? She leaned down, gave him a kiss on his forehead. "But I do not miss it."

"Nor I." An incomplete answer.

What was the sun in Florian's life, except a reminder that another day had passed him by? So many days he had awakened in Crandon to the cold white light of another day breaking, and he knew he would need to find food, shelter, a coin if he could. Sunrise had been just the opening shot of daily battle. And though he mostly felt so far away from those days, still there were moments when his mind would return, as if the tide of his thoughts could not help but bear back ceaselessly. Happiness, he was learning, did not guarantee forgetting.

"How long have we been here?" Evelyn mused.

Florian followed her gaze upward, where the shadow of a great ship had, for a moment, eclipsed the moonlight.

"I don't know," Florian said. Time no longer passed in days but in great swaths—the time they spent with the humpback whales. The era of manta rays that passed overhead like great birds.

"Do you ever wonder what happened?"

Evelyn did not need to clarify. Days or months or minutes ago, Florian had become a child of the Sea, left his brother and Rake behind to fight a war that was still raging. Above them, the Emperor's men still hunted the Pirate Supreme. On the Floating Islands, a witch remained with all of Flora's secrets. On the Red Shore, enslaved people waited for freedom that would likely never come. In Crandon, there was always cruelty, always heartbreak. All the Known World still squirmed beneath the Nipran Empire's fist.

Distance, Flora was learning, did not guarantee forgiveness.

What was Alfie doing now? she wondered. Was he safe without Flora there to watch over him? Would Rake keep his word and protect him? She trusted Rake with her own life, but she was less sure she trusted him with Alfie's. They had never shared the same bond. And besides, they were up against more than anything Rake could take on alone. The Empire of Nipran had crushed thousands of men just like them in a single breath and never stopped once to wonder at what it had done. The thought caught in her throat, and she felt sick.

Was her life truly so separate from all that now?

Flora pushed her worries down as best she could. Time may have passed, but not so much that she could not recall how to feed herself with her own fear. *Let it nourish me,* she thought. *Let it pass through me.*

"No," Flora lied. "I don't."

Evelyn watched her with a curious face. Then, with one finger, she touched the crease between Flora's eyebrows that formed when she was worried.

"Liar," she whispered.

◆ CHAPTER 5 ◆

*Koa*

Ahead of them, Chima and Tupac led the way back to Yunka. Chima in the lead, of course. She was bigger and dominant over Tupac, who seemed to want both to be as close as possible to her and to stay clear of her powerful jaws.

The girl fell again, her feet unsure in the sinking sand of the dunes. Koa tried to offer his hand to help her up, but she ignored him, and Kaia scoffed at him, and so Koa chuckled, because what else could he do? He'd take the blame for Kaia's disobedience, and everyone in town would think, *Oh, that Koa, he's a lovable idiot*, and no one would know that he, too, had the Wariuta's best interests in mind. And both the girls were treating him like he was either diseased or stupid even as he saved them both, in his way. If he didn't laugh, he'd scream.

He knew that with the Colonizers, the men were in charge. It was mostly men who came to Puno. And while Koa, like all the Wariuta, regarded all Colonizers with equal parts pity, fury, and disgust, he did wonder sometimes what it would be like to be listened to. To be taken seriously. Like his father had been. It was not that Wariuta men never led, but it wasn't a given the way it was with the Colonizers. He had no urge to lead. But it would be nice, he thought, to be listened to.

But the thought was gone as quickly as it had arrived, and Koa went back to wondering what would become of the pink girl he'd found. And just how much trouble he'd be in. And if she'd receive the healing she obviously needed. And where she'd sleep.

He'd offer her space in his hut, except he was pretty sure that—given the opportunity—the girl would stab him in his sleep. Which, he thought, was fair enough. As far as she knew, she was just a prisoner.

As far as Koa knew, too, he supposed.

He smelled Yunka before he saw it, smelled the smoke of cook fires, the warm scent of roasted meat rising in the wind. The girl was likely hungry, and he was glad the wait for food would be short. Though she should receive attention from the healers first.

"You'll eat soon enough." Kaia gave him a withering look, her face smug.

Koa tried his best to ignore the sting of hurt her words brought, but he failed. He wasn't even hungry; he was just worried for the girl. Kaia knew that. She was angry with him—for what? taking her blame? being right?—and lashing out, as was her way. She wanted him to be as sour as she felt. The only thing Koa could really do was refuse to take the bait, so he smiled at his sister until she—reluctantly—smiled back.

"Sorry," she said at last.

When Koa smiled again, it was for real.

He turned and walked backward so he could try to make friendly eye contact with the girl. "Do you smell that?" he asked her. "The night meal'll be ready when we arrive in Yunka. Do you eat cows where you're from?"

He didn't expect answers, and he was given none. Still, he wanted the girl to hear his voice, as soothing and as affable as he could make it. He smiled his big smile, the smile that made Kaia laugh, but the girl didn't smile back. That was OK. He wouldn't want to smile, either, if he were her.

"I really don't think we need to keep her tied up," Koa said to Kaia. "She hasn't tried to run for hours."

Which was true. After the one time, the girl had not tried to bolt again. Koa would not have tried twice, either. Chima had chased her down, and the girl had shrieked in terror at the sight of her jaws. Koa may not have screamed if faced with Chima, but he certainly understood being fearful of the creature. Chima was young, but her forelegs were already burly with taut muscles. He looked to Kaia hopefully.

But Kaia just gave him a poisonous glare and yanked the girl forward for good measure. She staggered but couldn't quite brace herself properly before hitting the ground. When she stood again, half of her face was coated in the red sand of his home. She spat a mouthful of it out and coughed, a horrible, dry, hacking cough. She needed more water. Koa winced apologetically at her and offered her the waterskin. He tried to look small as he handed it to her. He thought small thoughts. But she flinched away from it and didn't accept it. She looked to the ground.

Which was too bad. First, she was dehydrated, and badly. But also, Yunka was beautiful as it rose over the dunes. The fires flickered orange in the dwindling light of day. The huts leaned together like the people who lived within leaned on one another, each dwelling as individual and unique as the person who owned it. It was lovely the way nothing was exactly the same, the way each hut was built to its own dimensions, took its own shape. And there, in the distance, the bathing pools shone with the bleeding rays of the sunset. Koa wished the girl would look up, see where she was headed, see what he saw. How could any place so beautiful be frightening?

Nearing the town, both Chima and Tupac sprinted ahead of the group until they were just black dots in the darkening landscape. Perhaps with the animals gone, the girl would be less afraid. If only for the remainder of their walk.

"See?" he asked her. "Yunka. You'll like it."

The girl did not meet his eyes or respond. But she did look into the distance at Yunka. He wondered what she was thinking, wondered if she thought it was beautiful, as he did. He hoped so.

Wariuta cities were as varied as the people who lived there. In Puno, he knew, the houses were built of stone. In Nema, on the far lakes, the houses were built into trees, and fishermen hung their lines from their balconies at night. But Yunka was special. He would have chosen it as his home even if he had not been born there.

"The best city in the world," Koa said. He meant it.

"How would you know?" Kaia snapped.

Koa watched her back as she made her way to the city he loved and she resented, his lips pressed into a thin line of irritation.

Someday, he hoped, she would appreciate what they already had.

He reached out a hand to help the girl, but she gave him a quick, hateful glance that made it clear she did not need or desire assistance and made her way on her own.

• CHAPTER 6 •

*Kaia*

Ica already sat in her place before the bonfire that raged in the center of Yunka. At her side, her hyena, Puka, groomed herself with long, steady strokes of her thick pink tongue. Kaia had hoped that maybe she would catch her mother without the whole town watching, but no such luck. She braced herself at the trouble her brother would surely be in and stepped forward into her mother's view, dragging the girl in her wake.

Not long ago, Wariuta were split into townships, each with their own leadership and rules. But when the Colonizers came, the necessity for unity had arisen. No one was confident that anyone could lead the once-disparate groups, but Ica had won leadership through her cunning and also her strength—she was undoubtedly Yunka's finest warrior, but she was known to be merciful, too. So nearly all the former foes had raised their fists for her, and Ica had led all the Wariuta ever since.

They had lost Puno, though. Ica blamed herself—she thought the years of violent conflict between Yunka and Puno had soured their relationship past the point of any potential reconciliation.

Violent conflict that, in her youth, Ica had often led, often instigated. But Kaia knew better. The greed of the Colonizers was a contagion, as infectious and terrible as the sores and fevers that often came with them. The Wariuta of Puno were no different from all the others who had been colonized before them. But she'd die before she let Yunka go the same way.

Ica's silver eye glinted in the firelight. Long before Kaia had been born, Ica had lost that eye in battle. A scar from where her opponent's battle ax had nearly ended her life cut a straight line from her hairline to her chin. But she was still sharp-eyed, even in her older age. And so it did not take long for her to spot her daughter, and the prisoner she had with her.

Following Ica's gaze, Puka regarded the prisoner with a curl of her lip, letting out one whoop into the night. Like her master, Puka had lost one eye in battle and, like her master, had a silver eye in its stead. The mirroring of their eyes, the Wariuta said, spoke of the divine relationship the two shared—as the finest fighter and the most ferocious familiar that lived.

Ica stood and motioned to the girl.

"Who is this you've brought us?" she asked. At the sound of her voice, the rest of the Wariuta hushed, their eyes all pointed at Kaia and Koa. Without looking, Kaia could feel Koa shrink under their collective gaze. He hated to be looked at. Not Kaia. She stood with her chin up, meeting her mother's eye. Someday she would lead these people. She needed them to know that she would do so with courage, just as her mother had.

"A prisoner, Mother. Found on the shore." Kaia yanked the leather straps, forcing the girl to step forward. She could see the suspicion creep across her mother's face as she beheld the girl's pink skin.

"She needs the healers," Koa chimed in. "She was shipwrecked and nearly dead when I found her."

"Shipwrecked?" Ica's voice was like the pass of metal over a whetstone. She took a step toward her children and their prisoner, and even in the darkness, her might was obvious. She wore the same leather tunic of all the people in her town. Yet on Ica, it looked like armor. Pride swelled in Kaia's chest, forcing the curl of a smile to her lips. For all their differences, she knew that the best of her came from her mother.

"Tell me, my son. What were you doing on the shore?"

Koa did not answer. Ica looked to Kaia, who said nothing. Kaia could feel her mother's eye as if it were boring through her.

"My mistake is not this girl's fault," Koa said at last. His voice was stronger now, and Kaia fought the urge to encourage him in any way. He needed to stand up on his own if he would ever garner respect and not just affection. "We know nothing of her, and yet we treat her as a prisoner?" He looked around at the gathered Wariuta, meeting the eyes of his people.

Ica nodded. "You make a kind point, son. But this is no Wariuta girl you have brought to us. She hasn't earned our trust."

"I will," the girl said. Her voice quavered, but her words were clear. Kaia whirled on her. She could speak their language? Why hadn't she said anything? What trickery was this? "If you will hear my story."

Ica looked to Kaia, who tried with her eyes to tell her mother that she had no idea the girl could speak the Sky Tongue.

"Go on, then." Ica leaned forward, and Puka did, too.

The girl eyed the animal with visible fear. She took a deep breath.

"My name is Genevieve," she said haltingly. "I am on a ship that did battle with the Pirate Supreme. We lose. My lady killed. I"—her voice cracked—"am not. I am in the sea, and now I am here. I am not bad. I want to survive."

Ica nodded. "How is it that you speak our tongue, girl?"

Many merchants and pirates spoke the Sky Tongue, but that was from multiple visits. It was clear from the girl's evident fear of the familiars that this was her first time among the Wariuta.

Genevieve bowed her head. "My lady says education is speaking many of languages," she said. "She tells me great things of Wariuta. You raise cattle from dust. Your alchemists have no equal in the Known World."

"Ah." Ica's face hardened.

The girl had said the wrong thing. Kaia smiled to herself.

Colonizers had long wanted to know the secrets the Wariuta alchemists kept. They made salves that cured wounds, oils that burned for days without depleting. And, probably of the most interest to the Colonizers, a brutal explosive called kau. But the Wariuta had no intention of sharing their secrets with those who showed so little regard for life.

Koa sensed the change in his mother's disposition as well. "Are you here," he asked the girl carefully, "to colonize?"

Genevieve mulled the question over carefully in her mind. "I am sorry," she said. "I do not know that word."

At this there was a murmuring among the gathered Wariuta. Koa looked triumphant.

Kaia had had enough. "Her ignorance isn't evidence against malice. When has a Colonizer's ignorance ever limited his destruction?"

The murmuring grew louder. Kaia did not let herself meet Koa's eyes, even though she could feel the heat of his gaze on the side of her face like flames. He was too soft for this conversation, too weak. His kindness—regardless of the situation—was like an open door to pain, and Kaia meant to close it. It was possible to be Koa, to be so sweet, and not also be easy prey. He needed to learn this. Kaia had to protect him and her people. The deal they had made was aside from all that.

"You say your lady was doing battle against the Pirate Supreme," Ica pressed. "Tell us why."

A flicker passed over the girl's expression. Kaia could see it for what it was. Guile.

"To end the slave trade."

But that wasn't the whole truth, and Kaia knew it. The girl knew that Kaia knew it. She could see her eyes dart to Kaia and then back to Ica.

"See?" Koa asked a little desperately. "Let's show her that we are better than the Colonizers. Let's give her safe quarter. Perhaps she can be of some use. You speak Colonizer, too, yeah?"

Genevieve cocked her head a little, confused. "I speak the Common Tongue. And the tongues of Tustwe, Iwei, and the Floating Islands."

Kaia felt her heart fall into her belly. If there was anything the Wariuta genuinely needed from an outsider, it was someone who could speak the many languages that arrived on their shore. Though several of the merchants surely spoke the Colonizers' language, none wished to stand between them and the Wariuta. And in this regard, the pirates were doubly useless.

Koa had won, and she knew it. Koa knew it. All the gathered Wariuta knew it.

Ica turned on her son then, her face hard. "I wish I could trust you to guard this girl," she said. "But your heart is too soft, and until we know if we can trust her, you will see to her care and comfort only."

Kaia knew what was coming before it did. She closed her eyes as if she could guard against it, but it still came.

"And you, my daughter," Ica said, "will be responsible for her security."

"Of course, Mother." She shot Genevieve a look of pure venom. "I'll keep a very close watch on her."

But when she met Genevieve's eyes, she did not see fear anymore. The girl was smug in her victory.

That was fine.

Kaia could change that.

• INTERLUDE •

# The Sea

*At night, she comes alive. Everywhere the hum of life, the buzz of activity.*

*The Sea hears it all, but she listens to her mermaids.*

*The Sea knows her children all, and she sighs for her newest pair, her happiest. They are so small. How can she tell her children that love may not be enough?*

*In a kelp forest, a bioluminescent speck floats through Florian's outstretched fingers, and his eyes follow it as it illuminates the deep lines in the palm of his hand. Those lines look like great chasms in the world of that little glowing speck.*

*How can she tell her children of scale; how they are like the speck in the palm of her great hand? How she is like that speck in the great canvas of time?*

*Close to a harbor for merchant vessels off the coast of Crandon, a small, slippery seal darts directly into a fisherman's careless net. This is happening and concerns her, and yet it is also happening and will continue to happen without her interference. How can she tell her children of priorities or impossible choices?*

*On the Red Shore, the child from Quark has made it to land, and perhaps to safety. The Sea cannot know, not now that the child's so far from what she can see. How could she explain to her Pirate Supreme that she saved this child but not so many of their men? Just one of countless choices she makes in an instant, every instant of every day of every era, unending. There is no rest for the Sea, no respite, just a world that keeps violently ending and perpetually continuing.*

*She has begged her daughters to keep to the deeps, to find the trenches and the canyons. How can she tell them that their sisters, her daughters—her daughters whom she swears always to protect—are being murdered not one by one but en masse now? How can she explain such wanton destruction?*

*If she once had the words for this, she has lost them along with her murdered children. She knows, in some distant part of her mind, that the Empire of Nipran is responsible, but she cannot always hold this fact in her memory. Her grip on this truth slips, fades, is transformed into all humans. With their avarice and their greed and their unending propensity for violence.*

*She awaits the Pirate Supreme's call, but she cannot hear them.*

*And she fears they have forgotten her.*

• CHAPTER 7 •

*Thistle*

The walk back from the river was an odd one. Clearly hurt that Thistle did not share his enthusiasm for the totally illegal guns, Dai had been cold and testy the whole walk back. Annoyed that he had made her a criminal by proxy—knowing there were guns was a crime against the Imperials in and of itself, and snitching would make her a criminal against Quark just the same—Thistle did not have the energy or inclination to soothe him. Instead, they'd stalked back in heavy silence.

A bad omen for their eventual marriage.

When she returned to the house, her mother was a whirlwind of activity. Their guest would be there shortly, so Thistle was rushed off to wash her face and comb her hair and change her clothes and otherwise make herself look respectable and presentable, which she did without argument. She needed a moment alone.

Still marveling at what a strange day it had been, Thistle stood by the door and waited for the guest as her mother had bidden her do. Her name was Lady Minami, apparently, and Thistle was to be on her absolute finest behavior. They'd never had a *lady* stay with them before. If this went well, Mrs. Vo said breathlessly, perhaps there would be more.

Unspoken: *So don't mess this up.*

For the second time that day, there was a highly anticipated knock on the door, which Thistle answered with a deep, Imperial bow.

"Welcome to our humble domicile, Lady Minami. We hope you find it and our hospitality to your liking." She looked up and felt the breath catch in her throat.

The Lady Minami was tall and imposing, unlike any person she'd ever seen in Quark. Her hair was knotted in a complicated pattern on top of her head, her back straight, her eyes sparkling yet impassive. She wore a corseted kimono in the Imperial style, of course, but hers had thin gold thread woven into its pattern of flowers so that it glinted in the early-evening light. She smiled.

"You must be Thistle Vo." She made a quick motion with her hand, and two young Imperial soldiers bustled into the house. Each carried several bags. Thistle motioned to them where their rooms were, and they sped off, needing little help from her.

"Yes, milady."

"My lady," the Lady Minami corrected, but in a gentle tone. "I hear you are to be wed."

Thistle looked at her feet, embarrassed on a multitude of fronts.

"Lady Minami!" Mrs. Vo bustled into the room and bowed low, her back curved incorrectly. Thistle could tell from the way the Lady Minami's eyes tracked her mother that she had noticed this and didn't approve. She surely did not approve of her thin black hair tied in a low tail at her neck, either, or the shabbiness of her dress. Or Thistle's dress, for that matter. How had Thistle never noticed how . . . poor they were?

"Please," her mother said. "Come. I have dinner all set for you."

The Lady Minami gave a small tilt to her head, the bow of a superior to an inferior, and followed Mrs. Vo into what now was, in Thistle's opinion, a completely inadequate dining room.

Her mother had set the table with their best porcelain bowls, with the actual silver. It was not often she turned the key to the cupboard that stored all their finest dishes. A bottle of rice wine sat to the side of a sparse bouquet of her mother's favorite purple flowers.

"My goodness," said Lady Minami. It was not that the woman was beautiful but that each detail that comprised her whole was expertly chosen to communicate her wealth and class. Thistle catalogued her every sartorial choice and stored them away for future reference. "Quite the spread."

Thistle, who had never even imagined a lady of such . . . ladyness, was at a loss for words. All thoughts of Dai and the guns faded as she stared, open-mouthed, at the goddess who had just materialized in her home. The Lady regarded her with a warm but amused smile, her black eyes twinkling.

"Such lovely flowers," the Lady added. Finally, Thistle recognized that she had been prompted to speak—several times now—and, not wanting to seem dense, she shook herself back into the world of the living. And the cognizant.

"They're thistles!" Thistle blurted. Her voice was altogether too loud. "For me. Or my mother, really. They're her favorite flowers. Because my name. That's why she named me that. But be careful and don't touch them. They've got spines. Not terrible ones, but they're very. Poky." She was rambling, and she knew it, but at least she'd mastered the volume of her voice now. She wanted to close her eyes against the shame of acting such a fool in front of such an illustrious guest, but the woman emitted a tinkling laugh. It was a friendly sound, high and light.

"They're almost as lovely as you are," she said.

Thistle loved the way she spoke, each word precise. She grinned at the compliment.

"Mm. You are too kind to us, Lady Minami," Mrs. Vo said quietly. There was an ice in her voice that Thistle did not recognize, nor did she like it. Was she trying to mess this up?

"Is there a specific seat I should take?" the Lady asked after some time.

"Oh! Right!" Thistle led the Lady to the nicest spot, the one with the only nonlumpy pillow. "Here, my lady." Thistle took care to enunciate both *my* and *lady*.

The Lady nodded her approval and gracefully swept into her seat, the silk of her kimono soundless with her movement. She sat, as Imperials did, with her knees discreetly tucked under her. Thistle made a mental note to sit this way from now on.

Mrs. Vo poured the Lady Minami some rice wine. "What business do you have in Gia Dinh?" she asked.

"Just some shopping," Lady Minami said. She flashed a small smile. "Quark does have all the best soaps in the Known World, after all."

Mrs. Vo gave a polite smile, but Thistle could see the flicker of suspicion across her mother's face. She hoped it was subtle enough that the Lady did not see it, too. Dinner passed without any egregious faux pas, and just after it, the Lady Minami excused herself to bed.

As they washed the many dishes from the evening, Thistle noticed her mother's brow furrowed in worry.

"What's wrong?" Thistle took a clean plate from her mother and started to dry it.

"Nothing—just. Nothing." She sighed, looking behind her as though someone might be in the doorway. There was no one there. She leaned in close to Thistle so that their foreheads nearly touched. "Watch your mouth around this one."

"Lady Minami?" Thistle tilted her head, a little surprised. Hadn't everything gone well?

"She's not . . . hmm." They could both hear the Lady moving about upstairs in her room. Mrs. Vo took a deep breath, then continued in a hurried whisper: "I don't believe she's told us the whole truth about her visit here. And it's been my experience that one should never trust an Imperial who's clearly keeping secrets."

Thistle nodded, but she didn't understand.

It had been a very long day of not understanding things.

◆ CHAPTER 8 ◆

*Koa*

When Koa was a boy, his father had told him that one day a girl would come back to his hut with him and everything would change, and he'd become a man.

Clearly, he had not imagined it'd go like this.

Genevieve had pushed herself to the very wall of the hut, her eyes darting between Koa and Kaia with undisguised hatred. Kaia was taking the downtime to sharpen her ax, which was unnecessarily menacing and annoying. First of all, she'd sharpened it, like, the day before. And also it made it harder for Koa to braid her hair because she was constantly shifting around. Her braids were loose because of it, and Koa figured that was what she deserved.

"She speaks our language," Kaia said. "Think she can fight like us, too?"

Koa rolled his eyes. Everything with Kaia was a fight. It was the worst side effect of her training, like the only tool she understood how to use was her ax.

"She's our guest," Koa said. His voice was quiet but, he hoped, also firm. He was not interested in Kaia starting another fight in general, and he was extra not interested in her starting a fight in his hut. "There's no reason to be rude."

"Do you remember the first Colonizers that came?" Kaia asked. Of course he didn't. They had come before either of them had been born. But he had heard the stories. All the warriors of Pilau, massacred. Over a quibble about fishing boats. "They were guests of the Wariuta once, too."

"That was years ago." He did not like the waver in his own voice, the weakness of it. He hated the way Kaia could bring that out in him, and he hated that Genevieve could hear it. He felt his cheeks prick hot and stupid, and he hastily completed Kaia's braid.

"Do you think they have fundamentally changed in the years since?" Kaia asked. "Or do you think this girl is the same as all the other grasping, ugly little foreigners who come to our land to get sunburnt and rich?"

"Please do not talk like I am not hearing," Genevieve said, her voice quiet.

"I bet she can't," Kaia said, as if to no one but clearly to Genevieve. "Fight, that is. I hear all those Colonizer women just lounge about all day, waiting in their big cold homes for the men to come home and lie with them."

"Kaia," Koa hissed.

Why did she always need to start shit? What good would it do her? Do anyone? She was supposed to be a leader, not a stupid kid itching for a fight. She was supposed to be better. She was better than he was in so many ways. How come she was so small in this one regard? Was she really that scared?

"My lady," Genevieve bit out, "is a great warrior."

"Was," Kaia corrected. She wore a snake's smile.

"Kaia!" Koa stood. He didn't know what to do, but he had the sense that he needed to stop whatever was about to happen from happening.

"What?" Kaia said. "Our tongue can be difficult to master. I'm just helping the girl with her grammar so she doesn't look like a complete fool in front of the others." She gave Genevieve a deeply condescending smile. "It'll be our little secret."

"I do not know this word," Genevieve said slowly.

"What, *fool*? It means—"

"Someone new to our land and our language and our customs who is still learning, that's all!" Koa interjected. He gave one of Kaia's braids a gentle tug, a nonverbal *Please, for the love of all things good and nice in our world, shut up.* Kaia shrugged in a completely transparent *Whatever you say* gesture that only a real fool would have missed.

"I do not think this is true," said Genevieve. Her expression was unreadable. "I think she calls me stupid."

"Not just you, to be clear," Kaia said. "Your entire empire. From your dead lady to your emperor, wherever he sits ordering his minions to our nation just to ruin our lives." She paused, examined her nails. "But I guess especially you."

Koa might have missed it if he had not been watching Genevieve so closely, so concerned for her hurt feelings; and though he saw it, he was utterly powerless to stop it.

In a lightning-fast, practiced motion, Genevieve pulled a dagger from her thigh and flung it at Kaia. It landed in the packed-dirt floor of his hut with a reverberating thud that stole the breath from Koa's chest. Next to Kaia but not *in* Kaia. For a moment, both Kaia and Koa simply blinked at the dagger. Then Kaia pulled it from the ground with what, Koa could see, was more effort than she had anticipated. A very thin trickle of blood dripped down Kaia's thigh where the blade had just barely grazed her.

"Only 'fool' leaves an enemy armed," Genevieve said coolly. "This is something my lady teaches me long ago. Perhaps a lesson you will not forget?"

"You," Kaia roared. She was on her feet, her hand raised and ready to strike, but Koa was ready, too.

"Whoa!" Koa crooned as if he were trying to calm an ornery bull. He was glad in moments like this for how big he was. He could physically block the women from each other by merit of size. "Hey, now. Let's all just take it easy, huh?" He tried to ignore the sweat that rolled down his face and back. "Have some chicha drink?" His mind raced, desperately trying to find purchase on something pleasant, something nice they could do that didn't require any weapons. "I'll rebraid your hair! You were moving around so much that I did a crap job and we both know it."

Kaia lowered her hand. She was still furious, but Koa knew there was some part of her that was aware she should not kill Genevieve, however much she'd like to. It'd cause hell with their mother, and though he knew well Kaia was not afraid of him, she did still fear Ica. She regarded her brother coolly.

There was a horrible beat of silence during which Koa had a seemingly infinite amount of time to picture the many courses of action Kaia might take next that would end in blood and death and suffering. He could only hope that Kaia's fear of Ica's authority would hold strong against her desire to fight the Colonizers.

"Give me the dagger, Kaia," Koa said. He was proud of the steadiness in his voice. How firm he was despite the wiggling doubt in his belly.

Kaia glared at Genevieve.

Genevieve glared at Kaia.

"Please."

"I could kill you with your own weapon," Kaia yelled at

Genevieve. "Only a fool would throw her weapon into her enemy's hand for pride's sake. But I suppose only the gun was worth anything to your kind, and yours is rusting on the shore."

"You will not kill me," Genevieve replied. "You need me."

Kaia spat on the ground, then tucked the dagger into her belt and, much to Koa's relief, sat back down.

"I want four braids this time," she said to Koa. "And make them tight."

• CHAPTER 9 •

*Kaia*

Ica walked steadily.

Kaia stumbled.

She was glad to see her mother's back, to know that Ica did not witness how gracelessly her daughter followed her lead, even if she knew their forebears saw. That could not be helped. The forebears saw all, and most clearly in the Canyon.

The narrow path into the Canyon of the Moon was treacherous even in the day. The cliffs were steep and falls fatal. But for those who sought wisdom, the trip had to be made at night. Throughout Kaia's childhood, Ica went alone, but as Kaia had gotten older, Ica brought her more and more. The invitations always filled Kaia with equal parts pride and dread. The path was not the only thing terrifying about the Canyon of the Moon.

Kaia knew why they went. They were losing the war.

They had lost the mountain city of Puno when Kaia was a child. More recently the shore. And now they had a Colonizer in their midst, and while Koa may have been hopeful for what Genevieve could offer, Kaia knew better. The girl was a snake. Kaia still had her dagger in her belt. She would die before she gave it back. She felt her hand reach for it involuntarily, checking to make sure it was still there. As if a dagger could protect her from what she might see tonight.

Elders visited the Canyon of the Moon to seek the wisdom of the forebears. It was where the veil that kept the dead and living apart was the thinnest, where those who came with pure hearts could seek answers in their times of need. The answers were not always encouraging, but they were always true. Kaia hoped that tonight they would help her mother see reason. To guide her away from her guilt, and to remind her of the powerful warrior she had always been. The one Kaia had always looked up to. The one who had taught her to live with courage.

Ica's familiar, Puka, led the way. Her enormous haunches relaxed even as she traversed the perilous terrain. Whereas Yunka was nestled into the red sand of the shore, the Canyon of the Moon was carved straight out of the moon-white rocks left by volcanoes long since sleeping. The Canyon of the Moon had been there ever since the first of the Wariuta had found this land. It was the most sacred space for her people.

Behind Kaia, Chima followed at a short distance. She could tell her familiar was as frightened as she was. The relationship between warriors and their familiars was an intensely intimate one; it was said that the familiar's personality was a portent of the warrior's destiny. And so far, that bore out for Kaia. Chima was small. She would never be as big as Puka or as strong. But she was fierce and stubborn. Kaia had seen flares of red-hot anger in her familiar, and it had been like watching herself. The animal was powerful, despite her size. Kaia was, too.

She waited a beat so Chima could catch up to her, and she rubbed behind the hyena's ear. Chima growled quietly, reassured.

"We're almost there," Kaia whispered.

A whoop from up ahead told her that Puka had reached the Canyon. Kaia swallowed her unease. She was aware of every breath she took, could hear the rush of blood in her ears.

Her mother waited for her at the entrance to the Canyon. She stood nearly a head higher than her daughter, and her hands were rough from years of handling a spear. Kaia would never be Ica. Ica was a legend. Kaia liked to tell herself that she had squared herself with this years ago, but the truth of it still made her stomach turn over. Someday, when the war was done, she would likely ascend and lead the Wariuta. If it had not been for the war, the vote may have been taken already. And everyone knew Kaia would be the presumptive winner, when the time came.

What would happen, she wondered, if she failed?

Ica squeezed Kaia's shoulder.

"When we walk into the Canyon of the Moon," Ica said, "we walk in with our minds clear."

Kaia made to keep going. But Ica did not move. She looked at Kaia as she so rarely did these days—as her daughter, not as her protégé. Kaia fought the urge to hug her, to let her mother's arms fall around her like a spell of protection, like she was still a child scared of the dark.

"You can do this."

Kaia nodded. She was only sixteen, but her childhood had ended long ago. War had seen to that. Whether she could or not, she *had* to do this.

She watched as her mother's figure cut a straight line down the rocks to the bed of the Canyon. It was as if the Canyon had been made for her, cut to her dimensions. It was the only place where a person as powerful as her mother made sense. As if her mother had been carved from the very same rock.

Kaia followed carefully, more mindful of her feet now.

In the center of the Canyon, equidistant from the great rocky cliffs that rose on either side, was the firepit. Who had dug it, no one knew. Who had lit the fire, none could say. But the fire there never extinguished, no matter the rains or the wind. It had been burning for as long as the Wariuta had been on this land; legend said the first Wariuta explorer who had disembarked her canoe and called this land her own had lit the flame. And there Ica sat, waiting for her daughter, Puka at her side. In the firelight, their twin silver eyes glinted.

Kaia took her place across the fire from her mother. As Ica prepared for the ceremony, Kaia watched as the moon moved into place overhead. When it was directly over the fire, it would be time.

Stars appeared as the sky darkened, each a cold pinprick in the heavens. Kaia knew, as all the Wariuta knew, that the stars were like the firepit—great fires that burned eternal. But while the firepit showed the future, the stars were so far away that by the time they appeared in the night sky, those who looked upon them with wisdom knew they looked upon the past.

A satisfied growl from Puka told them all it was time.

Ica passed Kaia the cup full of tea she had steeped in the firepit. It was a mixture of calafate root and dried mushroom stems. Kaia winced as the hot liquid burned her throat.

"Slowly," said Ica. She sipped her own tea methodically, silently, her chin tilted toward the sky.

The roots in the tea tasted of wood and sick and ants. As Ica and Kaia drank the tea, the shadows cast by the ancient fire sent strange shapes dancing across the cliffs. In them, Kaia knew, they would see their answers. If they looked hard enough. If their minds were clear and their hearts were pure, they would see. As ever, she prayed she would not disappoint her mother, her people. Herself.

Time dilated.

Kaia saw the night sky in fast motion, the night turning to day turning back to night, stars falling and blinking out as new ones shot across the sky, only to recede back into clouds that rushed with unfelt wind. There was a part of her that knew, rationally, that perhaps only a few minutes had passed, but the part of her that mattered, the part of her that saw through her eyes and smelled through her nose and felt through her fingertips, no longer lived time in a straight line. No matter how many times she did the ceremony, Kaia did not think she would ever grow accustomed to the strangeness of it.

When she looked down at Chima, her familiar's eyes were two bottomless black pools that contained all her anxieties: That she was unfit to lead. That she could never live up to her mother's legacy. That she would fail her people. That the Wariuta would lose everything that made them distinct in this world that trended toward sameness. That she was simply the one-handed girl who should never have been taught to fight as some in Yunka had always whispered she was. That no one respected her. That she would lose her mother and Koa to this war. That she would lose everything. She looked away before her fears engulfed her.

Kaia watched as a shadow on the eastern cliff formed the shape of a great city on a scale she could barely comprehend. Buildings, cold and sharp, loomed enormous over the people. She could barely stand to look at them, for the way they cut into the earth was so thoughtless, so savage. Beyond them, a great battle raged upon the sea, composed of all manner of ships: Long and narrow Wariuta canoes. Cold World galleons. The Colonizers' gunships. But. There. On the shore. A girl dressed in Imperial clothing skulked about the perimeters of the scene. Kaia watched her with suspicion.

It was Genevieve. It had to be.

All around her, destruction reigned. The buildings came crumbling down. But Kaia kept her eye on the girl as she slithered away from the unending darkness that swallowed the city until she met a great tall figure in an open field.

It had to be Ica. The figure had the bearing of a leader. The confidence of years of battle. Kaia watched with her breath held as the girl and the figure circled each other. Her eyes hurt from watching, unblinking, as their hand-to-hand combat began.

The girl won. Ica was dead.

In a howl of rage, Kaia flung the girl's dagger at the eastern cliff. In an instant, the images evaporated. By the time the dagger hit the ground, time had returned, the visions were over, and her mother was looking at her with something like fury or disappointment or disgust in her eye.

"She killed you," Kaia panted. "Genevieve, that little snake, she—"

"That is not what I saw," said Ica. She stepped over to where the dagger had fallen and picked it up. Her eye followed the blade, pausing on imperfections so minute Kaia had not seen them. Then she met Kaia's gaze once more. "You have sullied this place."

"I . . ." Kaia felt stupid. What she had thought throwing a dagger at a vision would accomplish was suddenly a mystery to her. She was a child. Out of her depth. Unfit. Everything she feared she might be.

"You must be better," Ica said. She wasn't cruel about it, her tone was even, but Kaia felt each word like a stab in her chest. It seemed these days she could do nothing but court her mother's rebuke. "For our people, you must be."

"I'm sorry." As if Ica had never been angry. Her fury had been legendary. The people of Puno carried many tales of it, and the people of Yunka were safe and fat and happy because of it. Her mother never seemed to remember.

"What good that may do us."

"What did you see?" Kaia asked finally. She did not know what else to say.

"I saw a coalition of many. I saw unity in purpose. And I saw the girl."

"Yes!" Kaia grinned. "Yes, I saw her, too!"

"We must work with her. Without her, the Colonizers can never be beaten."

"What? No. Mother, please, I saw her kill you, I saw—"

"She will not kill me," Ica said calmly.

"But I saw you die!"

"Death comes for us all, Kaia." Ica cupped her daughter's face in the palm of her hand. Her silver eye shone in the moonlight. "It will come for me, too. And when it does, you must be ready."

Kaia pulled away from her mother's touch. "No," she said.

Ica only smiled sadly. "Well. Whether you will be ready or not, it's coming. Until then, we will work with this Colonizer child. Not just for our own people but for all those who live under the Imperial violence and their greed all over this world. My life is nothing stacked against so many. A good leader understands this."

With dawning horror, Kaia realized her mother had seen what she had seen. She knew her own death was assured. And yet here she stood, looking like nothing unusual was happening. Why was her mother so resigned to martyring herself?

"But—"

"This is the path I choose. And until I am gone, you will walk it with me. Do you understand?"

"I understand that you have forgotten who you are," Kaia seethed. "You were a warrior once, the best of us. What happened to you?"

Ica pressed her lips into a thin line of disappointment. "I grew up, Kaia. Painstakingly, and often too late." She took a calming breath and met Kaia's eyes once more. "I made so many mistakes, so many terrible and cruel choices. But you . . . you need not make the same mistakes I did. You can be something better than me. If you'd just *listen*. Ferocity is not the only thing that makes a warrior great. Knowing this will make you a better leader."

Kaia shook her head. "Not a day went by when I was small when you wouldn't tell me to use my own judgment, not to be swayed by popular opinion. But now you lecture me about just doing as you say. Do you not see how infuriating that is?"

Ica smiled, and Kaia felt heat prickle at her cheeks. Was she amusing? She was not some precocious child; she was the next leader of the Wariuta.

"I wish you had not done such a good job learning to be yourself," Ica said finally. "Somehow you have turned into both the best and the worst of me."

*The worst of me.*

Unable to name the feelings roiling in her throat, Kaia simply turned away from her mother and stalked out of the Canyon of the Moon.

• CHAPTER 10 •

*Thistle*

Thistle had heard the rumors. That her father had been part of the noble and defeated Resistance and that he had betrayed them. That it was the Resistance, not the Imperials, who had either killed him or run him out of Gia Dinh. She was barely a year old when he died or left, so Thistle didn't know what to think. She had never met him.

But she also had never known her mother to lie.

And though her mother now ran a guesthouse that catered almost exclusively to Imperials, she still held her dead husband's supposed heroism in her heart. Each year on the anniversary of his death, she would light a candle for him beneath the shrine of Death and whisper his name.

The shrine was hidden from guests, of course. Shrines to the many gods were forbidden after Colonization. And though Mrs. Vo was rarely prone to rebellion, she did have her one statuette, hidden in the stone basement along with the stores and the gold coin she had squirreled away in case of emergency.

Thistle sat before the shrine of Death. They said that those who lived in peril could feel him stalking, but Thistle had never felt anything like that. She looked upon the marble statue. He was small, maybe just the length of her forearm, but imposing regardless of size. Death could take many forms, but when captured in a statue, he tended to be a young man in soldier's garb, and this was what Mrs. Vo's Death wore. He held a spear close to his chest and glared down at Thistle from his plinth.

"He was always the most imposing of the many gods."

Thistle whirled and, to her abject horror, saw the Lady Minami standing behind her. But Lady Minami smiled warmly and beckoned Thistle to stay seated. Thistle was shocked when the Lady, in her immaculate silk kimono, knelt next to her on the cold, dusty stone floor.

"I always thought it was lovely, the way you people speak of death. Like he is an old friend." She placed a warm hand on Thistle's. "Who is this statue for?"

"My father," Thistle said. Her throat felt very dry.

"Ah. Mr. Vo. I wondered where he might be."

"He died when I was still a baby," Thistle said. "I never knew him."

"A pity, I'm sure."

And then, as if someone else controlled her mouth, Thistle felt words come tumbling that should never have been spoken. "Mother says he died in the Resistance." Why was she talking? Why would she tell an Imperial of all people that the illegal shrine in their basement was for a dead Resistance fighter? "But I've heard the Resistance killed him. Dai says that the Resistance killed a lot of people who were just suspected of betraying them, and that maybe that's why there's rumors that my Dad did, and that actually he might not have done anything wrong at all. He says that was the way it had to be then, because there were so many betrayers. But I don't know. The Resistance lost."

"Dai as in Dai Phan, your future husband?"

Thistle turned to the Lady Minami then, her heart pounding with alarm at her potentially fatal mistake. "Please don't tell," she whispered. "That I was down here. That we have a shrine. That my father was in the Resistance. He's dead anyway. And I'll throw out the shrine, I promise; Mother will understand. We just. I don't mean any harm. I'm glad Imperials are here. Girls get to go to school now, I get to go to school now, and I know that's thanks to the Emperor. Please, I—"

"Shh." The Lady Minami squeezed Thistle's hand. "This will be our little secret."

"OK," Thistle said, but still the blood drummed loud in her ears.

The Lady pulled a long, slender pin topped with a pearlescent sakura flower from her hair and placed it—just as was tradition—before the statue of Death. An offering. "In his name, we ask for his blessing."

It took Thistle a few moments to realize what the Lady Minami had said. Not because she didn't recognize the words—they were the customary prayer for the many gods—but because she spoke them in the Old Tongue. In the language of Quark, long since outlawed. Thistle knew only snips and snatches of it herself, gleaned from listening to her mother's prayers.

"You speak our language?"

"Not as well as I'd like," the Lady admitted.

"But . . . how? It's illegal to speak it."

"Not in Crandon, it's not. And it's good for the mind to learn other languages. To be nimble."

"Oh." Thistle sat with this for a moment. How strange to think of Imperials learning the languages they forbade in the colonies.

"Perhaps I can earn your trust if I lend you a secret of my own?"

Thistle nodded her agreement, eager to know any secrets the Lady might hold.

"I don't think it's right to outlaw worshipping the many gods," Lady Minami whispered. "Or to outlaw speaking the Old Tongue."

Thistle smiled. "Really?" Her mother did not think so, either. It was nice to think of the Lady Minami and her mother agreeing on something. It gave her mother rather more credibility.

"Really. I believe the Empire of Nipran is strongest when we celebrate our diversity rather than eliding it. And I for one am proud to have Quark in our Empire."

"I'm proud to be in the Empire," Thistle said. She was startled to find that she wasn't lying, exactly. Not entirely. Her mother, just like all the adults in Gia Dinh, bit her tongue in public. But in private she gossiped and maligned her Imperial customers. They were a bossy, brutish lot, loud and demanding and often rude. Ignorant of their ways, though everyone in Quark knew how to bless the Emperor. An ugly people. Supposedly. But this was not what Thistle had seen.

She thought of the soldiers who tossed her candy, of them marching in their orderly formation.

Of the smooth roads the Imperials had built.

Of all the money they spent in businesses like her mother's and like Dai's family's restaurant.

Of the fine things—leather and apples and glass—that were now imported from all over the Empire.

Of the Lady Minami, who was interesting and smart and good.

Perhaps Thistle was not lying at all.

"You know, when I was a child, my nanny's name was Genevieve. She was from Iwei, strong woman, smart woman. She knew the Emperor's words better than any official, could recite the royal line all the way back to the First Emperor. She had hands like a man's." The Lady chuckled, and so Thistle did, too. "And she instilled in me a profound respect for the immigrants who come to Crandon. We are all part of the Empire's might, thanks to the Emperor, but it takes real courage to come to the center of that power and find your own."

Thistle thought about this. She wondered if she had that kind of courage, if she could be strong and smart, too. If she could make it in Crandon.

"What happened to her?" Thistle asked.

The Lady Minami looked down at her hands and gave a rueful smile. "She passed, sadly. But not a day goes by that I don't think about her."

"I'm sorry for your loss."

"And I for yours."

They both looked in silence at the shrine for Thistle's father for what felt like a very long time.

"Thank you for sharing your shrine with me." Lady Minami stood. "It's beautiful." She gave Thistle a deep bow of respect, which Thistle did her best to re-create. "I think you and I will become very good friends. What do you think, Thistle Vo?"

• CHAPTER 11 •

## *Koa*

Koa was pretty sick of Kaia's shit.

She had taken to looming over him and Genevieve, her presence like foul weather. Koa loved his sister, and even liked her most of the time. But she made it impossible to talk with Genevieve, to soothe her into comfort. How would they ever work together if she was constantly afraid for her life?

Koa tried that morning, unsuccessfully, to get Genevieve to bathe in the bath pits. It was Koa's favorite place in Yunka. Dug deeply out of the earth and packed with hardened clay, the pits were filled each day with steaming-hot water and emptied each night. No one talked in the bathing pits. It was a quiet place but not a lonely one.

However, Genevieve only regarded him with chilly horror when he pulled off his tunic, and it became very clear that she did not think being naked was normal. Which. OK. So that's why Colonizers always smelled so bad. Koa was willing to skip a single day if it meant getting Genevieve to be more comfortable, so he pulled his tunic back on and tried not to think about the warm, sour scent that came off his body.

Instead, he took her to the oasis.

There were many oases tucked away, too deep within the mountains for Colonizers to find. It was the secret to the Wariuta's success raising cattle—the oases were all uniformly rich with fresh water and with water lilies and seagrasses for the cows to graze upon. But one was different. It was full of seawater, and it was Koa's daily charge to keep the Wariuta away from it.

Genevieve stumbled as she followed Koa along the rocky pass, but she kept up. Before they got too close, Koa turned to her, already apologetic.

"So. You're going to hate this. But there's just no other way. I have to tie your hands."

Genevieve glared at him, her face red with exertion, exposure, and now anger. "You have to," she repeated, and even in her heavy accent, her disdain was clear.

"I have to," Koa said. "For your own protection. My job here is . . . weird? Please don't be mad." He placed his spear on the ground and bound her hands carefully, tight enough that she couldn't break free but as loose as he could manage. He did his best not to let their skin touch, kept his body as far away from hers as possible. A gesture of respect.

But Genevieve was still mad.

Koa didn't know what to say to her but figured once she saw, she'd understand. Or rather, once she heard. They walked in silence, Tupac padding alongside them, his big paws leaving craters in the sand.

When he could see the green of the oasis, Koa led Genevieve toward the lean-to he had constructed so he could have shade while he tended his post. The oasis itself was lovely. There were worse places to sit for the day. Three lanky palm trees on the water's edge leaned in the direction of the nightly winds. Distantly, he could already hear the singing that told him his charge was awake. Her voice was high and light as it drifted across the dunes. She must have sensed that Koa was not alone.

"I am going to touch you," he warned Genevieve. Though it pained him, Koa reached out and took her hand. "I'm sorry," he said, and he meant it. But she didn't tug or protest. She flinched when their skin touched but allowed him to lead her to the shade.

Why didn't she react to the song? Koa wondered as he tied her to one of the four wooden posts. It was as though she couldn't hear it.

"Hello, boy," called the siren. Her voice was soft like a baby's skin. "Have you brought me something good to eat?" She pulled herself to the edge of the green water of the oasis and rested her head on her arms on the red sand.

Koa looked at his charge. She was beautiful—she had smooth black skin and a mischievous mouth. Her eyes and hair were the same dark green of the water that was her home. But she had drunk the blood of enough Wariuta for Koa to know she was dangerous.

To all but him.

Her song was a lure. He was told it promised pleasure, but he couldn't hear that. All he heard was a melody, no more interesting or alluring than any sung under full moons or on naming days.

"You know my name, Lilith," he said. This was a game she played each day. She pretended not to know him, pretended he had not been her only company for the past five years. Each day, Koa sat by her lagoon. Some days she did not come to the surface at all. If Koa was honest, those were sad days. She may have been a murderer, but she was amusing—if occasionally rude—company.

"Oh, my," Lilith drawled. Her eyes dwelled hungrily on Genevieve, who stared back at the siren, agog. "Do you finally have a lover? I never thought I'd see the day."

Koa laughed his big laugh, felt the humor true and deep in his belly. "That's Genevieve," he replied. "And I'm pretty sure she hates me."

Lilith cocked her head. Her long green hair fell over one green eye. "Does she." It was not a question.

The siren regarded Genevieve with open curiosity. Koa could see that Genevieve's shock had already passed, and now she looked at Lilith with cold appraisal.

"I will not hate you so much if you do not tie me up." Genevieve glared at the siren. "What are you?" she asked.

"The better question is, What are you?" Lilith retorted. Her tail, long and elegant and covered in glittering green scales, thwacked against the surface of the water. She let her eyes wander over Genevieve, unblinking, and Koa lowered his spear so it was level with her head.

"No eating our guest," he said calmly.

"Wouldn't dream of it," said Lilith, who absolutely would.

"Lilith, this is Genevieve. Genevieve, this is Lilith," said Koa peaceably. "Lilith is a siren. Like a mermaid, but her song is dangerous. It's my job to protect people from her so she doesn't eat them, because she will and she has, and she'll eat you if you get too close to the water." Koa smiled at Genevieve. "That's why I had to tie you up."

Lilith pushed back from the shore and disappeared beneath the cool water of her oasis.

"But . . . you don't seem affected by her song," Koa said. He looked at Genevieve. She was calm, if annoyed. Usually those who heard Lilith's song were frenzied in their desire to reach her.

"It is nice," Genevieve said, but this was all.

Genevieve was like him.

Koa hated the word. *Unwanting.* It wasn't true, for one thing; he wanted all kinds of things. Good company. A nice place to sleep. For Kaia to be happy. Respect. But he understood it, too, probably better than the rest of the Wariuta did. For everyone else there was only one *want* that defined their lives. And Koa didn't want it. Or maybe it just didn't interest him. Sometimes he felt curious about it the way he might feel curious about a lizard. But, he figured, he was mostly curious why it mattered so much.

Whatever the reason, the fact that he didn't "want" meant Lilith's song had no effect on him. Koa was as safe by her side as he was in his hut. If he ever forgot the danger she posed, he needed only to remember Jia—a weaver by trade and a nuisance the rest of the time—who had assumed that since she did not typically favor females for lovers, she would be safe from the siren's song.

That was not so.

Koa found her, what was left of her, on the bank of the oasis. There was a word for what had happened to her, Ica said. *Exsanguination.* Her skin had gone ashy and terrible and vacant, all the warm color of her gone, gone, gone, her eyes still open, still wide with fear and realization, her mouth contorted in pain. Koa knew she was going to die before she died, had felt every drop of her blood leave her. Koa had retched, not when he first saw her but when he realized what and who she was. When he realized it was his own failure—to simply be at his post—that had allowed her to die.

Before him, Lilith had resurfaced and now rested her face on her thin arms, looking both harmless and lovely for her harmlessness. He tried to imagine her drinking blood but couldn't, even though he knew that was how she lived. On every seventh day, he brought her a calf to eat. But she always waited to eat it until he left.

Today was not the seventh day, however. That didn't matter. Lilith was still hungry. She was always hungry.

"Why not just kill her?" Genevieve asked.

The question startled Koa. She was a Cold Worlder, she didn't understand, but still. To be so callous.

"Because she is alive?" Koa replied. "Because it's not her fault she's like this."

Lilith openly glared at Genevieve. So she'd heard. Great.

"Because I am a gift from the Sea, girl," Lilith hissed. "Banished from my home for the crime of loving one of *you*." She licked her teeth, and Koa looked away. He hated when she was like this. Bitter. Cruel. "I sought the help of a witch, and my mother knew it. She always knows."

Genevieve smiled at Lilith, and Koa regretted her words before they were spoken. "That is your own fault. For trusting a witch."

To Koa's great relief, Lilith laughed. "What a little bitch you are," she said. Koa's relief dissipated immediately. "With your Quark face and your Crandon accent. You've trusted the wrong people, too, little miss. You'd be a fool to think otherwise."

She disappeared under the water again, and Koa looked to Genevieve.

"You're a part of the Empire?" So she was a Colonizer. He didn't realize how much hope he'd been holding out that she was not. There were so many immigrants from the Cold World who'd folded into Wariuta life with little problem. He had hoped she would be one. But the Empire's Colonizers were different.

It was the Colonizers' fault that the Wariuta had been relegated to only the largest of their cities. Outsiders had always been welcome, their best customs adopted—but there was one thing the Wariuta held fast to: the belief that life was sacred. It was the only demand they made of newcomers.

And Colonizers didn't respect that.

"Yes," she said tartly. "Proudly."

And they did not speak after that.

• CHAPTER 12 •

The Colonizers were a blight that predated Kaia's birth. They were a part of the world she had always known, a cancerous growth in her heart that was, unfortunately, as much a part of her as her stubbornness or her athleticism.

Kaia did not hate all outsiders, as Koa often accused her. She was half outsider herself. Her father had come from Tustwe and simply never left. Pirates came to make trades for leather and beef and alchemical goods. The many merchant ships carried glass or apples or rice or cheese. And mostly this was peaceful. They came to trade, and then they left, or they stayed. And that was that.

But the Colonizers were different. They did not want to trade. They wanted to take.

And they'd been taking for more than twenty years now.

The Colonizers fought cold and dirty, with guns and little care for collateral damage. It was the Wariuta way to respect even your enemies, but Kaia did not respect them; she hated them. She also did not know what life might be like if they ever left.

But the idea of keeping a Colonizer safe so she could help negotiate, to help haggle for what was rightfully the Wariuta's, didn't just irritate Kaia; it was like a wound, open and weeping and untreated by healers. Gangrenous and toxic.

Her father, Muteteli, had been killed by Colonizers. He had not even been armed, had been on the shore with his fishing nets and his canoe, simply seeing that the Wariuta would have trevally for the night meal. He was not a warrior, never had been. According to the other men who survived the attack, he had waved to the Colonizers, ever cheerful, before they shot him. The trevally he had caught rotted in the open sun, wasted, in the canoe Muteteli left behind.

Koa's father, Chimu, had been killed in the skirmishes that followed Muteteli's death. Though the Wariuta were more prepared this time, armed, at least, they still underestimated the Colonizers' blind disregard for life. They killed wantonly. Without thought or care. There was nothing holy in the way they snuffed out lives, nothing sacred. They pointed guns and pulled triggers, and Wariuta fell.

Chimu had been the greatest of the men—he loomed enormous over everyone, his body giant and his might met only by that of Ica. And so when he was killed—by a man crouched and hiding—shot in the back, the Wariuta knew the time of conflicts solved the old way had died, too.

The Colonizers looted alchemical stores, leaving behind all the healing ointments, the skin oils and protective creams. They searched only for the sticky black tar called kau, an explosive the Wariuta made that was ignited by water. The alchemists used it sparingly, made very little of it. It had been invented for terraforming but was used in battle to scare off enemies rather than kill them. It had been very effective at this for centuries. But the

Colonizers took every drop of it they could find, and the Wariuta knew they would use it for murder.

If they had not had such a singular goal, Kaia noted with disdain, they could have kept their delicate skin safe from the sun that ravaged them in the Wariuta land. There was an oil for that. But they left those jars behind or, worse, destroyed them.

And now Koa showed the girl, the Colonizer, Genevieve how to use that very same oil her people had almost entirely destroyed.

"Just put it on! This is why you people always burn," he said. He spread some on his own arm as an example. "Put it everywhere the sun'll touch."

"It smells," Genevieve said.

It took all of Kaia's self-control not to smack her.

"Not as bad as you do," Koa said, and Kaia laughed.

The girl, now with the Wariuta for several weeks, had still not bathed. Just looking at her made Kaia feel itchy. Koa's hut was thick with the smell of her.

Genevieve glowered and set about applying the oil to her filthy body. The skin on her nose and forehead was peeling. She looked disgusting, smelled disgusting. But Ica said they needed her. And so Kaia kept her safe. She could follow orders, even if they were mind-bogglingly stupid.

It wasn't only Kaia who hated her. Plenty of the Wariuta would see her punished for the Colonizers' many crimes. Kaia could feel the eyes of her people tracking the girl's movements as they walked around Yunka. She wanted to tell them all, *I know I know I know*, but she also knew she could not do that, could not defy or rebuke her mother in public.

Did Genevieve appreciate that her skin was now safe? Did she give thanks for the Wariuta healers who had mended her wounds? Was she grateful for her life?

No.

Koa ducked out of the hut to rustle up some food. It had become clear that Genevieve was a disruptive presence at the night meal, so the three had to eat away from everyone else, like pariahs. Like criminals. Another thing to hate the girl for.

Kaia sharpened her ax. She kept the weapon propped between her legs as she ran the whetstone along the sides. It was comforting work. She had been doing it a lot lately.

"You ruin that weapon," Genevieve said. "Sharpen too much."

Kaia glared at her. "If I could bury it in your back," Kaia replied, "I would."

It took a moment before Genevieve understood the drift of what Kaia had said, and when she did, she looked away. She did not seem afraid, exactly. Something else passed over her face. Kaia wished she could break her head open and read the scattered remains of her thoughts off the floor.

"I do a bad job," Genevieve said slowly. "Being a guest. I am sorry."

Kaia felt one eyebrow raise. "Colonizers are not guests. You are vermin."

This passed over Genevieve, and Kaia could tell she had not understood entirely. "My lady tells me that the strength of our Empire is there are so many *kinds* of us. It is stupid of me not to see that now."

"The Wariuta are not a *part* of your empire."

"You will be." And she had the audacity to smile. Not her normal snake's smile but a warm smile, a nice smile. As though she bequeathed Kaia with kindness. As if she were being generous. "The Empire of Nipran is the greatest Empire in the Known World. It always is. It always will be. This is not bad."

"We have very different notions of greatness," Kaia muttered.

She returned to her ax. Genevieve was right. She'd been oversharpening it. She put it down and met Genevieve's gaze.

She was bigger than the Colonizer, taller. But she could see a kind of wiry strength in the girl's build. Could tell from the way she handled her own blade that she'd been trained. If it came to a fight between them, would Kaia's victory be certain?

"I do not wish to harm you," Genevieve said as if reading her mind. "Or your people."

There was a tenor of truth in the girl's voice, and it was not that Kaia did not believe her. It was that she knew that what Genevieve wanted to believe was separate from the truth. She picked up her ax again, let it rest against her legs.

If there was anything Kaia knew, it was that it was unwise to let your guard down around Colonizers.

When Kaia was small, she had overheard her mother discussing her future with one of the women who handled training the children who would become warriors.

"She is not fit," the woman had said.

Kaia had looked down at the stump of her arm and cried. The other children had occasionally asked questions about it, but mostly there was no difference in Kaia's life from those around her due to something as trivial as a single hand. That it could now, suddenly, bear such terrible consequences was crushing. All she had ever wanted was to be like Ica. And here was someone saying she simply could not, could never be.

But Ica did not accept that. And so Kaia did not, either.

Kaia began her training. When she was very small, it was mostly about mindfulness and balance, and having one hand did not hinder her at all. But still she practiced whatever she had learned in the day each night so that she would be better, she would be stronger and faster than all the other children who had nothing to work against.

As time went on, her determination to be the best only calcified. It was like a rock in her heart, and she loved it, loved the hard work and the practice and the discipline. It became such that the only competition she could truly look forward to was with herself.

Until the day Ica challenged her to spar.

It was not unusual for older warriors to challenge warrior apprentices. It was typically a friendly gesture. A generous thing an adult might do to help a teen they respected or wanted to encourage. Kaia was in her thirteenth year then and had plainly outstripped all her cohorts. So it was expected that, someday soon, she would be challenged by an elder.

But it was not expected that the challenger would be the leader of them.

It was not long after both Muteteli and Chimu had fallen. The warriors had sustained so many losses that it was whispered that the apprentices would be given familiars early to take their places. Kaia had heard the gossip and wished fervently for its veracity. She had been begging Ica for exactly this since her father's murder. And now, with the chance to spar against her mother, it felt like her moment to prove herself.

Ica normally fought with two axes, but for the sake of sparring, she replaced them with a long, thin sparring stick. And in an unorthodox move, she allowed Kaia to fight with her actual ax.

Kaia was so excited she could hardly breathe. After years of lessons, and faced with her first foe of consequence, she couldn't keep her mind clear. But she didn't let that stop her.

She lunged straight at her mother, the only person who stood between her and her chance for revenge against the Colonizers.

For a split second, Kaia saw the white of Ica's eye go wide and she thought, *I have her.*

She did not.

Ica parried her easily; with one graceful motion, she took a partial step back, narrowing her body, evading Kaia's ax, and leaving her daughter, having now accidentally overshot her target, on unsteady footing. Kaia whirled and attacked again, this time with the full strength she had developed from countless nights of practice. Her ax sliced through Ica's sparring stick, leaving her with two.

Ica raised one eyebrow, and Kaia knew she was done for—her mother was a demon with two weapons. Her only hope was attack. She could not possibly win in defense. And so she tried again and again, the ferocity of her attacks gaining in rage and futility. It was not long before her mother had knocked her weapon from her hand and had a shard of stick beneath Kaia's throat.

"You let your rage guide you." Ica did not move the shard but still held it to her daughter's neck. "And it will lead our people only to death."

"A glorious one, if you'd let me fight."

"There is no such thing as a glorious death," Ica spat. She let her hand drop and turned her back on Kaia. "If you don't understand that, then you do not understand anything."

She picked up Kaia's ax and handed it back to her. For a moment, Kaia did not take it. Her cheeks burned with humiliation and disappointment.

"You are not done learning," Ica said, kinder now. "That is all."

Kaia snatched the ax. Her mother held her gaze. She wanted her to see something, to change who Kaia was and how she felt, but Kaia could not, and the uselessness of it made her whole body restless with fury. She wanted to scream, wanted to hit Ica, wanted to throw her ax into the nearest Colonizer and watch the Imperial ships go up in flames.

"Life is precious, Kaia." Ica's voice was soft, almost pleading.

"What about Chimu's life?" Kaia could feel tears forming, but she ignored them. "What about Muteteli's?"

Ica's nostrils flared. "No better reminders exist for me of the precariousness and preciousness of life."

"You make decisions all the time that lead to deaths. Ours and the Colonizers'."

"Yes," said Ica. "And every one of those deaths rests on my heart. I do not close my eyes any night without seeing the faces of those whose lives I have stopped short. I hope to build a world where they need not rest so heavily on yours. That should always be the hope. To lead in peace."

"But that's not real!" Kaia shouted. "It never has been!"

"What is and has been is not what will always be." Ica heaved a sigh. Kaia could see she was angering her mother, but she didn't care. "You have so much to learn. I can only hope that you will before I am gone."

And with that, she left her daughter on the field of her defeat. They never sparred again.

• CHAPTER 13 •

*Thistle*

At school, Dai did not act any differently, and so Thistle did not, either. There was some light teasing tossed their way—news of their betrothal had spread, naturally. All news spread quickly in Gia Dinh. But it wasn't even personal, really, just the kind of general teasing one had to expect, and that Thistle certainly had.

But after school, when he came over to the house and saw the Lady Minami's excess belongings being stored in the upstairs hallway, things felt different again. Stiff. The trunks were obviously Imperial—they bore her family crest. Only Imperials did that. Or rather, only the wealthiest Imperials did that.

Dai ran his finger over the three leaves that comprised the gilded crest. "Imagine having so much gold you can waste it on the boxes just to hold your crap."

"It must be nice," said Thistle.

This was, apparently, the wrong thing to say. Dai glared at her like she was willfully stupid.

"I guess," he said. Idly, he popped open the chest.

"Hey," Thistle said, a hissed whisper. "Don't do that!"

"I just wanna see."

The Lady Minami had unpacked in her room, but there were still some random bits and ends in her trunk. Despite her better judgment, Thistle peered in, too. A stray obi, embroidered with silver thread. A comb with pearlescent inlay that could probably pay for her stay in the Vo house for a month.

But then Dai pulled out a rolled paper, still loosely held by a broken wax seal. A letter.

They looked at each other. It was one thing to poke around the trunk. Another to read the Lady's correspondence.

"Put it back," Thistle said. But she did not say it with much conviction.

Dai unrolled the letter.

"It says . . . that Commander Niijima will find her in Gia Dinh. And that . . . she should stay at the Vo family guesthouse?"

Dai looked at Thistle as though he were seeing her for the first time. Commander Niijima was well known in Gia Dinh. Of course he was. He was the commander who'd sacked the city all those years ago and who now served as its acting lord. Thistle snatched the letter from him and read it furiously.

It was written in the most formal script of the Common Tongue, which was to be expected. But the seal bore the Imperial Lion. And the letter was addressed to someone named the Lady Ayer, not to the Lady Minami.

"It's not even addressed to her," Thistle said, as if maybe this could explain everything.

"I knew it," Dai whispered. He looked as if someone had rung a church bell right next to his ear.

"Knew what?" Thistle rerolled the letter, shoved it back beneath the obi, and shut the trunk a little louder than she'd intended to. Something like anger, hot and prickly, roiled in her belly.

"You father *was* a traitor," Dai said at last.

Thistle rounded on Dai, her friend, her best friend, the boy who was supposed to be her husband someday, and in that moment she hated him. "You can't be a traitor to something that doesn't *exist* anymore, Dai," she spat. "We're all Imperials now."

"No," said Dai simply, as though this could be simple. "Some of us aren't." And he started to back away from her like she were a dangerous thing, something aflame.

Thistle felt tears building, but she wasn't sad. She was furious. *He* was the traitor, not her.

"Your family lives on Imperial coin just the same as mine!" She stepped toward him, and he took a step back. She could feel a tear escape, and she batted it away. "Don't blame my mother for doing exactly what your parents do!"

"Why did Commander Niijima tell her to stay here, then?"

"But he didn't tell her; he told some other lady! It's the Lady Minami who's staying here."

Dai shook his head. "Thistle." His voice was soft, full of pity. "Is that even her real name?"

"Of course it is," she said. But she had no idea; she just didn't want to concede anything to Dai. He had called her father a traitor, and what did he know? He still had both his parents, who she knew served Imperials expensive food Quark natives could never afford.

"I . . . I don't think we can be friends anymore." Dai's voice was small. He took another step away from Thistle, toward the stairs, presumably toward the front door. "I'm sorry."

"What are you talking about?"

"We aren't all Imperials, Thistle. But you are."

"You're such a hypocrite," Thistle spat. "Look at your leather shoes. How do you think your parents paid for those? Where do you think they *came* from?"

"Your father was a traitor, Thistle. We all know that. And your mother—"

But before he could finish, Mrs. Vo came storming up the stairs. "Get out of this house this instant, Dai Phan." She grabbed him by his skinny wrist and pulled him down the stairs. "You," she said, her voice punctuating each step they took. "Are. Not. Welcome. Here." She flung the door open and tossed Dai out. "Anymore."

Thistle had never seen her mother so angry. And she had been in trouble loads of times. It was as if a whole new mother had come up those stairs, and a stranger had dragged Dai out of the house.

Distantly, she could hear Dai's voice as he shouted "Traitors!" at the house. Thistle looked out the window to see him running away. A few people stopped to watch him go. Mr. Bole peered at the house and caught Thistle's eye. He spat once on the ground and walked away with his wheelbarrow of fish.

Mrs. Vo came back upstairs, her cheeks flushed and her hair a bit askew.

"Don't you listen to that boy," she said. She grabbed Thistle by the arm, hard.

"Mother, ow—"

"Do you hear me? You do not listen to gossiping simpletons. Your father was a hero. Do you hear me? A hero."

"But Mother," Thistle said quietly, "the Resistance lost. *Quark* lost."

Mrs. Vo dropped Thistle's arm then and stood to her full

height. They could nearly see eye to eye, but she was still a bit taller than her daughter. For a moment, she did not say anything, just looked at Thistle appraisingly.

But then she raised her hand. And it was only in the moment just before she brought it down that Thistle realized what was going to happen.

The slap stung, bringing fresh tears into her eyes. Her cheek burned. Thistle put her hand to it, felt the heat from it as it throbbed.

"We may wash their clothes and fill their bowls, but remember this, child: We are not them. They are not us. And someday, this country will be free again. Do you understand me?"

"Yes," said Thistle.

But for the first time in her life, she knew her mother was lying to her.

• CHAPTER 14 •

*Koa*

After the messenger was sent and the meeting arranged, all the Wariuta, from the mountains to the shore, gathered in Yunka on the agreed-upon day. And so Koa was forced into the ceremonial headdress and cape that befitted his role as Ica's son. It did not fit him well. The headdress felt as though it was forever tilting off his head. Genevieve snickered a little under her breath as it nearly toppled off once more just as the Colonizer envoy approached. She had been teaching Koa the Colonizers' tongue, and Koa was surprised to find that he liked it, a little. It sounded much nicer when it wasn't being yelled at you amid bullets. It made his mouth take curious shapes, and it was the first thing in his life he learned quickly. And so now he knew he was what the Colonizers called a *prince*. The term fit him about as well as his headdress.

The Colonizers arrived with their armor glinting in the sunlight, sweat dripping down their faces in the heat. They were not dressed for the day's weather or the landscape or the season, and they suffered for it. One man, presumably the leader, since two other men had been carrying a piece of cloth to block the sun from him, approached Ica and bowed.

The Wariuta watched in silence, their faces uniformly pulled into masks of distrust. All had their weapons easily reachable on their backs, just in case, though now they stood behind Ica with their hands loose. The echoes of hyena giggles rose, but save for that, Yunka had never been so full or so quiet.

"*I am Commander Callum,*" the man said. This much Koa understood. The rest of what followed was garbled and confusing, and even if he understood some of the words, the context didn't fit, and Koa quickly lost the thread.

Genevieve stepped forward. "*I am Genevieve, maid to the Lady Ayer.*" At this, the look on the man called Commander's face changed. His eyes were only on Genevieve now, and if Koa was not mistaken, he was suspicious of her, too. There was a brief exchange between the two, but Ica quickly lost patience with it.

"Ask him if he brings us new terms," Ica interrupted.

Genevieve nodded. Another brief exchange. "He says it is the Emperor's will to own this land," said Genevieve. "But that, if it pleases the Wariuta, this can be achieved with peace. And all will benefit."

Commander snapped his fingers, and two men carrying a heavy chest came forward and dropped it at Ica's feet. As they did so, Commander barked words at Genevieve, who nodded her comprehension. Koa did not like the way she kept her eyes on the ground while Commander talked, as if his life were more important than hers.

"He does not expect Wariuta to trust right away. He comes with gifts. He hopes they will help the Wariuta see that the Emperor is generous. That to trade with the Emperor is good for the Wariuta. Good for everyone."

At this there was a ripple of laughter from the Wariuta. This was offensive. The Emperor must have known full well that his men did not trade with the Wariuta. That they came with guns and death and disease. But the laughter did not seem to bother the Colonizers. They opened the chest. Inside were many glass bottles, safely stowed in tidy cloth clasps that lined the chest in rows. Commander pulled up a bottle and handed it to Ica, who took it reluctantly.

"It is Kiyohime powder," said Genevieve, and her voice was reverent. "Enough to kill a thousand men, and each will die screaming. One bottle takes a year to produce in Iwei. This chest takes decades of work to make."

Koa did not need to see his mother's face to know she was disgusted. She handed the bottle back to Commander. "We do not have need of this," she said.

Genevieve translated, and Commander shrugged. His men collected the chest, and a new soldier came forward with a blood-red satchel. From within it, Commander removed a long, curved tooth the length of Koa's shin and offered it to Ica.

"This is a dragon's tooth," said Genevieve. "Very rare."

Koa waited for her to explain its use, but she did not elaborate.

Ica did not take the tooth. "What I am learning," she said slowly, "is that your emperor thinks we are simple people. That we can be bought with weapons and trinkets. He knows nothing of us, or our ways, yet he seeks to have our allegiance."

With a nearly invisible tilt of her hand, she gave Puka the command to join her. Puka giggled high and loud at Ica's side. Commander backed away a little from the hyena, his eyes fixed on the animal with undisguised disgust.

"The Emperor has one last gift," Genevieve translated. At Commander's words, her eyes widened. Commander pulled a chain from his neck, and at the end of it was a silver-hued glass vial the length of a finger. "This is mermaid's blood."

At this, even the Wariuta looked among themselves. Mermaid's blood was not favored among the Wariuta, but it was extremely valuable in the open market. The alchemists in Puno would be deeply interested in obtaining the blood for their experiments. Koa thought of the pirates who occasionally made port and knew that among them it was a highly controversial subject. Although they all knew that drinking the blood made them unsafe upon the Sea and some considered it a grave trespass, there were some who loved it. He didn't know what to think. But all his favorite pirates, the ones whose company he enjoyed, whose stories brought him joy, seemed to think it was bad. Koa was inclined to believe them.

Commander grinned with pride. "One drop on a wound, and soon all that will remain is a scar. Drink it, and you will see wonders you could never imagine. You will escape your life, if only for a few hours. Many believe it is holy and that the visions you see will bring wisdom and luck."

Commander handed the vial to Ica, who rolled it between her fingers. "How do I know this isn't just well-packaged wine?" She held the vial up to the sun and looked through it. "Or poison?" She gave it back to Commander.

Commander said something to Genevieve, and her face went white. But, doing as he ordered, she stuck out her hand. He pulled a dagger from his belt, and Puka took a step forward, but Commander did not aim at any Wariuta. Instead, he cut a gash in Genevieve's palm. She let out a small gasp of pain, but that was all. Koa looked to Kaia, who was less impressed with her stoicism.

Commander pulled the stopper from the vial, covered its opening with his finger, and, with the utmost care, upended it so that the contents just touched his skin. After corking it with painstaking slowness, he ran his finger down the cut on Genevieve's hand.

The Wariuta gasped as the wound stitched itself shut before their eyes. Genevieve rubbed her hand against her filthy dress. It came away with a smudge of blood but no other sign of her injury.

"Mermaid's blood does not keep," said Ica. "How do the Colonizers have so much?"

"The Emperor orders his navy to fish for mermaids as highest priority of the state. Their capture makes the Known World a safer and better place for all those who sail," said Genevieve.

Commander said some more words and put the chain with the vial on it back around his neck. "In his wisdom, he knows that this is in the best interest of all, and so he pays high prices for the blood. His alchemists learn to make it last. Vials like this one are from his personal stores. He offers a hundred of them to you. To the Wariuta."

"If we agree to let you on our land, you mean. If we agree to trade."

"Yes." Genevieve smiled. "It is a very generous offer."

Ica's face was impassive. She made a small motion with her hand, and Puka took two steps back, away from the Colonizer, Commander.

"I do not speak for the Wariuta lightly," she said. "We will discuss among our own and reconvene with you to go over our terms if we wish to agree to anything. Until then, you and your men will return to the shore, and no Wariuta will bother you."

Genevieve translated this, and Commander bowed, low and low-key stupid in the Colonizer way.

"He wants your reply in two days," said Genevieve.

Ica scoffed at this, which set Puka off, which set all the hyenas in Yunka off, and soon the Colonizers were running from the sound of the Wariuta familiars, who were laughing and laughing and laughing.

Koa looked at the blood in the sand from Genevieve's cut. She was not a soldier, not a warrior. She did not wear the Colonizer crest. But still, he had cut her. And if he would cut her, Koa wondered, what was he willing to do to the Wariuta?

• CHAPTER 15 •

*Kaia*

The Wariuta were not a nation the way the Colonizers were a nation. There were factions by trade and location; and while war had seen Ica elected as the leader, she still made a point to consult leadership from each of the other factions.

Representatives from the alchemists, the cattle drivers, the fishermen, the healers, and the potters all sat in the Canyon of the Moon. Ica had led them and Kaia there to discuss the future of the Wariuta and the Colonizers' offer. It was an unusual move. For one, only Ica and occasionally Kaia were permitted into the Canyon of the Moon. But also, Kaia had assumed—as most of the Wariuta had assumed—that Ica would simply make the decision for them all.

But invite them she had, and now everyone sat in a circle around the firepit. The ancient fire cast craggy shadows across all their faces.

"Imagine what we could do with that blood," said the leader of the alchemists. She was a tall, jittery-looking woman with a reedy voice whom Kaia didn't trust. But then, Kaia did not trust the alchemists under normal circumstances. They had traded with the Colonizers even during the most violent times of conflict, until they were caught. And though Puno had been sacked years ago, Kaia was not the only one who remembered how little of a fight the alchemists had put up to stop them. And now the trade of enslaved people flourished in Puno. "If we could study it, it's possible we could replicate it, and then—"

"Then what?" said the leader of the healers tartly. This was Karal, and Kaia loved her. She was practical and kind and had helped Kaia as a child as she learned to navigate the world with a single hand. Kaia trusted her opinion intrinsically. "We become invincible? We take over the world? We become the Colonizers?" She shook her head with deep disapproval that Kaia decided she shared.

The alchemist bristled. "I cannot see how you would squander such a unique opportunity."

"I cannot see how you would be so myopic," Karal shot back.

"I'd hear from you," Ica interrupted. She gestured to the leader of the potters, Aya.

Kaia knew her distantly in the way that she knew anyone who lived in Yunka. It was a city, but a small one. Aya was old now, the eldest among the elected vocational leaders. Her stark-white hair was kept in three tidy braids, and the wrinkles in her face were deep and myriad.

Aya sighed and rubbed her thick hands together in worry. "The opportunity to trade without blood spilled is a good one," she said carefully. "But I don't trust the Colonizers to leave it at that. I fear if we let in their nose, their feet won't be far behind."

"And let's not forget," said the leader of the fishermen, "how many of my people they have killed! All for the crime of what, doing their job? On our home shore? Do you forget Muteteli already, Ica?" Her voice bore the tone of accusation.

But Ica did not rise to the bait. "I will never forget Muteteli," she said, her voice calm. "He was and is one of my great loves, and even if he were not, I do not let slip the memories of our fallen." She turned then to Kaia. "Tell us what you think, child. This is your future we discuss."

Kaia took a deep breath. It was the moment she had been waiting for since this meeting had been called. She stood and looked at each of the leaders. "I say we use what little kau is left in our stores and we burn their ships and kill their men." She met her mother's eyes, tried to discern what she thought. But, as always, the leader of the warriors was inscrutable. "Every life is precious. Let's give these Colonizers' lives value. To tell their Emperor the Wariuta nation is not his to take."

The leader of the fishermen stood to show her assent. "They will never leave unless we force them to."

And, to Kaia's surprise, Karal stood, too. "The healers will stand ready to treat our wounded." She gave Kaia a discreet nod of approval. Kaia could feel the pride build in her chest, roaring and billowing. She could lead these people after Ica, and she would do so fiercely.

But Aya shook her head. "Putting aside our anger, which is fair and righteous," she added with a nod to Kaia, "we must confront the reality that we may just be outnumbered and outmatched here—they have more soldiers than we have warriors, they have guns, and they do not blink before killing. I don't believe we can beat them. Not because we are not fierce enough, but because in order to win, we'd have to abandon everything that we are."

Kaia felt a little of the air in her chest deflate.

The representative of the cattle drivers, and the only man present, nodded his agreement with Aya. "What does victory even look like for us," he said, "if we lose half our people in the fight? I believe you'd fight bravely," he said to Kaia. "But I also believe you would lose. And I would grieve for you, and for my own daughters, too."

"The Colonizers have so much to gain from trade with us, and, frankly, we have so much to gain from them," said the alchemist.

A surge of dislike hit Kaia like a stone. Of course that was what she thought.

"You'd sacrifice everything that we are," Kaia shouted, "for some new toys to play with."

"Kaia." Ica's voice was stern. "We are here to discuss in good faith. If you can't, then you'll have to leave."

Kaia fumed. She glared at the alchemist but did not speak more. The vote was tied—the youth, the fishermen, and the healers on one side; the alchemists, the cattle drivers, and the potters on the other. Ica's vote would decide the future of the Wariuta. Ica's gaze drifted to the canyon walls, where the shadows cast by the firepit danced. It had not been long since Kaia and Ica had been down here, seeking counsel. Not long since they had both seen Ica's death in the flames. Surely Ica would fight—for her people and for her life. Surely Ica knew that was the only way. Surely.

But Ica did not stand.

"It is possible that we could stave off the Colonizers for another few years. But the cost would be unfathomable. Catastrophic. I do not believe that, ultimately, we can win. Choosing violence now means choosing violence for years, possibly decades to come. And as the leader of the warriors, I can't in good conscience and clear mind let that happen."

And that was that. There was no more argument to be had. Ica's words were final. The representatives all stood and left.

Maybe Kaia imagined it, but it seemed that the ancient flame in the firepit flickered out for just the blink of an eye.

Koa was not in the hut when Kaia returned, so Genevieve was alone.

Good.

The Colonizer sat cross-legged on the floor, braiding her filthy, greasy hair into two plaits. Her dagger was nowhere to be seen. "The Wariuta decide?" she asked, her voice all innocence and hope and ignorance. Cloying. Infuriating. "I hope you trade," she added. "It is good. Trust."

Kaia did not answer. Instead, she kicked the girl onto her side and, before she could scramble up, pressed her knee into her neck. Genevieve thrashed and gasped but could not free herself. Kaia snatched one of the braids and forced her to meet her eye.

"I do not trust," she hissed. "I will never trust you. You're a Colonizer, and Colonizers can*not* be trusted."

Genevieve's face was red and starting to purple.

"I don't care what my mother says," Kaia went on. "We may make this deal, but know this and know it well: I will kill you and all of those stinking, small little men you call your own if and when you betray my mother's trust." She leaned harder into the girl's neck, felt a sick smile stretch her face. She did not like herself in this moment, did not feel proud. But she did feel right. "Do you understand me?"

Genevieve's eyes fluttered.

Kaia opened her mouth to speak again, but before the words could come out, she was knocked, hard, onto the ground. Several things seemed to happen at once—the air was slammed out of her body just as she heard the Colonizer girl gasp for air. A great weight clamped over her arms. And she heard Koa's voice but couldn't make out the words he said.

She opened her eyes and saw her brother. Saw him anew.

He was holding her arms. He was the one who had knocked her down.

His own sister.

To defend *that girl*.

"Don't," he said simply. A few moments passed as they stared into each other, Kaia seething, Koa tearful. "Please," he added.

"She'd kill us all." She wriggled beneath his grip.

But Koa held strong. "She's a prisoner here," he said quietly. "And I won't let you beat prisoners. This one or any other. You are better than that. *You are better than them.*"

Koa was bigger than Kaia, always had been. But he had never leveraged his size or his strength against her. Against anybody, really, despite Kaia encouraging him to do so for basically his entire life. That he chose now to start felt wild, wrong. Against her. Against *her*.

"You're a traitor," she said through clenched teeth. To the Wariuta of course. But also to her. His sister. She was held down by her brother. She could feel tears falling down the side of her face and onto the floor.

"No. I'm not," Koa said. "I love you, Kaia. Please don't do this."

Outside the hut, Kaia could hear Tupac and Chima circling, panting, and giggling. She tried to imagine their familiars battling each other, tried to picture Chima's teeth tearing into Tupac's flesh, the yelps and cries and the whoops of pain and combat. It was a horrible vision, and it made Kaia's stomach turn. She let her body go slack, and as soon as she did, Koa released her arms and stood.

Slowly, Kaia sat up. Her arms were sore from where Koa had held her, but there were no marks on her skin. She wiped her face with her arm, ignored the slick of mud the floor and her tears had made. On the opposite side of the hut, Genevieve watched, her eyes darting between the siblings anxiously.

"You're lucky," Kaia said, "that my brother's got a soft heart. You don't deserve his faith." She pushed down the shame that itched in her throat and the urge to take it back. To make right what she had clearly just made wrong. She had been exactly the person her mother had wanted to guide her away from being. A person of might but not of honor. She should apologize, at least.

But doing that felt like a concession to the same empire that she would see burned to the ground. And she could not do that. She also could not meet Genevieve's eye.

To her surprise, Genevieve bowed her head. "Callum is a fierce man. I . . ."

"You what?" Kaia didn't yell, but her voice made the girl flinch all the same.

"She won't hurt you," Koa said.

"Do not feel . . ." But Genevieve could not finish her thought. "But he is a commander! The Emperor has chosen him. Yes. He is a man of his word. I am only." She looked at her hands. "I am nobody."

"Nobody," Kaia said. "And if he breaks his word, I will kill you. And nobody will mourn you." If she died, it would be a kind of justice.

"I mean—" Koa interjected, but Kaia put up her hand to silence him.

"No one," she said again, firmly.

• CHAPTER 16 •

*Thistle*

The Lady Minami requested Thistle specifically to brush and braid her hair. Thistle was very bad at braiding hair, and she was not even sure she was much good at brushing it, but she did as her mother bade her anyway and went upstairs to where the Lady Minami's guest room was.

When she opened the door, she hardly recognized it as a room in the house where she had lived her whole life. There were throw pillows with silk cases embroidered with patterns. Lady Minami had hung a large piece of gauzy fabric over the window so the morning light came through in a pleasant, gentle way. And she had even propped her own mirror on top of the small table Thistle's father had built. It lent the room a kind of elegance the rest of the house did not have.

"Come," said Lady Minami warmly.

She was sitting before the mirror with her long hair down. It did not look like it needed brushing. It was smooth and perfect and clean. Thistle picked up a brush anyway—one of the Lady's, with delicate gold inlay in the handle—and started to pull it gently through the Lady's hair.

"I so appreciate your help." Lady Minami smiled at Thistle in the mirror.

Thistle smiled back. "Of course, my lady."

"You're a very fast learner, aren't you." It was less of a question and more of a prompt.

"Yes, my lady. Teacher says I'm too smart for my own good."

Lady Minami chuckled. "My tutors said the very same to me. Never seem to say that to the boys, do they?"

"No, my lady." Her hair smelled like the lavender shipped in from Iwei.

"I couldn't help but notice," Lady Minami said, "that someone had rifled through my trunk. The one in the hallway?"

Thistle kept brushing but averted her eyes from the mirror. Her heart beat very fast as she scrambled for the right thing to say.

"You're not in trouble," Lady Minami went on. "It's OK to be curious."

"I'm sorry," Thistle said. She did not know what else to say.

"Now, now. I've been staying here for over a month, and you never poked about my things before. It seems like something changed, doesn't it? Perhaps you weren't alone?"

Something like relief washed over Thistle. "Dai came over," she said, and fresh anger at him burned in her throat. This was all his fault. Everything was all his fault.

"Ah, see, that makes more sense. Dai Phan. Your betrothed."

Thistle pulled the brush through the Lady's hair, but it was rote. She hardly thought of what she was doing. "We'll see. I don't think either of us wants to be married to each other anymore."

"Oh, why is that?"

"He called me a traitor. Called my whole family traitors."

"Very harsh words. Why would he say such a thing? I was under the impression you two were good friends. Best friends, even. That's certainly not a generous way for best friends to speak to each other."

Thistle did not cry. "We aren't best friends anymore. We aren't even friends anymore. He said we're all traitors just for taking Imperial guests, even though his family owns a restaurant that only Imperials can afford to eat at. He's so stupid."

"That does seem quite hypocritical."

"Exactly!" It felt so good to be understood. "I don't see why wanting to make a good living makes us traitors."

"I should think not. It's perfectly normal. Admirable, even."

"Yes! If anything, he's the traitor for not reporting those guns he found."

As soon as she said it, Thistle wanted to shove the words back into her mouth in great heaping handfuls.

"Guns?" the Lady said. Her tone was one of forced lightness.

"They weren't his," Thistle added quickly. "He just found them."

"Well, that's hardly his fault," Lady Minami said.

"He wasn't even looking for them. He was looking for truffles. For his family's restaurant. They grow by the river."

"It sounds like he was just doing his job when he found them."

"Yeah," Thistle said. "They were buried beneath a tree, and he was able to knock off the lock."

"My, my. What a startling discovery."

"That's how I felt—you know? Because they're illegal, and I didn't want to get in trouble. I didn't want Dai to get in trouble, either."

"Of course not."

"I think it's good that no guns are allowed."

"That's very wise of you."

"Dai says they were there because the Resistance is coming back."

"What do you think?"

"I don't know." She thought of the Death shrine in their basement, of the sting in her cheek left by her mother's hand.

"Well, would you like to know what I think?"

Thistle nodded. The Lady's eyes found hers in the mirror.

"I think that a clever girl like you can only improve her lot in life by knowing what's really going on. I know we women are taught to keep our heads down and empty, but I disagree. I think the whispers only we are privy to make us powerful. It takes a lot of self-control to swallow our feelings and discreetly investigate, a lot of cunning. But if we can, then. Well, as I said. We can be quite powerful."

Powerful. It was not how Thistle would have ever described herself, but she liked it, liked the way it felt in her chest, liked the Thistle she could become if it was true. Powerful.

The words were out before she could help it. "Is Lady Minami your real name?"

The Lady smiled in the mirror, a full smile, her eyes twinkling. "Too smart for your own good, indeed," she said. "Tell me, Thistle, what is my true name?"

"Lady Ayer." She liked the way the name shaped her mouth, the sound of it.

"Very good," said Lady Ayer. "You know, I think you're far too smart to be a simple innkeeper's daughter. Such potential. I won't promise anything just now, but do you think you could be my . . . special friend? During my time here in Quark? To help me. To keep my secret. To collect those whispers that only the cunning can find?"

"Yes." She imagined herself like the Lady Ayer, elegant and

poised, full of powerful secrets and mysteries. She liked that version of herself immediately. Liked her much better than the Thistle who peeled carrots and got married off to Dai Phan.

"Well," said the Lady Ayer. "This must be my lucky day."

Thistle grinned as she continued to brush the Lady's long hair. The glint of the gold inlay on the brush caught the light, and Thistle looked at it again; she had not noticed when she first picked it up. Shining back at her was the Emperor's roaring-lion insignia.

This new Thistle was something to behold. A brave and clever girl, the finder and keeper of secrets. Much more impressive than the dead coward's daughter. She was fastidious in calling the Lady by her fake name, especially in her mother's presence, but she kept her true name, Lady Ayer, cradled close to her heart. The Lady had entrusted her with it, and she intended to protect it.

She had managed to smooth things over with Dai—she had told lies about how disappointed she was in her mother, and how much she hated the Lady Minami and all the Imperials who marched in Gia Dinh each day. How she hoped the Resistance *was* coming back, and that they'd make quick work of it, to boot. And when the guns were found by Imperial soldiers, she feigned despair.

And somehow that was enough to mollify the boy.

It had been so easy. He was so easy to trick.

Lying was easy.

She wondered how she had been best friends with him for so long without realizing how naive he was. How childish. How gullible. Not like her at all.

She had promised the Lady Ayer more information about the guns if she could find it, and so she was thrilled when, after school one drizzly, muggy day, Dai whispered that the Resistance was on the move. There were more guns, he said, even after those left by the river got rumbled.

"Where are they now?" Thistle asked.

Dai grinned, and she knew she had asked him the question he most wanted to answer.

"Come on," he said. And, like a fool, he led her to them.

Beyond the rice paddies, the Ó Baoill family kept an ironwood grove and lumberyard. Trees in varying stages of life and dismemberment grew in tidy rows or were stacked in neat piles. Thistle didn't like the grove or the yard much—both were full of large spiders that Dai knew the names of and Thistle did not care to ever learn. But she took her trepidation around the neck and stuffed it down, deep into her belly, where she hoped it would smother and die beneath her bravado.

The smells of sawdust and dying and dead underbrush were thick in the air. Dai, who had been walking a step or two ahead of Thistle the entire time, stopped in his tracks. He turned to look Thistle in the eye.

"Can I trust you?"

Thistle blinked at him, put on her best face of offense. "Obviously."

He smiled, wide and stupid. Trusting. "OK."

He knelt in the shade of a more established ironwood tree and, with his hands, moved some loose soil around until wooden boards were revealed. He pried these open to reveal a deep hole, at the bottom of which was another crate.

"Are those all of them?" Thistle asked.

"I dunno." Dai opened the lower box and extricated a large rifle. It was longer than the length of his arm, and it looked too big in his hands. "There's about ten different caches of them around the yard. This one's got all rifles, but I saw some other ones that were a mix of things."

Thistle picked up a rifle, too. It was heavier than she expected it to be. She didn't like the way it smelled. "How'd you know they were here?"

"Just digging," Dai said.

But Thistle could see him hiding something behind his teeth. She didn't push, though, didn't want him to get suspicious that she was mining him for information. She pointed the rifle at a tree, squinting to peer through the sight.

"Take your finger off the trigger," Dai warned.

Thistle put the rifle down. "Are they loaded?"

"I don't know how to check," Dai said. "But my dad says you should never rest your finger on a trigger unless you're ready to shoot."

"What does he know?" Thistle said. She hoped she sounded playful. "He's a cook."

But Dai didn't take the bait. He shrugged and put the rifle he'd been holding back in the box.

"We should leave before Mr. Ó Baoill sees us."

"Think he knows what's out here?"

"No idea, but I know he won't want to see *us* here."

That was inarguable. Mr. Ó Baoill was infamously cranky. But with so much land to cover, he could rarely find and stop the kids who played there and the teens who made out there.

They covered the rifles back up with the loose soil and snuck out of the grove. Despite her excitement to report what she'd learned to the Lady Ayer, Thistle could feel something cumbersome hanging between her and Dai. Once they cleared the grove, she took his hand. He flinched, surprised, but didn't pull away.

"Dai—are you mad at me?" She did not add *again*.

"No. Just." He squeezed her hand, held her gaze. His eyes were serious, and if she didn't know Dai better, she would have thought he was worried. "Don't tell *anyone*, OK? Not even your mom."

"Of course not," she said. And for a moment, guilt prickled her skin like mosquito bites. But certainly he wouldn't get in trouble after she told the Lady Ayer—the members of the Resistance would. Dai was just a boy, just a bystander, and the Lady understood that; she'd been very clear about that with Thistle. And so Thistle smiled at the boy who had been her best friend.

"I promise," she lied.

And she could tell by the way his shoulders dropped, the way his smile touched his eyes, the way he breathed out in a whoosh, that Dai believed her.

The raid on Mr. Ó Baoill's grove happened within the week. He was arrested, of course. The Imperials did not believe that the caches of weapons could have been hidden all over his land without his consent. And if Thistle felt a twinge of guilt when she saw Mr. Ó Baoill marched through Gia Dinh with his hands bound and his head down, she pushed it aside. She had found the information the Lady Ayer needed, and she'd found it fast. And anyway, it did seem implausible that Mr. Ó Baoill hadn't known. Sure, he had a lot of land, and he was old and walked slowly and with much effort, but it likely took hours to bury all those guns. He must have known.

The Lady Ayer had been so pleased with Thistle when the guns were found.

"What did I say?" she had told Thistle. "Too smart to just be the innkeeper's daughter."

Thistle glowed with pride.

But it wasn't until dinner some days after the raid that Thistle saw the true value of her contribution to the Lady Ayer. The Lady had requested to eat dinner with Mrs. Vo and Thistle together, which was odd. Typically, the Lady ate either in the city or alone, with Mrs. Vo or Thistle serving her. Thistle bristled with excitement. She brushed her hair with extra care and braided it in the best imitation of the Lady Ayer's style that she could muster.

Mrs. Vo was less excited, but that was to be expected, Thistle thought.

The Lady Ayer still sat in her typical spot at the head of the table, the seat with the most comfortable cushions. Mrs. Vo had steamed some fish and made a sticky tamarind glaze that was spicy and sweet. It was usually one of Thistle's favorite dishes, but somehow it felt cheap, or tacky, or too sweet, or too spicy on a plate before the Lady Ayer, who picked at her serving gingerly.

"I want to thank you, Mrs. Vo. For your hospitality these last months."

"Of course," said Mrs. Vo mechanically. "We are honored you chose to stay with us, Lady Minami."

"It has been my pleasure to get to know your daughter in this time."

Thistle smiled. The Lady smiled back. Mrs. Vo took a bite of white rice and kept her face placid and impassive.

"I will be returning to Crandon within the week."

At this, Mrs. Vo's eyes flittered up, and her face betrayed her relief.

Thistle's heart started to beat very fast. "Oh," she said. She felt as if her heart were breaking. "Do you have to?"

"Now, now, Thistle," said Mrs. Vo. "I'm sure the Lady Minami misses her normal life. We cannot force her stay here just because the two of you are friendly."

"Well, that's just the thing," said the Lady Ayer. "I'd like for Thistle to come with me."

"Really?" Thistle practically yelled. "You mean it?"

"I think she's proven to be an excellent assistant," the Lady Ayer went on. "Good help is so hard to find, even in Crandon. And I would ensure her a life of hard work and honor. Thanks to the Emperor." She kissed her two fingers in salute, and Thistle did, too. Mrs. Vo did not.

"No," her mother said simply.

Thistle felt her mouth drop open. It was the opportunity of a lifetime.

"What do you mean, 'No'?" Thistle demanded.

"Surely you'd like to think on it," said the Lady Ayer peaceably. "This would guarantee her financial stability for life. She may even find a suitable Imperial husband if she returns with me. To move up in the world. Certainly you wouldn't begrudge your daughter that."

"No," Mrs. Vo repeated. "I will not allow you to take my only family away from me."

"Ah," said the Lady Ayer. "What if we moved you, too? To Crandon. We could certainly find you some lodging in the Sty's End. Colorful district, lots of immigrants there."

This was better than anything Thistle could have ever imagined. She whirled to meet her mother's eyes, expecting to see her enthusiasm mirrored, but instead she found her mother's jaw set in anger. She was breathing very hard, and Thistle realized how pitiful she looked. How provincial. Her hair was messy, and her dress was worn down from being washed so many times. She hated her in that moment, hated how small she was, with her small guesthouse and her small dreams and her small view of the world.

"Absolutely not." And before there could be more argument, she pushed herself to her feet. "This is our home, Lady Minami. It may not seem much to you, Quark may not seem like much to you, but we aren't leaving."

"The thing is," Lady Ayer said, "I'm not sure you can stop her." She turned to Thistle then. "Thistle, would you like to come back to Crandon with me?"

"Yes!" Thistle yelled. She glared at her mother. "Yes, I would! And yes, I will!"

"You are my daughter," Mrs. Vo said slowly, clearly. "And you will obey—"

But Thistle jumped to her feet, too. Fury beat a song of resentment and fire in her ears. "You can't stop me," Thistle hissed.

"Thistle, dear, please take a seat. Mrs. Vo, you, too," said the Lady Ayer. Thistle obeyed immediately. Her mother remained standing for a moment, then reluctantly sat. "Now, Mrs. Vo, I'm afraid you've been outvoted here. But I would so prefer to have your blessing."

"We both know that you're not in the market for a lady's maid. Let's drop the pretense, milady."

The Lady Ayer quirked a smile. "I see where she gets it from."

"You have been using my home for the Emperor's business for three months now, and I have said nothing about it. I have guarded the Imperial interest, like a good citizen. But I will not see my daughter serve Nipran." She turned to Thistle then, and Thistle was startled to see tears in her eyes. "Your father died so that you might be free. And this is how you'd repay his sacrifice?"

"Careful, Mrs. Vo. You tread perilously close to treason." Lady Ayer's voice was heavy with warning, but Mrs. Vo did not acknowledge her.

"They killed him, Thistle. Your father, my husband. Took him in the middle of the night, without even the decency to return his body so that I could see him buried. He fought, so that—"

"He lost." Thistle felt her lip tremble. "He picked a losing battle, and I never got to know him because of his foolishness." She wiped away a tear and pressed on. "I won't mourn a man who chose a lost cause over his family."

"Thistle, please—"

"No." This time when she stood, the Lady did not stop her. "I won't make the same mistake he did."

And before her mother could argue with her more, Thistle left the room.

• CHAPTER 17 •

*Koa*

The hyenas, whooping and hooting, circled the Wariuta envoys as they made their way to the shore. They had no reason to be anxious, but Koa did. Genevieve had promised him that all would be well, that this was good, and he really wanted to believe her. But there were times when her mouth would say this was the right decision and her eyes would say it was not, and Koa did not know which part of her to trust. Or if he should trust her at all. His mind would not let go of her words at the oasis.

*Why not just kill her?*

And he wondered if he'd been a fool.

It was an odd kind of day, one of the rare ones when the fog rolled in from the sea over the sand dunes. Koa did not like the way the mist hung in his hair, obscured his vision. Next to him, Tupac declined to run around with the rest of the familiars. Instead, he hung close to Koa, as though they were the only two nervous beings in all the world.

"Hold steady, pal," Koa said. Tupac growled his assent.

Ahead of them, Kaia led the group with Ica and the other leaders. Her ax was strapped to her back, and she had a great, heavy shield around her left arm. She didn't trust the Colonizers, that much she'd made abundantly clear. But she didn't seem nervous like Koa was. Didn't seem to feel the possibility of violence hovering over them all, ready to drop. Or maybe she did, and this simply did not scare her. She'd always been the better warrior. She was smaller than Ica, but she walked just as tall.

Next to him, Genevieve stumbled in the red sand, and Koa could tell that she'd rolled her ankle a little. He offered his hand to steady her, and she reluctantly accepted his help. For a long and silly moment, Koa was thrilled that she'd finally begun to regard him as a friend.

Though all the warriors were armed, Kaia had made the decision not to allow Genevieve her dagger. Just in case. And so her hands were empty, except for the sand that clung to her palms from bracing her fall.

"I am perfect," she said.

Koa was pretty sure that wasn't the word she meant to use. He buried his amusement behind a smile and was pleased when Genevieve actually smiled back. Maybe once the deal was done, Genevieve would stay. Maybe they could finally be real friends, the kind that did not need to keep up their guard around each other. They could take turns watching over Lilith's oasis. It would be nice, Koa thought, to have someone like himself around. The dream of not being so alone filled him with hope.

They made slow progress, walking only as fast as Aya could go, and it had likely been years since life demanded Aya make the trip to the shore. But soon enough, they could see where the Colonizers waited in a half-circle formation.

Koa watched Genevieve's face as she looked down at them.

Her brow was drawn in the middle. If he was not mistaken, she looked suspicious.

But all she said was "Odd formation."

And they followed the leaders toward the shore.

Once, when Koa was very young, his father had brought him to the shore.

The waves crashed around their feet. His father was so big. Koa wondered sometimes, Was he as tall as his father had been? As fat? He remembered his father as enormous, with shoulders like the rocks that built the mountains.

"Your mother will want you to be a warrior," said Chimu.

"OK." Koa did not have much of a sense of what that meant, just yet.

Chimu knelt in the sand, let the water roll over his legs, so that he could be at eye level with his son. Koa barely remembered his face now, could not recall what kind of nose he had or the shape of his father's lips. But he remembered the eyes and the lines around them.

"You will have a choice," Chimu said. "Always remember that. You have the choice. You do not have to be what Ica wants."

"Ica's in charge," Koa said.

Chimu laughed, and even though his laugh was big and booming, it was lost in the crash of the waves.

"And for good reason. She is the greatest of us." He put his giant hands on Koa's little shoulders then. "But Koa. She will not always be right, and that is especially true when it comes to deciding who you should be. Do you understand?"

Koa watched the water rolling away, watched the sand gather between his toes.

"No," he said.

Chimu sighed and stood. Koa had the sense he had done something wrong and wanted to take it back. But he *didn't* understand.

"You're going to be big and you're going to be strong. You already are big and strong," his father added when Koa frowned. "But that doesn't mean you have to be a warrior. You are your own person. And I suspect your heart is too gentle to be like me."

"Is that bad?"

Chimu smiled, and so Koa smiled. "No, my love. No, that's a wonderful thing. And I hope, even as you grow and become your own man, that never changes."

When they reached the Colonizers, all the Wariuta except for Aya—who was just too old—took a knee in the sand. A show of respect, of their peaceful intent.

"We agree to trade with you," said Ica. "On the condition of peace, and the cessation of any further encroachment by Colonizers onto Wariuta land."

Genevieve translated this in the staccato rhythm of the Colonizer tongue. Commander nodded and bowed, but it was not the low bow of respect Koa expected. It was hurried. Next to him, Genevieve made a small hiss. She met Koa's eye, and fear dropped in his belly like a stone. She looked panicked. Something was wrong.

But before he could raise his voice—to say what? he didn't know—the leader of the alchemists stood and stepped forward to where Commander waited, and she raised her hands skyward. A signal.

At once, there was chaos.

Explosions of kau went off all around them, enclosing all the non-alchemist Wariuta with the Colonizers. The Colonizers raised their guns.

"No!" Ica shouted, and she stood with her hands up.

But the Colonizers fired.

Koa's mind went silent. There was so much noise, but it all rose into nothing in his ears as he watched, horror-struck, what unfolded. Aya was the first to fall, her body still on the ground, her legs crossed at the ankle as if she were just dozing in a hammock, as if she could stand again at any moment.

And then Ica fell.

Her hands were still above her head when the bullets found her. For a terrible moment, her body seemed to dance, but Koa knew this was death, this was death finding his mother and taking her from this world, with what seemed like a thousand bullets that tore through her body and left the woman who was their leader, was his mother, an empty shell upon the sand.

All around him there was death, death, death, as if life didn't matter at all, as if there was nothing sacred about the breath in their chest or the thoughts in their heads. Just blood and fire and smoke.

A burning in his arm told him he had been shot, and he looked down, detached, to see blood pouring from his biceps. Nothing had penetrated; it was just a glancing blow. He blinked down at the wound, trying to understand it, trying to understand what was happening, when he was knocked to the ground, and it was a moment or an hour before he realized that Genevieve was lying over him, trying to protect him with her tiny body.

"Come on!" she screamed. And her voice pushed open the gates for all the other sounds to come rushing in at once, a cacophony of screaming and gunfire and kau. His eyes searched wildly, and he saw Chima's body. His heart stopped, but Kaia was still alive, and she felled a Colonizer with her ax, her face covered in blood that dripped down her neck and her chest. He hoped, he hoped, he hoped that it was not her blood, but he couldn't look longer to decipher it before Genevieve pulled him and they were crawling away from everything. Koa was hyperaware of the feel of the sand on his knees, of the fog and its chill, of Genevieve as she led him away from the massacre.

She was still tugging at his arm when they cleared the explosions of kau, still yelling "GO GO GO" when Koa turned back to try to understand what had happened. From a distance, it was hard to see anything except smoke. There were bodies strewn about the shore, the Wariuta and their familiars, but a spattering of Colonizers, too. Just death, death, and death. He looked at it as if it were something happening to someone else, saw that they had set all the old crab traps and fishing canoes on fire, too.

But then there was a snuffling at his side, and Koa couldn't help it; he let out a howl that boomed across the dunes. Tupac sniffed his hand. His reluctance to join the other familiars had saved his life. Koa hugged his familiar close to him, and Tupac panted, his breath hot on Koa's wet face.

"Not now," Genevieve said, and her voice was quiet but urgent. She guided Koa back to his feet with her hand soft on his uninjured arm. "We warn Yunka."

Koa's eyes went wide with fresh horror. "No," he whispered. "They wouldn't."

But Genevieve only pulled him along. She did not need to tell him that if they would massacre the Wariuta on the shore, they would certainly massacre them in their homes as well.

They ran.

They did not have weapons, and there were only two of them. But still they ran. If they could just warn the others in time. Koa could lead them to the oases, no Colonizer would ever find them there, the trail was too long, too difficult, too circuitous for them.

There was fresh water there, and frogs, they could survive there if they must, could wait out the occupation if they had to. They could be safe; he could keep his people safe.

He smelled Yunka before he saw it. Smelled the smoke, not of the cook fires but of the fire of destruction. Yunka was a scene of disaster, of apocalypse, as it rose over the dunes. Fire engulfed it in its entirety, the thatched roofs of the huts uniformly ablaze, casting the late-morning sun into darkness. Ash fell from the sky like rain.

Koa made to run into Yunka, and Genevieve tried to hold him back.

"Koa!" she yelled.

But Koa did not listen to her. He ran, as fast as he could, his long legs carrying him faster than he would have believed, Tupac at his side, giggling loud and scared. There could still be Wariuta left. There could still be lives to save. And Koa would not let some smoke keep him from finding them.

• CHAPTER 18 •

*Thistle*

Mrs. Vo didn't knock, she just pushed the door open into Thistle's room. Thistle lay on her bed, her eyes focused on the little crack in the plaster of her wall. She did not stir at her mother's entrance but held her body as rigid as her fury would allow. She felt rather than saw her mother sit on the bed, but still she did not move.

"I know you're disappointed," Mrs. Vo said. "I know you think . . . hm. I know you think the Lady Minami is very glamorous."

"That's not it," Thistle groused. "That's not it even a little bit." If her mother thought a nice outfit was all it took to impress her, then she didn't know her own daughter.

Her mother lay a hand on Thistle's back. Thistle tensed away from it. "You can't trust her, my dear." Mrs. Vo sighed. "You can't trust any Imperials; they—"

"Killed my father, so you keep saying." Thistle sat up and glared at her mother. "But how do you know it was them and not the Resistance?"

Thistle could tell she was trying her mother's patience, but Mrs. Vo held her composure. She took a deep, steadying breath. "I know because I'm in the Resistance."

Thistle blinked. This was not the answer she had been expecting.

"You are . . . what?"

"Mm. I always have been. Always will be."

Everything felt very still. Outside, Thistle was dimly aware of the normal sounds in Gia Dinh—the fruit vendors closing up shop, the clop of horse hooves now and again. But it all seemed so distant.

Before her sat Mrs. Vo, in her endlessly mended dress, with her messy dirt-brown hair. Thistle, she knew, must have looked much more like her father than her mother, whose family had emigrated from the Cold World some generations back. She had his face and his hair and his build—must have, anyway, because she scarcely looked like the woman she was seeing anew. Mrs. Vo's jaw was clenched, her eyes serious.

They had the same eyes, though.

"I've never told you because just knowing is dangerous. And I . . . I wanted to keep you safe. You're my baby. I never expected you would want to leave with one of them, one of—"

"She's not like the old Imperials, Mother," Thistle said. Heat rose in her cheeks. Between the Lady Ayer and her mother, only one had lied for Thistle's entire life, not trusted her with the truth. As though she were a *child*. "She thinks the Empire is strongest when it honors its diversity."

Mrs. Vo let out a loud snort. "Sure. Once they've killed and conquered us, they're willing to say it's nice that we have a few dinner dishes they enjoy. That's not the same as freedom, Thistle; you've never known it, you've never—"

"I could, though," Thistle said. Her voice was louder than she meant it to be. "If you'd let me go."

"Not with her. Not ever with her. It's not a coincidence that Mr. Ó Baoill's grove was raided while she was here."

Thistle's face burned a deep and traitorous red. She tried to look away, but Mrs. Vo was not fooled.

"What have you done." It was less a question and more a demand.

"What was right." She still could not meet her mother's eyes, but she could feel the heat of them boring into her. "Guns are illegal and—"

"Laws made by tyrants are not laws worth following," Mrs. Vo spat.

It was, Thistle could tell, something she had said many times in her life. Never to Thistle, though, never before this horrible night. All around her she could feel the comfort and normalcy of her life crumbling down. Maybe they had never been there at all. Maybe her whole life had been a convoluted lie her mother worked daily to uphold. A facade.

"What do you know?" The contempt in Thistle's voice boomed like cannon fire. "You're just the widow of a coward with dishpan hands and no power. Of course I told the Lady Ayer; she's actually a person of consequence, someone who matters, someone—"

"The Lady who?" Mrs. Vo's face was shrewd, her eyes focused on her daughter.

Thistle shriveled inside. "Minami."

"That's not what you said. You fool child, you're toying with forces you couldn't possibly comprehend." She stood and made to leave Thistle's room, but Thistle lunged for her, catching hold of her mother's wrist. The force of her grip startled Mrs. Vo, who whirled on her, her whole body rigid with fury and disappointment.

"Don't tell them!" Thistle pleaded.

Mrs. Vo wrenched her arm from Thistle's hands.

"You've made your choice, Thistle." And with rising horror, Thistle could see the new reality of her life cresting in her mother's eyes. Regret. She could see her mother's regret, and in that instant, she knew her mother would choose the Resistance over her. Was choosing the Resistance. "I can't change what you've done."

"Please!" Thistle cried. "They'll kill me!"

"Why could you not have just minded your business like I told you?"

"You would let them kill me?" Thistle's voice was hysterical, Thistle was hysterical, could feel her breath leaving her, her vision narrowing so that all she could see at the end of a long tunnel of blurred nothingness and dark was her mother, her mother leaving her, her mother leaving her for dead. "I'm your daughter!"

Her mother moved to the door and did not turn. Without facing Thistle, she murmured: "I have no daughter."

And she closed the door behind her.

Thistle heard Mrs. Vo's footsteps quietly padding down the hall.

Thistle was dead asleep when she was shaken awake and a hand was clamped over her mouth.

"They're in the house." It was the Lady Ayer. It was the middle of the night, so she was in her nightclothes, which was the only thing that made any sense. Everything else was off, wrong.

"Who—" Thistle tried to ask, but the Lady's hand only clamped down harder.

A clatter of dishes breaking downstairs made it clear to Thistle that whoever was in the house wasn't making much effort to be quiet. Who would be in their house, and why they'd knock dishes onto the ground, was beyond Thistle's imagination. She felt very much as if she were still in a dream, except that the pain in her arm where the Lady's other hand gripped her was very real.

"I don't think we can hide," whispered Lady Ayer. Thistle could hear the door to the cellar being opened and boots clambering down the stairs. "So we're going to make a run for it."

Thistle nodded, fear just starting to creep along her spine like a spider crawling upon a branch. She thought wildly of the spiders in Mr. Ó Baoill's grove, of the guns that had been hidden there, of the smell of the gunpowder, of the weight of the rifle in her hands. It had been so heavy. She couldn't imagine hefting one, let alone aiming it in earnest. Having one aimed at her.

The Lady Ayer's body was rigid against hers but not, Thistle realized, afraid. Her movements and her breath were steady, sure. She let the Lady's courage bolster her own. She was not alone. There was no need to be afraid. She gulped down a hiccup of fear and focused.

Down the hall, she did not hear anything, which was odd. Why wasn't her mother responding to the clatter?

She met the Lady Ayer's eyes, and understanding passed between them.

Her mother didn't respond because her mother must have known this was coming.

"Are you ready?" the Lady asked.

"Yes."

Lady Ayer carefully, slowly, silently twisted the doorknob and pressed the door open. After a quick dart of her eyes, she gave Thistle a brief nod. Thistle kept her own eyes trained on the Lady as she led her at a run out of the house. When they were halfway down the front stairs, Thistle distantly heard a man's voice call "HEY!" but neither she nor the Lady stopped. Thistle's heart drummed in her ears like the Emperor's own taiko, loud, loud, loud, as she and the Lady Ayer spilled out onto the street, and the Lady flagged down an Imperial patrol that happened to be passing.

"In there!" she shouted. "They're trying to attack us!"

Three of the men who'd been casually patrolling ran into the house, their rifles drawn. The Lady and Thistle remained on the street with one of the soldiers, who put himself between the two and the house. Lady Ayer clutched Thistle close, and Thistle watched the house as though she could see through the walls, as if somehow the stone walls would reveal what happened within.

Then there was yelling inside the house. Indistinct but urgent.

Then a gunshot. A scream.

More yelling.

"It's OK," the Lady Ayer whispered into Thistle's hair. "It'll all be OK."

It felt like days had passed by the time the soldiers emerged from the house. One led a cuffed young man Thistle did not recognize—his handsome faced half-obscured by new bruises—and the other led an openly weeping Dai.

The part of Thistle that was still a child evaporated at the sight of her erstwhile best friend, blood dripping from a wound in his scalp, his face wet with tears and what might have been vomit. They were supposed to have been married, Thistle and Dai. Dai and Thistle.

"What has happened?" the Lady demanded.

"Found these two inside," the first soldier said gruffly. "This one"—he shook his captive, the young man, who seemed too dazed to fight back—"shot the woman."

"No, he didn't!" Dai wailed. "No, he—" But the other soldier hit him with the butt of his rifle, hard, on the back of the head, and Dai cried out in pain but did not speak more.

Thistle felt as though she were watching it all from very far away.

*The woman,* the soldier had said.

There was only one woman in the house. She and the Lady Ayer were outside.

There was only one woman.

The woman.

"She's dead," the other soldier said.

"Take these men to the Consulate and have them interrogated immediately. Let them see the Emperor's justice," Lady Ayer said. If the men were surprised to be given orders by a random woman in her dressing robe, they didn't show it. "And send back at least two men to stand watch over us," she added. "There was an attempt on our lives tonight, and I don't intend to suffer a second."

"Yes, my lady." The soldiers each held up two fingers, and the lady kissed two of hers and touched them to her heart in response.

"Thanks to the Emperor," she said, and the men echoed her. They led Dai and the staggering young man off to be interrogated. And probably, Thistle realized, hanged. Perhaps Dai would be spared for being a child—perhaps not. He was nearly a man.

The Lady Ayer turned to Thistle then and put her hands on her shoulders so that Thistle had nowhere to look but into the Lady's eyes. They burned into Thistle's.

"I know that this has been a terrible, terrible night," she said. "That there will be no salve for your wounds except time. But I think you should come with me to see your mother, one last time. Come and see what those men, this *Resistance*"—she spat the word—"have done to your family."

Thistle did not speak, did not argue. Lady Ayer led her into the quiet house, the too-quiet house, to where her mother's body waited.

They found her in the kitchen. There, on the floor just next to the stove, was the body, crumpled and wet. The smell of copper and sick, and a terrible smell Thistle did not recognize hit her just as the realization did. The smell was blood. There was a split second of madness in which Thistle thought she saw the body move, the gentle stirring of a breath. But that was just her imagination. There was too much blood, pooled and terrible, beneath the body that had been her mother.

"Look," said the Lady Ayer. "Look at what those men have done. Thanks to the Emperor, his justice will find them. Thanks to the Emperor, they will pay for this."

Mrs. Vo was facedown so all Thistle could see was the familiar shape of her body, in a horribly unfamiliar position. She could not look into the face of the woman who would have seen her own daughter dead, the face that had betrayed her and then been betrayed. Instead, she turned from the body and stepped past Lady Ayer out of the kitchen and then out of the house, as if in a trance.

There was nothing left for her there.

Thistle and the Lady Ayer left for Crandon only a few days later. When the Lady asked her to pack her things, Thistle did not. Not because she was disobeying the Lady—she would never, not on purpose, for the entirety of the time they knew each other. But because there was nothing of her old life she wanted to keep.

The Lady understood this and helped Thistle buy an entirely new wardrobe for Nipran. As they sailed into Crandon's port, Thistle looked up at the statue of the Emperor that loomed enormous over the city. It was the grandest thing she had ever seen in her life, which felt right. She felt grander, too. Bigger. She had a purpose now, as the Lady's maid.

She was dressed in the new clothes the Lady had had made for her, a fine silk kimono in the Imperial style. The Lady had braided Thistle's hair herself, so that she might learn the newest Imperial style. When Thistle had seen herself in the mirror, she'd looked like a whole new person. And Thistle liked the new person.

"It is a shame you're from Quark," Lady Ayer said. She said this without feeling, without any regard for the insult it did Thistle. Rather, she said it like a fact as simple and true and objective as *lousy weather today*. She was right, Thistle knew. "But you could pass as at least part Imperial if it weren't for your name. We should change it before we return to Crandon."

"What to, my lady?"

"Something Imperial but maybe not Nipranite." She paused thoughtfully, considering her options. "What do you think of the name Mary?"

Despite herself, Thistle crinkled her nose. The Lady Ayer laughed.

"Right you are, far too simple a name for a girl like you." She lapsed into silence once again, and Thistle could feel the air growing thick with opportunity. She had a whole new life ahead of her. She could be anyone she wanted.

"What about Rose?" Thistle asked. There was a Princess Rose from a book of Nipranite fairy tales that Thistle enjoyed very much. But the Lady Ayer shook her head.

"No, no. Too fussy. Too precious. You've outgrown the garden fence now, my dear. You're thinking too small." Thistle smiled at this. A big name, then, for her new self. "What about Genevieve?" the Lady Ayer offered.

"Like your nanny."

"Strong woman. Good woman. She'd have liked you, I know it."

Thistle felt her face crack into a grin. "Yes," she said. "I like that name very much."

"Good. That's a very good name for my apprentice."

*Apprentice.* The word felt warm and good and important in Thistle's heart.

Before they left Quark, the news had come that the young man had indeed been sentenced and executed by hanging. Dai's trial still had not happened, but Genevieve could hardly muster curiosity about his fate.

They were not Thistle and Dai anymore, and she was not even Thistle.

And if sometimes, late at night, when sleep would not come, she would see her mother's body on the kitchen floor, crumpled and wasted and gone, well. That was something from Thistle's life, too. And Genevieve did her best to leave it all behind. She had a new life now.

Thanks to the Emperor.

• CHAPTER 19 •

*Koa*

There were only a handful of survivors, and they were all children, small enough to have hidden during the attack or lucky enough to have been inside a hut that kau had not hit. Koa swallowed the bile that threatened to rise again. This was no moment for weakness. He carried Kalei in his arms. She was a baby, still nursing, still so delicate and small. Her mother's body was right outside their hut, Kalei inside, somehow, miraculously, asleep. He did not know how he would see her fed, did not know how to care for a baby, but he held her close all the same.

He would learn. He'd have to.

The children did not want to walk with Genevieve, and so she walked at the very back of the group as Koa led them to the oasis, his oasis, the hardest oasis to find. The Colonizers would not track them there, and they were too young to be affected by the siren's song.

When they arrived, he counted them.

There were only twelve.

All of Yunka contained only twelve children. Babies. The weight of the loss stood beside him, but he couldn't bear it yet, could not look it in the eye or it would crush him.

Lilith poked her head out of the water and then emerged, her face unusually soft.

"What is this?" she asked.

"Nipran attacks," said Genevieve. Her voice was thick with tears. "They kill Yunka."

Lilith's eyes snapped to Koa, who only nodded. In his arms, Kalei stirred, and then her face crumpled into a wail. Looking for her mother, Koa thought. Her mother who was dead and gone.

Just like his own mother.

He could not save Ica, he reminded himself.

But he could save these children. He could honor her in this way, by protecting the children she couldn't.

He shushed Kalei, bounced her in his arms the way he had seen mothers do, but she kept on wailing, high and plaintive and piercing. Her crying set off more crying from other children, and it seemed that soon the oasis would be nothing except the sound of their grief.

"And this is all that is left?" Lilith asked.

"Yes," said Genevieve. "Bodies. Everywhere." She was weeping. *Good*, thought Koa. She had told him to trust them. She should weep.

"They do not change," growled Lilith.

Koa did not respond to this; he just did his best to soothe the baby. Some of the children had already gone to sleep on the warm sand, exhausted, no doubt, by the trauma in their wake. Koa's body felt the drain, but he couldn't sleep, not while he needed to guard the children, not when he needed to decide how best to proceed.

"You must get that baby some milk," Lilith said. "Goat is best, until you find another woman. Cow will work, but not forever."

Koa sagged with relief. There were cows nearby, and goats in Puno. But would they be safe in Puno? He didn't know. But he did know he could steal a goat. And for the first time since they made the trek down to the shore, Koa felt some ounce of resolution, of control. He was so relieved by it that it took him a moment before he realized that Lilith—*Lilith*—was being helpful.

"Thank you," he said.

Their eyes met, and he was surprised to see something like anger thrumming in the siren's gaze. It was not her usual bitterness, it was something different, something raw and fresh and burning.

"I can help," she said.

Koa couldn't resist, he laughed. "Eating the children is not help."

"When have I *ever* preyed on a child?" Lilith snapped. Koa flinched, abashed. "You think that not one has ever come to the edge of my waters, curious and unafraid? You abandon your post too often to believe that."

"I'm sorry," said Koa, and he was. But, he thought, Lilith was still a monster. He knew this, just as she knew this, and though nothing was said aloud, that understanding passed between them.

"How can you help?" Genevieve asked. Her voice was ragged, and her words bore the weight of her effort. "You are stuck."

"My blood," said Lilith plainly. Koa tilted his head, confused. "My blood carries the memory of a weapon that can destroy the Empire."

For a few moments, no one spoke. Kalei's wails punctuated the otherwise quiet that had fallen over the oasis. Koa let his eyes drift to the distance, where the smoke of what was once Yunka rose into the night. He wondered if Kaia survived, then pushed the thought away. There was no way. And there was also no space in his heart to grapple with that just now.

"I do not understand," said Genevieve finally.

Koa snapped back to the present, to Lilith, who was glaring at Genevieve.

"One of you must drink, and I can show you," said Lilith, as though Genevieve were very stupid. Which, Koa thought, she wasn't. The idea was as appalling to him as it clearly was to her. They exchanged a look of suspicious bemusement.

"What, like. Cut you open?" Koa asked. He couldn't imagine doing this, for one, but also, nearing the edge of her water was a death wish. She was stronger than a human, by far, and her offer could easily just be a trick to lure one of them close enough to drain.

"If there were a less painful way, I would take it. But I lack the words." Lilith looked as frustrated as Koa felt. "My wrist would be easiest." Lilith reached one elegant arm out of the water like a gift. And a gift from the Sea, Ica had always said, was not to be trusted. *Ica.*

"Why would you give us this?" Koa asked. "Is this a trick?"

"I would see Nipran fall."

Koa looked to Genevieve but couldn't catch her eye. Her gaze was fixed on the siren, her jaw set. There was soot smeared on her sunburnt face, except in clean tracks forged by her tears. She took a breath.

"I will help."

Koa's brow furrowed. "Help with what?" None of the children wanted to be near her. She did not know the land. From what he'd seen, she did not know how to cook, or forage, or cast pottery, or herd, or fish.

She locked eyes with Koa. "Make Nipran fall."

Koa wanted to laugh, but the look in Genevieve's eyes was too bright with fury, too incendiary to be stoked with mocking.

"I will fight," said Genevieve. "Lady Ayer promises me . . . promises me Nipran means justice. Order." She motioned to the children, most of whom were deeply asleep. "This is not order. This is not what she promises. This is murder."

And before Koa could stop her, she pulled her dagger from where she must have secreted it away on her leg and went to Lilith. Koa felt his stomach roil as he watched her drag the dagger across the skin on the siren's wrist. Lilith barely flinched. There was a pause in which Koa wondered if Genevieve had cut deeply enough, but then the siren's blood, thicker than he expected, redder, began to spill.

Just as Genevieve's lips closed over the open wound, Lilith grabbed a fistful of her hair. Koa drew a shocked breath, Genevieve made a sound between a gulp and a shout, and Lilith pulled her under the glassy green water.

PART TWO

# The Song

· CHAPTER 20 ·

# Alfie

Alfie had never eaten so much butter in his life. Or meat. Or vegetables. Or fruit. Or cheese. Or rice. Or bread. But the butter. The butter was the best.

He looked better for it, too. His cheeks were full; the bags under his eyes were gone. He slept more soundly, and without the drink to help him get there. Working in the Emperor's kitchen was easily the best gig he'd ever held down in his life. Not a lot to compete with, honestly—pickpocketing was brutal, and pirating was... Well. It'd nearly killed him. He wasn't cut out for that kind of life. And the older he got, the more he thought that probably no one was. That no one should have to be.

The fact that he'd been placed in the kitchen as a spy for the Pirate Supreme wasn't exactly the life of ease and safety he might have hoped for. It meant that just as with every other job he'd ever had in his life, his survival depended on not getting too comfortable.

Which was hard. Because the Emperor's palace was *so* comfortable.

The servants' quarters were so lush they made the Nameless Captain's cabin look dim. Alfie could hardly imagine what the Emperor's chambers might be like. Heaven, or some such. The nursery gave a small glimpse, and it had initially been so dazzling that he'd rather forgotten what he was supposed to do upon arriving there with a plate of cold sliced plums and delicate mochi stacked on porcelain dishes for the Emperor's many children.

Or, it should be said, many daughters.

The Emperor had only recently sired his first and only male heir. After decades of daughters, of discarded wives. The palace was abuzz with relief and excitement.

Alfie was on his way to deliver some freshly smooshed berries and ice milk to the child when it occurred to him that—even knowing he was there to bring death to literally everyone who lived in this palace, probably and unfortunately including his coworkers and the many princesses he often served—this was the happiest he'd been in his whole life.

He pushed open the door to the nursery—opulent red lacquer with gold inlay, a door more expensive than Alfie's life was worth, surely—and was delighted to see that Keiko was there.

"You!" he boomed. Keiko laughed, and it was somewhere between embarrassment and delight. She was his favorite of the nurses who worked in the palace. Alfie put the tray of treats for the Crown Prince and future emperor down on the table. "Light of my life! Fire of my loi—"

"Not in here," Priyanka interrupted. Priyanka—the head nurse—was old, and Alfie liked her even if he didn't like her in the same way or quite as much as he liked Keiko. Apparently she had been a nurse to the Emperor's children since she was practically a child herself, which, Alfie figured, must have been at least a hundred years ago. She gave him a beleaguered smile before returning to the little princess whose hair she was braiding. "You know better than to talk your nonsense in here, Philip."

Ah. That was the other thing. He had to go under a fake name, a fake life story, a fake . . . everything, basically. So even if he liked Keiko, she couldn't like him, because she didn't know who he was.

But that was a thought for another time. "I've got the same question I have for you every day, milady," he said grandly.

Keiko rolled her eyes. "I'm not going to marry you."

Alfie feigned taking a shot to his heart and staggered theatrically. One of the princesses (Alfie could never keep their names straight, and anyway they were all named some variation on Jingū) giggled behind her hands.

"No matter!" Alfie crowed. He gave a long and unnecessarily deep bow. "Tomorrow will come and perhaps it will bring me a better reply."

"Hmm." Keiko pulled the Crown Prince from his golden crib (solidly gold—how was this lifestyle sustainable?), and he immediately started to wail in protest until she managed to get him to take a bite of the ice milk from his (again, literally solid) golden spoon.

"How is our majesty today?" Alfie asked.

"Oh, you know," Keiko said. He saw her eyes dart around the room, but the princesses and other nurses were all uniformly distracted with their many toys and books and instruments and impending toddler disasters. "Majestic."

Alfie was just opening his mouth to make a joke about royal diapers when the door to the nursery burst open with a crash. Several of the princesses cried out, and all others looked toward the threshold fearfully. Seven of the Imperial Guard were there, hands on the hilts of their swords.

"Princess Jingū," said the captain. Alfie suppressed a laugh. He really needed to be more specific. "Daughter of the Emperor's Eighth Wife, the Disgraced Lady Michiko."

Ah. There it was. As of earlier that morning, Lady Michiko had not been disgraced. Alfie and Keiko shared a look. He wondered what she had done—or, more likely, what slight the Emperor had perceived from her.

Alfie watched as one of the princesses, maybe eight or nine years old, stood shakily. She was, he thought, being rather brave about it. Here were seven men with deadly weapons ready to collect her, and she acted with more courage and grace than he had the last time he'd been assigned to clean the staff latrines.

Another princess, maybe four or five, tried to pull the Princess Jingū in question back down by the hand, but she shook her off. She met the men halfway, and Alfie was stunned to see them grab her by her arms, hard, as if she were a criminal and not a scared little girl in a pink kimono.

"Where are you taking her?" Priyanka was on her feet now, her face taut with worry. Alfie had never seen her look anything other than sanguine. And it was her fear, he guessed, more than anything else, that made the rest of the nurses scared, too.

"Away," said the captain. His men hauled the little princess out by her elbows. Several of the other princesses were weeping now, but the men paid them no mind. "Thanks to the Emperor," he said with an almost sarcastic bow.

"Thanks to the Emperor," all—even those who were crying—echoed.

The door slammed shut behind the men, and Princess Jingū, Daughter of the Emperor's Eighth Wife, the Disgraced Lady Michiko, was gone.

The arrests and executions had been ramping up lately, that was undeniable. Alfie knew from his sporadic correspondence with Rake that rebellions in the colonies were mounting, with the help of the Pirate Supreme. The unprecedented amount of dissent was, clearly, making the Emperor angry. And though Alfie had seen his anger exercised on the streets of Crandon throughout his whole life, he'd never imagined he would see it within the walls of Emperor's own palace.

Directed at the Emperor's own child.

Keiko wiped a tear. Alfie reached out to comfort her, then pulled his hand back. There were rules about the palace staff, about men and women, about touching. It felt so inhumane to watch her crying and not try to comfort her.

"She'll be all right," he lied. He tried not to think of his sister. She was happy, at least, but she was also gone.

"She's just a baby."

He could hear the strain in Keiko's voice, the worry. She bounced the Crown Prince in her arms, his giggles ringing incongruously.

*Well*, thought Alfie. *No, she's not strictly. And her life has been literal gold and peaches and butter, and so what's a touch of bad luck now after a lifetime of such fortune?*

As if reading his mind, Keiko glared at him. "Children shouldn't pay for their parents' mistakes."

"No," said Alfie ardently. "That's true."

Alfie woke that night in a mess of wet sheets and cursed.

It had been so long since this had happened! Shame bubbled hot and humiliating in his throat. As quickly and as quietly as he could, he pulled the sheets from his bed. He would die of embarrassment if Juan or Charles—the other kitchen boys he shared a room with—awoke to see him covered in piss. Again. He'd been able to bury the first incident in a tall tale of sake and bad choices, but he hardly thought he could pull that off convincingly for a second time.

And though part of him was silently carrying his soiled bed linens to the laundry, one foot remained firmly in his dream. In the world where Fawkes was still alive, his hands looming enormous, like the Emperor's statue over Crandon. Rake had seen the body, had assured Alfie that Fawkes was well and truly dead, but for some reason that did not provide Alfie the peace he hoped it would.

It wasn't like Rake was an expert in lending comfort, though. He was about as soft as a pistol's barrel.

As he crept back from the laundry, the evidence now buried deep within the enormous daily load of linens the palace produced (anonymous and gone), he heard men's voices in hushed argument in the atrium, which was—as a rule—empty at night. He stepped silently to the edge of the door frame and listened to the two figures who stood beneath the rib cage of the articulated dragon's skeleton that hung from the ceiling; it was longer than the room was wide, curling back on itself in a neatly arranged spiral, and visitors from all over the Known World came to witness it. It was, they said, the last of the dragons, killed by the 900th Emperor's own naginata.

A man with an accent Alfie recognized as from Iwei but trained in Imperial tongue was saying, " . . . because now Callum is headed back here for some kind of girl savage show-and-tell, and frankly I don't think the Senate will—"

"When has the Senate ever done anything?" the second voice interjected. That voice, Alfie realized, was not a man's but rather

Senator Tsujima's, rasping and harried with xyr age. A chance to listen in on xyr conversation was a rare and ripe opportunity. Senator Tsujima knew everything that happened in the court. Xe had spies everywhere xe was not. "We are hamstrung by bureaucracy. All the true power lies with the Emperor, thanks to him. You must be patient. Men like Callum are always barking about wars and new lands."

"But if we send men to the Red Shore, then—"

Ah. Alfie listened hard for information that could be passed back to the Pirate Supreme.

"—who will tend to the Resistance in Quark? Or the rebellion in Sty's End for that matter? The Guard is stretched thin as it is, what with the assassination attempts on the constabulary, and morale is dwindling. I fear the Empire will lose the battle for our men's hearts, which will lead inexorably to loss of our land. *My land.*"

"Dissidents come and go," said Senator Tsujima, xyr voice dismissive. "You should worry more about your wife's reputation than about skulduggery abroad."

"And what's that supposed to mean?"

"That you should cut her allowance. She has been drinking too much of the mermaid's blood, I hear. So much, in fact, that she shames herself in public with her intoxication."

The argument mounted from there, but Alfie slipped away, his heart hammering with pride. He would have to find time tomorrow to get to the docks, where several of the Supreme's men were tucked away, undercover and ready to receive intelligence from their many operatives scattered throughout Crandon.

For once, he'd have something to report.

But as he scurried back to his room, he felt something catch in his throat. If the Supreme found out that the Guard was already onto the plans for picking off the various constables around Quark, then surely they'd switch targets.

And the other target under consideration was the Crown Prince.

Alfie tried to push the imagining away, but he could not—his mind treated him to various terrible and bloody scenarios, all ending with a dead baby and worse: a dead Keiko. She was his nurse, after all. If anyone made an attempt on the Prince, she would need to stand in his defense. If the assassins didn't kill her, the Imperials would. He knew what it was to fear for his life, to have a pistol pressed against his temple. He could remember, always, with startling clarity, the feel of Fawkes's hands on his throat, of the world going gray and wrong around him.

It was nearly morning.

He stopped at a window and looked out at Crandon. The orange and flickering lights of blazing lampposts shimmered as far as he could see, tiny fires that begged to spread. The city deserved to burn. The Empire deserved to burn. But the collateral. He had not considered the collateral when he first made his promise to the Pirate Supreme. To serve them faithfully.

To help destroy Nipran.

He shook away his discomfort. It was fine. It would be easy enough to distract Keiko, to pull her away when the time came. She was not some Imperial lady who'd never seen a bad day in her life—she'd worked, been cheated, and still worked some more. He pushed the memory of the Lady Hasegawa down and away. Flora may have loved her, but Alfie didn't. She was just like the rest, and even if he was happy that Flora was happy, he still missed his sister.

But Keiko. Perhaps, his mind whirred with the possibility of it, Keiko could be recruited. Perhaps she could help.

He smiled into the horizon. Already the sun was just beginning to glow in the distance, dimming the orange lanterns as it rose.

He would send the message to the Pirate Supreme. He'd be useful. For once.

◆ INTERLUDE ◆

# *The Sea*

*Her mind is slipping.*

*So many of her daughters have been taken; mankind's thirst for mermaids has always been greedy. But now it is something else, something mechanized, weaponized. She cannot remember so much now. Where there ought to be a memory, there is only emptiness, and she is angry, but at whom? She cannot remember anymore.*

Mother, please, *Evelyn calls. The Sea tries so hard to listen. Evelyn's voice is an anchor, and she bends toward it.* Mother, how can we help?

*This is something the Sea remembers. How much Evelyn wants to help. How willingly she gives of herself for others.*

*But it is not Evelyn's help she needs.*

*She searches. Off the Skeleton Coast in Tustwe, a crabber checks xyr traps. In a kelp forest, a sea otter snags an abalone and returns to the surface with her bounty. A shark finds a whale carcass and feasts until he is sated enough to find a mate. An eel curls into her cavern.*

*They are not who the Sea needs.*

*She needs them. If only she could remember how to find them, if only she could pick through the deafening noise of her awareness and hear their call. Surely they search for her, too.*

*She does not find that chosen person, the person she plucked from all the humans of the world to be her champion; she cannot remember their name. But she does find a rock. A smooth lump of quartz. She rolls over it again and again, listens to its story. It is a story she has heard before, a story she can still remember now that she is reminded of it. This rock has had secrets whispered into it, ugly and hopeful and full of love.*

*Flora's story.*

*If the Sea cannot find her chosen one, then perhaps her children can. At least one of her daughters has met the person she seeks.*

Flora, *says the Sea.* I need you to find the Pirate Supreme.

• CHAPTER 21 •

## *Genevieve*

She watched it as if it were a dream—visions that flashed devoid of sound or smell or taste or touch. Down through the purple depths of the sea, below where the light existed, down, down, down she was led, deeper than mountains were tall, deeper than the sky was high. There was no life here, no darting fish or swaying sharks, past even the strange glowing creatures that dwelled in the darkness.

She heard it only once they reached the Sea's floor—like a clicking at first, far away, then a creak, then a groan, like an ancient ship treading water but bigger, louder. It shook the blood in her veins, rattled the bones in her ears and her feet.

She saw it only once her heart felt as though it had stopped. A shadow in the shadows, black in blackness, but there as sure as she was of anything. It was enormous, as big as the Emperor's statue in Crandon. It exhaled a puff of blue flame, and for an instant, its face was illuminated: craggy, iridescent black scales and curved teeth, as long as a man was tall.

A dragon.

She opened her mouth to scream, but no sound emerged.

Instead, her lungs filled with water. She fought against it, tried to find breath, but for a time she could not comprehend, a time that felt like infinity, no breath would come to her, just the burning pain of drowning.

She thrashed but could find no purchase.

And then, finally, the light came back, dazzling and blinding, burning and bright. Fresh air hit her lungs like a punch of relief. She gagged, spat water, felt herself being dragged from the oasis and onto the hot sand. Her body recoiled in shock at the violent change in temperature.

A shadow loomed over her, blocking the sun. "Are you OK?" asked Koa's voice.

Genevieve rolled onto her side and retched bile.

"Imperials," came the siren's voice. "So fragile."

Genevieve had seen the dragon skeleton before in the Emperor's palace. The last dragon's skeleton. After what may have been an hour or ten minutes, Genevieve turned to the siren.

"You tried to kill me!" She meant to shout it, but it came out as more of a wheeze.

Koa slapped her on the back, and she nearly vomited again.

"If I wanted to kill you, you'd be dead," said the siren, her voice sanguine.

"You're OK," said Koa, but Genevieve ignored him.

"Why did you show me this?" she spat. "The dragons are all dead."

"Idiot child. That's an Imperial lie. The First Dragon remains. She always does."

Another lie? Genevieve could barely stand the anger in her chest. How many lies was the Empire built upon? Wariuta bodies still littered the shore. How many times had that happened? How many bodies lay on the shores of nations all over the world, lured under the pretense of peace? She tried not to think of Dai, of the young man who'd been hanged. Of her mother. Dead, and for what?

Another lie she'd believed. Humiliation burned in Genevieve's throat.

"Yeah. A thousand miles beneath the sea. Maybe a million. Great," Genevieve said. "What good does that do anyone?"

The siren rolled her eyes, impatient now. "The Nipran Empire has more soldiers, more resources, and more footholds around your world than any other humans have ever had. You will need what only the First Dragon can offer in order to beat them."

"Dragons," Koa marveled. Then, looking thoughtful, he said, "I don't actually really know what they are, other than large."

"Creatures from the Sea," said the siren. "But not *of* the Sea."

Genevieve folded her arms. "You talk nonsense."

"Where mermaids are bound to their mother, dragons are not. They make their own choices. They can fly, they can breathe fire, and their song brings justice to the world."

"That's neat," said Koa.

"Indeed," said the siren.

"Nobody has time for songs; we need weapons."

The siren looked at Genevieve with something like pity before taking a deep, steadying breath. "Yes. And that's precisely what a dragon's song is. Convince one to fight alongside you, and you can win. If you intend to take your fight to the Emperor, you'll need something more than your pluck."

That was true. Genevieve wiped her nose on her sopping-wet sleeve and tried desperately to get her mind around the issue. Nipran was not what it seemed. The Empire and its justice were lies. It had to be stopped. There were still dragons. Perhaps the dragons could help. She would need to tell someone who could help her find the dragons.

"Koa," she said carefully, "I know . . . I have no right to ask for anything. From you. From. Any Wariuta person."

"Correct."

"But. Can you take me to Puno? So that I can find passage back . . . to Quark, maybe?" The Resistance could still be there; it was possible. Dragons were still around, so perhaps anything was possible. She had to fix the infinite mistakes she'd made in her short life, and going back home seemed like perhaps the only way to do so.

Koa did not appear to be listening anymore. His eyes were on the baby he'd been cradling since they'd left Yunka. She was asleep now, her long eyelashes resting on cheeks that bore the salted tracks of dried tears.

"Koa?"

"I suppose we have to go to Puno anyway," he said after a time. "I need to find additional carers for the children. They need proper food and shelter, not just frogs and milk."

"Thank you."

"I'm not doing this for you." He met her eyes then, and she could see that they had closed off to her, gave her none of his normal, characteristic warmth. "You're on your own. But I won't stop you from coming along with us."

"Koa, I—"

"No. I'm not interested in what you have to say. I don't think you mean to, but with every breath, you lie. You're a—" And here he said that word she did not recognize. "A well-intentioned one, maybe, but an ignorant one. And I won't see more dead because of you."

Genevieve watched as he cradled the baby with one hand and,

with the other, assembled an additional makeshift lean-to with fallen palm fronds so that a couple more children could rest in the shade. It seemed impossible that only hours ago he'd been silly and smiling.

Next to her, his hyena rumbled a quiet growl. Startled, she pulled her skirt closer to her body. The animal watched this with its black eyes. Watched her and did not blink.

Puno was nothing like Yunka.

Genevieve felt as ignorant as Koa had said she was. She had assumed, despite any evidence or reason, that the cities along the Red Shore would all be identical. But this was not the case at all.

Yunka was set into the sand dunes, with homes perfectly suited for the brutal desert sun and winds. Little huts that kept in the warmth at night and the cool in the day. Puno was wildly different. Carved out of the west side of a set of craggy mountains, it seemed both ingenious and a little precarious. Most of the land had been cleverly terraced so crops could be farmed along the slopes. What buildings did exist were made of the same dark-gray stone as the mountains and the terraces, slick from fog and moss. But there was something about it that lent the sense that it could all come tumbling down. It made Genevieve a little nervous.

The Lady Ayer may have taught her the language, but she hadn't thought to mention that the society was enormously varied. Pink people, Black people, even some she could tell were from Quark. In this way, it looked, she thought, rather more like Crandon than the insular, savage culture the Lady had prepared her for. When studying up for this mission, the Lady had described vicious battles to the death between highly skilled warriors, strange ceremonies, and superstition. What Genevieve saw here was just . . . a city. With people minding their business.

More lies.

Koa had not spoken to her once since they left the oasis, but now he turned to her. "You'll find more"—that word again—"on the south side of town."

Genevieve gulped. She did not want to ask anything else of Koa, but she was also, suddenly, so afraid. What else didn't she know? How else could she ruin everything? She paused, unsure of what to say, what to do. Behind them, one of the little boys pointed excitedly at a baby goat and giggled.

"Go on," said Koa. His face didn't look certain, but he did not falter.

This was fair. Genevieve knew that, knew the blood of his family was on her hands. She had not seen Kaia fall, but she had seen Ica. Dead and broken. Heard the howls of hyenas gunned down. Smelled the blood and gunpowder.

"OK," she said. "OK."

But as she turned away from Koa, she felt a horrible yank on her hair, heard Koa's cry of anger.

"You," hissed a familiar voice. She could not quite place it. Genevieve tried to thrash, but her every movement only exacerbated the pain in her scalp. Koa stepped forward, but the click of a safety being released on a pistol stopped him in his tracks. She could see the war in Koa's face—he seemed bothered by the use of violence, though perhaps not bothered by whom it was being used against.

"It's OK," she said in Wariuta through gritted teeth. "Go."

But Koa didn't move.

The hand loosened its grip just enough so that Genevieve could see who held her. Her eyes widened. Red hair, a face leathered by years at sea.

Rake.

The Pirate Supreme's operative aboard the *Dove*. The man who had killed the Lady Ayer. Who had beaten her. Who had essentially told her—correctly, she now realized—that she did not understand the violation of the Nipran Empire in Quark. Only a day ago, she would have given anything for a chance to kill this man, to avenge the death of her mentor. But now. She didn't know what to feel as she looked into his hardened face.

"I . . ." She tried to find her words again, to find purchase in her own mind.

Koa stepped forward carefully. "You cannot—"

"You were right," Genevieve said to Rake. "You were right about Imperials. I just saw . . . They killed them. They killed them all."

Rake's eyes narrowed at her suspiciously. "Killed who?"

"The Wariuta," she said, her words tumbling now. Koa watched, bewildered, unable to follow enough of the Common Tongue to understand. "They lured them to the shore with mermaid's blood and the promise of peace, but then they shot them all down. Old people, women. They burned Yunka to the ground, killed the children. These ones here, they're all that's left."

Rake's eyes darted to the dozen kids, then back to Genevieve.

"Mermaid's blood," he repeated.

"They're all dead, Rake. They killed them all."

"Mm. Imperials will do that." He let go of her hair but kept his pistol trained on her. He looked to Koa then, and in a strangled kind of accent said, "Sorry for dead," in Wariuta. "But girl come me."

Koa raised one eyebrow. "You know this man?" he asked Genevieve.

"Yes."

"He doesn't like you," said Koa.

"Most people don't."

Rake's hand encircled her arm and started to pull. "You'll need to come with me," he said.

"Yes," she said distractedly. Seeing that she was being pulled away, one of the little girls had started to cry. Not, Genevieve thought, because she liked her but because another change was simply more than the little girl could bear.

"Tell me where to find you," Koa said to Rake. "Once I've found a safe spot for the children."

Rake blinked at him, clearly out of his depth.

"Tell him where we're going," Genevieve translated. "He doesn't trust you. Or me."

"Then why's he care?"

"Just. I think he's not so keen on murder?"

Rake shrugged. "Fair enough. Tell him we're staying in a guesthouse on the southeast side of town. By the alchemists' lodge."

Genevieve translated this, and Koa nodded, mollified. Without another word or look to Genevieve, he led the children in the opposite direction.

"You've got some explaining to do," said Rake as the children trailed away.

"I know." It was, she realized, quite lucky that Rake had found her. Not lucky if he murdered her outright, but then, if he was going to do that, he would have done so already, right? And anyway, she had information to share. Certainly he wanted to destroy the Empire. She could pass the knowledge the siren had given her on to him, and through him to the Pirate Supreme. "I have so much to tell you."

"This isn't a campfire," he said coldly. "We are not friends."

Genevieve rubbed her scalp, which was still sore. "Yeah, clearly."

He did not release his grip on her as they moved through the crowded roads. Genevieve's stomach roiled with hunger she had not noticed until she smelled the cookstoves that seemed to be going everywhere.

"Is the Pirate Supreme there?" she asked. "I want to talk to them."

"I'm sure you do," said Rake. "But I wouldn't let you anywhere near them if my life depended on it, you traitorous little snake."

"But—" Genevieve wanted to explain; she'd changed! She knew better now! She'd learned! But how to say that without sounding like an operative. "I can help."

"Yeah, sure. I'm taking you to the Fist. You can tell that to her."

"The Fist?" Genevieve scoffed; she couldn't help it. "What kind of stupid name is that?"

Rake turned, and the smile he gave her robbed her of what little bravado she had left. "She doles out the Resistance's justice here," he said. "You can plead your case to her."

"The Resistance?"

Genevieve's blood ran cold.

"Like I said," Rake said, his voice barely containing his amusement now, "you've got some explaining to do."

• CHAPTER 22 •

*Tomas*

Tomas Inouye knew he'd fallen out of favor with Commander Callum when the Lady Hasegawa had escaped her imprisonment on the Floating Islands. If the commander had known how intimately involved Inouye was with that escape, Inouye would have kissed a noose for sure. But it was enough that it'd happened on his watch. And so now, while the rest of the soldiers enjoyed the first pass of rations in the galley, Inouye was trapped in the moldering, stinking brig, watching over the barred and locked cage that held an unconscious one-handed girl.

The slaughter of the savages on the Red Shore had not sat well with Inouye. Seemed ugly. There'd been so many women. Old people. Children. If the Empire could be brought down by girls and kids, then it wasn't much of an empire, was it? Or at least it certainly wasn't the Empire he'd been brought up to believe in. He hadn't said this aloud, of course—not to anyone. You could never tell who was a snitch hoping to curry favor. Hadn't Tomas ratted out a fellow before in the hopes of promotion? And when he was outed, Callum'd see him whipped for impertinence. Big fan of whippings, Callum. Inouye was not such a fan of Callum for this, and several other reasons. Chiefly his haughty demeanor and frankly prickish attitude.

The girl stirred a little in her sleep. Inouye watched her. She was still filthy with dried blood, but without her ax, she didn't seem so fearsome. He'd seen her in battle. Seen her take down Lieutenant Bisset with one swift swing of that ax. Had watched as she buried it into his back, his body, once whole and breathing, suddenly cold and gone.

"You'll see death," his father had told him when he enlisted. "And you'll never be the same."

His father had served for nearly all his life until he lost several fingers to frostbite on an exploratory mission that had yielded nothing of value to the Empire. Had set their family up passably if not comfortably for Tomas's whole childhood. His father's words had not been a warning so much as a statement of fact. He believed in the duty of good Imperial men to serve in the Guard. And though his father had never amounted to much in his many years, he believed, despite their family's low standing and Tomas's lack of any real martial talent, that his son would make it further than he had. Seeing death was, by his reckoning, just one of the many ways boys became men.

Inouye did not feel like much of a man. But again, this was not something he spoke of aloud.

The boat creaked, and above him, Inouye could hear the heavy footsteps of his brothers-in-arms heading off to their cabins to sleep. His watch was only just beginning.

The candle that illuminated the dingy brig flickered in its lantern mutinously.

Bringing the girl back to the Emperor was, Inouye thought, stupid. What'd the Emperor care that a one-handed girl could wield an ax? Surely, as a god, he would be unimpressed. Surely he'd seen more amazing things. There was a dragon skeleton in his palace! But Commander Callum seemed to believe this would entice the Emperor into sending troops over to more fully colonize the Red Shore, and it wasn't Inouye's place to argue.

Bored, Inouye kicked at the iron bars that separated him from the savage girl. She startled awake and was on her feet with frightening speed.

"What's your name, anyway?" asked Inouye.

But she only glared at him and sat back down on the cold, damp floor. She didn't speak Common Tongue, that much was clear.

"I'm TAW-MUS," he said loud and slow. "TAWWWW-MUSSSS."

The girl just stared at him as though he were the stupidest person she had ever seen.

"My NAME," he shouted, "is TAW-MUS."

She blinked. There was a chamber pot in the corner of her cell, which she regarded suspiciously. It had not been well cleaned since the cell's last inhabitant, Inouye knew. He knew because he was supposed to have cleaned it and had not. Not that he had disobeyed orders so much as he had edited them down somewhat. And anyway, she was likely used to squalor, so what was a musty chamber pot to her?

Without shame or hesitation, she sat on the chamber pot and took a long, loud piss. Inouye looked away at first, but when he looked back, she was still glaring at him. What a wild thing she was, unconcerned with his gaze even in this private moment. She was pretty, in an odd, savage way. The tilt of her eyes above her jutting cheekbones. Not pretty like a lady, but beautiful like an animal, maybe.

Distracted by the search for the most apt comparison, he realized a moment too late what she was doing. She had stood and picked up the chamber pot, and as he scrambled—seemingly in slow motion—to get clear of the way, toppling over backward and hitting his head on the floor, she swung the chamber pot at him.

He felt the hot splash of her piss all over.

Soaking into his uniform. In his hair. In his mouth.

And even as he spat and yelled abuse at her, as he banged his rifle against the bars of her cage, she only stared at him, impassive and unflinching except for a shadow of a smile in her eyes. The piss had gone cold, and he shivered in the gloom and the chill of the brig.

"Unbelievable," he muttered once he had yelled himself hoarse.

He righted his stool and sat back down, using his handkerchief to try to scrub some of the mess from his face and hair. If the other men figured out what had happened to him, he'd never hear the end of it, and the shame, preemptive and scalding, burned through him in a blaze. Just once, he'd like to guard a prisoner and not have his life ruined over it.

The girl sat back down on the moldering pile of straw that was her bed and said something in the strange staccato language her people spoke. He couldn't understand, of course, but he could still hear the impertinence in her voice. The hatred. That was fine. He hated her, too.

And then, in what sounded like a curse, a malediction, she spat one word he did understand:

"Tawmus."

• CHAPTER 23 •

# The Pirate Supreme

The Pirate Supreme did not like Barilacha, the capital city of the Floating Islands. That is to say, they did not like what Barilacha had become. Everywhere, Imperial Guards stalked about like loose dogs, teeth bared. The Pirate Supreme wanted to comfort every person they saw, to whisper: *Someday these men and their guns and their boots and their ignorance will be gone, I'll see to that; the Floating Islands will be free.* But they couldn't, and so they didn't, and they swallowed the disgust they felt when they saw two soldiers leering at a local girl, no more than fourteen. Pushed down the urge to pull the pistol they had secreted away in their coat and ensure that the Imperials would never enact their violence upon her, or anyone else, ever again.

The Pirate Supreme had to be discreet.

They rode the rickety and unsettling elevators away from the shore, from the Sea, and toward her. Their skin crawled. Every step away from the Sea felt like a mistake that compounded itself. Every step toward her felt like a mistake best left in the past. She would not be happy to see them, they knew this. They had to seek her out regardless.

It had been years. Decades, now.

Her door was the same, with its golden-hand knocker that they knew had been pilfered off the captured ship of a Cold World slave trader. They knew this because they were the one who took it, who brought it back from the Sea and gave it to her. It was a gift to her as much as a punishment to that slaver, and they had both delighted in its duality. A perfect present. They wondered if she still had the slaver's head, too.

They knocked. Their hand reunited with the gold one if only for a moment.

Why did they feel anger already, annoyance that billowed, when she had not even yet opened the door? She had stopped begging them to return long ago. Stop writing, stopped calling out to them. So why did it feel as though she had made them come back? Why did they feel manipulated?

She opened the door, and for a moment they regarded each other like strangers. She had aged. So had they, they knew, knew the creases in their face had become deep and permanent, knew their muscles had gone wiry and long beneath their sun-worn skin. And yet it was still startling to see her, her black hair laced with white, the skin on her neck loose and puckering. But Xenobia was still beautiful.

She gasped.

"Kwizera." She did not speak their old name so much as she breathed it.

"No one calls me that anymore."

She stepped aside, and they wordlessly followed her into the home they had known so well for so long. Little of the house had changed, not the darkness, not the cramped ceiling. Not the tea she served them in a small ceramic cup. At least the cup was new.

They knew better than to unquestioningly drink the witch's tea.

"I wondered—I hoped, I mean—that you would ever—"

"I'm not here for us," the Pirate Supreme said. "I am here for the Sea."

"Ah." Xenobia sat down opposite them at the little wooden table, and her face would have been a blank wall if they did not know her better, did not see the flicker of fury in her eyes. "Were we so bad for each other, Kwizera? Truly?"

"You tried to kill me."

"Only the twice."

"The situation is the same. I've got just enough room in my heart for one tempestuous bitch, and it isn't you."

Xenobia smiled her shark's smile. "How is your lady love these days? I hear she's been very testy."

The Supreme pushed down their irritation. Xenobia knew, of course; they could tell, could see the smug victory in her eyes. The Sea had been alternating between furious and distant. With her mermaids disappearing at such a terrible pace, she couldn't help but blame the Supreme, whom she had charged with their protection. Their bond wore thinner and more strained each day. They wondered if she could even hear them when they called anymore. Or if she would listen. They had resolved to call upon her less, telling themself that it was best for the Sea, when really it was their own fear that the Sea would not respond.

"I need your help."

Xenobia fingered the string of pearls at her neck. "Of course you do."

"If I had any other ideas, literally anything, even the inkling of another plan, I wouldn't be here."

"Don't go whispering sweet nothings into my ear or I might get too full of myself."

"I need you to help me find the banished mermaid."

Xenobia's face fell, and they could see it in her eyes. Fear.

"No," she said simply.

"The Sea will not listen to me. And I . . . I suspect that the memory the banished mermaid holds is the essential one to defeat Nipran. For once and forever, Xenobia. Imagine it. A world without the Emperor's shadow looming over us all. A free world. You used to believe in such a thing."

"I also used to have tits up to my chin. I'm sure you remember them."

They pushed away the memory, which was crystalline and bothersome in its clarity.

"It's possible now. There are Resistance cells all over the Colonized World ready to fight at my word. We just need your—"

"Why would I help you? Help the Sea?" Xenobia interrupted. "She has taken everything from me. And you." She did not finish that. She didn't need to. *Chose her over me,* she could have said. *Left me,* she could have said. *Abandoned me. Betrayed me. For power. For the Sea.*

"This life here. It can't be safe. There are Imperials all over the place, and we both know what they'd do if they found out about your business. About what you are."

"Not everyone needs to be a revolutionary, you know. Always so grandiose. We don't have guns secreted away, but that doesn't mean we don't have power. It's quiet rebellion, so I'm not surprised you don't understand it. No one in Barilacha would ever betray me."

*Unlike you,* she didn't say, did not need to say. The words hung between them anyway.

"Your safety is precarious here, and you know it." They picked up the cup as though they intended to drink, but at the hungry look in Xenobia's eyes, they put it back on the table, their suspicions confirmed. Whatever was in that cup—poison or potion—couldn't be trusted. "As long as the Imperials have unfettered power, no one is safe, especially not you. And the Emperor's appetite for new subjects is ever growing. Just a week ago, his men committed slaughter on the Red Shore—"

"What do I care of that ill-begotten trading post?" Xenobia muttered, but the Supreme pushed on.

"And captured the near entirety of the Wariuta stores of kau. I can't imagine you need me to explain that it is objectively bad for the Emperor to have large stores of deadly explosives."

There was a pause, and the Supreme could feel Xenobia's mind churning. She didn't like the idea of the Emperor developing weapons of mass destruction any more than they did.

She stood, poured more tea from a different kettle. Whereas the tea in their first cup smelled of linden flowers and dittany, the new tea smelled of clove and something else savory, woody. She took a conspicuous sip of her tea before she placed the cups down for herself and the Supreme and then left the room for a moment.

When she returned, she carried the mirror that had always hung in her bedroom. It looked the worse for wear, the frame around it cracked. But the glass was still whole. She placed it on the table between them, and it reflected the mud ceiling back at them.

"I'm only doing this," she said tartly, "so that maybe one day I can poke my toe in the Sea without fear of her sending a tidal wave to murder me on the spot. I assume that's something you'll communicate to her?"

"Of course."

"I'm not doing this for you."

"Of course not."

"Because you're an asshole."

"Well—"

But before the Supreme could argue that point, Xenobia closed her eyes and began to murmur the words of a spell. Kwizera felt a twinge of nostalgia in their chest, for nights spent watching Xenobia hone her craft. They brushed it away.

The ceiling flickered and then faded from the mirror face, and the Supreme watched it intently as green water slowly became visible. Green water that rippled, then splashed violently. Xenobia kept murmuring, more urgently now. The green water was surrounded by red sand. The banished mermaid must have been in one of the many oases of the Red Shore.

But then they saw why the water was thusly disturbed.

The siren was hauled onto the sand by several men. Several men of the Imperial Guard. She thrashed and spat and tried to bite them, but they were unhindered by her fight. The dead guardsmen that floated facedown in the green water told the Supreme that the mermaid had not been caught easily. Each of them had been smart enough to plug their ears. They were immune to her best weapon. She was pulled onto the sand and then dropped.

As she tried to drag herself back to the water, the men of the Guard raised their pistols.

They could not hear the bullets, but they could see their effect. The life drained from her eyes.

Xenobia stopped murmuring. Only the mud ceiling remained in the mirror.

◆ CHAPTER 24 ◆

*Alfie*

Keiko would tell him about it after. Alfie was not so foolish to pretend that he would have been brave enough to watch it unbothered. He had been fortunate that he was off reporting to his contact for the Pirate Supreme at the Crandon docks when the entire palace was gathered into the great courtyard to bear witness to the executions.

No one was surprised that Lady Michiko was sentenced to death. She had lain with a senator while married to the Emperor. This had happened before in history, and—Alfie thought, given the Imperial predilection for taking on many wives even well past the time in the Emperor's life when he was likely able to perform any husbandly duties—it would happen again and again and again. And again. And just like every other time it had ever happened, the wife was sentenced to death and the senator, too, for betrayal. They were hanged in the courtyard before all who knew them, a warning.

But this time, so was Princess Jingū.

They'd had to stand her on an empty shipping crate so that the noose could reach her neck.

It was not enough to simply punish the criminals. Their families must be punished, too. The senator had been a young man, not yet married or father to any children, his parents already gone. But their graves were exhumed and their remains thrown into the sea.

And still, the next day, the three bodies hung in the courtyard as all tried their best to pass them without seeing them, trying to ignore the smell of them as they went about business that invariably took them through the courtyard, which was at the center of the palace grounds.

Alfie secreted a bottle of sake from the kitchen. It was easily taken—there were so many bottles, and everyone was a little distracted. And he took it to Keiko, who had a rare day off from watching the Prince. A kindness from Priyanka, no doubt.

Alfie knocked on Keiko's door. There was no answer.

"Come on," Alfie said as kindly as he could. "I know you're in there. And I've got a present for you."

Silence.

"Keikooooo," he crooned.

He knocked again. "Beautiful Keiko, if you don't open this door, I'll have no choice but to serenade you from the hallway. I have been practicing my finest Iwei opera voice, and I think both you and everyone who happens to walk by will simply—"

There was a shuffling, scurrying sound, and Keiko opened the door. Her eyes were narrowed in annoyance, her hair disheveled, and Alfie could see that she'd been crying. A lot. He lifted the bottle of sake and two glasses with a smile, and, after a perfunctory glance down the hallway to ensure no one saw, she let him in.

The nurses got their own rooms, and Keiko kept hers very tidy. Her bed was made, and there were a few books stacked in a neat pile on the small tansu where she presumably kept the rest of her belongings. A tiny window let in the last bit of red light from the dwindling sunset. It was a sparse room and a small one, and Alfie's heart wrenched in envy at the idea of space of his own.

"Your room is as lovely as you are," he said instead.

Keiko gave him a withering look. "Honestly, Philip, stop. I'm not in the mood." She put a couple of flat cushions on the floor, and they both sat down, Alfie chastised, Keiko miserable. He poured them each a glass of sake and was a little shocked when Keiko downed hers in one gulp and held out the cup for more.

"I'm sorry," Alfie said as he poured. And he meant it. He was sorry that Keiko had seen a child she'd helped care for killed. He was sorry it made her so sad. He was sorry that it would probably happen again.

"She was a very sweet girl," Keiko said mournfully. A fresh tear rolled down her cheek, and she ignored it.

Alfie, thinking Keiko was too lost in thought to notice, rolled his eyes.

"What." It was less a question, more a demand. *Explain yourself.*

Alfie sighed. "Easy to be sweet, isn't it? When you have everything you want all the time."

"Except her life," Keiko spat.

Alfie wanted to help, but he couldn't help it, couldn't help himself. "One bad day," he said. "She never had to wonder when her next meal would come, never lived without adults to care for her. It's sad she's dead, but so are countless other kids that didn't get to live in the palace and died too early as well."

Keiko laughed. "You live here, too, you know."

"But I haven't always, have I?" Alfie could feel the heat on his neck. He wanted so badly to shut up, and he just couldn't seem to do it. The memories of his own childhood, not far from this palace, scrounging for food, begging for anyone to care. A set of cold, dead ears in his hands. Fawkes. "And anyway, I work here; that's different."

"Yes," Keiko took a solemn sip of her sake. "I suppose it is."

They sat together in silence. Alfie did his best to drink his wine slowly. He could feel the bad mood, the anger swelling inside him, and if he drank too much, he'd unleash it all on Keiko, which was the last thing he wanted. He was supposed to be comforting her, he knew that; why was he so bad at everything?

"They're not all cruel, you know," Keiko whispered. "There are good ones."

"I've heard that before." He could not keep the bitterness from his voice.

To his surprise, Keiko's hand found his and squeezed it firmly. "I don't know where you've been. I don't know what you've seen. But I'm sorry it hurt you."

Their eyes met, and Alfie was too taken aback by her kindness to notice that he was crying. Wordlessly, he leaned toward her. It could just be exhaustion, if she wanted. It could just be a gesture of friendship. She gave him a rueful smile, reached her hand up, and cupped his cheek. She did not kiss him. She also did not need to speak to the sorrow they shared. How strange it was to know just from this that she had lost someone she loved, too. How strange to have a friend.

Alfie knew the plan to have the Crown Prince assassinated was likely speeding along the docks, careening toward the time when Keiko's life could be imperiled. And Alfie recognized two things at once. The plan must go forward. And Keiko must not be hurt. He would have to get her out of harm's way, have to remove her from the bloody path that would find its way to the tyrant's heir.

And he'd have to do so without Keiko knowing it.

It was risky, Alfie knew, to return to the docks so soon. One trip out of his way was reasonable as a kitchen boy. Maybe he'd saved enough for a visit to the whores who prowled there. But two so close together would be harder to explain. Still.

Funny how, after all the years he had been on the *Dove*, the streets of Crandon were still indelible in his mind. He could find the fastest route at any time of day, knew how to dodge the constabulary patrols. So even if it was risky, he could do it; this was one thing he could do.

He'd failed to keep his baby sister safe.

He'd failed to keep himself together.

Failed to be strong. Failed to be brave.

But he wouldn't fail this time. And not just to keep Keiko safe—to keep all the nurses safe. Priyanka. The irritable one. That one he'd caught looking at his butt several times. She deserved clemency for her good taste at the very least. All of them. There was no reason for any of these women to suffer because they, too, lived under the boot of a tyrant.

The sun was high, and the air was thick with the dust and grime kicked up by the horse-drawn carriages. The tang of sea salt in the air found him, and he knew he was close.

His contact worked as a crabber and would not tell Alfie his name. But he was easily spotted—fully a head taller than everyone else who worked on the docks and tattooed from brow to toe with the blue ink so popular among men from the Cold World. His pink skin was mottled with scars.

He was taking a break, leaning against one of many stacks of shipping crates, smoking a pipe. The smoke curled above his bald head in great winding tendrils. All around them, seagulls called and the men of the docks went about their business, hauling crates and yelling to one another. Alfie ran to his contact.

"Hey!" He nearly tripped over his own stupid feet as he neared him. "Hey, man, I gotta tell you—"

But before he could finish, before his contact could even turn to meet his eyes, several men from the Imperial Guard emerged from behind the great shipment, their pistols drawn.

"Carden Moi," their leader barked. To Alfie's horror, his contact startled. "You're under arrest for collusion against the state."

Alfie immediately made to run away, but one of the guards called, "Hey!" And Alfie knew he was cooked. He turned slowly and gave an obsequious bow. Carden was being cuffed, none too gently, and hauled off, but the leader and one of his underlings remained.

"You'll be needing to come with us for questioning." The underling grabbed his arm.

"Wait, hold on, then!" Alfie said quickly, his mind racing. "I was just . . . he sold us bad crabs!"

The two men of the guard exchanged a dubious glance. "What's that?"

"That man—his crabs." Alfie's mouth couldn't quite catch up with his mind. "They were spoiled. Got them to the palace, and they were no good."

"The palace," said the leader.

He gave Alfie an appraising look. Alfie did his best to look respectable.

"Easy enough to check," the other said, and Alfie's stomach dropped. It was a lie, of course. The palace hadn't bought any crabs. He was hoping the invocation of the palace would have been enough to keep him safe.

No such luck.

They tossed him in the back of a barred carriage with his contact and headed off to the city jail.

"So," said Alfie, conversationally. "Your name's Carden?" After all their time in contact with each other, Alfie had never known his name. He'd called him Cranky McJerknuts in his thoughts, but that wasn't something he could say aloud.

The man whose name was apparently Carden glared at him with his unsettlingly blue eyes. He reminded Alfie a bit of Fawkes, so Alfie looked away. Carden was not Fawkes, and this was not the *Dove*. He needed to keep his head about him if he was to wriggle out of this.

"Don't tell them anything. Not a thing," Carden said as they slowed to the jail. "Remember, there are fates worse than death, and cowards always find 'em."

"Right." Alfie gulped.

Carden was dragged out of the carriage first, and then more men came for Alfie. He smiled at the men, trying to look innocent and compliant, but the men did not smile back.

"Right."

• CHAPTER 25 •

# Genevieve

She wondered what the Lady Ayer would do. She was smart, had taught Genevieve everything she knew about manipulation and guile. And yes, maybe she'd fought for the side Genevieve now wanted to see defeated, but that didn't mean everything she'd taught Genevieve was bunk. She'd been an excellent mentor.

And Rake had killed her. Shot her through the neck during that terrible battle aboard the *Dove*.

The Lady Ayer's murderer led her to a small stone house, where a ragtag group of people milled about. Pirates, no doubt. Too many piercings and tattoos and strangely flamboyant clothes to be anything else. Didn't even try to look respectable.

But then, Genevieve thought, maybe that was the point.

Inside, the house was small and dank and smelled faintly of mold. Rake bade Genevieve sit on a small wooden chair, and after she did, he cuffed her to it. Genevieve did not struggle against this and did not even argue. She did not need to like Rake to know that he could serve as an effective conduit to the person she so desperately needed to reach.

And even as deep dislike, possibly hate, bubbled in her chest, Genevieve stayed still, stayed obedient. She was a better person than he was, she reminded herself. She could be a better prisoner than he'd been as well.

Rake set about making a fire in the hearth.

"So why's he called the Fist?" she asked conversationally.

"She."

"Why's *she* called the Fist?"

"I suppose due to her predilection for knocking out Imperials," he said. He fanned the small flames he had made. "And those who lick their boots." He gave Genevieve a meaningful look.

"I didn't know," she said solemnly.

"Bullshit. You're from Quark." The fire was stable now, so he backed away from it, pulled up a stool, and sat down. He took his pistol from his boot and started polishing it with a greasy rag stowed in his other boot.

"The Resistance killed my mother, you know," said Genevieve quietly. She'd done her best to push the sight of the blood, the body that lay in the kitchen, down, down and away, but still it rose, in the quiet of the night and in the stillness of the morning.

Rake stopped polishing his pistol for a moment, and their eyes met. He looked so much like the men Genevieve had grown up with—wiry and weatherworn. She wondered what his childhood had been like in Quark. If he'd gone to a school like hers, known boys like Dai. How odd it was, to have started in the same place and then taken such wildly different paths.

"I'm sorry," he said. "It's no small thing to lose your mother."

And for a moment, they were just two orphans, alike if not identical in their loss.

But then he looked away, and the moment of empathy, of sameness, snapped out of existence. He squinted down the sight of his pistol and resumed polishing it.

They sat in silence for what felt like hours. Genevieve's hands went numb in her cuffs, her arms sore from being stuck in the same position. The fire crackled and danced, and Rake had to add more wood to keep it going. Whoever the Fist was, she was sure taking her time.

At long last, the door creaked open, and Genevieve heard the footfall of someone behind her. Trying to maintain what little dignity she could muster as a person handcuffed to a chair, she did not strain her neck to try to see the person.

"Rake." It was a woman's voice, low and rasping.

Rake stood, and—was he blushing? He straightened his coat and squared his shoulders. Genevieve suppressed a laugh. He had a crush on the Fist, that much was blazingly and immediately obvious.

"Got a prisoner for you here. Says she has some information that could help fight the Empire. Be warned, though; I've met her before. An Imperial bootlicker if I've ever met one. Was working beneath an Imperial operative, so I suspect she could easily be a spy."

"I'm not," said Genevieve.

"That's what a spy'd say, though, isn't it?" said Rake coolly.

Genevieve could hear the Fist take off her coat, throw it on the floor. "Either way, information is information," she said. "We can dispose of her after, if need be."

"Ah," Rake said. "Not so sure on that count. There's a Wariuta boy who seems to be watching out for her."

Genevieve wasn't convinced Koa would be all that mad if she got killed, but decided against mentioning that.

"Hmm." There was something familiar in the voice, but Genevieve could not place it. The vague Quark accent, maybe. "We'll cross that bridge when we get to it."

The Fist circled around, and when their eyes met, Genevieve felt the breath catch in her throat. They stared at each other, both too dumbfounded to speak for some time. Very distantly, Genevieve was aware that Rake was still talking, but for the life of her she had no idea what he said.

"Thistle," said her mother.

Her mother, who was not dead. Her mother, who was very much alive. There was a puckered bullet scar on her throat that explained the change in her voice, and she wore a patch over her left eye now, but that was her mother, that was Mrs. Vo, the same woman who'd taught her to peel carrots and braid her hair.

"Mother?"

"What?" Rake practically shouted. "You little snake, you *just* told me your mother'd been killed by the Resistance!"

Mrs. Vo laughed, and it was a bitter laugh. She made no effort to undo her daughter's binding but rather sat down on an empty chair as though Genevieve's presence had knocked the wind out of her. "Is that what she said? Well, not quite. Was the Imperial Guard that shot me that night, not the Resistance."

This time it was Genevieve's turn. "What?"

"Mm. Came in, guns already pointed. Could tell they felt bad, shooting a woman. Said 'Sorry, ma'am. Lady Ayer's orders.' Left me for dead. If it hadn't been for the Resistance, I would've died, but they came and found me. Nursed me back to health. And you"—she gave Genevieve a venomous look—"were already long gone."

"The plot thickens." Rake's voice was like ice.

"I . . . She told me—I saw your body! You were dead!"

"Thistle." Her mother motioned to herself, still quite alive.

"She said that the Resistance had shot you, said—"

"And you believed her."

The memory of that night came back in a rush. The Guard had gone in first, hadn't they? Then the shots had rung out. Dai had tried to say something, but a soldier had hit him. And as she sat, a new, clearer picture of the night came into focus. Of Imperial troops shooting without question. Just as she had so recently seen them do. And yet, unlike the Wariuta on the shore, somehow her mother had lived.

"Mother, I . . ." She could not find the words that would suitably explain the rush of realization that was still tearing through her. "I'm sorry."

And then she wept. For herself, and for her foolishness, and for the loss of the Lady Ayer all over again, and for the Wariuta who likely still lay on the shore because of her idiocy, her naivete, in believing in an Empire of justice that had never truly existed.

"Uncuff her," her mother said.

Rake did as he was told.

And then she was folded into her mother's arms again. And even if now they were laced with muscle, even if the voice that soothed her was damaged and strange in her ears, she was in her mother's arms once more.

And so she wept.

• INTERLUDE •

## The Sea

*Has the Pirate Supreme called for her? She does not know. She cannot hear them anymore. She can hardly hear her own daughters, their voices overlapping and minute as the echo of waves in a seashell.*

*There: A daughter has found a cool bed of sand in the mangrove lagoons of Tustwe. But she is not calling to her mother; she is simply lolling, her body languid and her eyes closed. At least she is safe.*

*And here: Another of her children fights against an abandoned net that she has become accidentally entangled within. The Sea is distracted by her panic but cannot attend to her just now. She will survive.*

*But where? So many of her daughters are gone, gone, gone. Once she knew them each by name, knew their hearts, held their memories close. But when she reaches for them, there is only the nothingness of loss, the infinite void that grief has left her.*

*Over there: Florian and Evelyn move together. She does her best to guide them, but she is so scattered now, so confused that often she is not sure that her own guidance is true anymore. She is glad there are two of them, glad they can depend on each other if not on her, though it rankles her not to be dependable to her children. What is she, if not a mother?*

*If she could just reach the Pirate Supreme.*

*Why have they abandoned her in her time of gravest need?*

*So arrogant, humanity. To kill her daughters as if she did not encircle their world, as if their food and their lives and their safety did not depend upon her whims and her serenity.*

*In her fury and her frustration, she raises a mighty hand and lets it fall on a small fishing ship off the coast of a nation whose name she can no longer recall. Who are these men to her? No one. She fills their lungs and lets her grip wind around their little kicking legs until they are still. As gone as her memories.*

*In a moment, she will forget them.*

## CHAPTER 26

## Geneviéve

When Genevieve woke the next morning, her body stiff and creaking from the thin mattress she had slept on, she was only a little surprised to find that, in her sleep, her hand had been cuffed to the bed frame.

The cuff clanked against the wooden frame as she sat up and rubbed her puffy eyes with her spare hand. They were sore from crying, from exhaustion that felt like no amount of sleep could cure.

"You're up," said Rake, which. Yes, clearly. "Your mother had some business to attend to. She'll be back shortly."

"Business?"

"None of yours."

Genevieve suppressed the desire to groan. He may have been a double agent under the Nameless Captain, may have been a Resistance fighter, may have kicked the ever-living crap out of her and murdered her mentor, but he was still corny.

"Was it your decision or hers to cuff me?" She tried to make her voice sound impassive, blandly curious.

"Hers," Rake replied with obvious amusement.

It stung, but Genevieve kept her face still. "There anything to eat?" Her stomach ached with hunger.

"Later."

"So. Just you and me, then?"

"And you'll remember how that went last time. So no funny stuff."

"To be fair, last time it was you who did the funny stuff."

Rake made a sound between a laugh and a growl. "I can't believe you're her daughter."

"Make you feel at all guilty for kicking me in the head?"

"No."

The door opened then, and there stood the most improbable trio. Her mother, who was wearing a highly suspicious-looking cowl and hood. And Koa, with his enormous hyena by his side chittering a high giggle. Koa looked exhausted, his face drawn. She'd nearly forgotten about him in all the shock of the previous night. But there they both were, two figures from such different times in her life.

It was a moment later that Genevieve realized her mother had a vise-like grip on Koa's enormous arm.

"Do you know this one?" she asked in her new, rasping voice.

"Koa," said Genevieve quickly. He'd noticed the cuff on her hand and looked a bit alarmed. "I'm OK," she added in Wariuta.

"You speak their tongue?" her mother asked.

Genevieve nodded. Her mother let go of Koa's arm and showed him to a seat. He looked so out of place perched on a small wooden stool, the hyena sitting by his side. He regarded Rake dubiously.

"Always a prisoner," Koa said, more to himself than to anyone else. "Are you really OK?"

"I'm fine. Koa, this is my mother."

Koa looked at Mrs. Vo with such clear surprise on his face that her mother laughed. "I see he's just as surprised as you were."

"Not quite." She turned back to Koa. "Are the children safe?"

"With some carers. Found a woman with milk for Kalei."

"What's he saying?" her mother asked.

"That he's found care for the children orphaned by the Imperial attack." And the horror of what she had seen, only two days ago now, hit her anew. She swallowed it down. "Yunka was decimated."

"Must want revenge," said Mrs. Vo. "Must want to make the Imperials pay, no? Ask him that."

Genevieve did, but Koa shook his head. "No more blood," he said.

When Genevieve translated this to her mother, she scoffed. "Blood's the only language they speak, boy. And they didn't just kill everyone; we hear they also took at least one captive, maybe more. A warrior girl to show the Emperor."

Genevieve's heart set to racing. "With one hand?" she asked her mother, hoping against hope.

Mrs. Vo's eyes narrowed at her. "How did you know that?"

"They have Kaia," she told Koa, and Koa's whole body reacted, suddenly taut. He looked from Mrs. Vo to Genevieve desperately.

"Tell her to let her go!" he demanded.

"No, not my mother. The Imperials."

"I have to get her."

"Does that girl mean something to him?" Rake asked.

"His sister." Genevieve did not like Kaia, exactly, but the idea that there were any survivors from that massacre was so heartening, so wonderful, she could barely contain the bubbling hope inside her.

"Big boy like him could be useful," said Rake. "Warrior, that's why he's got the animal."

"Hmm. Tell him they're taking his sister to the Imperial Palace. In Crandon."

Genevieve did.

"I have to go get her," Koa said. "But . . . the children. I have to protect what's left of Yunka. What little is left."

He cradled his face in his hands. He looked much older than he had even a few days earlier, his face and body carrying the weight of his grief and his burden. Genevieve was hit with the desire to hug him, but of course she could not.

"He's conflicted because he wants to guard the children and also rescue his sister," Genevieve translated.

"I see." Her mother bent and whispered into Rake's ear then, and he nodded, whispered back. Resentment that somehow her mother trusted this pirate over her rankled Genevieve, until she was reminded, forcibly, by the bullet scar in her mother's neck, that she had little reason to trust her own daughter.

Her mother did not look at her but rather at Koa as she spoke. "Tell him we're going to Crandon. And that he can come, and that we will help him find his sister. If he's willing to fight."

Genevieve translated this, and she could see the visceral, physical pain the idea of more bloodshed cost Koa. He regarded his hands sadly.

"I'll have to get the children sorted first. I can find them temporary care, at least," he said, more to himself than to Genevieve. "But then I'll go. For Kaia."

"He says he'll go," said Genevieve. "If I come, too."

Rake and her mother's eyes met. "Why should we trust you?" Mrs. Vo asked.

"I . . ." She looked down at the cuff on her wrist, the cuff she'd earned. "I know I haven't given you a reason to trust me."

"You worked for one of the Emperor's worst operatives," Rake added for good measure.

"Abandoned your own mother for her," said Mrs. Vo.

"But I." Her mind spun. She knew if she simply told them the truth, that she had changed, that she had seen what the Empire was now, had seen that it was all lies, she would sound like a liar. Like a spy. "If I step out of line, I swear I will put up no fight if I'm to be killed."

"We could kill you now," Rake muttered. "Save ourselves the trouble."

But her mother put up a hand to silence him, and he resumed glowering.

"And I swear if you do," her mother said slowly, meaningfully, "I'll be the one to kill you."

• CHAPTER 27 •

*Tomas*

Commander Callum led the procession through Crandon to the palace on the back of a great gray horse. And even if Inouye was relegated to the back, on foot, he could still appreciate the looks of awe that greeted the men as they paraded through the city. Several yards ahead of him, the girl was carried in a prisoner's barred carriage, and the people gawked at her.

If the intention of the procession was to humble her, it was not working. She held her head high and met the eyes of those who stared. More than a few looked away, cheeks red with shame. Having been the recipient of more than a few blistering glares over the voyage, Inouye understood entirely.

Inouye had never been inside the palace before, but he'd seen it from the outside, all gleaming gilded details and great tall walls. The grounds, he was thrilled to see, were beautiful, with koi ponds and bridges and trees and flowers in nearly every direction he looked. A great white peacock waddled just beyond a copse of cherry trees. He had never been so proud to be Imperial. Truly,

Callum's replica in the Floating Islands had been a farce by comparison. All of the architecture, none of the grandeur. There was simply no imitating royalty.

When they reached the throne room, it took all of Inouye's self-control not to crane his neck to take in the many details of the walls, the ceiling, and the painted columns. Everywhere, painted and sculpted Imperial lions looked down from plinths and alcoves. It had a slightly claustrophobic effect—the walls felt close against them even in the vastness of the room.

The entirety of the palace had been gathered to watch Callum's reception. Senators and maids, lords and guards, stood lined against the length of the room. The Emperor's many wives and many children all sat on their knees at the base of a great dais, their faces and bodies completely still. And on the dais, beneath a stately, ornate octagonal pergola, enshrouded with heavy black curtains save for the space just in front of him, the Emperor sat on his golden throne, flanked by large jade lions.

It was an honor, of course, to even look upon the Emperor. And though Inouye was relegated to the back of the procession, he could still make him out clearly. He wore red robes embroidered with black and gold and green threads. He was old, Inouye realized. His head looked slightly bowed beneath the weight of his enormous jeweled crown. His small pale hands were folded on his lap.

Callum stayed on his horse even into the throne room as his many men marched in after him, laden with the goods of his exploits. The cases of kau. Strange fruits from the Floating Islands. Vials and vials of mermaids' blood. And of course the girl, who had been removed from the cage and was flanked by four men, who held her at sword point.

"Thanks to the Emperor," Callum boomed.

"Thanks to the Emperor," Inouye and the rest of the room shouted back.

"In your grace and in your name, I have gone to the farthest reaches of the Known World, and thus your wealth grows," Callum said. He enumerated the many treasures as his men hustled forward to display them to the Emperor, who showed little interest in any.

But then the girl was presented, marched to the front of the procession by her guards. Many of the wives and ladies gasped at her bare feet and bare muscled legs. One senator ignored all decorum and pointed at her missing forearm.

"And this creature," Callum said, his voice thick with disgust, "is a savage warrioress from the Red Shore. When we, thanks to you, defended our ships against her attack, she managed to kill four of our men before she was subdued."

More gasps, and murmuring now. Callum was making his case for sending more men to take the Red Shore entirely, and all knew it.

"The vile chieftainesses of the Red Shore castrate their males to subdue them. They leave their baby boys in the sun to die, either by exposure or eaten by the mad, frothing hyenas they keep at their sides. And then they teach their females, like this one"—he motioned to the girl, who stared, seemingly unafraid, up at the Emperor—"with one single purpose. Murder. Trained since birth to kill, bloodthirsty and cruel, the females of the Red Shore practice in dark magic and bloody sacrifices."

Callum looked around the room meaningfully. Every breath was held in anticipation of what he would say next.

"And so, if in your wisdom and your beneficence you will it, I will lead your men to destroy the scourge of their savagery. I will bring order and justice and civilization to the Red Shore." He bowed his head in practiced deference, somewhat dampened by his refusal to get off his damn horse. "Thanks to the Emperor."

"Thanks to the Emperor," the room echoed.

When the Emperor finally spoke, his voice was reedy, thin. "She will make a lovely addition to my menagerie," he said.

This was not an answer to Callum's call to arms. Callum seemed a little taken aback. His horse shifted, likely uneasy to be so surrounded by human bodies, and the sounds of the hooves on the great marble floor were so loud against the hush of the room that they shook the room like gunshots.

But the Emperor did not say anything more. And so after a few minutes of strained and confused silence, Callum saluted him, turned his horse around, and led the procession back out of the throne room and into the palace grounds.

Inouye tried not to think of the bitterness and the bile he could taste in his throat. All their work, all their fighting, all the blood—and the Emperor didn't even care.

Inouye could tell he was still in bad standing with Callum when, as soon as the demonstration was over, he was ordered to take the girl to the menagerie rather than joining the feast with all the others.

"Will you need extra men?" Commander Callum had asked. This was a barb, of course, an insult. Some of the other men chuckled.

"No, sir," said Inouye. He was an Imperial soldier, after all. His pride rankled at the very notion that she could get the better of him. Without a piss pot to throw, anyway.

She'd be kept in the menagerie, along with the other strange and wonderful creatures from abroad. At least there would be that, Inouye reflected, a visit to see, if only briefly, the jaguar and the oryx and the great white bear.

"There's no unicorn," Windsor said as he looked about the many gilded cages.

"Can you try and focus?" Inouye snapped. He couldn't believe he'd been paired with this buffoon. Windsor shrugged. The evening was waning, and Inouye hoped they could complete their task with enough time to join the other men for dinner.

The girl was proving to be much more docile now than she had been with a piss pot in her hands, her eyes downcast. This would be easy work.

Windsor picked his nose absently. "Don't think she'll run for it here, do you?"

Inouye looked around. The palace gates were tall, unscalable. There were guards posted all around them. They were mere feet away from the golden cage in the menagerie she would call home. In the cage next to hers, a tiger prowled. Where would she go?

"Probably. Grab her as soon as I open the cage, hear me?"

Windsor nodded, but not as attentively as Inouye would have liked.

"Windsor," he admonished.

Windsor flicked whatever he'd found in his nostril into the night.

The girl watched all this, her eyes darting between the men. Inouye felt a twinge of unease but then reminded himself she was bound. She had no weapon. There was only one of her. They were in palace grounds. They were Imperial men. They would not be bested by some wild and savage girl who was born in a hut.

He opened the door.

The girl burst over the threshold, and she was more blur than body. In the instant that Inouye registered she was moving, she'd kicked Windsor in the groin, and he was down, rolling on the ground, and the girl was moving again, and too late, Inouye put up his hands to guard his face, but she had already rammed him with her shoulder, knocking the wind from his lungs and possibly breaking one of his ribs. He tried to call out, but his voice would not come to him, and Windsor, useless Windsor, just cradled his balls and whimpered.

Inouye staggered to his feet.

As she ran, the girl wriggled from her bindings, and Inouye knew with a sinking feeling that she would be free of them in moments, that they had not tied her tight enough, that she'd put up enough of a fight as she was bound that she had effectively rendered the ropes useless. That he was about to lose another prisoner. Another girl.

"Guards!" he called, but his voice was just a rasp. And anyway, they'd mostly be in the courtyard, wouldn't they? For Callum's reception. He needed his breath, and so he shut up and ran as hard as he could.

He had not run so fast in his whole life, and it was no easy feat in the heavy leather boots he wore. They were like stones on his feet he had to drag along as the girl sprinted ahead of him. He'd never been jealous of someone with bare feet before in his life.

It was only because he was so much taller that he was able to catch up to her, just shy of the outer palace walls. He leapt for her as she ran, and with a stroke of luck caught one of her feet. They both landed hard, and then the true fight began. Despite his size advantage, he could not seem to keep a hold of her, could not seem to pin her down.

When he landed one good punch across her jaw, he thought he had her. But she blinked past the pain and used his momentary distraction to punch him back, in the throat. She would have wiggled away then, but he managed to throw his body on top of hers and use his weight, if not his hand-to-hand combat skills, to stop her.

As they wrestled, his hands trying to find purchase, her thrashing wildly but silently, the shame of his continued failure began to eat at Inouye's resolve. He was not the Imperial man he'd been promised his whole life he would be. All his life he'd been told he was strong because of who he was, and yet here he was. Losing to a girl.

It had all been a lie.

As if she could hear his thoughts, the girl wrapped one leg around Inouye's neck, her thigh and her calf pressing on his windpipe. He clawed at the bare skin of her leg but could not loosen her grip. She bore down harder.

"Sh," she crooned as she squeezed. "Tawmus, shh."

When the darkness started to contract around him, Inouye knew at least one thing he'd been told was not a lie. He saw death then, just as his father promised him he would.

He reached for death.

And death reached back.

• CHAPTER 28 •

## The Pirate Supreme

Even when they were young and in love and unable to keep from touching each other, Kwizera had known Xenobia was not necessarily trustworthy. That she would see to her own interests first. It was something they had loved about her, and a source of respect—she was a survivor, and always would be.

But it felt different now. It was one thing to survive at all costs as a young person, so new in the world. A different thing altogether to do it now. Selfish.

"I wish it weren't true, either," Xenobia said.

Their eyes met, and they could see that she had divined their thoughts.

"It's your fault she was there," they said. They knew they were being cruel just to exorcise their own anger, but that did not stop them. "If you hadn't—"

"I know." Xenobia's voice was firm. It was many years ago when Xenobia had promised the mermaid a spell to unite her with her human lover—and just as many since the Sea had punished them both for the betrayal, banishing the mermaid and cursing Xenobia with a loveless life. "But there's nothing I can do about that now, is there." This was not a question. It was a plea for clemency.

The Supreme stood, needing to move, needing to control something, even if it was just their own body. They had been so sure that the banished mermaid was the key. That she held the memory of the legendary creatures who lurked in the Sea's depths, who could be called upon for aid. But without the confirmation of her memory, that was just a legend. And what good could stories do them now?

Xenobia's eyes were downcast. "Someday maybe you will see that I was just trying to give that mermaid what we had."

She did not say the word *love*, but it hung between them anyway.

"Today is not that day." The Supreme did not want to talk of love with Xenobia, didn't want to be reminded of what they had been. They wanted to save the Sea, to free her from the grip of the Emperor. And with the death of the banished mermaid, it felt as though there was little hope left for that.

"I trained a new witch, you know," Xenobia said. "And my understanding is that she has joined your great love as a new daughter."

The Supreme's mind whirred. Only two people had joined the Sea recently, and they had seen them go with their own eyes. If Xenobia had a connection to one of them . . . "Florian?"

"That was one of his names," said Xenobia. "Perhaps he can be of some assistance?"

"How did you know—"

"I have my ways." And when it was clear that this was not enough to mollify the Supreme: "Our connection has been lost. But I could feel him submerge."

"Can you call to him?" Mermaids had a direct line of

communication with the Sea, a line that had all but been severed for the Supreme. If they could just reach her, if they could just beg her for help.

"Possibly."

They did not want to ask for help, but already the Emperor's men had taken the Red Shore. Already his ships prowled the waters near Tustwe, growing ever more bold. Tustwe had not yet been colonized, but it was the lone holdout among nations in the Known World. And it was only a matter of time before those many ships found the Forbidden Isles.

They were desperate for any edge. They did not need to say this aloud; the witch could see it in their face.

"They're the ones, I think," said Xenobia. "From the song. True love's might, and all that." She did not say what they each remembered.

That there had been a time when they both believed that song was about Kwizera and Xenobia.

"I think so, too," said the Supreme, to themself mostly, remembering what Florian's brother had told them—that the girl had died. That she had been, apparently, reborn as a mermaid. And though they could smell the taint of mermaid's blood on his breath, they knew he had told the truth. This once, Xenobia was not lying.

"We have to call to him," said the Supreme. "You have to."

"I can try," says Xenobia. "For a price."

"Always a price with you."

"I'll do whatever is needed, whatever you ask of me. For you. For the Sea. But when we are done, you must step down as her steward. You must return to Tustwe, with me. We go home."

*If we survive*, the Supreme thought.

*If we win.*

*We can't win. But we have to try.*

Heartened that the tea was not poisoned—Xenobia had had plenty now to be sure—Kwizera took a sip. The last place they wanted to go was Tustwe. Tustwe had stopped being home years ago, even before Xenobia stopped being home. Word had reached them that their father had died, and their brother, too. There was nothing left for them there. They were no one in Tustwe. They were the Pirate Supreme on the Sea.

But without the banished mermaid's help, they needed Xenobia. Memories of Xenobia, her arms wrapped around them, rose unbidden in the Supreme's mind. They tried and failed to push them back down. They had made their choice years ago—between Xenobia and the Sea, the Pirate Supreme had chosen the Sea. They had chosen power. But power did not make one feel safe. When was the last time they had felt at home, anywhere? Maybe it was time. Maybe.

"Come with me to the Forbidden Isles. We're convening Resistance leaders there."

"And our deal?"

"I'll honor it."

Xenobia pulled a small shining dagger from her cleavage and cut a jagged line in her palm. She held the dagger out for the Supreme, who took it with some trepidation. A blood bond. A powerful magic. No going back now. They would have to trust Xenobia.

They cut their hand.

### • CHAPTER 29 •

## *Alfie*

Alfie was tossed in a holding cell along with a very emacited elderly man who looked just a little too excited to have some company. He made a great show of having Alfie sit, as though he were inviting him into his house for dinner, not having him crouch on a boulder in the dark.

"Haven't had a cellmate in years!" croaked the man. His voice was like paper on paper, it was so strained and quiet. "Was starting to think they forgot about me."

The smell was overpowering. As his eyes got used to the dank, Alfie realized the boulder was next to the corner the man had clearly been using as a designated toilet area.

"They . . . they feed you, though, right?"

"When they remember, I suppose." The man scratched his scraggly white beard. Even in the dim light of the jail, Alfie could see that he had a number of sores along his neck and chest. "What're you in for?"

"Wrong place wrong time," Alfie said. He wasn't sure what could be overheard by the guards, and he wasn't keen to tip his hand to a stranger, nice though he seemed. "Was just trying to contact our crab vendor, let him know that he'd sold us some bad goods," he added for good measure. It didn't hurt to practice your lies. "Had no idea he was wound up in some mess."

"Whoring?" the man asked, and Alfie startled.

"What?"

"Was he into whoring?"

"I . . . I don't think so."

"I was."

"Oh."

"Yes," said the man seriously. "Was damn good at it, too. Half the Guard came to me in my time. Wouldn't know it now, but I was a real looker. And a real wizard with—"

"That's nice," interrupted Alfie. He didn't really want to know about the man's sexual exploits of yore. "Seems unfair to lock you up just for being good at your job."

"Oh, that's not why I'm in here."

"What are you in here for, then?"

"Murder."

"Did you do it?"

"Oh, yes."

Alfie laughed; he couldn't help it. "OK."

Alfie tried to conquer his unease. Being locked in a cell with a man who was clearly only sporadically fed and mostly left to rot and forced to defecate in a corner was not, he thought, a great way to get in the right headspace for what promised to be a brutal interrogation with the Imperial Guard. One wrong answer and he'd be stuck in this jail forever, like this poor old man. Poor old murderer. Whatever, no one deserved such a fate. He knew the constabulary were bastards, but their cruelty seemed to know no end. Fear and anger pricked in his chest and his eyes, and he wondered if he was crying because he was caught or because he was furious or if it even mattered which.

"I'm sorry they did this to you," Alfie said. He didn't know what else to say.

"There, there," said the man. He squeezed Alfie's hand. "You'll be OK. Chin up."

Alfie squeezed the man's hand back, oddly bolstered. "Thanks," he said. "I'm Alfie. What's your name?"

"My name?" The man seemed to be shocked by the question, and it was several moments before he answered. "Jung Hoon."

"If I get out of here," Alfie said, "I'll try to get you out, too, Jung Hoon."

"OK." Jung Hoon laughed, a dry-leaf sound. "Sure thing, Alfie. I won't hold my breath, though." And, still chuckling, he eased himself onto a pile of rags that he was clearly using as a bed. In the hours that passed, Alfie tried to sleep but found that he couldn't. If he tipped off the Guard, he was dead. If he didn't cooperate with them, he was dead. No matter how he sliced it, he couldn't imagine an outcome that didn't leave him dead.

He thought of Flora, stepping into the Sea. He wondered if she ever thought of him. He hoped not. She had done enough worrying over him for a lifetime. At least he got to see her happy before he died. That was something. Maybe that was everything.

Jung Hoon was snoring softly when a guardsman came down to their cell and unlocked it. "Philip Boucher?"

Alfie sprang to his feet as Jung Hoon stirred awake.

"That's me."

"You're free to go."

"What?"

"Do you want to stay here?" the guard asked, impatient.

"No, I—I'm not going to be interrogated?"

"Nope, palace vouched for your story."

"'Course." Alfie's mind raced. He'd been lying, so who had covered for him? Who had risked their neck? He prayed it wasn't Keiko. "'Course they did."

"Told you you'd be just fine," said Jung Hoon warmly.

Alfie smiled at him in the darkness. "Thanks, man," he said. "I—"

"You wanna leave or not?" the guard interrupted, and Alfie stepped to.

"Chin up," Jung Hoon called after him.

"Philip Boucher," said his rescuer. Alfie knew that voice, but it didn't make any sense; why would that voice be here? Perhaps he'd lost his sanity in the darkness along with his hope.

"Senator Tsujima?" he asked the light. His eyes had not adjusted, and he felt as though he were losing his senses.

"A simple misunderstanding," xe said, xyr voice apologetic. "The Guard has to be so vigilant these days. But I was able to confirm that you'd gotten me some crab from that terrible man." Alfie's eyes started to make sense of the senator, who was smiling at him with a crocodile's concern. "You know how the Guard is. Ever zealous, but perhaps a little hasty at the price of accuracy. Thanks to the Emperor, I heard the news and could clear it up."

Alfie didn't move. It seemed a trick, a prank, but one with terrible consequences should he fall for it. He imagined stepping out of the constabulary only to be bludgeoned to death for doing so.

"Come on, then," Senator Tsujima said. Xe stepped into the light of the Crandon street and reached out a manicured hand to Alfie. Xyr nails were painted with a green lacquer and inlaid with gold details. Alfie was mesmerized by them as they glinted in the torchlight. "Unless you'd rather stay here?"

"No," he croaked. His body ached from lying on the cold stone, so standing was painful. But he shook life into his feet, happy to take them as far from that cell as he could go.

"I should think not," the senator said. Xe proffered xyr arm to Alfie, and xe led the way back toward the palace.

"Go along then, Jiro," Senator Tsujima said, waving xyr hand dismissively toward a waiting servant. "Ready my carriage, won't you? It'll give me a moment to check in with poor, beleaguered Philip here."

The servant bowed and was off. Soon just Tsujima and Alfie stood together Once xe was sure they were alone, the smile fell from xyr face like a mask.

"What is your real name, Philip?" xe asked. "You don't sound like someone from Iwei; surely that's a fake name. You sound like you grew up here. In Sty's End, if I were to be precise, I can hear it. From the look of you"—xe pinched Alfie's cheek, hard—"I'd guess you grew up with not enough to eat, but that you've gained weight, a lot of it, and recently. So who are you?"

"I—"

"I mean, I know you're a spy for the Pirate Supreme. But curiosity bedevils me—my most favorite vice, you know. I do love to gossip." Xe smiled beatifically, and there was a glint of cruel, sharp teeth. "What is your name?"

"Alfie," he blurted. He could feel his cheeks burning. He'd been in the palace for only a few months, and he was already blowing his cover; if that wasn't proof he was a shit spy, he didn't know what was.

"See? What'd I say? I know a Sty's End boy when I see one. I grew up there myself, you know. Don't let anyone tell you that your birth is your destiny." Xe examined Alfie's face closely. "You don't look like a pirate, Alfie." Xe said his name with a dagger's sharpness.

"I wasn't a good one," he said truthfully. A bad brother, a terrible pirate, a worse spy.

Senator Tsujima cackled. "A pirate turned spy," xe said with an air of being impressed. "I'd have you make one more turn, young Alfie. As recompense for your freedom."

The senator had a reputation for manipulation, and Alfie was starting to see why. Xe did not need to say that if Alfie did not grant xem this request xe would see him thrown right back in the cell from whence he'd come. That was obvious. And so Alfie gulped and nodded, already dreading whatever task he was about to be dealt.

"You were already privy, I think, to a plan to assassinate the Crown Prince?" Tsujima whispered. Xe did not wait for a response. "I would see that done, if I had my druthers, and expediently."

Alfie blinked, stunned. But before he could answer, both he and Tsujima startled. In the distance, the sounds of cannons firing could be heard.

"Now, don't disappoint me. Bad things happen to boys from Sty's End who disappoint me," Tsujima hissed. And xe turned on xyr heel and stepped into the ornate carriage that awaited xem.

• CHAPTER 30 •

## *Geneviève*

After all the time the Lady Ayer had spent searching for clues as to the whereabouts of the Forbidden Isles, it seemed mad that she, Genevieve, was headed there now. The voyage was a short one, and mostly she was not allowed abovedeck—her mother did not trust her enough to let her see which direction they sailed, and it didn't escape Genevieve that she'd clearly been assigned a rotating schedule of guards.

Koa, who had never been on a ship before, was magnificently seasick. Pallid and sweating, he lingered abovedeck out of necessity, so that he could vomit overboard rather than in his berth. This meant Genevieve was usually alone. Which was fine. She had been mostly alone since she'd started informing for the Lady Ayer. She was used to it now.

Still, she could have done without the constant dirty looks from the various pirates, especially Rake. He seemed to yearn for another chance to kick her in the head. And, if she was honest about it, she wouldn't have minded a chance to repay the favor.

It was only week later when they reached the small cluster of islands where the Pirate Supreme held court.

Whatever she'd been expecting of the Forbidden Isles, it wasn't this. They were neither forbidding nor grand. Just very small islands clustered together, with a number of mooring points for a great variety of ships. The one thing that made them unusual was that each island seemed to be entirely unique. The largest was dense with fragrant green trees Genevieve could smell even as they sailed past it. One of the smaller ones seemed to be entirely made of starkly black rock that jutted from the clear blue water. At first she thought a trick of the light made it appear as though the rocks were moving, but as they neared it, she saw a great number of enormous black lizards perched all over the rocks, heads bobbing as they sunbathed. Some of the lizards bobbed in the water that lapped against the rocks.

"Iguanas," said her mother. She had crept up on Genevieve as they sailed on toward an island composed almost entirely of sheer cliff faces. "Taste like chicken."

Genevieve scowled. "Doubtful."

"Mm. There are enormous tortoises that live here, too. Bigger than the dogs in Gia Dinh. They say they live for hundreds of years."

"That can't be true."

"I believe it. Their meat is very tough."

"Is there anything on these islands you haven't eaten?"

"Pirates."

Genevieve smiled. "I am sorry, you know. For." She did not know what she should apologize for first, and the breadth of possibility winded her.

"I believe that," her mother said.

"But you don't believe I've changed my mind."

"Did the Lady Ayer give you that name? Genevieve?"

Genevieve looked back at the water. She could see a school of very large fish passing beneath them. Everything around these islands was so alive, teeming. How odd it was, to consider all these lives being lived with no concept of empires or operatives or betrayals.

Her mother put her hand on Genevieve's back, and the warmth of her touch spread through her whole body.

"I'll always love you. But you're not my Thistle anymore, are you?"

Genevieve met her mother's eyes, which were soft and sad.

"No," she said. "I suppose I'm not."

Several feet away from them, Koa sprinted to the side of the ship and vomited spectacularly over the rail. A few of the pirates chuckled, and Rake brought him a bottle of something clear that Genevieve hoped was water but could just as easily have been rum.

"Everything's different now," said Genevieve. The world felt like an ever-shifting place beneath her feet, and she could not seem to catch her balance.

"Yes," said the Fist.

The pirates had brought down the sails and were tying the ship to one of the few vacant moorings. They had reached the Pirate Supreme's stronghold, which was built into the side of the island, mostly hidden from sight. It was a smaller island than some of the others, but Genevieve could see why it had been chosen as the stronghold almost at once. The natural rock formations that defined it yielded innumerable caves and crevices. Exploring it would be difficult. One would need to know where to go upon approach.

But there, moored just before the island, was the ship that had changed Genevieve's life. That had seen her mentor dead and her shipwrecked on a distant shore.

The *Leviathan*. Her black flags with the white mermaid rippled in the light wind.

A prickle of hatred, but Genevieve pressed it down. She could still hear its cannons booming in her ears, could still see the great tentacles of the sea bashing men into the cold depths, never to rise again. The Empire was a lie, Genevieve could see that now; the Emperor had to be stopped. But those many, many men. They didn't all deserve to die—they had believed, just as she had, in a lie they'd been told their whole lives. In order and justice.

But then, did that excuse matter? When the lies spilled so much blood? She thought of the dead on the Red Shore. Of the children orphaned by the Nipran. Surely those men who had fired upon those women, those men who had sacked Puno, had believed the lie, too.

Genevieve didn't know what to think anymore. And the uncertainty of it churned in her stomach.

She did not speak of any of this, but she felt her mother's hand fall off her. And before she could say more to her, she saw the Fist walk away, barking questions and orders to the pirates with whom Genevieve had fought. Rake joined her, and the two shared quiet words that Genevieve could not hear, their heads tilted together.

"I don't know how you people stand it," Koa wheezed. He sat on the deck, looking exhausted, with his legs spread, as if he'd just run a very long way, very fast. His hyena nuzzled against him, offering his own kind of smelly comfort.

Genevieve sat down next to him. "I promise, you'll get used to it."

"I never know when to believe you." He petted his beast, who lolled onto his back so that Koa could scratch his belly.

Genevieve winced a smile. "No one does these days." They sat together for a moment in silence. "I never meant you or any of your people any harm. I hope you know that."

"Well." He looked at his fingernails. "What you meant doesn't really matter, does it? My people are dead."

"Not Kaia."

"No." And he smiled, a ghost of the big smile he used to have. "Not Kaia."

Genevieve had been to the Imperial throne room, and the Pirate Supreme's was like a storage closet in comparison. Treasure stacked against the walls like it didn't matter, wasn't precious. A wooden chair at the head of the room, not a proper throne, as if the Pirate Supreme themself wasn't that important. It was all much less reverent than she had been expecting.

Maybe, she realized, that was the point.

She had spent so long looking for them with the Lady Ayer, this supposed villain. And here they were. Whatever she had been expecting, this wasn't it. Maybe she had expected someone bigger. Or an Imperial. But there they were, small boned and Black and grinning as if everything was a joke only they were in on.

The Supreme was sitting on their chair, one leg hanging over an armrest. Less regal, more drunkard in posture. They were alone save for a tall, ample-bodied Black woman with her salt-and-pepper hair stacked high and messy on her head. She stood next to the Supreme, looking haughty. Rake led the Fist, Koa, and Genevieve to them, and their footsteps echoed against the plain stone walls.

"I know them," Koa said, and his voice was happy for once.

Genevieve did not need to wait for confirmation. Tupac lolloped forward, tackled the Supreme, and licked their face as they laughed.

"The Supreme comes to Yunka to trade now and again. Always has the best stories!" Koa waved. The Supreme grinned, standing and brushing themself off, scratching Tupac behind his pointed ears. "Had no idea they were so important."

"The name didn't tip you off?"

"People call themselves all kinds of things," Koa said with a shrug. "I don't verify; I just call them what they call themselves."

The Supreme stood and, in flawless Wariuta, addressed Koa with their arms outstretched. "My friend! I can't tell you how happy I am to see you." They wrapped Koa in a tight hug, and the two laughed a little with pleasure at the reunion. The Supreme was about a foot shorter than Koa, but they held on to his shoulders and met his eyes seriously. "I am so sorry for what has been done to the Wariuta."

Koa bowed his head. Genevieve wanted to hug him but held back. The burden he carried now was too great for one person, and yet there he was. She wished she could fix it for him.

"I will see justice done for your people. Know that."

Koa did not respond to this.

"I have important information I must give you," Genevieve blurted in Imperial. She felt as if a thousand years had passed since she had seen Lilith's memory, and she wanted to share it directly with the Pirate Supreme before there were any more cataclysms in her life.

The Supreme looked a little offended that she'd interrupted. They looked at Rake with raised eyebrows, and Rake glowered at Genevieve.

"This child was the charge of the late Lady Ayer," he said with hardly disguised disgust. "She claims to have had a change of heart and wishes to help us now."

"She's also my daughter," the Fist added, but she did not elaborate.

"Do you trust her?" the Supreme asked Rake.

"No."

"Then why bring her to me?"

"She's a child who's just awoken from years of lies," her mother said. "And while she has not yet earned back her trust with me, I still know my child. Whether she's right or not, she believes what she's saying is the truth."

It was not, Genevieve thought, as much respect as she deserved. There was a part of her, the part that had pushed Dai down in the mud in Gia Dinh all those years ago, that wanted to shout at her mother for undermining her at such an important moment. But if she wanted to prove herself, squabbling with her mother like a baby probably wasn't the way. So she clamped her mouth shut and fumed.

"I see. Xenobia," the Supreme made a little motion with their hand, and the woman who had been staunchly ignoring the visitors turned to them. "Any way to tell if she's lying?"

"I'll know once she tells her story," said the woman casually.

"Go on, then, child. Tell me your tale." The Supreme sat back down on their chair and looked at Genevieve expectantly. With all eyes on her, Genevieve shifted uncomfortably.

"There's a dragon," she said. The Supreme tilted their head, probably thinking she was stupid or mad or both. Genevieve pressed on. "There's a dragon at the bottom of the sea, and if you can call to her, she will come and fight for you."

"All the dragons are dead," said Rake.

"So are all the witches, supposedly," muttered Xenobia.

"I . . . the siren said—"

"Siren?" interjected the Supreme.

"At the Red Shore." She switched to Wariuta then, so Koa could vouch for her. "Koa, tell them. Tell them about the siren."

"Lilith?" Naturally he was confused. He'd understood very little until now. "She lives in the oasis. I guard her. She's been there for longer than I've been alive."

The Supreme and Xenobia exchanged a meaningful look.

"Guarded her," Xenobia said. "She's dead."

Koa grimaced. "Was it them?" he asked, and Genevieve did not need to ask whom he meant. "So much death," he added, to no one really. He looked older than he should, older than he had even two days earlier.

"Yes," the Supreme replied. And then, in the Common Tongue: "But. Before you came here—she told you about the dragon?"

"Showed me," Genevieve clarified.

"She gave you her blood?" asked Xenobia. "Willingly?"

"Yes." Genevieve took a deep breath. "Or, really, she offered Koa her blood, but I was worried she'd kill him and so I took it instead, and she dragged me underwater and it was so terrible, and I saw the dragon in the depths, and she was telling me, or showing me, I suppose, that her song can still be sung, whatever that means, and she showed me her teeth, and they were huge, and anyway she didn't say so, but I got the impression she meant to offer her aid for the Pirate Supreme, which sounds silly, but I could feel it, could feel who she meant to fight for, and I know the Emperor is bad now, and so that's why I'm here."

She had not said it all aloud since it had happened, and she realized how bizarre she sounded. So much had been told. Nothing had been said. Somehow she needed to communicate all that, urgently. So much was riding on her competence. She looked around at her audience.

Silence.

And then: "She's telling the truth," said Xenobia.

"How do you know?" asked Rake.

"When you spend your whole life crafting magic, you can hear the construction of an untruth in a story. Hers has none. She has told us what she has seen as best she remembers it."

On the one hand, Genevieve was glad to be believed, but on the other, she did rather wish the witch had given somewhat more substantial evidence. She could sense more than see the glance exchanged between her mother and Rake.

But the Supreme whooped and clapped their hands in delight. Everyone except Xenobia watched, bewildered. "I knew it!" they hooted. "We have to find those mermaids!"

"Whaaat," Rake said, looking between Xenobia and the Supreme, "is going on?"

"We've got a chance," the Supreme crowed. They shook Rake by the shoulders and planted an exuberant kiss on his cheek. Rake blushed a flaming red. "We gather the coalitions now. It's time to move."

• CHAPTER 31 •

## *Florian*

They were lost.
 Once Florian had known the stars in the sky like a map, but that felt so long ago. All the little bric-a-brac of his life above had started to run together, to fade or even disappear. And so he knew some little fraction of his mother's suffering. It was so painful to forget.
 In one hand, he clutched the quartz that knew his secrets. In the other, Evelyn's hand gripped his reassuringly. She could not find her way any more than she could make the Sea catch fire, but her constant company and encouragement staved off hopelessness. He squeezed her hand back, an unspoken thank-you.
 Distantly, Florian could hear a humpback whale's song echoing, mournful. A calf had been lost to a whaling spear. He could feel the whale's grief as though that spear had hit his own chest. They stopped to listen, to bow their heads, to honor the pod's loss.
 And it was then that Florian felt it. The quartz grew warm at first, just warm enough for Florian to take notice, before, in an instant, it turned so hot he nearly dropped it.

"What's wrong?" Evelyn asked.

"I . . ." Florian looked at the quartz. Was he imagining things, or did it glow? He felt a tug in his chest to the east, as if he were being called. As if he were being summoned. As if he were being demanded. He could not hear the voice that shouted his name, but he recognized it all the same "Xenobia?"

"The witch?"

"She's calling me."

"Do we go?"

"I think I have to."

Florian gripped the rock, and once again he whispered his story into it. He told the rock of his love and his mother and whom he needed to talk to in order to save her. He told it of Xenobia and her lessons and the trades he had learned to make and the bond they shared, whether he wanted it or not, of teacher and student.

"I will give you my memories of my birth mother," Florian said. They weren't all bad; Florian knew that. But he could not bear to part with any that might include Evelyn. Nor, he realized, could he bear to part with any memories of Alfie. And so the spell was cast. "Let me speak to her."

There was the sound of rending, of tearing. Florian cast an arm protectively across Evelyn's chest. Before them, a hole in the Sea opened. But it opened not into nothingness or sky or land. It opened into a narrow room with treasure stacked on each side of it. Florian squinted as the room came into focus.

There were people in the room, talking to one another. They did not notice the window that had opened between them just yet. Florian's eyes fell on the girl from Quark first.

"Genevieve?" Evelyn asked.

The whole room whirled at the sound of her voice. And that's when Florian saw him. Rake. He fought the sudden and powerful urge to throw himself through the window, to hug the man who had once been like a father to him. And from the look on Rake's face, he suspected the pirate felt very much the same. Rake ran to the portal and tried to reach his hand through. But he could not touch Florian.

"My boy," Rake whispered. "Look at you."

"There you are," said Xenobia. She tilted her head. "Have you missed me?"

"No," said Florian truthfully. "But I'm glad you called me. I need your help. I need you to find the Pirate Supreme."

There was a chuckle from the back of the room, and that's when Florian saw them. The Supreme stood and walked to the portal, their eyes alight with curiosity.

"Mother needs your help," Florian said in a rush.

"Too many of her daughters have been taken," Evelyn added. "And she wonders why you have abandoned her."

The Pirate Supreme's face fell, and Florian could see the pain as clear as the moon. "I will never abandon her," they said. "I keep calling to her, but she must not be able to hear me . . . Our connection has grown too weak."

"She can barely hear us," Evelyn told them. "Though I know she's trying."

"You can help your mother and us all if you will listen," Xenobia said curtly. Clearly she had grown weary of all the emotion. "There is a dragon. Deep in the trenches of the sea. We need you to go and beg her to come help us."

"To help you what?" asked Florian.

"Destroy Nipran," Rake replied.

"Save the Sea," said the Pirate Supreme.

"Set us free," Xenobia added.

"Of course," Evelyn said. No hesitation.

Florian whipped his head around to look at her, bemused. "We will?"

"Yes. We must do whatever we can to save our mother. And if saving her means stopping the Emperor, well." She shrugged a merry little shrug. "That's just a bonus."

"Doing this will keep you safe," Rake added. "And Alfie, too. If we can stop the Empire, then the mermaids will not be under such constant attack. You will finally have the life you've earned." To Florian's shock, there were tears in Rake's eyes.

Florian reached out a hand to him. "Thank you. Father."

This was apparently more than Rake could stand, and so rather than letting anyone witness him weeping, he simply turned and walked out of the room, the balls of his fists pressed into his eyes. A woman Florian didn't recognize followed him.

"Go," Xenobia said not too kindly. "To your mother's greatest depths. The dragon rests there in a great cavern not even the light can touch. The rock will light your way; I will see to that. Now go. You're our only hope."

And before there could be any more discussion, the window closed.

"Come on, then," Evelyn said cheerily. "Let's go save the world."

◆ CHAPTER 32 ◆

If she kept moving, the pain would not find her.

In every quiet moment, she would see it all again. Watch her mother fall, arms in the air like a child rather than the legendary warrior she was. See Chima, her familiar, her shadow, cut down by bullets she could not outrun. She would imagine Koa's corpse, and her whole body would curl into itself trying in vain to protect itself from grief so immense she could not stand it. Her own obvious failure would pummel her with its truth again and again. She had failed to protect her people, and now her people were gone.

So she kept moving.

Escaping had been easy. She'd taken the measure of Tawmus early on, and knew it was just a matter of time before he made some crucial and fatal error. She did not regret his death, even if she had been taught to honor life. He did not deserve her mourning. None of the Colonizers did.

Now that she had escaped, she didn't have a plan other than to get out of the palace. But where the palace ended was hard to say.

She'd done a good amount of slinking about at night to know that it continued outside the buildings. And hiding had told her that hundreds of people walked past her single vantage point during the day. Escape would not be easy.

But the other thing she noticed was that, for the most part, people kept their eyes down. They attended to their own tasks and nothing more. And so if she could just blend in. She needed to hide her arm. The palace seemed to have some kind of law against anyone with any sort of disability. No crutch, no cane, and everywhere stairs that proclaimed their indifference to those who might struggle up them. She needed clothes like the clothes these people wore. Her skin was not nearly covered enough to possibly blend in.

Luckily, the dresses the women around here wore all had long sleeves. If she held the pretentious posture they held all the time, shoulders in, eyes downcast, as if they were trying to make themselves disappear, she could probably carry it off.

And so she lurked.

It was not long before she found a small window to a bedroom that belonged to a pretty girl. Kaia wondered where she was from—she was pink-skinned, with wide hips and cow-like eyes. She looked to be one of the workers, perhaps; her clothes were not ornate and excessive like those Kaia had seen in the great and terrible room where she had been marched before all those staring eyes. She was lovely the way a hot bath was lovely, and Kaia did not mind watching her.

There was something in the way the girl moved. The gentle way she folded the blankets over her bed. She reminded Kaia of Koa. Like a person who would do whatever it took to do no harm. She felt the lightning strike of loss and clenched her jaw. She did not have the luxury of wallowing.

And anyway, this girl's clothes would be the perfect size.

Kaia waited until the girl had closed the door behind her, and slipped in through the window.

After a quick dig in a wooden box at the foot of her bed, Kaia found what she thought she needed—a long-sleeved thing and a thing to go around the waist. But how was it assembled? That was more complicated. Why was it so complicated?

She was trying to figure out how best to secure the things so that she was as covered as she could be with her one hand, when the door burst open and the girl entered, looking back at a boy. They were both laughing but stopped upon seeing Kaia there, half in and half out of the clothes she had stolen.

The girl's eyes were wide with fright. But Kaia could see that the boy was not unaccustomed to danger. He cast an appraising look over the situation, his eyes darting across Kaia's arm and her pathetic attempt to dress herself.

"You're the girl," he said. In Sky Tongue. Her tongue. Kaia was so shocked that she actually felt her jaw go slack, felt her mouth make a big, stupid *O*. He held up his hands in the universal signal of good intent. "I'm not going to hurt you."

He did not look like a typical Colonizer, though the Colonizers looked many different ways. He looked as though he might have family in Tustwe, just as she did. But that was not enough, Kaia knew from experience, to create solidarity. This boy was not her brother. Her brother was dead.

"How—" the boy started, a question he did not finish.

The girl seemed to ask the same thing at the same time, and the boy looked back and forth between the two, speaking as quickly as he could in both languages.

"She recognizes you from the procession. Your arm . . . makes you pretty distinctive. We heard you'd escaped, the whole palace knows, everyone's looking for you. And—I've traveled a lot, and I've been to Puno a bunch of times. She wants to help."

"Puno? Are you a merchant? Or a pirate?"

"Does it matter?" So he was a pirate. "I want to help you."

"Why should I believe you?" Kaia ached for her ax, a dagger, anything so that she would not feel so naked. She could easily get past these two, but if they raised an alarm . . . To say she was outnumbered was a farcical understatement.

The boy looked to the girl and then back to Kaia again. He had translated for the girl up to this point, but he did not translate what he said next.

"Because I'm only here to help destroy this empire from within. And I can't imagine that's something you'd take issue with. And besides, maybe you can help me. My name is Alfie. It's nice to meet you." He tried to hold out his hand to shake hers, but Kaia ignored the gesture.

"You're a spy?"

"Yes."

"A pirate and a spy."

"I sound pretty impressive when you put it like that."

"I don't know if *impressive* is the word I'd use."

The girl looked at the boy called Alfie, confused. She, of course, had understood none of this. Kaia eyed him shrewdly.

"She doesn't know?"

"No."

"So you do not even trust your friend, and yet you ask me to trust you."

"Listen, I could have called the Guard ages ago instead of chatting here nicely with you." He sounded a little annoyed. "And I still can. Get in their good graces. Would help my cover, wouldn't it, to be a good little citizen? Maybe even the Emperor would give me a smile. But I don't give a shit about that." He took a steadying breath. "I will help you if you'll help me. Does that seem like an arrangement you can trust?"

Kaia looked at the girl. "What's her name?"

"Keiko," Alfie said.

The girl bowed in the manner Colonizers considered polite. It did not become her, even if she was beautiful.

"She stays with me until you've made good on your word."

"She has nothing to do with this," said Alfie.

"If you have nothing to hide, then she has nothing to fear from me."

"Hurt her, and I will see you hanging from the Emperor's gallows."

"Give me reason to, and she'll be in too many pieces to watch me hang."

Kaia held Alfie's gaze. She had little interest in killing Keiko, but her patience for the people in this land was gone. They had taken everything from her, taken everything she had once been. There was no room left for honor, or pity. She looked at Keiko and tried not to think of Koa, of the way their spirits were clearly of a kind. No, she would not be able to kill her. But Alfie needed to think she would. And who knew? Maybe this Kaia, the Kaia with no people and no family, the Kaia who had lost everything, even her own familiar, wasn't a Wariuta warrior anymore. She was just a life, adrift in a sea of pain. Why not cause a little, too?

"OK," Alfie said. "We have an accord."

• CHAPTER 33 •

# *The Pirate Supreme*

She smelled the same. After all those years. They caught a glancing blow of her scent, and they were back in their youth, their body entwined with hers, bodies and breath moving as one. They remembered the sound of their name on her lips, the roll of her tongue as she whispered *Kwizera*. And even now it was like they could feel her standing next to them, even when they weren't looking at her.

Rake cleared his throat.

In their throne room, representatives from each of the many coalitions of the Resistance stood gathered. They surveyed the attendees with pride. The Sisterhood of Widows. Chieftains from the Cold World. Koa stood in for the Wariuta, shifting on his feet, unused to authority. From Iwei, Quark, and the Floating Islands, guerrilla leaders. Xenobia for the few remaining witches. The Fist and her daughter. And even an ambassador and her attendants from Tustwe, the last free nation in the Known World.

The Supreme called everyone to order. Thirty or so heads turned to face them, and they grinned. The time had finally come.

How long had they waited for this moment? Too long. They pushed Xenobia's scent from their mind as best they could.

"Friends," they said. "We are here to destroy the Empire of Nipran. To watch the palace in Crandon crumble and to burn their nation to ash."

The ambassador from Tustwe darted her eyes toward Koa's hyena, clearly a little unnerved by the animal. The hyena rumbled a friendly growl, and she looked away.

Abebi was the first of the representatives to speak. She was an older woman with her hair in dreadlocks. Her arms bore the scars of battle, and her hands were gnarled from years of hard labor. "The Sisterhood stands with you. We have several operatives in place in the Imperial Palace, as well as within the Crandon constabulary. They await my orders."

This was no surprise. The Sisterhood of Widows was a nationless, ever-growing army of women whose husbands or wives, lovers or partners had been killed by the Empire. They existed in every known nation, even Tustwe. Xenobia's mother had once been in the Sisterhood of Widows. And once, long ago, Xenobia had fretted that she, too, would be a member if Kwizera did not make more effort to keep safe.

The Supreme nodded their approval. "The Sisterhood has long been a powerful member of our coalition. I thank you."

"The nationless stand with you," said the Fist.

"And Iwei." Iwei was the first nation to be colonized so many hundreds of years ago. Their representative was young, more child than man still, named Gavroche. The Supreme had met him before and was immediately fond of him. A creature of spit and spite.

"The tribes of the mountain stand with you," said one of the Cold World chieftains. He was pink-skinned and covered—even on his face—with blue tattoos, as was the way of his people.

"As do the tribes of the bogs," said another.

"And the forests," said another.

"And the wastes," said the next.

And so it went, down the line of the representatives until they reached the ambassador from Tustwe. The room hushed, all eyes on her. She wore the traditional garb of a politician, a green umushanana with a yellow sash, a thin gold circlet around her shaved head.

Tustwe had refused to participate in any kind of direct action against the Empire for decades now, and Nipran had not so much refused to colonize them as been unable—the Skeleton Coast precluded invasion by merit of its terrible sailing conditions. The name was earned by the carcasses of ships too foolish to heed warning that littered its shore. It was said only those from Tustwe could master the routes in and out of that nation, and so far that had been true. Kwizera had sailed from that very shore, so many years ago, with Xenobia, their hearts open to a new life. How could they have known what was to come?

"And what of the Sea?" asked the ambassador. The Supreme's heart fell into the pit of their stomach. One of the many reasons for leaving Tustwe was, in their opinion, the national lack of grand ambition. Of course they'd find an excuse to balk at the last moment. "In Tustwe we hear wild stories. Of waves as tall as gods. Of ports devastated, whole towns obliterated throughout the Known World. Of even pirate ships that sink, men consumed by sharks. Do you no longer have her allegiance?"

"It is I who stand in allegiance to her, not the other way around." This was not an answer, and they knew it. The Supreme had hoped no one would ask about this. Their connection to the Sea was all but lost, and though two mermaids had enlisted to hopefully find a dragon, that was hardly the same as the might of the Sea.

They held the ambassador's gaze.

"Tustwe offers a fleet of our ships," she said. Her tone was firm, her cadence slow. She was speaking very carefully. A true politician. "And a small retinue of soldiers who have volunteered. However, Tustwe will not officially raise arms against the Empire of Nipran."

Murmuring. The Supreme and Xenobia exchanged a look. They had both thought that if an ambassador from Tustwe had been dispatched to attend at all, Tustwe was ready to finally bear arms. Still. The ships would be welcome, as well as any soldiers.

"Hedging your bets," Rake said. Not rudely, exactly, but not politic. The Supreme suppressed a smile. They had always liked Rake, especially for his rough edges.

The ambassador smiled in that way that politicians do. "We have long held a policy of nonintervention. While we do not condone the behavior of the Empire, particularly the recent invasion of the Red Shore, our queen cannot commit to any acts of direct aggression against them. She has her people to think about. And besides"—she looked to the Cold World chieftains with contempt—"Tustwe will never ally with slavers."

In response, the chieftain of the bogs spat on the ground.

"Anything her majesty has to offer will be gratefully accepted," said the Supreme. "Our coalition is broad. It has to be to win." There was nothing of their disappointment in their voice. The ambassador was not the only politician here. They turned to speak to the rest of the room now. "Already in place are plans for various assassinations. We will not speak of them here. The fewer who know the particulars the better. These are operations of incredible delicacy and secrecy, and they must stay that way. However, these plans cannot be depended on for victory. And so we are here. To set a day of attack. To plan as best we can."

"Coordinated attacks across the colonies, ramping up until the invasion of Crandon," said Rake. "Assassinations of high-ranking officials. The destruction of consulates. We can spread their forces thin if we do these things simultaneously. Create chaos."

"If we're lucky," said one of the chieftains.

"That's the thing about luck," said Gavroche, smiling. "We each have to get lucky only once. They've gotta be lucky every day."

"And that is where the witches can help," said Xenobia. "In Quark, the Red Shore, and in the Cold World, anyway. There aren't many of us, but those who remain are powerful. We will craft the tales of your heroes and help to make them true."

"Separately, we have all been forced to live beneath the Emperor's heel," the Supreme said. "But together. Together, we will see him dead and his colonies freed."

The room erupted in cheers.

Reflexively, the Supreme looked to Xenobia, and it was as if no years had passed at all. They were still just Kwizera and Xenobia, and together, the two of them would bend this world away from the Empire. They reached out their hand, and Xenobia took it.

Death had come for safer targets. Best, Kwizera thought, to give him a grand one.

• CHAPTER 34 •

## Alfie

Kaia did not look like a maid, even with her hair combed and in a kimono. Maybe it was the way she held herself, like she was ready to fight, her legs flexed and eyes roaming. Or maybe it was just because she was missing one hand. It was hard to say.

Keiko pulled a corset around her waist and yanked the ties back. Kaia called out in shock.

"What is she doing?" she demanded. She whirled on Keiko, who backed away as though from a wild animal. "Is this some kind of Imperial torture device?"

"Of sorts?" Alfie said. When Kaia looked as though she might only punch him out, he added: "It's called a corset. All the women wear them here."

"Barbaric."

"Sure. But you have to let Keiko work, OK? She's trying to help you."

Kaia closed her eyes as if to gather herself, then reached her hand out to Keiko and touched her shoulder gently. It was as good an apology as she could make directly without the Common Tongue, and Alfie was glad to see it.

"Can it be a little looser?" she asked when it was tied and done.

Alfie asked Keiko, who shook her head. "It's as loose as I can make it without calling attention to her."

Corseted, and with the obi on, Kaia looked somewhat more in place.

"Remember to keep your head down," Alfie said.

"Tell her to keep her hands together," Keiko reminded him. Then, realizing what she'd said, she added, "Or, to make it look like her hands are together."

Alfie translated this, and Kaia rolled her eyes.

"I have never hidden my arm before," she said. She sounded angry, but not at him. "It seems this place is determined to squash out any speck of dignity I have left."

"I know. But the palace would never hire someone who . . ." he scrambled for something polite to say.

"I know." Kaia straightened her shoulders and then bowed her head experimentally. It was, Alfie had to admit, a passable impression of the proper posture of an Imperial girl.

"One last touch," Keiko said. She grabbed a bonnet and fastened it over Kaia's hair. "She'll look like a laundry girl this way."

Kaia examined herself in the small mirror Keiko had propped on her tansu and shuddered. "I look like a complete fool." She touched the bonnet, a look of disgust on her face, but she didn't disturb it.

All in all, it wasn't a bad disguise. The bonnet hid her dirty hair. Alfie smiled at both Keiko and Kaia. "This is going to work," he said. And he believed it. He had to.

Keiko had done the best she could. Now it was time to test her labor.

"I don't know," said Keiko. She looked at Kaia, her brow crumpled in worry.

"It'll be fine," said Alfie. "Trust me."

Keiko looked at him then, and he sensed he had said the wrong thing. She seemed troubled, and not about Kaia. About him.

"You told her my name is Keiko," she said.

Alfie laughed a little, bemused. "'Course I did. Would you rather her call you something else?"

But Keiko was deadly serious. "You gave her my real name," she said pointedly. "Why didn't you give her yours?"

Alfie's heart stopped. What name had he given? He racked his brain, trying to remember what had happened. He'd been so stunned, so confused by Kaia's presence, and it'd been such a scramble to make sense of the situation, to defuse it. He didn't remember what he'd said. "Didn't I?" he said stupidly.

"No. You said. You said the name Alfie." She tried to hold his gaze, but Alfie looked away, cursing himself inside. "Is that your real name?"

There was no point in lying. And anyway, he couldn't think of one. "Yes."

"If you want me to trust you, you need to trust me," said Keiko.

"Are we going?" Kaia asked.

"Just . . . just shut up a sec," Alfie said to Kaia. She looked offended but did as he asked. His mind was spinning; he didn't know what to do, what to say. He couldn't believe he'd messed up so badly, but then of course he could believe it, because he messed up everything, all the time. What was wrong with him? "I'm sorry," he said to Keiko. "I—if I tell you who I am, you'll just be in more danger."

"I'm sneaking a prisoner out of custody," she said. "I'm already in danger."

This was true. Alfie closed his eyes. "I wish you weren't," he said. And when Keiko did not respond to this, he went on. "I'm here as an operative for the Resistance. The Pirate Supreme, specifically. As a spy."

Keiko sat down on her bed. "Shit," she said.

Alfie had never heard her cuss before, and it didn't sound right from her. It was like the auditory equivalent of seeing a dog in human clothes. It might have been funny if he didn't feel so awful. "I didn't mean. I mean, I never wanted to put you in any danger. I'm so sorry," he said.

"Well, you did," she said curtly. She stood and dusted off her skirts, which did not have dust on them. "Come on, then." She took Kaia by the arm. "Let's get this over with."

And in the midst of the most uncomfortable silence Alfie had ever experienced, they walked out of Keiko's room and into the palace.

Getting through the servants' wing was easy. Everyone was so busy attending to their own business that they didn't have time to watch Alfie, Keiko, and the stiff and uncomfortable laundry girl as they went. Kaia had snuck in through Keiko's window—a difficult task for one, an impossible task for three. And so the real test would be getting through the palace. Then the palace grounds. Then the palace gate.

Their story was simple: Alfie was escorting the young women on an errand for the nursery to buy new textiles for sheets and pillows. Only the best for the princesses and Crown Prince. This was a believable story, if a little strange that a kitchen boy had been sent on the job. If they were questioned by a guard, it'd make sense that Alfie would do the talking—he was the only boy present and the best liar of the three. It wasn't a perfect plan. But it'd have to do.

They passed the courtyard with only one stumble—Kaia held her head a little too high as she curiously regarded a few senators as they passed. Alfie could understand why—the golden robes they wore were ostentatious even by Imperial standards, so he couldn't imagine how they looked to a Wariuta person. One of them quirked his brow at her, offended at her impertinence, but he didn't stop arguing with his cohort.

"Don't look at people," Alfie hissed under his breath.

"Sorry," Kaia hissed back in a voice that didn't sound very sorry. But she kept her head down after that.

When they passed the atrium, though, Kaia couldn't help but pause, arrested by the sight of the great dragon skeleton assembled there. Keiko made a small noise of remonstration, and they moved along again before anyone noticed that a laundry girl seemed shocked by such a normal part of palace life.

"For gods' sake, keep it moving," Alfie said just as a senator turned the corner in front of them.

At the sound of a foreign tongue being uttered in the Imperial palace, the same senator regarded them suspiciously.

"New girl," Alfie said, his voice cheery. And then, for good measure, he added in an exasperated tone: "Immigrant."

"I see," said the senator. He looked at Kaia disapprovingly. This time, at least, Kaia had the good sense to keep her head properly bowed. "They'll hire just anyone these days, won't they?"

Alfie laughed as he swallowed his disgust. "You know how it is."

He bowed deeply to the senator, and the girls followed suit. The senator went on his way without sparing them another glance.

"We're not going to make it," Keiko whispered. Her voice was shaky, terrified.

"Yes, we are," said Alfie firmly. He wished she had not had to come along—but without another maid, Alfie and Kaia would look extra suspicious. Kitchen boys and maids did not just perambulate about the palace one-on-one, lest they appear to be canoodling on the Emperor's coin. "Just act normal, and we'll be out of here in no time."

This was a lie, of course. They still had the grounds to traverse. But they were at the grand entrance to the palace now, and the grounds were much less busy than the palace itself was.

When they walked through the great golden doors and down the front steps, Alfie felt a grin pulling at his face. They really were going to make it. None of the guards had even blinked at them as they'd gone. Scared straight by the senator, Kaia was doing an excellent job keeping her head down and eyes averted now, and Keiko—well, Keiko looked terrified, but he suspected he could see that only because he knew her so well.

He hoped that someday she might forgive him for all this. He knew she may very well not.

The grounds were empty save for some gardeners tending to the various trees and flowers, their backs to all as they worked. This was easy, this was pie, and they walked quickly but not too quickly through the grounds.

They were nearly to safety when, as if in slow motion, the gates were pulled closed by several guards. Alfie was not the only one confused. There was some murmuring of confusion among the gardeners.

"No one comes in or out!" a guard called. "Emperor's orders!"

The murmuring grew louder. Not everyone in the palace during the day lived in the palace. Something was afoot.

"What's going on?" Alfie asked a gardener.

The man grimaced. "I hear there's a plot to assassinate the

Prince . . . so till that gets sorted, we're all stuck here. Which is fine by me. Food's better here than it is at home." The man gave a loud chortle. "I'm gonna go see about some milk bread."

Alfie tried to laugh along but could not find the energy.

"What do we do?" Keiko whispered.

"I . . . don't know." Alfie looked around desperately but could think of no alternatives. All the entrances would be heavily guarded. And if what the man had said was true, then . . . the Guard was looking for him.

"Stay with Kaia," Alfie told Keiko. "I need to go. To see if there's any other way in or out."

Keiko gave him a look like he was the worst person she had ever met, which, honestly, he probably was. "Fine," she said. "Come back to my quarters when you can. We'll be waiting."

"I promise I will." He gave her hand a squeeze, tried to let the gesture communicate his earnestness. He would not let harm come to Keiko. If that was the only thing he could do before he was strung up by the Guard, then so be it. It would be enough.

To Kaia he said, "Be gentle with her. I will be back for you both as soon as I possibly can. They've locked down the gates."

"Are they looking for me?" Kaia asked.

"No. Or yes. But I think they're also looking for me."

### ◆ CHAPTER 35 ◆

## *Evelyn*

They swam down, down, down. Into the gaping abyss of the trenches far below the world they had so recently come to know. In Flora's hand the quartz stone glowed, lighting their way.

It was cold. Not cold like Crandon was cold in winter, not the biting cold of ice, but the deep, encompassing cold of nothingness. Without the illumination of Flora's stone, Evelyn knew, they would be lost forever. Maybe even with the stone.

As they descended, the water around them grew thick with tiny particles that shone white in the light cast by Flora's stone. Flora pointed the quartz over them, once, and illuminated an enormous shark languidly plodding through the water. Evelyn gasped. It was immense and scarred and paid them no mind. Occasionally, blinking lights flashed, but it was impossible to tell in the encompassing darkness whether they were near or far.

"Are we lost?" Evelyn asked. After all they had been through, still she was like an extra saddlebag for Flora to carry. And maybe she would have felt shame if she were not so cold.

"I don't know," Flora said. Her voice was gentle, was always gentle, with Evelyn. "I don't think so."

"I'm so cold," said Evelyn.

"Yes," said Flora. There was nothing else to say.

Flora took her hand, and for a moment, Evelyn's fingers were warm where Flora's lips kissed her. They held each other's hands after that for some ways, even though it did make the going slower. Clearly, Evelyn was not the only one a little afraid.

They swam farther down.

There was no sound anymore. No whale's song that echoed, resonant and sad. Only silence and darkness, cold and craggy rock. There was no silence, Evelyn realized, on land. There was always something: the sound of a leaf falling, a bird's call. Not so down here. Not even the tiny blinking fish of the deep came this far.

And then suddenly:

"Stop."

They had reached the bottom. The floor of the Sea was not like the ground on land—it began and ended in gradient, a spectrum of diatomaceous earth. Something breathed, the force of its breath sending waves over the undulating floor. Something enormous. And there: the yawning maw of a cavern somehow even darker than the darkness that enveloped them.

Flora's face was lit by the glowing stone, and Evelyn found fear there, worry. And she kissed her then, so that perhaps Evelyn could carry some of the worry for her. Flora would carry a burden forever without a thought to ask for help. It was Evelyn's turn to be strong now.

"Please, Dragon," Evelyn called. And her voice was so brave, she could feel Flora's pride in her swelling in her own chest. "Will you lend us your time?"

Silence.

"Perhaps she did not hear—" Flora began.

But before she could finish speaking, there was a great rumble, like stone on stone, like thunder just after a lightning strike. They both flinched as the great head of the dragon emerged from the cavern.

She was gigantic on a scale Evelyn did not have words to describe. Big like the sky was big, like she might have been limitless. She did not end and begin the way a person did; she was more like a cloud, blurred at the edges, ethereal. She glowed blue in the light of the stone, but she could have been purple or white or opalescent, or a color that Evelyn's eyes did not understand, could not categorize.

"Two souls," the dragon whispered. Her voice was soft for something so colossal, as though she were just a girl passing secrets. One great foot emerged from the cavern, and each of her three toes ended in claws as long as trees were tall. She lowered her head so that her eyes—slit-pupiled and silver—met theirs.

"We come to beg a favor," Evelyn said.

"Ah." The dragon's only reply.

"The fate of the Known World depends on it," added Flora.

"Who sent you?" asked the dragon.

"The Pirate Supreme," Florian said.

"They will destroy the Empire of Nipran," said Evelyn. "And end the Emperor's tyranny. He's been killing and lying and hurting for so long now." She thought of Flora the child, scrounging for scraps while so many had so much. While she had so much. Shame washed over her. "It must be done. Not just for us but for the whole world! To save children, and, and, and mermaids, and—"

"To save the Sea," the dragon finished for her.

At this the dragon emerged fully from the cavern. Her body

was long and sinuous, sliding from her hiding place like an eel. Her great scales flashed white as she moved.

"At last," said the dragon.

Flora and Evelyn exchanged a look. So Flora didn't know what that meant, either. Still, though, the dragon swam toward the surface, and the mermaids followed.

"At long last."

• CHAPTER 36 •

# Genevieve

She sat with her mother on a set of steps that led straight into the sea. There was nothing to do just then except wait, and so they waited together in uneasy silence. It was odd how quickly she had become accustomed to her mother being the Fist. Perhaps it was because it suited her so well. Her mother was a skilled leader, that much was clear from the quiet way she demanded respect. And Genevieve was left to wonder who she might have become if her mother had trusted her enough to tell her who she was, all those years ago, before the Lady Ayer had cast her spell upon her.

The Fist sat with her knees lazily spread, hunched over a steaming cup of something the witch, Xenobia, had made to help with her voice. It smelled odd, more like woodsmoke and copper than something edible. Her mother gazed out at the sea. In the distance, Genevieve could see whitecaps blooming like flowers beneath a brewing storm. The sea was angry, according to the Pirate Supreme. Genevieve didn't know what that meant, exactly, but it didn't sound good.

"Do you think they'll get the dragon's help?" Genevieve asked.

Her mother took a long sip of her drink. "Hmm. I don't know much about magic." Her voice was a little less raspy, though still deep and different from what it had been when she had been Mrs. Vo the innkeeper. "But I've seen enough now not to underestimate it."

"Why didn't you tell me?" It came out more like an accusation than the genuine question she'd intended. "Who you were," she added in a more conciliatory tone.

Her mother put down the now empty cup and looked Genevieve in her eyes. Their eyes were so similar, Genevieve knew, the same shape, the same shade of tawny brown. "You have to understand. Just knowing that I was involved was the same as a death sentence for you. I couldn't risk it."

"Dai knew," Genevieve said. And the resentment she hadn't realized she had bubbled to the surface, prickling her eyes. She looked away.

"That was his parents' choice," her mother said. "One that got him killed."

They sat in silence with this horror for some time. Genevieve had not known what had become of her former best friend, her former betrothed. The anger she'd felt toward him for years seemed hollow and cruel now. He'd been so young. She had grown so much since then, changed so much. And he would forever be the same. She didn't have the strength to ask how it happened, but she suspected she knew. Traitors were usually hanged.

All this death, all this suffering, and she'd helped cause it. Because a rich lady promised Genevieve she was special, that being a part of this cruelty made her better than everyone she'd grown up with. But the truth was she wasn't special. She was normal, gullible. Eager to believe that the Empire was successful because it deserved to be, because it was just, because it was great. Not because of its seeming unending predilection for murder. She'd forgotten so easily, so quickly, who she was, where she came from.

She'd even let the Lady Ayer change her name.

"Is there any coming back?" Genevieve asked. Her voice trembled, straining against the shame that constricted her rapidly beating heart. "From what I've done? From what I've become?"

"I have done things that keep me up at night," her mother said. "I can't sleep for seeing the terrible things I've done, the faces of the people I've killed or had killed. But I keep going because I know what I'm fighting for is right."

"But how do you know?" She felt a little desperate. To know anything for certain would be a salve. It felt as though nothing in the world was exact, and that everything was complicated, and that she would never be smart enough or good enough or wise enough to parse it. She had thought she was right all those years ago, when she had gone along with the Lady Ayer. She'd thought she was fighting for good. But she'd been wrong.

To her annoyance, her mother laughed. Not a chuckle but a big boom of a laugh, like a cannon being fired. Genevieve glared at her.

"I'm sorry, child. I'm not trying to be cruel. It's just that I don't know. I suppose you never can. But I believe people deserve to be free. And I can't prove that, and I don't know what that's going to look like. Mm? But that belief lives in the same part of my heart that loves you and loved your father. And so that's what I choose to fight for. That's who I've chosen to be."

"I don't know who I am anymore."

"You're my daughter." Her mother squeezed her hand, and she was not only the Fist then, she was also Mrs. Vo. She was still her mother. Was it worth it? To have been lied to, to have fought for the wrong side, to have shamed herself—all to be reunited with her mother, the family she thought she had lost? To see that person clearly, finally, for the first time? Was that enough? She didn't know. But it was the truth, at least. And it was nice to know something true. "No matter what you've done."

She smiled at her mother, let her eyes wander over the face that was at once so different—wrinkled and scarred, burnt by the sun, with lips gone slack at the edges, one eye hidden behind a patch whose story Genevieve did not know—and exactly the same. Her mother was a completely different person and exactly the same person at once. And so maybe she could be, too.

"I think . . . I think I'd like you to call me Thistle again." Thistle. The name was so familiar and so strange. Like putting a lost glove back on her hand and finding it fit just the same. A reminder that, even after all the mistakes she had made, she had something to be proud of. Thistle, daughter of the Fist, child of Quark. "I think that'd be right."

The Fist's eye watered, but she did not cry. "As you wish."

They sat in silence for some time, absorbing all that had been said. The golden light of dusk danced across the sea.

"It's funny," the Fist said. "So much Imperial time and money spent to educate you, to sharpen you into the little dagger's edge you are now. And you're going to use it against them." She chuckled. "Irony can be so delicious."

"You reap what you sow," Thistle said.

• CHAPTER 37 •

# Commander Callum

Commander Finn Callum was home. Though his estate in Crandon was not as comfortable as he remembered it. Less grand than what he deserved. Still, he felt a kind of relief as he sat in his library, which did not hold as many books as it held weapons. A sword from the era of the 990th Emperor, a naginata his grandfather had once wielded in the days before gunpowder. A dagger from the Cold World, forged in dragon fire in the days when there were still dragons. All mounted on the walls. His servants had brought him some mediocre tea, which sat on the table next to him, going cold.

When they found Tomas Inouye's corpse on the palace grounds, the girl gone, Callum felt only irritation. Keen and biting, a threat to his calm. Windsor was flogged, discharged, family connections be damned. He sent his men into Crandon to find the girl. It wouldn't take long, he was sure. She stuck out from the Imperial gentry like a donkey among horses.

His return had been an overwhelming disappointment. The parade was not nearly festive enough. He had expected sexual entreaty from at least a handful of ladies, only to receive none. The Emperor's reception had not gone at all as planned. The old idiot could barely keep his head up, let alone declare war. It was so exhausting, he reflected, to be the only competent person in his orbit. What he could have accomplished if only he had adequate help!

Still, it was good to be back. In civilization once more, where real people tended to real business, not just hawking their wares in the open air like perpetual vagrants. Crandon smelled of smoke and horses and the sea, and Callum loved it as much as he'd loved anything in his life. Not that there were many points of comparison. He was not prone to affection. He had, however, expected a somewhat warmer reception from the Emperor's court. Even though the old man was senile, demented, weak, he had assumed the nobles would have his back. But alas, they were as weak as the old man who led them.

Senator Tsujima was exactly on time, as xe always was. Xe wore a particularly decadent haori, and it didn't suit xem. It would be more fitting, Callum thought, on a man. A royal one at that. New-moneyed people were like that, though, forever dressing above their station. Impertinent, really. Xe may have earned enough money through buying and selling slaves in the Cold World to earn a place in the Senate, but that didn't make xem noble. Callum didn't like Tsujima, didn't approve of xem, but xe was useful even if Callum didn't know how to treat someone whose genitals were a mystery.

But Tsujima knew everything about everyone at court. Callum motioned for xyr to sit down, and xe did, with a flamboyant little flourish Callum found deeply annoying.

"Commander Callum," Tsujima said silkily. Xe was forever decorous. "Welcome home. I rather thought you'd invite me here to your lovely abode a little sooner. You must be so exhausted from your exertions upon the Red Shore."

"Battle will do that," Callum replied.

"From what I hear, it was less of a battle and more of a massacre," said Tsujima. Xyr voice was conversational, but there was a barb in there. The disposal of resisters was, Callum thought bitterly, the dirty business the military attended to so that the gentry of Nipran could feign ignorance of it. They were a just and polite society, after all. But murder was murder, and murder was required to keep the ladies in their silks and the men in their gold. Callum was the best at commanding all that bloodshed.

"Our men fought gallantly," said Callum. He gave a short, cold smile. Smiling had never suited him. "I do not imagine, however, that you hinted so aggressively for an invitation here just to give me your compliments."

"Alas, no," Tsujima said with a rueful smile. "Deserving of them though I'm sure you are." Was that sarcasm? "No, I'm here to gauge your interest on a matter of the greatest delicacy. One that requires your absolute dedication to secrecy. It's a secret I think you might be amenable to, if you were to hear it."

Callum quirked a brow. He did not trust Tsujima, did not trust anyone who had never served in the Guard.

"The thing is, it's so delicate, in fact, that in order to tell you about it at all, I must divulge a secret of my own, such that I might, ah, encourage your loyalty." Xyr tone was one of false reluctance, but Callum could feel xyr hunger to exert power over him as clearly as he could see xem sitting there, in his chair, in his home, making veiled threats.

"Go on, then."

"I know about your arrangement with Lord Hasegawa." Tsujima tut-tutted. "Naughty stuff. Sending his daughter off to be killed by pirates so that you would have an excuse to start a war. No, I don't think the court or the senators would be pleased to hear that you'd sent one of Crandon's own daughters to her death just so you could secure some explosives. She was one of us, after all. And it didn't even work. I hear she escaped your grip, slippery little thing, never to be seen again."

Callum kept a mask of impassiveness on his face, but inside, his guts were churning. Tsujima was right, of course. This agreement with Lord Hasegawa was the kind of thing that had to happen in darkness. And even if plenty of nobles had participated in such arrangements, or worse, they could never admit to it publicly. Reputation was everything in court. He'd be ruined.

"You have proof of this allegation?" he said calmly.

"Indeed, I do," said Tsujima. Callum's hand made a tight fist in his lap. "A written testimony from Lord Hasegawa himself. A written testimony I was clever enough to secrete away such that it cannot be destroyed except by me or my secret keeper, who will release it should I suddenly and inexplicably perish."

Callum silently cursed Hasegawa. *The little toad, the little traitor.* "Is that so?"

"Oh, yes, yes, yes. Hasegawa always needs money, doesn't he, more than your little arrangement allowed him. And I was generous enough to lend him some coin. A paltry amount, really, but it did the trick. A small price for such valuable information. So. Am I assured your silence?"

Callum took a deep breath. He didn't have a choice, and Tsujima knew it. "Yes."

"You have likely noticed that the Emperor is . . . not the man he once was."

This was a shocking thing to say aloud. Callum regarded the senator coolly. "I would not say such things if I were you."

"Luckily you are not, and unluckily for his majesty, I am not the only one who has noticed nor who is concerned. I imagine you were somewhat disappointed by his inability to recognize the great gestures you made, your clear entreaty for troops to take the Red Shore? Man like you, in his prime. Certainly leading the offensive there would keep you in gold for the rest of your days. If the Emperor had ordered it, that is."

Callum did not reply. His lips set into a tight line of chagrin at having been so transparent, but Tsujima was undaunted and, apparently, clairvoyant.

"There is a plot, you see," said Tsujima. "A Resistance plot to kill the Crown Prince."

At that, Callum's ears pricked. The heir.

Tsujima nodded. "My sense is that there are several factions of the Resistance working together to see it done. And my sense is also that, if we are careful, it could be aided in happening with precious little interference from us."

Callum saw it then, the hazy edges of Tsujima's motivation. He could not help it; he was impressed. Xe was full of surprises.

"With no heir, the Senate will take over once the Emperor dies." A clever plan, if xyr involvement was not spotted. As a senior senator, Tsujima would become incredibly powerful overnight. Xe had so much to gain. "And this is where you come in." Tsujima steepled xyr fingers and regarded Callum, xyr eyes fixed with cold calculation.

"There it is."

"You have long cultivated a glowing reputation for violence," Tsujima said in a tone that belied both disgust and respect, as if xe were conversing with a useful dog, a beast of burden. "And if you were to aid us in this little bit of tidy skulduggery, why, I imagine the rewards would be . . ." Xe searched for the right word. "Ample."

"I'll need specifics."

"Well, the Senate would be in charge of appointing the new general of the army, wouldn't we?" Tsujima paused, letting that sink in.

Callum could feel his mouth watering, and it tasted like blood. To lead the entire Imperial forces. To be top man in command. General Mirimoto was old now, nearly as old as the Emperor, though his mind was still sharp. He'd need to be replaced with someone younger. Someone hungrier.

Callum smiled, a real smile. Finally. A competent ally.

"I'll need you to put that in writing," Callum said. "Before I can commit to anything."

"Naturally, naturally. I'd expect no less. Anything less would be foolish. And you, my good sir, are no fool."

Tsujima stood, and the two bowed to each other.

"Thanks to the Emperor," Tsujima said.

• CHAPTER 38 •

# The Pirate Supreme

The Pirate Supreme waited, along with the representatives, Xenobia, the Fist and her daughter, and Rake. That morning they had awoken with Xenobia in their bed. Xenobia was already awake and sure, she said, that it would happen today. That the dragon was close. She could feel it. And so they waited, all of them, on the steps that led into the Sea, watching for any sign of movement. A pod of whales spouting nearby gave everyone a false start.

When the sun began to set, the Supreme turned to Xenobia. "Are you sure?" they asked at a whisper, for probably the hundredth time.

"Yes," Xenobia said.

The ambassador from Tustwe shifted on her feet, impatient and cold in the dwindling sun. The Supreme feared that she would lose interest entirely and leave before the dragon presented herself, but they kept that worry to themself.

And then, Koa's hyena giggled. High and anxious, the animal's nervous laughter was louder even than the waves that crashed against the stone of the Supreme's keep, a piercing *hee-hee-hee* that sent shivers through them. All watched, transfixed, as the animal started to pace, clearly afraid. Koa tried to shush his familiar, but Tupac would not be comforted.

"She's close," said Xenobia. Even she looked afraid; Kwizera could see it in the way she breathed, short and shallow, the way she held herself taut. They took her hand in theirs, and for a moment they were as they had once been, joined by their fear and their anticipation, together in an uncomplicated way. For a moment, they were just Kwizera and Xenobia, there to protect each other from whatever may come.

But then Xenobia's eyes darted away, scanning the horizon.

She need not have looked so far.

With unnerving quiet, the dragon's enormous head surfaced almost directly in front of the waiting crowd.

Maybe because they were in such shock, or perhaps because the dragon was so strange, so otherworldly that no one knew how to respond, not a one of the waiting crowd made a sound. Eyes wide, they watched as the dragon slowly blinked, taking them in. She could have easily opened her maw, swallowed the entire group whole. But instead, she simply looked at them, as if waiting for them to speak. Which, Kwizera realized, she probably was. They had called her, after all.

The Pirate Supreme stepped forward, and with their best semblance of courage, they squared their body to the dragon. *If you want to do great things,* they reminded themself, *you must be bold.* They were close enough to her that if they reached out, maybe they could have touched the scales that glistened silver and white and blue on her snout. But there was something so odd about her—the way she was both very much right there and also indistinct at her boundaries, more cloud than creature—that they wondered if they could touch her at all. When she breathed, the air around them smelled of rain on stone. She was beautiful the way a distant storm was beautiful, and with just her presence she seemed to tell the Supreme how small they were, how finite.

She was not death, but she was a reminder of it.

"I am the Pirate Supreme," they said, and their voice was loud and clear. "I am the one who calls, to beg your help."

"Yes," the dragon said. Her voice was impassive, but they guessed she was likely impatient at redundancy. Likely the mermaids had told her. She did not say more but waited, as if the Supreme were a child. Compared with her, they likely were.

"We have assembled fighters from all over the Known World so that we can free the colonies from the Emperor's grip and save the Sea from his greed." They motioned to the crowd behind them. "We have waited generations for a realistic shot at liberty," they said. "And the time is now. If, that is, you are generous enough to help us."

"The Emperors killed my children," the dragon said. "Hunted them down. Found them out and took each of their lives. My sons and my daughters, my children, my babies, all dead and gone."

None were brave enough to tell her that a skeleton of one of her children was on display in the Emperor's palace. The Supreme wondered if she knew.

"Nipran is rapacious," they said. "Whatever they consume they consume voraciously, no matter the cost, until it is gone. They must be stopped."

"Yes," said the dragon. She looked then to Koa, who startled backward, nearly tripping over his hyena, who had gone as still as everyone else in the dragon's presence. "What do you think, child?"

She asked this in Sky Tongue, and the boy was so surprised

that it took him a moment to answer. "I agree," he said slowly. "That they must be stopped."

"But," the dragon said.

"But . . ." He looked around at all the leaders and representatives cautiously. "Death makes me uneasy."

"The Emperor must be killed. His Empire burned. His soldiers defeated," the Supreme interjected. They liked Koa, felt an affection toward him, but they would not see him ruin their one chance at overthrowing the Emperor. "Will you help us?"

"Help you kill them all?" the dragon asked.

"Yes," the Pirate Supreme said.

"How small you are," said the dragon. "How limited your imagination."

The Supreme did not know what to make of this. They looked to Rake, whose eyes conveyed bewilderment as deep as their own.

"Is that a no?" they asked, unsure what else to say.

"I will bring justice," said the dragon. And before anything else could be said, she emerged entirely from the Sea, her long body rising like smoke. "Sail now, children," she called back to them. "I will meet you on their shore."

The crowd whooped and cheered as she flew away on the wind, more mist than bird. It looked as if she were swimming through the air, her body undulating to propel her away. In her wake, the Sea stilled, as though she knew that finally, a power great enough to save her was on the move.

And the Pirate Supreme grinned.

The battle of Crandon started now.

# PART THREE

## The Spy

## CHAPTER 39

## Thistle

How many times had Thistle looked at her mother and sworn she would never be like her? Countless. But now she watched the woman the Resistance called the Fist and marveled.

Maybe one day she could be like her. If she worked hard. If she was lucky.

If she survived.

Aboard the *Leviathan*, the Fist had started teaching target practice to those unfamiliar with guns. Some were too proud—the gruff chieftain from the Cold World bogs refused to let his people attend, but he was unusual. Much of the underground work of the Resistance had not required participants to learn weaponry at all, and they had but the weeks-long voyage to learn before they would be thrust into battle.

The Fist lined up empty glass bottles along the quarterdeck and barked instructions at her students. Thistle watched with her lips quirked in equal parts amusement and concern. Most of those who attended knew nothing, and it showed. When one of the Widows fired directly into the deck, she couldn't help it, she laughed. Not out of cruelty, truly, but incompetence would always be a little bit funny.

"I suppose you can do better, hmm?" her mother called. It was not an entirely friendly tone of voice. The smile fell from Thistle's face. She was loath to disappoint the Fist, but a sliver of her old irritation with her mother found its way beneath her skin. Objectively, what had just happened was funny. But she tried to take the high road.

"Just hope no one got hurt," Thistle replied.

Her mother stuck her with a challenging glare. "Show her, then," she said. "If you're such aces with a pistol."

She handed Thistle a gun that was much larger than the one the Lady Ayer had entrusted her with. It felt heavy and wrong in her grasp. An Iwei thing, she could tell from the barrel. A cursory examination of it told her that the sight on it listed a bit to the left. In her mind, the Lady Ayer's voice reminded her to count the bullets. She pushed the voice away but counted all the same. There were three bullets in the chamber. Three bottles on the quarterdeck.

Thistle aimed, breathed out. Just as the Lady had taught her.

Three bottles exploded into shards.

The assembled class clapped and cheered, and Thistle did an exaggerated Imperial bow for them. She grinned, and to her delight, her mother grinned back.

"At least she taught you well," she said. She thumped Thistle on the back, then resumed teaching.

Aglow, Thistle sat back down to watch along with Koa, who refused to handle a gun. It took a moment before she realized he was grimacing at her.

She knew he didn't like guns, but wasn't it better to be well trained with them at least? And anyway, she just wanted to enjoy herself. But Koa's eyes were too sad to ignore. "What?" Her voice was a bit more testy than she might have hoped.

"It could have been you," Koa said. "On the shore. Shooting us down. Just like those bottles." He made his hand into a gun and mimed shooting. "Bam. Bam. Me. Kaia. Bam. Tupac." His voice quavered with emotion. "That's what you came to our shore for, isn't it?"

Thistle felt as if she'd been slapped. Not undeservedly, but it stung all the same. "I had been taught . . . so many lies. When we left Crandon, the Lady Ayer told me that we were trying to start a war, yes, but with as little bloodshed as possible. It sounded so smart, she always sounded so smart, and I guess I was just stupid and—"

"But you're not stupid." Koa averted his eyes, let his hand find Tupac, whom he rubbed behind one crooked ear. "I know that, you know that. But you would have killed me on the shore. You pointed your gun at me. I see now you wouldn't have missed."

"No," said Thistle. "I would not. I'm sorry."

It was a weak apology. She tried to think of something else to say, but nothing came. Nothing sufficient. Nothing that could speak to the depth of her error, or the profundity of her ignorance. She had needed to learn so much and so quickly and in the worst way possible. She only hoped that maybe someday she would undo even a fraction of the harm she had caused in her short life.

They sat without speaking for some time. The guns sent a visible jolt through Koa's body each time they were fired. Thistle wanted to reach out to comfort him but worried that might be the opposite of what he wanted. Glass exploded on the quarterdeck, another target hit. The class cheered. Koa sat rigid. Finally, Thistle could not take it anymore and put her hand, tentatively, on his. To her surprise and relief, Koa reached his hand up and clasped hers. It was not an absolution, she thought, so much as an acknowledgment that she was there. That he wanted her there.

"I'm grateful for your friendship," Thistle said. "I do not deserve it."

"No," said Koa. "You don't."

Tupac stood and positioned himself between the two so they both could pet him, and Thistle pushed down a laugh. They were so alike. This boy and his beast. Cut from the same piece of cloth. She scratched Tupac under his chin, just below his enormous canine teeth.

"Do you ever worry," Koa asked, "that you have been made into a weapon without the wisdom to know where best to aim?"

Thistle let her hand fall from the animal. If Koa was indeed her friend, she could certainly count on him for bone-crushing candor. She thought of the Lady Ayer, of her mother. Both leaders. Both with specific ideas about whom she should be. Her mother thought she should have stayed safe. The Lady Ayer had thought she should be an operative, just like her, in service to the Empire.

"I do," Thistle said, and it was the truth.

• CHAPTER 40 •

*Koa*

The voyage to Crandon was difficult, even on the *Leviathan*—the ship that Koa had been told was blessed by the Sea herself. Rocky and uncomfortable, across waves too tall and too violent. The Sea made herself clear: She no longer favored or recognized anyone, not even the Pirate Supreme, and this was disquieting to all, but especially to Koa's old friend. Koa could see that easily, though it wasn't as though the one called the Pirate Supreme made any pretense of hiding it. They paced the ship, and when they weren't yelling orders to their crew, they sat looking either angry or worried, or most often both.

It was likely due to the witch that the small fleet of Resistance ships had not sunk. She was forever murmuring spells, which was unsettling. Now and then she'd prowl the ship for ingredients, randomly accosting people and asking if they had a blade of grass or a compass on them. And so the fleet made its way.

The witch and everyone else who was not part of the Pirate Supreme's crew spent most of their time belowdecks, watching the lanterns swing as the boat was jostled and tossed by the Sea.

Koa was grateful to have mostly conquered his seasickness, but Tupac was unable to find his sea legs, forever scrambling and toppling. It would have been funny if it were not so distressing to the animal. Koa alternated between frustration and guilt. He needed his familiar, and yet could he keep him safe? He did not know. It seemed not. He tried not to think of Chima, of Puka, of all the fallen familiars. He was stepping into danger, and he was taking Tupac along with him.

It was impossible to explain to outsiders the bond between a familiar and a warrior. It was not just friendship. It was something greater, more encompassing than that. They were partners, each other's shadows. He tried his best to comfort Tupac, to cuddle him and help him keep still, but the animal was forever giggling, squirming, pacing.

He wanted to yell at Tupac, *Do you not see how miserable I am, too? Do you not understand all that has been lost?* But it would have done no good, and so he did not. Instead, he did his best to help the witch when she needed it, which was often. He did not understand her magic, but he liked her and her propensity for cursing in various languages.

It was night when Rake called the passengers to the deck. The moon was high in the sky, though shrouded in the fog that Koa had been warned perpetually lay over Crandon. Koa shivered in the damp of it as they sailed beneath the shadow of an enormous statue.

"That's the Emperor," Thistle told him. She had changed her name back to the name she had been called as a child, apparently. Wariuta often changed their names if something fundamental about themselves shifted: their gender, or their sexuality, or in moments of terrible grief or triumph. He wondered what had shifted in Thistle. He hoped it was good. "They say he watches over us."

"But it's just a statue. Stone, no?" It seemed a monumental waste of effort to build a model of someone, when tales of starving within Crandon reached even the Wariuta shore. Surely there were better ways to spend resources?

"Yes," Thistle said. "Just stone." She shook her head. "I found this impressive once. No more."

The Emperor stared down to the Sea. His gaze did nothing to arrest the progress of the attacking fleet.

Koa had never been so cold in his life. He wrapped the poncho a pirate had given him tight around his enormous shoulders. He looked to the city with his eyes narrowed. Buildings seemed to be stacked directly on top of one another. It was nothing like home.

"It's so crowded," he said.

Thistle looked at Crandon, too, and nodded. The street lamps glowed orange, like the last rays of a bleeding sunset. It might have been lovely.

"Where will the people go?" Koa asked. "When the battle starts?"

"There'll be nowhere to go," Thistle said finally. Crandon was dense with human life, Koa could see that immediately. The hum of it all reached out across the water. Escape would be. Difficult. Impossible, maybe, for some. No passenger ship would be able to board the entire populace and set sail in time.

Koa took a shaky breath. "I'll never understand this world," he said. "They brought blood to our shore, and now what, we bring it to theirs? When does that end?"

"When we dock," she said, "keep your ax drawn."

"But I don't want to kill anyone. I just want to find Kaia."

"I know that. But the Imperial Guard won't. And they will shoot you on sight."

"Do you think . . . They wouldn't kill Kaia, would they?"

"We'll find her," Thistle said. But there was reticence in her voice.

Koa looked at her, but she would not meet his eyes. The Colonizers had brought Kaia all the way back to their own land, had bragged to the world about the warrior they had kidnapped; why would they just kill her?

Thistle opened her mouth but was cut short when Rake called out to the crew to ready the cannons.

Distantly, Koa could hear the city bells ringing their warning of impending attack. They had been spotted. Next to him, Tupac quivered with rising anxiety, his giggles going sharp and jagged. Koa laid a hand on his familiar's haunch, felt the familiar bristle of Tupac's fur beneath his fingernails. Whatever happened, they would go through this together. And though that was little comfort, it was better than nothing.

The *Leviathan*, being the biggest and best and most powerful ship in the fleet, was on the vanguard, carving a path of cannon fire destruction through the docks so that other, smaller ships could make for land. Koa's whole body tensed at the sound of the first cannons firing, and he jammed his fingers in his ears as Tupac ran circles around him, his giggles drowned out by the cannons. All around them it smelled of gunpowder, and Koa could not help but think of the men who guarded the docks, and the bodies and families they would leave behind.

He could hear the screams and shouts of alarm and panic, gunfire, and the slaps as the many rowboats hit the water, carrying the Resistance's forces. And all the while, the hyena laughed and laughed and laughed, his fear a terrible song over the cacophony of the unfolding battle. Koa tried to keep his mind from that horrible sunny day on his own shore, watching his own people fall.

"Come on, then," said Thistle. "Let's go kill some Imperials."

And Koa did not say no.

• CHAPTER 41 •

*The Fist*

She sailed ashore with the pirates, the Resistance from Quark, and her daughter, pride bursting in her chest. All those years ago, she'd never have believed that Thistle would raise arms with her against Nipran. And now they would fight side by side. As mother and daughter should.

All around them were screams and fire, bullets and bodies. She had never been to Crandon before, never once desired to visit the snake pit from whence the Imperials came. And so it was with great pleasure that she scanned the wide streets and the many tall and narrow buildings and saw them ablaze.

How arrogant they were not to expect this. Not to assume that one day the many nations they had subdued would seek revenge. To forever assume the war would never reach their shore.

The dirty work of the Empire had come home.

They would know the death they had spread throughout the Known World at last. At long last.

An Imperial soldier made the fatal decision to point his pistol at Thistle. The Fist roared, aimed her rifle at him, pulled the trigger. He lay dead in their wake, her daughter safe. They had made it this far together. She would do her best to see that Thistle made it through this. Though, as she watched her daughter, she could tell that the Imperial woman had taught her well. Her sense of tactics, her aim. She did not require her mother's instruction.

As they made their way to the palace, she could feel the heat as the gunpowder barrels—the gunpowder that she had, over years of hard-fought negotiation and battle won for their use—exploded through windows and walls, shattering glass and wood. Its purpose finally achieved. The whole sky was black and orange with smoke and flame. It was like the sun rising over a more just world.

She caught Thistle's eye as they cut their way through Crandon. She was illuminated with the light of the fires that raged. They smiled at each other. This was not the girl who used to peel carrots in her kitchen. She was not the woman who had taught her how. Not anymore.

"This has been too easy," Rake yelled. His face was black with grime and smoke, save for a swipe he had made across his brow.

The moment was broken.

The Pirate Supreme grimaced at their first mate. "The shore was poorly guarded," they said. "The palace won't be."

They would know. They'd been there before, scouted the many halls so that they would be prepared for this moment. A benefit of having kept their face a closely guarded secret for so long. The Pirate Supreme was rarely unprepared, a quality the Fist had long hoped to adopt. It was the mark of a good leader, she thought, to be humble in the face of challenge. To be thorough.

Ahead of them, the Cold World tribes cut a path of destruction, their battle cries sharp even through the deafening reports of guns and, distantly, cannons. She saw one of them, the chieftain of the bogs, take an Imperial bullet, his head snap back. He was gone. This only enraged his people more. The woman who fought at his side threw a spear, and the Imperial guard gasped, clasping at the weapon now buried in his belly. As he fell, more of the tribe swarmed the soldier, obscuring him. It would be a slow death, and a painful one.

It would be what he deserved.

The palace rose above the rest of Crandon like the moon, grand and white and forbidding. How strange that something so beautiful could be the locus of so much cruelty. It was an injustice to the stones it was made of.

A volunteer soldier from Tustwe reported to the Pirate Supreme, yelling directly in their ear. The Supreme nodded and yelled back their orders. A small retinue to the front gates, a distraction. But the bulk of the Resistance would attack the stable gate on the south end of the palace grounds. The Guard was thinner there. The Sisterhood of Widows, the tribes of the Cold World, the Fist, and the guerrilla fighters from Quark, Iwei, and the Floating Islands, as well as the soldiers from Tustwe, would attack there, and with luck they would win. This had long been the plan.

The witch had grabbed the string of pearls around her neck and yanked until the thread that held them broke, but the pearls didn't fall. Instead, they hovered, slowly orbiting her open hand, innumerable and glowing in the red light of war.

The Fist made to go with her people from Quark, but before she could, Rake's hand encircled her wrist.

"Be safe," he said, his voice strained.

She could only barely hear him over the chaos Xenobia unleashed. The pearls became projectiles, hurtling toward the enemy, and as they did, they changed—from pearls into tiny flaming suns, each as hot and as cruel as high noon. The Imperial armor was no match for the heat, and they heard screams and confusion and horror echoing down from the ramparts.

Momentarily distracted, the Fist had looked up to bear witness to this feat. But when she turned back to Rake, his eyes were intense on hers. His feelings were clear. She was still organizing her own. The Fist smiled, then leaned in and gave him a kiss on the cheek. She tried to ignore her daughter, who watched with plain disgust. It was so like children to deny their parents romance, and for a moment it was as if there were no battle raging around them. It was as if they were simply mother and daughter again. And the thought made her smile for just a moment before a fresh volley of bullets snapped her focus back on the battle.

They had hoped the dragon would arrive before they got to the palace, but she was not there yet. Which. Was not ideal. But the Fist had trained her people well, had forged them through battle after battle. They knew what they were doing. Now she needed to trust them.

Thistle and the Wariuta boy ran behind her as they neared the south gate. It was with some annoyance that she saw his ax still strapped to his back. She knew the Wariuta were slow to kill, but still. He was a warrior. Her daughter was adept enough to protect the both of them, and his familiar didn't hurt. So. She would have to trust them, too.

She watched—as best she could—and marveled as her daughter moved. Thistle had always been a fierce thing. Fights in the schoolyard, arguments with teachers, a willfulness that the world, her mother included, had been unable to break. She had just wanted to keep her little girl safe, give her a quiet, predictable life. Why had she not seen? That life was never for Thistle, just as it had never been for her.

It was no wonder she ran away when she got the chance. To

Thistle it would have seemed the best and likely only escape. And how much of a relief had it been to her, even through the pain of Thistle's departure, to return to the life that she was meant for?

And how could her daughter have understood the horror of occupation if her mother was so fastidious about keeping her safe? A safe child needed not question the world. But it was clear that Thistle had now. And it seemed she had settled on some good answers.

The Fist's eye caught a soldier, hidden behind a decorative parapet, aiming his rifle at Thistle. She had moved forward without checking her blind spot first. He was too slow in sighting, and the Fist's bullet caught him before he could squeeze the trigger.

She smiled. Thistle still had something to learn. And, if they survived, her mother would teach her.

## CHAPTER 42
# Commander Callum

All around Crandon the bells tolled. There was an attack upon their shore. But there was nothing Callum could do about that at the moment. Inside the Imperial Palace, he tried to cut his way through the many servants who ran around as they locked doors and cabinets and gathered provisions to bring to the nobles already cloistered away in the catacombs. It was pandemonium, chaos as all the bodies clambered about, so unused to threat, so terrified of battle. *Everyone dies,* Callum thought. And yet people were still scared. Madness.

Though the chaos was to his advantage. Even the guards were frightened, jumpy. Low-ranking men were often like this, Callum knew, a side effect of their poor breeding. And none questioned him, a commander in the Imperial Guard, as he moved through doors that should have been closed to all but especially to someone with a pair of daggers strapped to his leg and a pistol on his back.

It was almost too easy.

The Emperor would not be hidden away in the catacombs, which were liable to collapse if the ramparts were hit just right. He would instead be hidden in a secret cell within the Imperial Palace. Callum only knew where it was due to his time serving in the Emperor's Guard in his earlier years, a post often given to young men of noble blood hoping to carve a place for themselves in court.

Callum got there with such speed that it startled even him. When the coup happened, he would have to talk to Tsujima about better security. It was only when he got to the passage that led to the cell that he was given any bother.

General Mirimoto was in the antechamber to the cell, rather than leading his men. This was not unusual. One of the perks of high rank was to stay mostly safe from the bloody exertions of battle. He was able to send his commands from safety and comfort this way and concentrate only on strategy. *Someday,* Callum thought, *that will be me.* Mirimoto ordered a couple of his guards off to go see to this or that, leaving him woefully alone. This was a farce.

Mirimoto's wrinkled face regarded Callum coolly. "Ah, good. I need another message run to Commander Imanaka."

Callum couldn't help it; his face contorted into the shape of resentment. Mirimoto's eyebrows pulled up, shocked at his impertinence.

"Now, Soldier!" His voice impatient, as if Callum was someone he could command. Now. With them alone, and Mirimoto unguarded.

The pistol would be too loud. So instead, Callum stepped toward the general until they were so close they could have kissed. With dawning realization that something was terribly, terribly wrong, Mirimoto opened his mouth to call for a guard, but it was too late. Callum clamped a hand over the war hero's mouth and pinned him to his war table, their eyes locked in this strange and intimate moment, Mirimoto's wide, Callum's determined.

Once, the general had been something of an idol to Callum. But then he had ignored the young man again and again, his accomplishments never enough to gain favor in court. And so Callum had shipped off to the colonies, hoping to make a name there. It was only through the blood of so many, riches shipped back to Imperial stores, gold won, and land conquered that Callum had returned. And still nothing. From Mirimoto or the Emperor.

"Can't ignore me now, can you?" Callum hissed. He pulled the key that hung from a chain around the general's neck, the key to the Emperor's cell, pulled hard enough to leave red welts on the old man's skin and hard enough that the thin gold chain snapped. Callum pocketed the key.

General Mirimoto stared at him with bewilderment that simply stoked the flames of Callum's anger.

The dagger cut through Mirimoto's chest with ease. Callum had not fought for years, trained so many men, not to know where and exactly how to push a dagger into a man's heart.

A gasp, a groan, and the general was gone. His body crumpled at Callum's feet, just another carcass. Callum smiled. He stepped over what was once the great general of Nipran, careful not to let his feet track blood, and unlocked the door to the Emperor's cell.

There were no windows, of course, no egress or ingress that could not be guarded. So the room was much dimmer than the rest of the palace, alight with a decadence of ornate paper lanterns. The Emperor lay on a bed, dozing, as his two guards stood beside him.

Callum closed the door behind him, knowing that the room was soundproof. No sounds in, no sounds out.

"Who—" one of the guards started, but Callum was too quick for them. He pulled his pistol, and both men were dead before they could fully unsheathe their swords.

The Emperor stirred in his bed and blearily blinked his eyes open.

"Is it over?" he asked. His voice was so soft, so weak. Callum smiled. He sat down on the bed next to the Emperor, relishing this moment of trespass. To be so close to him, the supposed god, who smelled faintly of the stale urine his perfumed robes could not hide. The old man's face was vacant, his eyes clouded. Callum reached out a hand and brushed the man's face gently with his fingers. His skin was like paper beneath Callum's touch.

"Yes," he whispered, as if to a lover, his voice low. "It's over now."

Then he wrapped his hands around the Emperor's neck and squeezed.

The man thrashed a bit, but not with much force. He was so weak, his spindly fingers trying to pry Callum's hands off his neck to no avail, his legs kicking but finding no purchase. Callum watched, unblinking, not wanting to miss a thing, as the man who had determined so much of his disappointing life writhed beneath him.

Watched with delicious glee as the life faded from the clouded eyes.

"Thanks to the Emperor," he said. And he dropped the body back on its bed, eyes still open, mouth still agape, frozen in its final moments of horror.

Carefully, Callum stepped back through the cell, avoiding the pooled blood of the dead guards, and returned to where General Mirimoto lay dead. The bells were closer now, and he could tell that the Resistance had broken through the gates, much earlier than expected. He'd need to be fast if he was to find the Crown Prince first. He pulled a dagger from the general's hilt, and after only a moment of reluctance, stabbed himself in the side. He knew enough not to pierce anything vital; it was mostly a flesh wound. It would take time to heal, and it'd be uncomfortable, but it was a small price to pay.

He took a deep breath, clutching the wound at his side, letting it bleed over his fingers.

Then he thrust the door to the passageway open and shouted, "The Emperor is dead! General Mirimoto! He . . . killed him!" And he collapsed, theatrically, to the ground.

• CHAPTER 43 •

*Alfie*

The palace was mayhem, but Alfie could maneuver through that. His whole childhood had been a sustained flow of mayhem. The problem was that he wasn't sure what to do.

That wasn't exactly true; he knew what he was supposed to do. He was supposed to find the Crown Prince, and he was supposed to either hand him over to the Pirate Supreme's forces or kill the infant himself.

It was just that he wasn't sure he could.

If he didn't, the Pirate Supreme would have Alfie killed. Or Senator Tsujima would order him killed. But if he got caught trying, he'd be killed by the Guard. Most likely, he was not going to live through the night.

In the meantime, he figured, it would be good to be armed. The armory would be stripped. The guards' normal posts, too. The dungeons would be shut down, no one in or out. The only way to get a weapon, he realized, was to pull one off a dead body. It'd hardly be the first thing he'd pulled off a corpse, but it did mean heading directly into the chaos instead of, more sensibly, away from it.

Alfie steadied himself and then ran toward the battle that now raged within the palace itself.

Maybe he'd get shot before he had to make a decision. Maybe that would be some small mercy. Maybe his string of luck in surviving the unsurvivable would come to a predictable end, and no one would remember him, and no one would be disappointed by him, and maybe that was OK. Maybe that was fine, actually.

He ran.

He found what he needed in the atrium. The dragon's skeleton that had once hung from the ceiling was just a pile of gray rubble—equal parts bone and ceiling—on the floor. Beneath the enormous rib cage was a puddle of viscera and limbs that told Alfie the bodies below had been crushed to death by the fall. He would not be strong enough to lift the ruins, but if he could just find one whose weapon was close enough to the edge . . .

He was scrounging about unashamedly when he heard the clack of a pistol cocking. He froze. How had he not heard the approach? He must have lost his sense of what was close or far in the cacophony. Slowly, he put his arms over his head.

"Please—" he started.

"Who are you with?" demanded a voice. "What side do you fight for?" The accent was easy enough to place as Crandon born. But Alfie knew full well that plenty of Crandon natives fought for the Resistance. Without turning to see what the man was wearing, he'd have no way of telling which side he was on.

"I—" Alfie started, hoping he could make a pretense of conversation before having to commit, but the man jabbed him hard with his pistol in the back of his neck.

"Stay where you are!" he barked.

"I just want to get out of here," Alfie said. And for once he was telling the truth. "I don't want to fight anyone." Maybe the Alfie who had served on the *Dove* so long ago would have been embarrassed by his tears. But the Alfie who stood in the atrium with the blood of soldiers and the dust of a dragon's bones on his knees and hands was not. Could not be. He simply did not have the energy anymore. "Please."

Outside the atrium, Alfie could hear shouts echoing as those in battle called out to one another. In his rational mind, he knew who the fighters were. Guardsmen, of course, and plenty of them. But pirates, too. People from all over the Known World, all taking one last shot at the Empire before likely being crushed into oblivion, only to be remembered in cruel tavern songs about their flatulent corpses. And he was hit, hard, with the stupidity of it. The pointlessness of all of it. Probably nothing would change. Probably humans were too intractably violent in their nature to ever create any meaningful change. Too greedy, too hungry, too ugly. Fighting for right or for wrong, what did it matter? It all ended the same. Death, death, death, all the way down.

"I just want to live," Alfie said. His voice was quiet but without shame.

"Everyone wants to—" But the man's scoff was cut short.

The report of a rifle. A spray of something hot and wet on Alfie's back. He ducked, but the attacker clearly had had no interest in him; Alfie'd have been too late anyway. By the time Alfie turned all the way around, he was alone again, save for the man who had, until just moments ago, been holding him at gunpoint. There was a gaping hole in his back, still smoking gently from gunpowder. He'd been an Imperial guard after all.

The man looked to be perhaps ten years older than Alfie. Old enough to have a family, if he was inclined to one. He had the red hair of someone with parents or grandparents or great-grandparents buried in Quark. His eyes, open, were the ruddy brown of fields after the rain. How had he come to wear the uniform? Why did he come to die for his Emperor? *Everyone wants to live,* he had been about to say. Alfie was sure of it. And yet he had not, and Alfie had. Alfie wanted so badly for that to mean something, to make sense of the rat's nest of reality that swirled around him, but he could find neither sense nor meaning. The question of who deserved to live or die remained as arbitrary as ever.

Alfie relieved the corpse of its weapon and moved on.

· CHAPTER 44 ·

*Koa*

Koa hated it. Hated the cold, hard streets, uneven and untrustworthy beneath his feet. Hated the smells of smoke and burning metal and the strange chemical scents that coated his tongue. Hated the sounds of people, everywhere, too many people, shouting and yelling and shrieking, crying, hysterical as their lives either fell apart or ended. Hated that, as Tupac ran at his side, the animal felt so far away from him, as if they were running at the same pace but on different shores.

But most of all, he hated that he had anything to do with this destruction. Though he had not once lifted his weapon, he was still a part of this fight, was as guilty as anyone else as soon as the first cannon had fired and he did nothing to stop it.

*For Kaia,* he told himself.

For Kaia, at what price?

He wondered what Ica would have done.

He saw a child crying frankly, tears running pink streaks down his soot-covered face—his house was burning, and the child watched this calamity with unbridled despair. Koa wanted to run to him, to cradle him in his arms and whisper to him that all would be well, but it wouldn't be, would it? His parents may have died, probably had. He broke away from the group to go collect the child, but Thistle held him back, her fingers tight on his wrist.

"This way," she said firmly. "For Kaia."

When Koa turned to look at the child once more, he was gone.

Their destination was an enormous building that seemed to swallow an entire corner of the city. This was where the Resistance had said Kaia would be. But that was all he knew. It did not look beautiful, as was promised. It looked like the physical embodiment of greed: too big, too tall. Garish in the way that the Colonizer uniforms were garish, glints of gold and lacquer. And as he looked at it, the Colonizers finally started to make sense. They had worshipped at this palace, been told this was the greatest to which they could aspire.

No wonder their souls were broken.

It was the soldiers from Tustwe who made it through the gate first, leading the others. By the time Koa and Thistle walked through, only a spattering of dead bodies remained, and Koa was glad he could not see the blood that spilled in the dark of the night on the grounds. He could smell it, though, and hastened his step, did not look as Tupac helped himself to the carrion.

Thistle's mother was yelling at various people, who took her orders without question. She was a good leader, Koa could tell from the way people seemed to calm under her direction. Ica had been like that. It was easy to follow her orders because she always knew what she was doing. You could trust her with your life. And it seemed these people trusted Thistle's mother with theirs. He wished he felt the same. She yelled something at Thistle, who nodded.

"We go inside with the Sisterhood."

Koa pressed his lips into a thin line. Inside there would be slaughter, indiscriminate. As if reading his mind, Thistle flashed something like a smile—and a bit like a wince.

"Only soldiers now."

Koa took a deep breath. He whistled for Tupac, and they plunged into the building that was all wrong. If he thought it was cold and unnatural outside, nothing had prepared him for what was within—the walls seemed to hold the stale air in, suffocating and cloying, as if he were breathing only screams and bated breath. Thistle led him through strange and narrow passages, the clamor of their footfalls bouncing off the walls disconcertingly. Tupac stopped giggling, but his eyes swiveled everywhere, his head bowed as he ran. He looked as afraid as Koa felt. He should have lent his familiar courage, he knew. He had none to give.

It was hard to tell what sounds were coming from where in that dead building, and so when they turned a corner and ran headlong into two Colonizer soldiers, Koa's shock was double.

They all blinked at one another, but Thistle acted first. A deafening crack, and one of the soldiers fell. The gunpowder was thick in the air, and Koa gagged on it, spit filling his mouth as he tried not to look down at the soldier who lay dead on the floor—there was no question of that: he was definitely dead, and blood pooled around him—and soon it was not spit but bile that rose in his throat, and Koa could not stop staring at the body, the place where the man had once been. There was shouting around him, and activity, but Koa could not pull his eyes away from the death Thistle had made, final and permanent.

When he looked up, he saw Tupac in a fierce tug-of-war with the second soldier. Though that was not exactly what was happening—the soldier's hand was in Tupac's mouth, and Tupac was pulling, pulling, pulling as the man screamed and tried, with his one hand, to get the pistol at his side. If Koa did not act fast, the man would shoot his familiar, that much he could see, and it was as if everything slowed down as Koa pulled the ax from his back and threw it at the soldier just as the man pulled the safety back on his pistol.

There was a thwack as Koa's ax found home in the man's chest.

There was a heart-stopping bang as the pistol fired.

There was a cry of pain.

◆ CHAPTER 45 ◆

*Keiko*

Keiko needed to get to the catacombs, now. But where were the guards? She wasn't to carry the Crown Prince anywhere without a retinue of guards. The many princesses had, thankfully, been down at dinner when the attack had started, so hopefully they were already in the catacombs. But how had the guards neglected the Crown Prince?

She could hear the gunshots, and they were so close, maybe even in the palace already, and she rocked the baby in her arms as he mewled grumpily. She hoped he could not feel her heart as it drummed in panic.

She had left Kaia in her room, but that was before the attack. She could have been anywhere now and was probably gone. The chaos of the battle would have been more than enough cover. Good riddance. She had enough to worry about without harboring a fugitive, even a beautiful one. All the other nurses were gone. Alfie was, too, and a spy to boot. She hadn't even had a moment to take in this information before her world was torn apart again when the bells rang of invasion on the Imperial shore.

When an explosion went off just outside the nursery window, sending shards of glass and wood and stone flying, Keiko knew she had to move, guards or no. The Crown Prince howled in fear. She tried to hold back the tears that ran down her cheeks, but she couldn't. Gently, she kissed the Crown Prince on his little sweaty brow. If not for herself, then for him. She needed to be brave.

Clutching his highness to her chest, Keiko peeked out the door to the nursery but pulled her head back in quickly as a man came running down the hallway, laughing maniacally, smashing the many vases and kicking over the statues that lined the hallway. She wasn't sure what side he was on and didn't care to find out. He didn't seem interested in anything other than gleeful destruction, and soon the sounds of his voice and the crashes died down and were gone.

The nursery and the catacombs couldn't have been farther apart, which on a normal day made sense. Why keep life so close to death? But that terrible night, it felt like an insurmountable distance. She would have to move quickly and carefully, and so she darted out of the nursery, thankful for the years in the Hasegawa household that had taught her to move in silence.

She pretended then, as she went, that she was back there. That she was simply slipping down the hallways to Evelyn's room, that soon she would be snuggled against Evelyn's warm body, her fingers tangled in the hair Keiko herself had brushed with a thousand strokes before the lights went out. Evelyn was waiting, she told herself. Go, quietly, go.

Keiko scurried past a hallway where she could hear screams and shots, her stomach rolling. There was a part of her that wished she could stop and help, to save whoever's voices were being cut short, but there was a much larger part of her that knew, beyond any doubt, there was nothing she could do. She had one life to save, and if she could do that. Well. Her life would have been worth it.

She felt strangely out of her own body as she ran, as if she were watching herself from above. She had not been, for her entire life, a person of much consequence, and she had been just fine with that. All she wanted was to go about her own business, love whom she loved, and leave the room a little nicer than she had found it. And yet here she was now, ducking invaders and hiding behind doors as she carried the fate of the Empire in her arms. If she hadn't been so terrified, she might have laughed. How had it come to this?

They were about halfway through the palace when she heard her name called by a familiar voice. The pure shock of it stopped her in her tracks. She was suddenly very much back in her body again, her blood pumping, her breath shaky. She turned.

Alfie stood there, a pistol in his hands.

"Keiko!" he said, and he smiled, but she did not wait to hear more. She turned to run.

She had not made it far before she felt his hand on her arm, his grip tight on her skin. She tried to writhe away but could not without risking the Crown Prince, and so she had no choice but to let him catch her.

They regarded each other for a surreal moment, both panting, both ignoring the shots fired and the yelling and the explosions that rocked the palace.

"Well?" Keiko said, her voice alien to her own ears. She felt such a burning and consuming fury at this boy, this boy she had trusted, who was going to ruin everything. She clutched the Crown Prince ever tighter to her chest. "Are you going to kill me, too?"

"No, Keiko, I—" His eyes were sad. Good. She hoped he felt it every day for the rest of his life, hoped it crushed him beneath its weight. "I wanted to—"

But she did not find out what he wanted. There was a cry of delight, and Keiko whipped around to see two people turning the corner.

"The Crown Prince," the woman said.

"Good work, Alfie!" said the other. They were grinning the wide grin of the victorious. "I knew you could do it."

Alfie didn't so much whisper as he breathed: "The Pirate Supreme." His grip fell from Keiko's arm, and she turned to run in the opposite direction, but a wiry red-haired man came from that direction, his pistol pointed.

"I wouldn't," he said coolly.

Keiko gulped down a sob. It was all over. She was surrounded. She was practically crushing the Crown Prince in her arms, but what else could she do? They would have to pull him from her cold, dead hands.

So consumed with the sureness of her own impending death was she that Keiko did not notice when Alfie carefully, subtly moved her behind him, so she was marginally blocked from the Pirate Supreme and a more difficult target for the man with red hair.

The woman quirked a brow at them. "I do not think he's on our side."

"I am," said Alfie, but his voice was unsure. "But. I—I can't let you kill him."

The Pirate Supreme laughed, a big, merry laugh that was so wrong amid the despair and destruction of battle, it made Keiko flinch. "Come on, kid," they said. "That's the Emperor's son! You know what evil he'll bring into the world. He's everything we're fighting against."

"He's a baby," Keiko said. Her voice was so much bigger than she thought it could be, bigger even than the hiccupping sobs of the Crown Prince. He may not have understood exactly what was happening, but he clearly knew to be afraid.

The woman laughed. "Now he is. But it won't be long before he's a tyrant, just like all of them before him."

"Rake," Alfie said, turning to the man with the red hair. "Please. You know this is wrong."

But the man just shook his head sadly. "It's gotta be done. You know that."

"You promised," Alfie said to him. "You promised Flora you would protect me."

"I said I'd do my best," said Rake. "But I can't protect you from yourself. If you're asking me to choose between you and the Resistance"—he cocked his pistol and pointed it at Keiko—"I choose the Resistance."

"Rake—"

"Don't make me choose."

Keiko turned and saw the Pirate Supreme stepping quietly closer to them, their arms outstretched, their hands open, ready to receive the Crown Prince. "Give me the Prince, girl. There's no reason you need be hurt, but I will if I have to."

"OK," Alfie said, and Keiko's heart dropped into her feet. "OK, just . . ." He turned to Keiko then, his face unreadable. "Duck," he whispered.

Keiko looked back at him, puzzled. Alfie met her eyes, and she could see his message in them. She ducked.

Many things happened so quickly that Keiko could hardly track any of them.

Alfie fired his pistol at Rake, catching him in his shoulder. As

Rake fell to the ground, his own pistol fired, and Keiko could feel it more than hear it as it flew past her head and grazed Alfie's arm.

Alfie cried out in pain as the Pirate Supreme advanced, their hands scrabbling at the Crown Prince as Keiko thrashed away from their grip until there was another bang and a cry, and the Pirate Supreme staggered back, blood blossoming from their belly.

Alfie's pistol smoked, and he looked as shocked as everyone else that he had fired again. The woman howled and caught the Pirate Supreme as they fell backward, their face a mask of shock and pain.

"Run!" Alfie cried.

Keiko did not need to be told twice.

• CHAPTER 46 •

*Kaia*

Kaia abandoned the room where Keiko had left her and ran into the palace, which was shrouded in chaos and cacophony. It was never the Wariuta way to revel in the death of anyone, even an enemy, but Kaia did not care. It was not enough, but it was still a small justice for her people that left Colonizer soldiers' bodies scattered throughout the palace. It would not bring her mother back. She did not care. The more of them that died the better; let them taste blood in their own mouths for once, let them wallow in a fraction of the pain they had left in their wakes.

If she had to kill some, then so be it. She could square herself with that. This was not the time to be the gentle-hearted leader Ica had encouraged her to be, and she knew in her heart that Ica would agree. Death blows were raining down on the Empire. It was more merciful at this point to kill it quickly. Decisively.

She tried to remember the route Alfie had taken them on before to get out, but all the many corridors looked the same, and she had no idea where she was—even the windows offered little help, since the grounds were dark save for the spots where things were aflame. It was near impossible to tell what was what in the unfamiliar landscape and amid all the destruction.

She picked a sword off a fallen soldier and gave it an experimental slice through the air. It wasn't her weapon of choice, but she could wield it. It was lighter than her ax, anyway. She felt a pang of sadness—that she did not have Chima by her side, that she was, in this strange place, only half the warrior she had been before.

And because her familiar was in her thoughts, Kaia did not think anything of the hyena giggle she heard at first. It was her mind, her memory, playing tricks on her in this desperate circumstance.

But when the giggling got louder, Kaia's breath caught.

That was a hyena.

Here.

She ran toward the sound.

If it was possible that other people kept hyenas, Kaia didn't know, didn't have the breadth of mind to consider as she sprinted through the cold halls of the palace, because it was possible, so possible that maybe, maybe, maybe a Wariuta person was here, in this nest of the Colonizers, and if there was, then she was not alone, after all this time, she was not alone, and perhaps maybe, maybe, maybe she was not the sole survivor of her people, and then maybe, maybe, maybe she would survive. They would survive. She would see to that. She could feel tears streaming down her face but paid them no mind. She had something to live for now, something greater than the fall of Nipran, something pure and good and loving and right. She would find her old self, the one who could imagine a future. Maybe.

The giggling was high and loud in her ears. She turned a

corner, and before she could fully understand what she was looking at, a great force knocked her over and pinned her down.

Kaia gasped but then felt the rough kiss of a hyena's tongue across her cheek. The animal pulled back, and Kaia's eyes focused.

"Tupac?"

The animal growled his pleasure at seeing a familiar face. And as he did, the great possibility of what could be set Kaia's heart racing. She could hear the rush of blood in her ears. She shakily got to her feet. She felt herself moving as if she were moving through sand, impossibly slow and unwieldy.

And there he was.

Koa.

She let out a sharp cry, a noise she did not know her body could create. She had never let her heart even entertain the idea that her sweet, good brother had survived the massacre, it was so unlikely, so impossible. But there he was, his big, warm body so out of place in this terrible, cold country. Koa and Tupac, as intact as if the Colonizers had never come. Like a dream of a better life, a better world than the one she lived in. She had never loved him more than in this moment, when he was here and alive.

But he had not seen her. His hands were covered in blood, and he was trying his best to stanch a freely bleeding wound in Genevieve's thigh. The girl. Why was Koa trying to save her? Surely she would fight even now for her beloved Empire. Only Koa would try to save an enemy's life in the heat of battle. It was his foolishness, his soft heart that made her see that this was not a dream. This was real. Koa's softness had always been real. She tried to stifle the relief she felt when she realized that was another thing the Colonizers had not killed.

"Koa." Her voice sounded far away in her ears, an echo from the horizon. "Step back."

Koa's head snapped around, and his face lit up like the sun but only for a moment. His eyes narrowed at the sword in Kaia's hands. "What are you doing?" he asked, but it was clear that he thought he knew exactly what she was doing. He stood and put his body between them.

"Kaia," Genevieve croaked. "I am so . . ."

But Kaia did not want to listen. "You—" she raised her sword.

Koa put his hand on her arm, forced her to meet his eye. And just like that, she was back in Yunka again, her brother's gaze calming her from one of her many rages. The thrumming blood in her ears quieted. "She's on our side," Koa said.

Koa pulled her into a tight hug, his big arms around her. She hugged him back, barely registering the warm slide of blood on his skin. He kissed her forehead.

"You're alive," she murmured again and again. She could feel her tears pooling between them and she did not care, did not care that her nose ran or that they were in the middle of a battle or that Genevieve lay on the floor bleeding to death.

"I'm not the only one. There are more of us," he whispered. "In Puno."

More. She had been so sure she was all that was left of her people. It was as if she had been struck by lightning. She pulled back, her shoulders square again, the Kaia who needed to lead her people emerging from the ashes of the massacre. She could do this. She had to do this. And distantly, she was aware that the thought no longer scared her. It was time.

"Why are you here?" she asked finally.

He gave her a quizzical look, then smiled his big sunrise smile. "To rescue you, obviously. To take you home." He knelt back down next to Genevieve and resumed tying the makeshift bandage he'd been attending to earlier. "I couldn't have gotten here without her."

Genevieve's eyes were going soft around the edges. She was losing a lot of blood, and consciousness was clearly becoming elusive. Her eyes fluttered, and Koa's hands shook as he tried to make sense of the wound and the blood that would not stop pouring. She could let Genevieve bleed to death, let her bear witness to the slow evacuation of life from her own body. But if Genevieve had brought Koa to her . . . then she was not the girl Kaia thought she was.

"Give me that," Kaia barked, and Koa stepped aside. He had done some good, getting the wound well covered. But he had been too gentle to tie the bandage tight enough to actually stop any bleeding. The girl would lose her leg, but she could survive. Together, Koa and Kaia tied the bandage tight, tight enough to wake the girl momentarily, tight enough to exorcise some small fraction of Kaia's hate. She had to be better than that now, for her people. She needed to survive, and she needed to get home. And maybe Genevieve could help her get there. "Done," she said, proud of her handiwork. She'd always been excellent at patching wounds. "That should stop the bleeding."

With a grunt, Koa lifted Genevieve's body. Her face was white, but Kaia could see her chest rising and falling with breath. She was alive.

"Come on," Koa said. "I think I can remember how we came in. Let's go." He started in the opposite direction from which Kaia had come.

Kaia hustled after him, sword at the ready. "Where?" she asked.

"Home," Koa said.

As if it were as simple as that.

Kaia hoped he was right.

◆ CHAPTER 47 ◆

## *Kwizera*

Xenobia's arms felt like home. Kwizera looked up into her eyes. She was crying freely, her face a mess of tears and spit and snot. They had never loved her more. They reached up, ran their fingers across her cheek, tried their best to wipe the tears. There was not enough strength left in them to do this. They let their hand fall, tried to focus their mind, to find the words.

"Hold on," Xenobia said.

Kwizera knew they could not.

Distantly, bells rang, different bells now, the bells that marked the death of the Emperor. For a moment, it seemed that the world went still as all of Crandon realized what had happened.

"We won," Kwizera rasped.

"Yes," Xenobia said. "Yes, my love, you did it."

Kwizera smiled past the taste of the blood in their mouth.

"Do something!" Rake yelled, but both Xenobia and Kwizera ignored him. Not even Xenobia was powerful enough to stop death.

"I should . . ." Kwizera tried to find their breath, it was so hard to speak. "I should have never left you."

Xenobia coughed a laugh through her tears. "No," she agreed. "You shouldn't have."

"Do you forgive me?"

"Yes," Xenobia replied, so easily, so fervently that Kwizera knew she was telling the truth. "And look what you've done," she said, her voice steadying. "The Emperor is dead. Nipran will fall."

It was so hard to hold their head steady, and Kwizera felt it loll to the side. Outside the window, the first sliver of sunlight was just bleeding into the blackened horizon. They smiled. The sun would rise on a new world today, a world they had helped make.

"Use my blood," Kwizera said.

But Xenobia shook her head.

"End it—" They coughed, felt blood dribble down their chin. "With both our blood, she will hear." Xenobia caught their face again and kissed them hard on the mouth. She pulled away, and their blood was streaked across her lips. She was so beautiful, and Kwizera wanted to tell her so, but there was a rattling in their chest, and they knew the blood was in their lungs now.

They tried to say *I love you.*

They could not.

• CHAPTER 48 •

*Rake*

R ake watched in mute horror as the life faded from the Pirate Supreme's eyes. Death had come, and it had come for the wrong person.

He fell to his knees. He could see the witch screaming her grief, but he could not hear it. He could not hear anything except the ringing in his ears, the high-pitched tone of rage as unceasing as a toothache.

Xenobia lifted a dagger then from the Supreme's body and held it aloft. The sounds of the world came rushing back to Rake then—the battle, the distant explosions, the beating of his own heart. And the witch. She was chanting words Rake could not follow, in a language he did not speak, her eyes streaming tears, her nose flaring with effort. She cut herself then, a clean line across her wrist. Before Rake could try to stop her from doing more damage to herself, she plunged both her hands into the Pirate Supreme's wound. Rake watched, open-mouthed in revulsion.

But as she chanted, Rake started to hear screams rising from outside the palace. He looked out the window and immediately saw why.

A wave, an enormous tower of water, taller even than the statue of the Emperor, loomed over Crandon's coast.

"Xenobia," Rake whispered, fear rendering his voice faint. "You can't—"

"Let it be done," she said. Each word was like a bullet. She slammed her hands onto the ground, smearing the mix of her and the Pirate Supreme's blood upon the palace floor.

The wave fell.

The crash was louder than the firing cannons, bigger than the sky. He watched as the water slammed through buildings and rushed its way up the many cobbled streets, an ever-expanding spread of destruction. Even there, so far from the water, he could smell the brine of the Sea. For the first time in his life, the scent did not bring him comfort.

Rake did not have to see the docks to know they were gone. Did not need to see the small fishermen's houses that lined the water to know that nothing would remain. He would not mourn the Emperor's navy, but this. This was such a wide swath of people, and he could not be sure they all deserved to die. But they were gone. He blinked in shock. They had already won.

"This is the boy's fault. Your little spy," Xenobia hissed. The sound of her voice made the hair on Rake's arms stand on end. He turned slowly to face the witch, found that he could not resist her words. "Find him," she said, and it was a command. A command he could not decline. "Kill him."

And so he ran. To find Alfie. The boy had run, naturally, run for his life. Rake would see that Alfie would not make it. His feet pounded the beat of vengeance on the marble floors of the palace as he ran. The boy. That stupid boy. How stupid Rake had been to trust him.

He did not think of the promise he had made to Florian.

He could not protect the boy from himself.

A trail of drips of blood led him to Alfie, who had made it all the way to the kitchens on the first floor. He'd nearly made it out but had been foiled by his lack of care. Incompetent as ever.

Rake roared. He aimed his pistol at Alfie, but when he pulled the trigger, nothing happened. He was out of bullets. Alfie, eyes wide, tried to run off, but Rake was too fast for him. He was taller, bigger, stronger. He tackled Alfie, and both their bodies fell hard on the stone floor. Rake could hear Alfie's head smack the ground, and he felt no regret. He wrestled the boy down—it was easily done—and pinned him beneath his body.

"Please!" Alfie cried.

Rake punched him, his fist slamming against Alfie's jaw. His temple. His chest and his belly.

Alfie's face was a bloody thing, his breath ragged and wet.

Hadn't Rake taught him better? All those years aboard the *Dove*, had Alfie learned nothing from him? *Keep your head down. Do as you're told. Be safe, please.* Years-old anger burned inside him as he looked at the boy, the boy he couldn't teach, and saw his own failure looking back at him.

No. Alfie deserved this. He had killed the Pirate Supreme, and for whom? An Imperial prince? That kindness had only created more pain, had punished the wrong people, and he would pay, he would pay with his life for his terrible judgment, his stupidity, his—

Rake felt it before he heard anything. A disturbance, a change in the air, like his body was light and his mind was blank. Vaguely, he was aware of Alfie sputtering, his breathing ragged and desperate, but he paid the boy no mind. He stood and followed his feet out of the palace.

They all did. Everyone who was still inside filed out from their hiding places, their hands limp at their sides. The survivors of Crandon. They stepped over the bodies of the fallen, no one even pausing to look down. They all looked up.

The sun cast its light over Crandon, blinding except for the coiling shadow as long as the horizon.

She sang. A song with no melody, but undeniably a song, music that caught in Rake's throat. He could feel it as much as hear it, and it was like loneliness and kinship, loss and love, the emptiness he felt when he looked at the Sea, the possibility the Sea promised. No one spoke. They all listened.

And as the First Dragon flew, her song washed down over them.

To his surprise, Rake knew the words.

> *Two souls fight*
> *For love, to be*
> *True love's might*
> *To save the Sea.*

## CHAPTER 49

# The First Dragon

I do not come because they asked. I come because it is time.

Every epoch, this day comes. When some destructive force becomes too great. When I must remind the humans of who and what they are. Of what they have done. So that the Sea can be restored once more. So that creation can return to this world.

This time is no different than all the other times. Every time I return, they learn. And every thousand years, they forget. My life is long, and always the same. I breathe in, and oceans rise. I breathe out, and empires fall.

I know they call what I do a song, but it is not that, exactly. My song is a song because that is the closest word for what it is, but that is an approximation. They will hear me, and they will hear what I have heard. They will see what I have seen. They will feel what is real. And the balance will be made. This is not justice—the dead will stay dead. There is no eye for an eye that will do true justice.

There is only reckoning. And that is what I will give them.

As I call down to them, I can see and hear and feel each and every one of them.

Still clutching the Crown Prince in her arms, Keiko staggers. She has never raised her hand to another person, never once allowed another to suffer if she could help it. But all the same, she lives here, lives comfortably off the backs of strangers on distant shores whether she thinks of them or not. Now she sees the children forced to dive into dangerous, rocky waters in Iwei, to catch those oysters she likes to eat. She shivers with their cold, she trembles with their fear. But still she stands. She is stronger than she thinks.

The witch, Xenobia, does not stagger, does not fall. She knows who she is and what she has done. There is no part of her engaged in self-deception. Still, tears cut down her face, through the blood of her beloved. She feels the blast of icy water as it hits the shore, feels the last gasps of air of the drowned. She cries out with their shock and their pain, feels the terror of so many lives cut short in an instant. The anger that burns inside her, the flame of rebellion ebbs at long last. There is no need for defiance in this world she helped make.

Rake does fall. He crumples to the ground, crushed beneath the weight of all the corpses he has made. He feels each death as if each were his own. And when that is done, he feels the fear he put in Alfie. Feels the constant shame he instilled, the shame that should have been his own. That he could not protect him or Florian, that he failed them as the only father either of them would ever know. That he could not protect their innocence, or their bodies, or their minds from cruelties too vast and unending for children. That in his singular purpose to redeem himself with the Sea, Rake allowed Alfie to be the collateral damage. He howls his agony.

Kaia—the warrior, the leader—kneels. She does not weep, does not cry. She accepts the pain of Tomas Inouye's death with what humans might call grace. She sees his parents receive the news, watches as his body, cold and still, is revealed to them, feels their hearts break in her breast. If she feels regret, it is not for Tomas but for all the lives she was willing to take this day. She makes her hand into a fist and raises it to me. A salute that I accept.

Safe at home outside the manor xe bought with ill-begotten coin, Senator Tsujima witnesses the many people xe enslaved. I make sure xe sees each and every one of them, every man, woman, and child xe traded and sold, their sadness and their soul weariness. I make xem feel the salt water in their throats when they were tossed overboard to evade antislaving navies. I lay down on xem the pain of watching their children walk away in chains, knowing they will never see them again. My reckoning passes through xyr body like flames, and xyr body cannot bear the magnitude of the suffering xe has caused in the world. Xe asphyxiates on it, xyr breath leaving xem slowly, xyr eyes bulging with pain. I do not mourn xem when xe dies.

Xe is not the only to die under the weight of this reckoning, but xe is the one that pleases me most.

The woman who calls herself the Fist gasps with pain. She has not killed many in her time, but she has ordered the men who did kill. She feels the blight on their souls, feels the taint of blood spilled that haunts their dreams. She sees the faces of the fallen. Feels the loss of their families, their mothers. She fights for freedom, has always known it is a bloody business, that power seeks only to retain power, no matter the cost. And so she can stand this pain, can weather its storm. It is a grave responsibility she is willing to carry for Quark, and for all those who writhed beneath Imperial boots.

Koa weeps. He sees the children of the soldier he killed, his little girl and his baby boy. Sees them as he scoops them up in his arms and covers their face with kisses. He feels the pain they will feel when they are old enough to understand that they will never see their father again. And while I sing, he shares their tragedy. He will never kill again. I hope he will never have the need.

In the Sea, the mermaid called Evelyn writhes in torment, her body racked with Keiko's hurt at being forgotten, with the children in the Cold World's devastation as they watch the forest they called home destroyed for the wood in the trees they called their friends, the same wood Evelyn's own casket was built of. But her love is there to hold her, to soothe her. She will be comforted, even if she is not comfortable.

Flora has already punished herself enough. How many nights has she replayed the murder of that merchant? A crime committed for survival, a crime she has never once forgotten, not even in the moments of her greatest happiness. This is how it should be. Humans never have clean hands. But she has already reckoned with herself and her regret—my song for her only treads a well-beaten path.

Though she cannot stand, Thistle lets her body go slack, lets herself slip from Koa's arms. She does not feel her body hit the ground. The cries of the Wariuta children echo in her ears. She feels the flames of their homes being burnt lick against her skin. She feels the rope of the noose tied around Dai's neck, feels his urine run down his leg, as he realizes he is about to die. She feels the bullet cut through her mother's neck. She retches.

Clutching his hand to his chest, Alfie hiccups a sob. His toes go numb with the biting cold of a winter he survived but those two children he stole bread from did not. He feels the crushing sadness that Flora felt when he stole their gold to spend on mermaid's blood, the keen slash of disappointment but not surprise. The destruction of her hope. He feels the sharp betrayal Keiko felt when she found out what he was. But worse, he feels Rake's betrayal after he pulled the trigger, feels the witch's pain as her lover crumples to the ground. The pain is crushing, so much so that he yearns for death, and he does not know if he will survive. He can, of course, we both know. He has lived with guilt before.

Outside the home paid for with his daughter's life, the Lord Hasegawa screams in pain. He has never truly suffered, despite having caused so much suffering, has never had any real consequences for his frivolousness and his malice. It is not my reckoning that will kill him—but when he passes out, he hits his head hard on the stone fence that surrounds his good fortune, and it is that blow that ends his life. His wife, the Lady Hasegawa, weeps into her kimono as her daughter wept, knowing she was unloved by her mother. But she survives.

Within the depths of a constabulary jail, Jung Hoon laughs. It is not happy laughter, but he cannot cry, not anymore. His tears dried long ago. He does not laugh for the man he killed—the pimp who beat him, who had to die so that he could possibly be free—he laughs for the child he once was, the one he walked away from and never thought of again.

All across Crandon, the humans that comprise Nipran weep and scream, they collapse and they lose consciousness. Those who walked by the homeless and the destitute without even a moment's fleeting sympathy. Those who shooed the starving orphans from their storefronts so they would not disrupt business. Those who traded in goods they knew caused destitution and war in nations far enough away that they simply did not care.

There are deaths, of course, many in the Senate and the constabulary. Those who viciously bolstered Imperial supremacy, those who knew, on some level, that their place on the top of the world was precarious and had to be jealously and violently protected. Those who knew that their greed wreaked human and natural destruction but did not cease. Those who understood that the price of their great nation was paid for in the blood of shamans, witches, and priestesses, their wisdom snatched from life and memory in the name of a false god, a small man, already unthinkably rich. They leave behind this world they tainted, and though some will be mourned, none will ultimately be missed.

I do not spare the children of Crandon. If they do not know, if they do not see, then they will live to see all this suffering done again. But I am gentle with them. I show them the children not unlike themselves, made into refugees by Imperial troops. I show them the myriad injustices committed in their names. Some of them weep. Some of them fall. But they will all live to remember this day, to speak of it to their children, and to their children's children. Generations later, the children will forget, but I cannot stop that.

Only Finn Callum glares up at me, curious but unmoved. Every epoch there are those like him. Broken, somehow. Unable to hear me, unable to be reckoned with. It is exactly this deficiency that allows him to kill without bother. To seek power and fortune through the blood of others. His time will be short, but the shadows cast by his victims are long. There is no salvation for someone like him.

Like I said. This is not justice.

I sing and I sing as I circle over Crandon. I am responsible for their remorse, and it is my duty to bear witness to them. I hear their cries. I feel their pain, immense and sharp. Their reckoning fills me, my belly swells with it. In one hundred years, I will lay a new clutch of eggs, and once again, my children will fly through this world. Once again, they will be hunted down and killed. I always hope this time will be better for them. The words to my song are always the same. Each time two souls fall in love. Each time their love sets the world in motion to seek redemption. Each time the powerless topple the powerful. It is always the same, has always been the same.

The Sea is forever destined to forget. And I am forever destined to remember.

The remembering is my labor, and I shoulder it alone.

Perhaps if I were stronger, if I could stand to do this more often.

Perhaps then the pain would not be so great.

I will never know.

### ◆ CHAPTER 50 ◆

## *Xenobia*

After the song, the First Dragon landed on the Imperial Palace, her claws crushing the ancient stone in their grasp. All watched as the legacy of the Emperors crumbled down, nothing left except rubble, and the bodies within.

Xenobia knew that now the people of Crandon and the Resistance alike would find and bury the dead. That Kwizera's body was somewhere within those stones. But she could not bear to see them battered and gone, not again. Her hands were still sticky with their blood.

So she walked to the Sea.

Across Crandon were the sounds of turmoil, of grief. People still wailed their horror and their regret, their pain and their sorrow. Xenobia paid them no mind. She knew what she needed to do.

The Sea was calm now, though pieces of what used to be Crandon's coast washed gently against the new shore. Xenobia watched a bloated body come in with the tide. A woman in a tattered yukata, her face submerged. Xenobia moved on.

The water was cold around Xenobia's feet, though it smelled more of oil and smoke and destruction than the Sea. She scanned the horizon. The great tidal wave had decimated the statue of the Emperor. All that remained were his feet, standing bodiless, reigning over nothing. She could not smile, but she did feel as glad as was possible.

She looked down at her hands. They were red, her skin stiffening as the blood dried.

She walked into the Sea.

The mermaid that would be born of Kwizera's blood would not be Kwizera. But they would hold the memory of them, of their service to the Sea. Of their love and their bravery. Of their great deed in ending the Empire of Nipran.

If the mermaid would find her, she did not know.

If the mermaid would remember her, she could not ask.

If the Sea would resurrect her as one of her daughters, she doubted.

But it was a small price to pay, to know that some part of Kwizera would live on. That they would be rejoined with the Sea they loved so much. Her power for their memory. Her life to breathe life back into theirs.

Without them, there was nothing left. No purpose.

The water swirled around her neck as she walked farther into the Sea, and just before her head was submerged, she thought of Kwizera's wide smile, the smell of their hair.

When the Sea swallowed her, she smiled.

• CHAPTER 51 •

## *Koa*

It felt at first as if there was no moving forward. That they all would simply perish where they stood or lay or knelt. But slowly, there was the quiet hum of activity across what was left of the palace grounds. Melancholy movement. Koa had picked up enough of the Colonizers' tongue to understand some. Whispers of how to find the bodies and where they could be buried. No one spoke of what had just happened because no one needed to.

He watched as a Colonizer girl approached Kaia, and was a little surprised that they seemed to know each other. She was carrying a baby, who was sleeping soundly. Koa felt a pang of affection for the baby's soft little face, his complete separation from what had just happened. He deserved his sleep. He was innocent.

The girl did not speak Sky Tongue, and Kaia did not speak the Colonizers' language, but they stood together in silence and in solidarity. Kaia ran a gentle thumb down the baby's cheek. The girl smiled at his sister, and Koa smiled, too. Maybe life would go on. Maybe one day Kaia would fall in love. Maybe that had already started.

Thistle's mother cradled her in her arms, Thistle openly weeping. Koa stepped away. It was not his place. He scratched Tupac behind the ear. The animal was bewildered but calm. Koa knelt next to him, trying to grapple with the feeling that nothing made sense and everything made sense simultaneously. He wondered if Ica could see him now, in this moment when he missed her so deeply.

He looked up only when he heard the terrible commotion. A man yelling, shouting, screaming at everyone. It was a man he recognized.

Commander Callum.

Koa stood. He had dropped his ax long ago, but he was still big, bigger than Commander. And he would not let him hurt anyone else.

"Lies!" Commander shouted. "Weakness!"

People gasped and turned away from him, horrified by his lack of respect in this holy moment in time. His desecration of the sacred event they had all shared. He defiled the peace that had washed over Crandon.

When Commander saw Kaia, he picked up a fallen sword, pointed it at her.

"You!" he yelled, and his voice was like a malediction. A curse. "You will let this savage take the Prince?" the man shouted at the crowd of people who scurried away from him.

Koa knew that Kaia did not understand this, but she didn't need to. She stepped between the Colonizer girl holding the baby and the man who was now screaming at her. Koa tried to move in front of her, but she pushed him back with her short arm. And Koa knew better than to disregard his sister.

She readied her sword.

Commander's eyes were wild as he charged at Kaia. With a great swing of his sword, he aimed a slash that would split her head in two. But Kaia's blade met his with a mighty clash, her strength a match he did not expect. He stumbled back in shock.

"You will kill no more of the Wariuta," she said. Her voice was not angry so much as certain. Firm. It was like a command. It was like Ica's voice. "Not today. Not ever."

They circled each other like hyenas, and Tupac giggled with anxiety that Koa shared. Kaia was a fearsome warrior. But the sword was not her weapon of choice; it was the weapon of Colonizers. And he also knew that it was easier to kill if you had no conscience. Commander clearly did not.

Koa blinked, and in that momentary distraction, he missed Kaia make her first move, a feint to the man's left, and once again their blades met, the clash of metal echoing over the now silent crowd. People watched, their mouths open, but no one spoke as Kaia and Commander fought. Commander kicked Kaia's stomach, and she stumbled back, winded. He tried to take advantage of this, tried to drive his sword directly through her belly, but she moved out of the way at the last possible moment, their bodies practically entwined. It was like a dance, except without joy.

Koa didn't want to watch, but he also couldn't look away.

He winced at the sound of the swords as they slid against each other, the shriek of steel on steel. But it was when Commander's sword slashed Kaia's sword-bearing arm that Commander cried out in triumph and Koa cried out in dismay. It was involuntary, a cry of fear ripped from his chest. There were gasps as Kaia's sword clattered onto the stones.

With a malicious grin wide across his face, Commander lunged with his sword once again, but this time when Kaia moved out of the way, she grabbed him around his neck and hurled him to the ground.

Commander's body slammed down, and the impact of it jolted the sword from his hand. It skittered away from him, and he made to crawl for it, but Kaia was too fast for him. She tackled him, and their bodies became a blur of punches and biting and growls and grunts, until, to Koa's infinite relief, Kaia wrapped herself around Commander from behind, her legs holding his body down, her arm around his neck in a tight stranglehold. A move their mother had taught her.

She squeezed.

Commander thrashed and writhed in her grasp, his hands seeking purchase but finding none. Kaia was too strong for him. She gripped him tight as the fight slowly drained from him. First his legs, then his arms. His mouth gawping like a fish's.

When she stood, the man who had killed their mother, who had killed their people, was gone. His eyes still open, frozen in his final moments of fury and fear and agony. No one stepped forward to press them shut.

• CHAPTER 52 •

*Thistle*

The *Leviathan* still sailed. Improbably. Impossibly. Her many sails still intact. Her mermaid figurehead still beautiful, hair forever flowing in a windy moment captured so long ago. She rocked gently in the sea, her anchor still holding fast. Rake, Thistle, her mother, and the few pirates who remained of the Pirate Supreme's crew had paddled out to her to see what remained.

Though seaweed and a few dead fish were strewn across her deck, she was entirely whole. Rake surveyed the scene with open-mouthed wonder. He seemed unable to find the words he needed to command the men.

"Clean up the decks," the Fist said. Not unkindly, but the men still followed her orders without question. "And check below for water damage."

Thistle found that somehow it was easier to keep her balance on her crutches and new wooden leg on the ship than on the shore. Maybe it was the cradling of the sea. Maybe it was simply that here she need not balance on uneven cobblestones. Whatever it was, she felt oddly at ease here on this pirate ship she had spent so long seeking to destroy.

Overwhelmed by the magic of the *Leviathan*'s survival, Rake staggered to a barrel that was tied to the deck and sat down. He ran trembling fingers through his bright-red hair.

"What do we do now?" Rake asked the Fist.

Thistle's mother put her hand on his shoulder, gave it a little squeeze. "We bring the Wariuta home. Koa has said that they are willing to take in the Crown Prince and the princesses, raise them among their own. At least there those girls will have a chance at a good life."

Thistle smiled. Koa would be a great carer for them. It was what he wanted, after all. To care for the children. And Kaia, Thistle knew, would be the leader the Wariuta needed to come back from the devastation. The princesses' nurse, Keiko, would be joining them, which would hopefully make the transition somewhat less abrupt.

"And then what?" Rake asked.

"Then . . . we hunt down every vial of mermaid's blood in the Known World." The Fist looked out over the Sea, her eyes thoughtful. "And we return it to where it belongs. The Pirate Supreme may be gone, but that doesn't mean we need abandon their cause. We will do what's right."

Rake stood then, and he was the steady, sure man Thistle had first met not so long ago. He wasn't smiling, exactly, but it was as if there were a smile caught in his eyes as he looked straight at Thistle's mother.

"The Pirate Supreme isn't gone," he said. "She's right here."

The Fist raised a brow. "If anyone would take up their mantle, I'd think it would be you, Rake. The crew already answers to you. You were their first mate."

But Rake shook his head. "I can't. Not after . . ." He took a deep breath. "I can't be trusted with that much authority. But you. You could lead us. If you're willing."

The Fist pressed her lips into a thin line. "Hmm. We'll ask the crew to take a vote. I won't take a throne I haven't earned."

Rake smiled this time in earnest. "Fair enough."

"And you?" Thistle's mother asked her. "Will you serve aboard this pirate ship?" She smiled warmly at her daughter. "Your life is your own. It's for you to decide."

Thistle thought of Koa and the Wariuta. Of Quark. Of Crandon, still fraught with devastation and trauma. "Can I think about it?"

"Of course." Her mother took her hand and brushed a gentle kiss across Thistle's knuckles. "You have all the time in the world now."

The girls who had been princesses all peered over the side of the *Leviathan* as the Red Shore came into view. They cooed and whooped with excitement, making the hyena calls Kaia had taught them. Koa had helped them choose new names for themselves, and Rake had taught them to tie knots in his spare time. They seemed to have come alive on the voyage, happy and content to be allowed to decide things for themselves, to let their hands get dirty, to be as loud as they pleased. For his part, Tupac seemed content to receive whatever snuggles the princesses were willing to sit still long enough for.

The first rowboat carried Kaia and the vast majority of the girls. Kaia gave Thistle a perfunctory goodbye wave, which Thistle was glad to receive. It was more regard than she expected.

"Are you coming?" Koa asked. He had one foot in the second

rowboat that would carry him, Tupac, and a handful more girls, the other foot still on the deck.

Thistle swallowed hard. She had been considering this moment for the whole voyage, changing her mind daily, hourly, about what was the right thing to do. Now that it was here, she felt sure but sorrowful. She shook her head.

"I'm sorry, Koa," she said. She brushed a tear from her cheek. "I don't belong in Yunka. I'm . . . I'm going to stay with my mother. I'm going to help make sure this never happens again."

Thistle wasn't sure what she was expecting, but Koa bounding across the deck to wrap her in a hug so tight it whisked her off her feet was not it. She laughed through her tears as he squeezed her in a warm embrace.

"I'll miss you," he said. He was not crying as Thistle was, but he looked wistful. "You know, pirates used to stop on our land all the time—always had the best stories. It's a tradition you should continue."

Thistle smiled. "I wouldn't want Tupac to miss me too much."

"Don't be a stranger." He gave her one last smile, then boarded the rowboat with the girls and disappeared over the edge of the *Leviathan* as they were lowered down.

Thistle watched as they made their steady progress to the shore. She watched until all the girls were safely on land. They waved back at the *Leviathan*, and then, following Kaia, they took off at a run toward Puno.

The Pirate Supreme came and stood next to Thistle. She put her arm around her daughter.

"Are you ready?" her mother asked. Behind them, Rake was barking orders to the men, to lift the sails, to batten things down.

Thistle grinned. "Let's go make something of this world."

◆ INTERLUDE ◆

## The Sea

*The blood of so many of her lost daughters returned in a flood, and now the Sea can do nothing except birth them anew, one by one, until she is restored. Only not entirely. So much is still gone. So much is new. So much is still in flux.*

*She can hear her mermaids, but she cannot speak to them, not yet. She wants to offer them words of love, of comfort, but finds that she cannot yet command her voice. She has too much healing to do. So instead, she watches and listens to them. Some rejoice. Some mourn. Two entirely new mermaids, Kwizera and Xenobia, find each other, find home at last, at last, at last. Someday the Sea will join them in their happiness. But not today.*

*This will happen again, she knows.*

*There is nothing she can do to stop it, she knows.*

*But the First Dragon is back in her cavern, nestled into the scar tissue of the Sea's own formation. The dragon alone knows her mother this intimately, understands that the architecture of where she lives is the scar tissue of the Sea's becoming. The echoes of volcanoes that changed the shape of the world are carved into the Sea, forming valleys that are deeper than mountains on the land are tall. And that is where the Sea must focus her attention now, on her dimmest, most secret corners.*

It hurts, *says the Sea.*

It always does, *says the First Dragon.*

I will never recover, *the Sea laments.*

You always do, *the First Dragon replies.*

*Far from what some called the Known World, the reverberations of her great trauma hit the shores in rogue waves, too large and deadly to be understood on a human scale. They will never know what caused this disruption to their lives, never understand the many forces that fit together to create their sudden tragedies. Some will call it the work of gods. Others will call it fate. The result is the same. Death, destruction, loss that they did not earn but suffer anyway. Perhaps one day a world will exist in which no one is punished for the crimes of others. More likely not.*

*But there, in a kelp forest: a baby otter is born, completely unaware of all the turmoil that preceded it. Her mother licks the fluids of her own body off her child. They are unbothered by circumstance. The Sea watches them with interest.*

*She does not know if the baby otter will survive. Many do not. But she hopes it will.*

## ◆ EPILOGUE ◆
## *Alfie*

### FIFTEEN YEARS LATER

Jung Hoon dumped a steaming pot of thick white noodles into the bubbling fish broth Alfie had spent all morning preparing. The lunch rush would start soon, and Alfie's food cart had gained a large and loyal clientele of fishermen and merchants. Now and again, when the *Leviathan* made port in Crandon, Rake would come visit. He was a softer man now, and Alfie was glad for that. They hugged whenever he left.

It was more than Alfie could have ever dreamed to ask for.

Alfie sliced scallions by rote as he watched the people of Crandon walk by. Most days were the same. Alfie would wake up before the sun, head to the fish market, and get what he needed from the same people who'd come later for his signature noodle soup. He'd gut the fish and boil down their bones along with the various aromatics he'd collected in the marketplace as he called hello and how are you to the other early risers. Eventually Jung Hoon would join him, and the day would start in earnest.

It was a good life. Quiet and gentle.

It was the life Alfie had always wanted. Almost.

"Here they come," Jung Hoon said as the line started forming. "I'll just take my break now."

It was the same joke every day.

"You leave and you're fired," Alfie responded, his script unchanging.

"Oh, you don't mean that. You'd miss me too much."

Alfie shook his head. "I'd miss you like I miss a pebble in my shoe."

Jung Hoon chuckled and started dishing out soup.

Alfie made cheery small talk with his customers, doled out their chopsticks and their napkins. But the smile drifted as he heard the beating of a single drum and yelling. He craned his neck and saw a small procession of men with their fists in the air.

"THE SONG WAS A LIE," they chanted. "THE MERMAIDS MUST DIE!"

Alfie closed his eyes. Callum's Army, they called themselves, but they were more like a cult. Now and then they hosted these processions, and usually people turned away from them in disgust. The people of Crandon had, for the most part, accepted the dragon's song and struggled to reshape society accordingly. There was no more Empire, only free nations that traded with one another as they pleased, each responsible for their own laws and their own customs. There was also no longer any kind of certainty, of consensus; conflict bloomed—though at least now each nation fought for their own rights and interests as opposed to the Empire's. And there were still some Imperial holdouts, and Finn Callum had become their martyr.

And lately it seemed like there were more of them.

Jung Hoon followed Alfie's gaze to the procession as they passed. "Just ignore them, boss," he said. "There's no fixing stupid."

"MIGHT IS RIGHT!" they chanted. Some of the onlookers hissed their disapproval at them. One customer threw a bowl at them, and it shattered on the ground at the feet of the procession, splashing Alfie's painstakingly cooked broth onto the cobblestones. A brief tussle ensued, and Alfie had to dash forward to pull the shoving match apart. One of the protesters spat at Alfie before moving on, and he was grateful that that was the worst of it.

Alfie watched with relief as the procession turned the corner, still shouting, still beating their drum. He wished he could brush them off as easily as Jung Hoon did.

When the lunch rush was over, Jung Hoon took the dishrag from Alfie's hand and pushed him out from behind the cart. "Go on," he said. "You need a break. And I'm sick of looking at you."

"You sure? It's a lot."

"You can pay me extra."

Alfie laughed.

He took off his apron and walked, as he often did, down to the docks. The afternoon sun was just warm enough to cut through the fog, but the sky was gray. Alfie liked it that way, liked the chill of the air, the scent of the Sea. He walked to the end of a fishing dock, sat, and took off his shoes. The damp wood of the dock was cold beneath him. The tide was in, the water high, and so his feet just skimmed the surface of the Sea. It was too cold, really, to put his feet in the water, but he did anyway. He always did, no matter the weather.

A disturbance in the water ahead of him told him he'd made the right choice coming down that day. His luck wasn't always so good. The visits were becoming more and more sporadic as time went on. But today. Today was lucky. Something like solace washed over him, and he felt his shoulders loosen, his jaw unclench. He grinned.

    A familiar face surfaced, wearing an easy smile. Her voice was less like a voice these days and more like the echo of waves trapped in a seashell. And though Alfie had filled out, his stomach boasting a comfortable roundness, his eyes just starting to wrinkle at their corners, the mermaid looked exactly the same as she had more than fifteen years ago when she stepped off the *Leviathan* and into the Sea. Somewhere not too far, Alfie knew, was another, and the knowledge she was close by was a great comfort. He wanted their happiness.

    But Alfie was here to see the missing piece in his life.

    "Hello, brother," Flora said.

# The Mermaid, the Witch, and the Sea

### The exciting prequel to
### The Siren, the Song, and the Spy

The pirate Florian, born Flora, has always done whatever it takes to survive—including sailing under false flag on the *Dove* as a marauder, thief, and worse. Lady Evelyn Hasegawa, a highborn Imperial daughter, is on board as well—accompanied by her own casket. But Evelyn's one-way voyage to an arranged marriage in the Floating Islands is interrupted when the captain and crew members show their true colors and enslave their wealthy passengers. Both Florian and Evelyn have lived their lives by the rules, and whims, of others. But when they fall in love, they decide to take fate into their own hands—no matter the cost.

Edison Public Library
Main Branch
340 Plainfield Ave
Edison, New Jersey 08817

# Honey Russell:
# Between Games, Between Halves

# HONEY RUSSELL

◆

# Between Games
# Between Halves

◆

JOHN RUSSELL

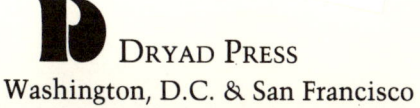

DRYAD PRESS
Washington, D.C. & San Francisco

Copyright © 1986 by John David Russell.
All rights reserved.
Printed in the United States of America.

*Acknowledgements*
The author thanks Sebastian Yorke for permission to quote from Henry Yorke and Cynthia Bee Farley for permission to quote from Clair Bee and for their cooperation the Naismith Hall of Fame and the Seton Hall University.

*Photography Credits*
International News, facing page 18; Marvin Newman, facing pages 19 and 188; Naismith Hall of Fame, facing pages 35 and 52; *The Cleveland News*, facing page 53; *Bettman News Photos*, facing pages 87 and 120; Century Flashlight Photographers, Inc., facing page 98; Handy and Boesser Photographers, facing page 120; *Lousiville Courier-Journal*, page 121. Cover photograph by Irv Goodman.

This project is partially supported by grants from the Maryland Arts Council and the National Endowment for the Arts, a Federal agency.

Library of Congress Cataloging in Publication Data

Russell, John, 1928-
    Honey Russell: between games, between halves
    Includes index.    1. Russell, Honey, 1902-1973. 2. Basketball players — United States — Biography.   I. Title.
GV884.R85R87    1986    796.32'3'0924 [B]    85-29252
ISBN 0-931848-64-4
ISBN 0-931848-65-2 (pbk.)

DRYAD PRESS
15 Sherman Avenue
Takoma Park, Maryland 20912

P.O. Box 2916 Presido
San Francisco, California 94123

To David's Memory

*Tom Fool "makes an effort and makes it oftener / than the rest"*
— Marianne Moore, "Tom Fool at Jamaica"

# Contents

Commencing    1

Second Mainstays    11

Fifth City —Monsters of the Midway    49

Depression Schemes — The Son Also Rises    91

With His Guard Down    149

Concluding    193

*Chronology*    213

*Index*    217

# Commencing

◆

During the last months of my father's life — when our family did not know if his illness was mortal, though the signs were increasingly bad — I was talking one day with him of past times, and told him (as on one earlier occasion) that I had thought of writing about him. He was not feeling good, and the idea, as I saw on readvancing it, did not intrigue him. I spoke a little further of it, though, because of having struck on a way of beginning. It was remembering two attitudes I'd seen him in — physical postures which had hit me with unexpected force. One went back to a moment between games of a doubleheader in New York when he was a college coach; the other, to an incident between the halves of a Boston Celtics game when he was managing them.

At the same time, I had the idea of amusing him — as anyone might be amused when told of being remembered for a particular stance or bearing, unsuspected by himself, that had kept its image in the observer's eye over a long span of years. I bet him he couldn't remember walking out to the floor-level seats at Madison Square Garden after a consolation game he'd been involved in — but that that occasion had made an image for me for whatever story I might eventually write about him. He wasn't particularly inquisitive. Then I asked him if he recalled a between-halves lecture to his Celtics players, most of whom were new to the team, early in the second year he coached them. He did remember that, but, with a laugh, jumped on past it to the Chicago-Boston playoffs of that year, and came up with an image and memory of his own. It was about how he had tried to keep his opponent, Harold Olsen of the Chicago Stags, from making a certain substitution. "Will you ever forget that?" he said — and had moved to a third dimension.

That is, he had conjured up a moment on the floor, between plays. It was something I'd forgotten about, though now it came back to me. His remembering brought zest to his face, something of the old animation. It made me glad to have mentioned my own ground-breakers, with which this book does begin — helping to give it its "Between Games, Between Halves" title. But his was the incisive memory, of a decision made closer to the heart of things, for a player or coach, during action in a game. In this talk of ours he was affable, yet showed no interest, really, in how I might contemplate getting a narrative launched. His own recollection, though — that was invigorating. All his life he had been the purveyor of his own tales. Most likely he appreciated my wish to write about him; but even had his illness not been pulling against him, he'd undoubtedly have taken my overture in that same way. Consigning his stories over to a second hand, mine or anyone else's, must to his mind have made them sure to lose their savor. With this view — if he did hold it — I am in sympathy, knowing his monologues to be unrecapturable. I am glad he reverted to that one memory, though, of a ploy he tried in the Boston-Chicago playoffs, since otherwise I would not have recalled it. It was the only straight assist I was to get from him for this book, for that October afternoon marked our last talk together.

Between that final Celtics year and his resumption of his career as coach of Seton Hall came one "trough" year. To conclude his three-year contract with Boston, he was managing their 1949 farm team in the Eastern League, Schenectady. I was in my sophomore year at a college nearby upstate, and was being redshirted that season. There were enough of us in my category to make up an unofficial squad, which managed to get in a handful of JV-level games. My father knew I'd been practicing all year but hardly playing, so toward the end of the Eastern League season (when ours was over) he surprised me by having brought an extra uniform along when I came over to a Schenectady game. This wasn't really too daunting, since I'd always scrimmaged with his teams whenever I happened to be around. However, I didn't actually expect he'd put me in a game — only thought I'd be taking some shots in the warm-ups.

Through the first part of the game I was my usual spectator self, but afterwards I did play, for one long stretch in the second half: not a critical period of time since Schenectady had a decent lead, yet it still came as a surprise to hear my father tell me, "Jack, get in there for [I forget who] and play number [I forget]. Keep trying to get the ball into Gunther" (Coulby Gunther, who used to play for Brown and was a deadly hook-shooter).

I reported to the scorer, giving my name out of the side of my mouth with my eyes on the court. Afterwards, since I did score a basket while I was in, I couldn't resist going over to the scorebook when the game was over, to see if I'd been credited for my shot. (There'd been no public address announcing the running score.) I peeked over the scorer's shoulder and couldn't find my name. The last name on the Schenectady roster was Mahoney, with one "x" marked next to it as a second-half entry. We had no Mahoney on our team, so that had to be me.

Of course it all came clear right away. My own discouragement as a redshirt sophomore had never let the thought of future eligibility enter my head (and besides I had not thought my father would play me). Once I was in the game, the scorer had inquired of our bench who I might be, and my father called back, "Mahoney."

The Brooklyn-Irish ring of the name, but even more, its almost "hired-hand" quality, tells something about my father, or so it seems to me. It was entirely unsentimental of him — though very kind — to stick me into that lineup with a tag like that. He must have improvised it on the spot. Yet he'd been the one to remember the need for a false name (to protect my eligibility), not I. Nor could he have attended to something like this in advance, because ten other things would have been on his mind before and during the game. Thinking of me must have occupied that strict little space coaches reserve for their umpteenth player when all else has been looked to — or when everything has got out of hand.

An aftermath to the episode occurred twenty-five years later, when I was driving with my mother and sisters, for only the second time, to my father's gravesite. There was a large headstone at the end of his own row, which bore the romanized inscription, "MAHONEY." I'd begun to write about him by then, but had not thought of that old story till I saw the name. I told the others about it; they'd never heard that one. Meanwhile, in the early stages of my writing, I had noticed that quite a large number of my father's associates had Mac's to their names. I do not mean just Irish friends. Many boys of second-generation Jewish families, in emulation I suppose of the sports-competitive Irish, had Gaelic-sounding names or nicknames. (Mac Kinsbrunner and Mack Posnak, for example, of the old St. John's Wonder Five — a team my father coached after they'd moved into the pros as the New York Jewels.) The many variants of *Mac* of course all imply "son of." One variant simply drops off the "c": for names like Magregor, Matheney, Malone. On that analogy, there came a flashing thought — looking at the tombstone, I saw the name Mahoney as a patronymic. My father, caught up with demands of the moment, never had time, nor did he have inclinations, for such things as etymologies. Yet in the one basketball game I participated in when he was the coach, he managed to call out an appropriate name to protect me, on that day a long way back. After all I was "son of Honey."

Honey Russell was the name he went by from the time he was a boy, and he always included the nickname in his signature: John "Honey" Russell. (Not on legal forms or income-tax returns, of course, but everywhere else.) On all the plaques he received, on all captions under his picture, even on the backs of watches, that would be the name. I only saw two exceptions. One comes from the oldest clipping my mother has of him, a 1917 photograph representing him as a high school all-star, and under it the name John. The compiler of that team must not have known of the already current nickname. The other exception has an appropriate permanence to it. If you sought out his niche in the Basketball Hall of Fame at Springfield, you would find John D. Russell printed under the picture of him there. This adheres to the protocol adopted by the Hall of Fame, to have its inductees commemorated by their formal names (you learn what some of them are for the first time). It is Bernhard (not Benny) Borgmann you meet there; Nathan (instead of Nat) Holman. These were the great offensive players of my father's day, and he joins them among the first five professionals to be selected—he as the all-time defensive standout. So it goes—and you begin to think of them as men with real lifetimes, instead of athletes having the sports counterpart to a lifetime. Adding to the formality is the stained-glass window reserved to each entrant. But the panels are set up in bent-screen arrangements that relieve what could have been a churchly atmosphere; and under each man's picture his achievements are recorded in plain light.

 As luck would have it, the man next to my father happens to be Walter Brown. This is because the panels for each group of inductees are arranged alphabetically; and while Walter Brown's name came up first in 1965, my father's was last in 1964. From his point of view, nothing could have been more fortuitous. He was a keen admirer of Brown, and credited him as the force behind the National Basketball Association, which came into being as the BAA. Brown founded the Boston Celtics and hired my father as their coach. A testimony to Brown's sagacity is that the first four Celtics coaches reached the Hall of

Fame — though they are there for different reasons. Doggie Julian was elected as a college coach; Red Auerbach as the coach who won so many titles for the Celtics (their names show up as Alvin and Arnold). Then comes Bill Russell (whom my father would sometimes call "the other Russell"), famous as a collegian as well as for his all-pro years at Boston. My father's election came on the strength of his career strictly as a professional player. There were plenty besides Borgmann and Holman whose scoring averages suffered after entanglements with him — no other player turns up to compete with him in longevity, even if some later defenders may have been as tenacious on court.

The Hall of Fame was five years old when my father was inducted, by which time he was 62 and out of basketball. Not long after his retirement from college coaching (at Seton Hall and Manhattan, where he won over 300 games), he'd been elected to the other Hall of Fame, honoring amateur sports: the Helms Foundation in Los Angeles. He thus became the first to receive double recognition, as coach and player; but it was his election as a player that meant the most to him. Those playing days had soon enough been clouded over, what with lapses in record-keeping and, in the 1920s and '30s, the rather unremarkable sports photography. (I don't mean to imply that my father throve on mementoes, nothing of the sort. Two action photos of him are all our scrapbook contains. Which may merely confirm how early careers, by comparison to modern ones, can fade.) Soon after the news came out of his Helms selection in 1962, he ran into a New Jersey fan who'd followed his coaching at Seton Hall and was brimming over with congratulations. Had he ever *played* the game, the fan asked my father. Though able to conceal his surprise, my father was made to feel pretty rueful by this well-wisher. For of all men, he was the last who should have been asked that question — being the one, as his plaque at Springfield attests, who played more years, 28, in more professional games (and for more teams) than any other player in history.

Yet he was not a famous man. A phrase from the *Times* obituary of him comes to mind: the "pale-faced and colorful Mr. Russell." The adjectives, though not meant to do so, tend to cancel each other. Within the world of sport, certainly, my father was colorful, but mostly in an "after-hours" way. What made him colorful were his wit and gregariousness, but these have to be consigned to his private side. Publicly he does tend to pale. The *Times* editor meant his complexion of course — my father was long-faced, bald except for a peninsula of dark hair running back from his forehead, and rather an expressionless man in public. As a young player his speed gave him some flair; when I saw him play it was a sense of efficiency that he gave out, no wasted motion, not much accommodation for flair. When coaching he kept his mouth and gaze steady, his posture straight — reminiscent of the way he umpired baseball games, his voice rolling out "strah-a-ahk" in a gravelly monotone, his arm going up forcefully but without tension. He would not intrude his personality onto games, though never other than totally involved in them. That umpire's judgment of his seemed to carry over to the player and coach, in both of which roles his concentration was bent on what was coming next. So in public he could be counted on for this steady comportment. Privately it was another matter — he grinned instantaneously (sometimes coming across like a joker in a card deck); he teased and clowned, and could register just about every shade of mock-surprise or horror — his brows had a whole field to themselves for this, where no hair ever fell forward. Those who knew him almost always recall first that impish side. But only for a comparative few, I think, is he a tremendously memorable man, because there was never anything controversial about him. In this respect one might think of him as "pale," despite his accomplishments.

To put it briefly, he had no interest in those routes open to sports figures that create currents of publicity about them. In terms of physical antics, bench-tirades, vows, locker-room orations, over-estimates of his opponents, or post-mortems with the press, my father never could have been labeled the "colorful" Mr. Russell.

What did appeal to reporters were his yarns about the past: a repertory of bizarre situations that came his way during a whole lifetime given over to sports. But as to whatever might be next on his agenda, my father was colorless. A winning streak in jeopardy, say, or the fact that he was in a tournament or playoff game, would not get a rise out of him. He treated all contests the same. Though as a player and coach he did set several records, it was never with a sense of having records in mind. Averages, margins-of-victory meant little if anything to him. If it worked out that 70 percent of the time he proved accurate in expecting to win, that was fine but some other overall tally might have sufficed as well. He did not really *point* for anything in his career, my father; except perhaps in the one mundane respect of keeping his job. And as to that, he once said the ideal college coach should be smart enough to want a 50-50 record, which would give room for praise in successful years, without creating expectations of solid winning — which coaches can't guarantee, and is a reason their jobs are fairly hazardous.

While my father may have entered each game really expecting to win it, that was because he was a concentrator on the moment. For that reason, maybe, to try to get at anything cumulative about him — say to present his exploits according to chronology — would hardly generate any intensity. Where he was in time didn't mean much to him. Arriving at places he was supposed to be, holding good to bargains — these were his preoccupations. He was a nonpareil scheduler, train-and-plane catcher, easer of the way for others. (I once remember him traveling from New Jersey to Madison Square Garden so as to *hand* complimentary tickets to friends, because he thought there'd been a change in ticket windows that might throw those people off.) Since he was a steady man, not a charismatic one, it seemed in the cards for me to trace a pattern that would be faithful to this steadiness. So I began to put the book together on a basis of vignettes that had their way of revealing highlights of his character to me. But what I found was this: trying to present him *steadily* came to mean *surprisingly*. It was as though depths, however they might have seemed soundable with him, were the source of buoyancies that continually foiled expectations. Reliable though he was, my father always kept surprising me; straight as his posture and firm as his jaw were, I missed their import as often as I thought I had marked it. I suppose that would have had to happen when the point of view, no matter at what age, remained that of child to parent. As a son, naturally, I could not see him develop in time; rather, it seems to have been in space — in seeing connections across times — that a principle of development emerged and kept the story going. Its impetus owes most, I suppose, to my wish not to see him pale.

While this account does not move chronologically, there happen to be many decades' worth of anniversaries that help rough out the stages taken by my father's career. Almost seventy years ago, when that 1917 clipping was fresh, he was an all-around high school athlete competing for the last time as an amateur; he turned professional a year later, at age sixteen, and from then on made his living from sports. The end of the war in 1918 brought a sports boom and my father was caught up in its vortex — he was a seasoned pro by eighteen, as the country shifted into the roaring twenties.

In the midst of them, nearing his tenth pro year, he was traded from the world champion Cleveland Rosenblums to George Halas's Chicago Bruins (January 1927) — a trade that initiated his career as a playing coach, for Halas bought him as the leading basketball player in the country, aiming to have him manage the Bruins. He was not yet twenty-five. Ten years further along, with plenty of experience as a playing manager, he was hired as a college coach by Seton Hall, for the 1937 season.

He probably would have continued there but for World War II, when the college dropped its sports programs (he was eventually to return); meanwhile, in yet another postwar boom, he was signed to coach Walter Brown's Celtics for the NBA's inaugural season of 1947. These were all basketball milestones for my father; the sport he participated in almost as steadily, baseball, was to bring him his best reward in 1957, when he received his World Series' ring as a chief scout for the Milwaukee Braves. On that championship team several of his discoveries had played leading roles. And one decade later, in 1967, he would complete his last full year in his "everyman's" job — which a great many fans of his teams would be surprised to learn he had — as an insurance adjustor.

It seems only convenient to think of these accomplishments in ten-year steps for their way of suggesting what is the *sine qua non* for any athlete: staying power. Such milestones are merely ways to docket a life given wholly to sports — he was working for the Chicago White Sox right up to his death, at age 71. He began, as I said, all the way back at the end of World War I; his own father, hostile to the idea of professional sports, having died on Armistice Day, of influenza, in the first year of his son's earning money for play.

But it is the memory of the joy he gave as a father that underwrites this book. He would have been capable of saying to me, or to my sisters, the kind of thing that John Butler Yeats said to his son William, in almost the last letter he wrote to him. It was apropos of times planned and unplanned when the paths of the two would cross. Said Mr. Yeats, "There never has been a moment in my life of meeting you, even though it was by chance in the streets of Dublin, that it did not give me pleasure."

# Second Mainstays

During the war when we were growing up, my father's mainstay job as a college coach was interrupted. Having turned forty, he realized it was about time he hung up his shoes. But since he continued managing for different pro franchises in the east, he found himself having to suit up regularly for these short-manned teams. "Old Man River" — so a wartime program from Philadelphia describes him — "just keeps rollin' along." All that had to stop when the NBA came into being, a year after the war — at 44 he was too old to play in such a high-powered league. It was the packing of the big-city arenas for college games (even though many schools had canceled their schedules) that really gave the NBA its impetus — that plus the popularity of service teams like the celebrated one from Great Lakes, which could funnel seasoned players straight into the new league.

As for the college boom, between 1941 and 1945 practically every doubleheader in Madison Square Garden was a sellout. For one thing, people could pay — war work had filled their pockets, and they came not only to see the games but to bet on them. An added attraction was the appearance of the first big centers on college basketball courts. The scarcity of mature players — the upperclassmen having gone to war — probably had something to do with this crop of huge saplings, considering the fact that players over 6'6" weren't eligible for the armed forces. For the first time really tall youngsters (skinny or slow, but their chance for developing had arrived) became the kingpins of college teams.

Though not associated with Madison Square Garden in these years, my father was sent complimentary tickets for the college games and generally passed these on to me. (None of the sports figures around New York needed tickets for sporting events — they were all recognizable men, and my father like the others simply went to players' entrances at the Polo Grounds or Ebbets Field and walked in: it was all easy and informal, the turnstile men friendly, no badges needed.) I was in high school then and would take friends along to the Garden, where we'd sit in the top balcony, our seats ending at a stanchion that partially blocked the view of the first person in. The cigar smokers and shouters up there had no unanimity (the student sections were down on the floor), and their catcalls were like muskets going off the whole time, probably because so much betting went on in the dark up there. Maybe the last game I viewed from that balcony was the Red Cross benefit of March 1945. It matched the NIT and NCAA champions, DePaul and Oklahoma A & M. Ray Meyer was at DePaul even then. Playing for and against him that night were two men who really did usher in the era of the big centers — George Mikan and Bob Kurland. I remember a friend of mine saying of Mikan's photograph, "He looks like Clark Kent." Burlier than Kurland and bigger than all the others, Mikan in action did resemble Superman, except for the Clark Kent glasses which he kept on. Superman status would come later, when he was voted the best basketball player of the half-century.

What used to strike me from that balcony were the well-appointed sections down below, reserved for the Garden's top-dollar patrons. These were a thin green band of loge seats circling the entire arena. To me they defined the place, maybe because of their permanence, since the floor of the arena was always changing. On one memorable occasion, a favorite day to my sisters, our whole family were down in those loge seats — it was for a final matinee the day the circus was leaving town. I remember my father keeping us there a good while afterward, having us watch the dismantling that went on. Did he do this out of respect for the workmen (himself possibly never having hit a nail with a hammer) — or was he just intrigued with the mutability of the place? If the latter, his feelings differed from mine: I keep a sense of the green seats where we'd been sitting, which didn't get changed as the rest of the Garden below and above us seemed to come apart.

Well, of course, it was floorside that counted when basketball was being played; and the metropolitan coaches, almost like members of a club, could be spotted any double header night in the last couple of rows of wooden seats, just in front of the loges, near the dressing-room underpass. There wasn't a better place to see a game from than these temporary seats. My story begins with them, half a dozen years after the war, by which time my father was back in college coaching.

His own assigned seats were on the aisle, top row. A couple of places further in on this row were held by Kenny Norton, the Manhattan coach. (My father had had that job in 1945; he was now at Seton Hall.) The seats in the row in front of ours were Nat Holman's, and down one step more, Danny Lynch's of St. Francis. Just across the aisle was Howard Cann, NYU. These were all amicable men, Danny Lynch the live wire among them, always swivelling around to pass up comments. By contrast Holman was staid, his homburg neatly rested on his overcoat beside him, his grey-black hair so well groomed that you'd figure the homburg couldn't have encased it. It puzzles me to recall that, on the night Nat Holman first told my father of his fears about his City College team — some weeks before the news broke of the 1951 point-shaving scandal — I can only fix their conversation as taking place in the upper reaches of the Garden. That was where bettors would congregate, as I said, but there would never be a reason for my father to be up there, much less for him to encounter another coach by chance there. I may have misplaced the incident — I was present, but only while driving home was I told what transpired — and wonder whether some trick of memory, which does not want me to place a more or less painful event down near the courtside seats, has caused me to relegate it to those smoky and dark upper regions.

Not that, in the ordinary way, much conversation got exchanged between my father in his reserved seat and the other basketball experts in their Garden-club section. This was because my father almost never sat down. His coat and hat would be keeping me company at Garden games more often than he would. That last row was just shoulder high, and it was natural for him, with his foot raised to the scaffolding on which the seats were elevated, to watch the court action from the aisle. That way he could wander, something like a cop on a beat. He knew all the ushers in the area and was often talking with them, or to friends in the green seats behind. As often as not he'd have his arm round some chance acquaintance's shoulder. Or it might be on my own shoulder that I would find his hand. For I was frequently down from college and, if so, would be over at the Garden with him on a doubleheader night.

The night that calls to mind these arrangements, however, was not one of the standard doubleheaders. It was the finals of the 1951 National Invitation Tournament. Though Brigham Young was to play Dayton in the feature game, the consolation game concerned us more, for Seton Hall was coming up against St. John's.

This was a New Jersey-New York rivalry of no acknowledged standing so far as local newspapermen were concerned. Naturally enough the New York colleges vied for eminence among themselves. Seton Hall had been a latecomer to national exposure, playing most of its games in its South Orange gym — which would hardly attract the New Yorkers.

On the other hand my father was a Brooklynite, did as much recruiting in New York as in New Jersey, and knew all these rival coaches from associations in the pro game. Holman and he, for example, both inducted into the Hall of Fame on the same day, had lined up against one another for upwards of fifteen years in the old American League and others. As for the younger coaches, some like Frank McGuire (who would be coaching St. John's that night) had played for my father on local teams like the Jewels, in the years just before the war. Pro basketball in the east then was largely a hit-or-miss proposition, the teams playing to small crowds in Brooklyn's Arcadia Hall or the uptown St. Nicholas Arena, places and schedules always subject to change.

Now, in 1951, with LIU and CCNY having run afoul of the scandals, and Seton Hall and St. John's having reached the NIT semi-finals before losing, this consolation game was going to determine an eastern — certainly the metropolitan — "championship." That may have been a fact of no real moment — Brigham Young was the best team in the building — yet something of consequence was still on the line. This was the Seton Hall team on which Walter Dukes and Richie Regan were sophomores — in two years it would be the country's best team, and establish a national winning streak for a single season (the record now held by Indiana State and Larry Bird). And this was the St. John's team on which Bob Zawoluk was a junior. It would be competing the next year in the NCAA finals.

The players knew one another for better reasons yet. They had scrimmaged at the beginning of the season — my father and McGuire had arranged the matches informally — though the outcomes were not conclusive. What is clear is that each team put together some very sharp halves, and each thought itself better than the other. Was there also a Catholic hegemony at stake? Probably, since here was my father, only a year back from his Celtics service, showing in early scrimmages a powerhouse in the making that might depose St. John's. There had been no way of proving this, until, as a result of their placement in opposite Invitational brackets, there'd come this unexpected game, the consolation, which would settle the question.

There was another reason the game should stick in my memory. I was by now about to graduate from my hideaway upstate (well out of it); yet I had attended St. John's Prep, right across from the college those days in downtown Brooklyn. I knew most of the players on McGuire's team, and bantered with a couple of them that night while they were shooting between halves. One of them was Al McGuire, St. John's captain — who was to make a move in the second half that would wreck my father's cause.

Years before I'd introduced Al to my father, since I was a substitute on the Prep team on which Al as a sophomore was the youngest regular. I didn't know how good he was then — all I knew was that he was rough — but this being a team competing for the city championship I'd got my father to come see its final game. I wanted him to have a look at our two all-metro forwards, both of whom played spectacularly in that final win. Al, who hardly scored, was in on the floor play and backboard action as usual. When afterwards I asked my father how he liked the team, meaning the star seniors, I remember his judgment: "That big black-headed kid — there's the ball player."

He had that kind of eye, which picked out the unspectacular. I would almost say his preference ran to the type of athlete whom you might call the "second mainstay." This was because basketball was to him strictly a team game, won in the end by defense and by players who'd give themselves up. He was certainly right about Al, as was proved to his cost the night of that consolation game. Al got damaged himself that evening, taking one whale of a fall near the end, but this came after he'd made his game-saving play.

The score had just been tied. With Seton Hall the coming-on team, St. John's was trying to keep possession and run out the clock. Al had caught a poorly thrown pass right at the sidelines, and, trapped by the defense, he'd begun to fall out of bounds in slow motion. The referee was standing there, our player would be given possession — *we would win* — when Al, ball against his chest, put up a T in front of that referee's eyes before he fell, and got granted a time out. It happened in front of our bench, and where I thought my father might contest the call, what he did instead was nod.

Two overtimes resulted from that play, and there should have been a third, except for what another "second mainstay" managed to do — another Mac, Ronnie MacGilvray — and this brings me back to the coaching. For my father saw this one coming, a game-ending situation in which the opposing coach would not be able to go to his star. The All-American, Zawoluk, my father could discount because his seven-foot center Dukes had neutralized him. On his own bench was a sophomore who had scarcely played in the NIT. He'd been a regular on the Dukes-Regan freshman team of the year before, which had a 39-1 record. (That figure tells something about my father; for what other freshman team ever played 40 games? After his return to Seton Hall from the pros, he'd done a crash recruiting job, and wanted to put his bonanza haul of freshmen under game conditions as often as possible — the heart of his coaching philosophy.) My father rated this sophomore, Joe O'Hare, as the smartest defensive player on his team. He had not been out of his leggings in the St. John's game, and now the second overtime was ending. With the score still tied, St. John's was to be taking the ball in and would need to bring it the length of the court for some last-second shot.

It looked to my father as though MacGilvray would be instructed to take that final shot, not Zawoluk. In his last time-out, he called O'Hare out of his sweatclothes to go in and take MacGilvray — told him Ronnie would try to take the ball downcourt himself. "He'll want to come up the middle and end up by the foul circle," my father said. "That's what we don't give him."

"What am I supposed to do?"

"I want you to play head up on him and keep throwing feints at him to his left. That's to your right, you got it? Forget about going for the ball. Feint him left the whole time and make him go to his right. From halfcourt on I want him crowded over till you've got him on his bench. That's where you head him unless he gives up the dribble."

When O'Hare, cold, went out to accomplish this you could see the confidence generated along the Seton Hall bench. And it was repaid. The script was exactly followed. At the end of the line, MacGilvray had had to tightrope in front of his bench and he'd wound up in the dead corner of the forecourt; time was gone, O'Hare was still there; the heave MacGilvray now took was not really a gamble because no harm could come from it: after the shot came down the third overtime would ensue, that was all. But of all things the ball went in.

To parochial eyes like mine, there went the metropolitan playoff. The score was 70-68. O'Hare felt particularly bad. For one thing, he thought my father had made a mistake putting him in. He felt he cost his team the game, not having played MacGilvray perfectly, letting him get a shot off. (Here he was wrong: he'd done exactly the job asked of him.) So ended what was long afterwards called the best consolation game in the Garden's history — maybe a dubious distinction, but these matched teams, tournament finalists over the next years, proved they could take almost anybody's measure.

For my father, though he'd lost to Brigham Young a couple of nights earlier, this one was tougher — or so I thought, always seeing him as a New Yorker working over in Jersey, and here having come so close to winning a long-wished-for game which wasn't likely to come up again as a rematch. I went back to the dressing room, mainly to tell one of the players that I would meet him up in the green seats, for his girl friend and a girl I had brought to the game were sitting there — in the reserved section right behind our two floor seats, as it happened — so I went on up there without saying much more, as I remember, than so long to my father in the dressing room.

The Brigham Young and Dayton teams were on the floor

*Second Mainstays In Action.* NIT consolation, 1951. St. John's Ronnie MacGilvray (15) contests a shot, as Al McGuire blocks out Walter Dukes at left. Number 27 is Don Dunn; Seton Hall's 15 is Bobby Hurt. The Seton Hall shooter is John Ligos.

*Between Halves.* HR's characteristic delivery.

when I got there. I was downhearted, the result I suppose of having to face this championship game, with our team having come off fourth best in the tourney. The girl who was with me had never met my father, she was from the West Coast and knew nothing about metropolitan rivalries. No doubt she found it odd that I had spent the first game down on the bench instead of where, as she might have phrased it, she and my friend's girl, total strangers, had been "dumped." But I wanted to speak of my feelings about the loss — could do so to some degree with the other girl, a veteran of such games — but it behooved me to try to engage the interest of the girl I was escorting. I said something about how rough it was on my father to come so close, and now have half a year ahead before it would begin again — with a lousy bunch of "if only's" left, after one damned shot by MacGilvray. I knew MacGilvray in a small way also. Past friends of mine had done it.

About this time the lights went down. The opposing players were about to be introduced. I pointed out Mel Hutchins, the center for Brigham Young (if I'd known his sister would be the Miss America that summer, I might have quickened this girl's interest). Soon came the overtures to the Star Spangled Banner. We were on our feet in the dark, when — as the opening bars came over the loudspeakers — I noticed that directly below us, in the aisle behind the two arena seats that were ours, my father had appeared. He must have emerged during the player introductions.

I nudged the girl and said, "There's my father," pointing down to where he stood. Immediately I had perceived something about his bearing, that she should be able to take in. Tension, thickened atmosphere, had been building these several minutes past for the spectators, but I was still thinking of the just-lost game and so, I inferred, was my father. I have said that he always stood behind that bank of chairs with a foot up. This time both feet were on the floor, he had his hand to his forehead as though shading it, and was looking down — standing there alone, no ushers in sight, the whole Garden still, save for the anthem. The girl could not have misread his attitude.

But what a flyer I'd taken, figuring him all filled up with emotion because he'd just lost. This set-piece of mine now collapsed. My father blent in with 18,000 stubholders; he might have been any Garden veteran, Nedick's patron, who'd emerged from that underpass and seen his chance in the dark. For he'd made his way over to that tier of seats, as the girl could clearly see, but it wasn't to indulge wounded feelings. He'd simply spotted a likely place to spit. And spit is what he very deliberately did — as though he had a nice sandbox down there. He couldn't have put more of a damper on my misguided reverence — not then nor any of the other times I'd brought him along in my mind, only to find myself miles off the track he himself was on.

"Hawk a lunger" was a phrase some of us sometimes used for it.

My father was a midnight snorer and a congenital early-morning throat clearer. Seven broken noses (which do not compare with the baker's dozen sustained by Jerry West) had made inroads over the years on his breathing. There may have been a side effect on his voice too. It had a medium-pitched dryness, especially noticeable over the telephone. His voice didn't square with the even-tempered man he was: deadly dismissive, it could make him sound. One freshman team he had, the one with Bob Wanzer on it, was a little more woman-conscious than most. Imagine their reaction when he silenced some comments about girl friends at the break-up of one of their practices: "If it doesn't look like a ball, don't go out with it." The sentence became a legend, but nobody laughed. To many in a spot like that he would come across as much tougher-hided than he really was, on account of the perfunctory way he had with words (matched by his small handwriting — an unwillingness to waste air or tabular space). If you didn't know him, you could be at a loss as to how to take him, what with that graininess natural to his voice, seeming to mean all business.

Between halves in the locker room this gave him an air of authority, his voice edged with an assumption left unsaid: that here in this room were ball players who had mentally (if they were losing) let opponents get the better of them. "What these two backcourt men are doing is this," my father might start off, never impressed by what might have been superior or even phenomenal performances by the opposition. His teams would more often be ahead than behind at halftime, but his standard demeanor regardless of score would be one bordering on reprimand for lapses in concentration. "That time" or "That play where, Bobby, you took one dribble too many" would mark the start of a corrective, and with no further reference my father would assume that the play in question was recallable to all fifteen listeners in the locker room.

Toward the end of a halftime break he would almost invariably wind up on the note that "The first five minutes of this second half are going to tell the story of this ball game." It was an axiom with him that you had to go back out mentally as though you were behind. "Fifteen points behind" was his rule of thumb — his starters were to play as if that were the situation. Cracking down in those first five minutes would be the decider on whether those in the room would be in for "an easy ball game" or would have to fight the thing down to the end. Easy games were what he was after (if exciting ones turned up it was with small welcome), so charging up his players wasn't kept first in mind. Once he cleared his throat between halves, it wasn't a group appeal he was about to go into anyhow. It was more like a putting-on-mettle of individuals. It went without saying that they were thinking only of team output. That anyone ever had a points-per-game average he might be privately ruminating was the kind of thought that would not cross my father's mind. The foul situation and how many time-outs remained — figures of that sort he kept a lock on; otherwise he wouldn't dream of making adjustments because of statistics, or because it might have come to him between the halves that someone's ego needed assuaging.

A game sticks in my mind in which he departed from his halftime routine. It was early in the 1947-48 season, his second and last year with the Celtics — they were to finish third and make the playoffs, but be knocked out by Chicago, marking the end of my father's job at Boston.

His chances to develop a real contender there had been hurt by conflicting loyalties. He had signed on with the Celtics, after the organization of the NBA, in July of 1946, while he was managing the Rutland baseball team in the Northern League. This was a summer league not affiliated with organized ball, so that college players could participate. There were plenty of professionals on the rosters, including some just back from the ruined Mexican League. Managing the Rutland club was natural for my father, who had coached baseball at Manhattan that year, and who had been a Northern League umpire for several summers before then.

Signing with the Celtics created a dilemma, because he knew he had to go out immediately and get ball players; but that would have meant dropping the Rutland job in mid-season. When he decided not to do this, and stick out the last month of baseball, the results were disastrous. He'd let his rival coaches get an important jump on him. Very much the result of this one-month postponement, he collected a last-place team for Boston. One major player he had been after was Ed Sadowski, who had played for him at Seton Hall and was in 1946 the biggest basketball player in the country. (Shorter than Mikan and Kurland; but Sadowski outweighed both of them.) Over the past years Ed had become a top professional center, leading his National League club, the Fort Wayne Zollners, to three straight championships in the annual pro tournament at Chicago (an event I'll mention again: my father had connections with it). Ed was a scorer — his hook shot as tough to defend against as Mikan's, considering how broad Ed was — but there was another reason to want him for the new Boston franchise. If Mikan looked like Clark Kent, Sadowski resembled a wrestler much in the papers in those days, the Swedish Angel. At 6'6" Ed was easily as formidable as the Angel, and in opponents' arenas often seemed put in the role of the "heavy." This made him a drawing card, in fact the leading attraction in the new pro league, which was a reason my father failed to get him. He thought he had lined Ed up for the Celtics, but Toronto hired him as playing coach and came up with $10,000 as well, the highest salary in the NBA. Most rankling of all, when Ed took that offer he also took to Toronto some players my father thought were already his (including another Setonian, Mike McCarron). Over the telephone he'd received some half-promises but, remaining in Rutland, he hadn't really gotten to those players with pen and ink and so lost the nucleus of the squad he was aiming to have represent Boston.

Queerly enough, Sadowski was wearing Celtic green by the next season — my father drafted him after the Toronto franchise collapsed. So he figures in the halftime story I am about to tell, as one of those blocking the door at the end. (I can hear my father mutter, "He blocked a lot of things that year," for the two of them now couldn't get along.) Another player new to the Celtics had joined them on account of that Northern League baseball season. This was Ed Ehlers of Purdue, the league's best hitter, whom my father got to know as a basketball prospect. Here was an odd repayment, as I sometimes feel it should be put, for staying on with the minor baseball job: he got an inside track on Ehlers, and was able to sign him for the Celtics' 1947-48 season.

Ed Sadowski and Ed Ehlers were two different types of basketball player, signaling the transition that was underway as a result of the formation of the new basketball league. You could almost feel the floor shake when Sadowski came down to take his pivot spot, from where he would spin methodically and deliver his flat-arched hook shot against the glass. Like an engine with a governor, Sadowski could be counted on for game-by-game production, and was the Celtics' mainstay, picked as the all-league center that year. (The team had a small-package version of Sadowski playing in the opposite frontcourt, Mel Riebe. He and Ed had flattish feet, prominent stomachs, and very white legs — both played with their backs to the basket.) Ed Ehlers, on the other hand, coming out of the free-lance college game, played in overdrive, all over the court, and his style was made for the big arenas in which the new pro league was operating. Actually the sport was attracting college players *en masse* for the first time, because the big halls promised salaries competitive at last with what other sports offered. And as the NBA had shrunk its number of franchises, talent was on the market. My father, like the other coaches, brought in newly graduated players plus draftees from the defunct clubs: he and the league were putting adversity behind them and readying for a second round.

Thus he was able to indulge a coach's dream: he worked up a two-team system. At least this was the way the Celtics began to practice in the old Boston Arena. High above its practice floor my father had an office where he slept on a cot: he had not moved our family to Boston, knowing his chances of staying were slim after the previous year's finish. Nevertheless, he went blithely into his experiment with his two squads.

One of the teams the Celtics fielded was a group of old pros, built around Sadowski at the pivot with Dutch Garfinkel controlling the ball in the backcourt. Later in the year, with the acquisition of Mike Bloom from the Baltimore Bullets, the team more or less jelled into an old-world style of play, featuring plenty of pushing and pulling and a slowly revolving offense. But in the beginning my father tried to alternate between this style and a wide-open game suited better to his rookies and second-year men.

It is curious that I misremember this other five, in that I

tend to put Kevin Connors among them. Connors did play for Boston in the team's first year; but by that time he'd become known as Chuck Connors. To our family, though, he was Kevin — going back to his Seton Hall days. For he, like Sadowski, had played there before the war. To the question, "Who was your best discovery?" my father had an adroit answer, which couldn't offend any of the top-drawer athletes he developed. He used to say, "Kevin Connors. Who else played two sports in the major leagues and then made good in the movies?" But in another mood, say when Kevin was responsible for a lost game in St. Louis and my father saw him reading *Twelfth Night* afterwards in the hotel, the budding actor didn't draw such happy comments. "This guy loses me ball game after ball game," my father is supposed to have raged out, "and he sits here reading Shakespeare." ("Twelfth Night," I can hear him grumble. The dialogue comes from *It's the Final Score That Counts*, Zander Hollander's book on sports figures who went on to other limelight careers, like Dr. Spock and Whizzer White — and the phrasing does sound authentic.) For reasons perhaps of art, Kevin didn't last twelve nights on the roster of the new Celtics. I tend to misalign him with the '47-48 team because of baseball.

Kevin was in the Dodgers' organization in those years, and always talked baseball. Since Ed Ehlers always did too, I tend to remember them as a pair of hot-stove leaguers, never away from the subject through a whole five-month basketball season. This was wrong, but probably triggered by an unerasable memory I have of Connors — as a man bedeviled by Jackie Robinson.

An odd name perhaps to connect with the practice gym at the Boston Arena, during training camp in October 1947. But many people forget that when Jackie Robinson broke the color line that summer, going from Montreal to Brooklyn, it was not to play his regular position. Instead he played first base. Kevin had learned at the Celtic tryouts that he'd be moving to Montreal himself the following season. But first base at

Brooklyn was blocked for him. (When Kevin did get to the majors, it was Chicago he played for.) So at the Arena one day when I was there, Kevin in a sweatsuit came running over to a bench where Ehlers and some others were sitting. He had a first-baseman's mitt on and a bright new basketball under his arm. When he reached the bench he gave a sort of torquewise jump enabling him to flip the basketball up into the air. He'd come down in the position of a first baseman stretching for a throw, grimacing at his friends as the ball fell in the glove. He looked like an accordion gone beyond its limit: six and a half feet of grey sweatsuit with a death's-head glaring out of it. The others were already laughing and would have continued no matter what he said, but he really broke them apart when he came out with his punch line: "*The new white hope.*"

Connors the deferred white hope did not last with the second edition of the Celtics. The four I place with him were Ehlers, Gene Stump, George Munroe, and Cecil Hankins, all recently out of college, though Munroe and Hankins had played in the league the year before.

The game I have in mind took place in Providence about a month after the Connors incident: I remember its being cold, and in that hockey town they laid the boards for the basketball court on top of their ice; they did not drain the rink. Also Providence was one of the weaker NBA teams, so if my father was to start his junior group, or else substitute wholesale with them, it would make sense that he'd try his two-team ploy in Providence. In any case the backup team was in there, early in the first quarter. This group was close in age to me, and I had made some friends, particularly with Gene Stump.

As a regular for DePaul on the Mikan teams, Stump had had to give up all kinds of headlines to the big man. But there was one thing he had in common with George Mikan — both wore glasses. And as it happened, during the '47-48 season players were trying out contact lenses.

On the Celtics, Stump played with contact lenses; by

coincidence, so did Ehlers and Munroe. These three always s 
next to one another; they'd have a row of small bottles on a towel and shared a little tilting mirror for putting in their cup-shaped lenses. Munroe had graduated at the top of his class from Dartmouth and later became a Rhodes scholar. In 1942 and 1943 he had almost single-handedly accounted for Dartmouth victories over Seton Hall. A well-hated adversary then, he was mild mannered, a student at Harvard Law School, and the most philosophical of those Celtics. The three of them made a tableau, not unlike the see-no-evil monkeys, blown up to life size in Celtics uniforms, about whom the other players cracked jokes every suiting-up. As basketball players they were runners, fast. Shock troops — and another one teamed up with them was Cecil Hankins, the fastest man in the league; ironically, he drove so hard on layups that he often had trouble scoring underneath. Hankins, who came to the Celtics by way of the St. Louis Bombers, a collapsed franchise, had been the number two player at Oklahoma A & M on the Kurland teams, just as Stump had been for DePaul. They'd even guarded each other in that wartime Red Cross game I'd seen at the Garden, and were the MVPs of their teams. Another case of my father and his second mainstays? Maybe not, but here they were competing on his backup team, which he decided to use as a unit that afternoon in Providence.

    Put in in the first quarter, they added to the lead and all seemed well; then suddenly their playing broke down and Providence started scoring, building up enough of a spread for my father to have to abandon his strategy. Before the period was over the whole "pro" team was in and had begun chipping away at the lead, closing to within a few points by the half; my father made no substitutions from the younger group during this time. It looked as if understudy status was in store for them from here on. At the half the team came into the dressing room, the younger players filing in first and looking for the far corners, the others grousing, talking up the recent floor play. The regulars took seats on chairs near the door, reached for towels, remained more or less semi-circular as a unit, faced toward a portable backboard, and my father came in. He was glowering. He called out his ritual first question, "What are the fouls?" and got answered by the equipment manager.

My feeling for the younger players made me dislike his mood, and I got further downcast when he made no reference to the start of the game. He began saying specific things to the individuals in the semi-circle, making one of them stand up so he could demonstrate a pick-and-roll play Providence was using and how to combat it. This incidentally happened often between halves; that is, a physical demonstration of one of his defensive maneuvers, right when it needed teaching. He had more of them than anyone I've ever seen — in this case the Boston guard being blocked was told to ram his elbow into the stomach of the opponent picking him off, and use this leverage to whip himself around and beat that man who'd be rolling to the basket.

It was natural for the Sadowski-Garfinkel group to listen along in what (to me) seemed a very usurpative way. Munroe and Stump and Ehlers were all sitting back out of the light, probably feeling numb in the legs after sitting on top of that ice for so long — certainly despondent and paying less and less attention as my father's directions got more and more detailed. Of course they couldn't sprawl, or look inattentive. They just kept their heads down, and my sense of how my father had written them off was making me seethe, except it seemed all so foregone and, admittedly, earned. But what he was doing to their morale, so I thought, was pretty unjustified.

All new defensive assignments were now clear with the Sadowski squad, and the warning knock came telling us five minutes. Sitting on a trunk in a corner, I'd seen my father only in profile all this time, as had the non-starters nearby. They began stirring, I got up, the big men from the "pro" squad were already moving toward the door when my father said something, turning inwards to the room, that made everyone stop. Except for one phrase, I remember mostly the timbre of his words. He was looking at the subs who had played in the first quarter, to whom he had said not a blessed word at halftime. He said something like, "What in the name of God are you stalling around back there for. You're starting this half. Take your eighteen eyes and get out on the damned court. Get the hell out of here and win the game, for God's sake. Get off your tails, get out of here, get up on the court."

They yelled, they were already running, even Munroe was yelling, thumping on a green sweatjacket ahead of him, there was plenty of commotion because the exit was narrow and these ex-wallflowers were fighting past everything, all the beef up in front, to get out and win, no circulation problem now, and win they did. Whether they played every minute of the second half intact I don't remember — they well may have. Stump played a longer game only once, later on at New York, when he went the whole 48 minutes. Win though they did, the two-team system was consigned to the lumber room soon enough. That was not what my father gained that night. Ideal arrangements, long-range plans, don't work out for coaches; the problem of here-and-now remains the test after all. Just when he decided on his psychological ruse — before he came into the room, at some point during the directions to the others, or at the moment of swerving itself — is less important than the fact that somehow a departure from regimen was called for, resulting in an anti-strategy that, not so incidentally, foiled me once more from thinking I knew his ways.

Drawing poorly and never able to get out of third place that season, the Celtics would give my father only one chance to retain his job, and that was by doing well in the playoffs. Throughout the season he was more or less embattled with Sadowski, up among the league's top scorers. Dutch Garfinkel, who became the team leader, was making good passes to

Sadowski, but plays off the pivot were not being made, and my father — later Garfinkel — became convinced Sadowski was playing for himself. The fact that Sadowski had been player-coach the year before at Toronto was the real thorn. The idea began to grow in my father's mind that Ed wanted his job.

An observer had no way of being anything but neutral on the issue. The most painful thing was the fact that Sadowski was the first outstanding college player my father had developed — they'd always been paired up as winners, and now with each loss my father could feel another nail being galvanized for his coffin. Once I saw him, upstairs in the Arena, confront Sadowski — saw but did not hear them, a dumbshow behind plate glass, and they almost came to blows. (I have never seen my father swing his fist.) The problem was, it was too easy to see a momentary bad play in the wrong light, as selfish or worse. But what then about the enormous amount of hard effort also turned in by Sadowski? One fact can be stated — when my father was replaced, Sadowski was not the man (it was Doggie Julian of Holy Cross), and the two became friends again in later years.

Near the end of the season, Garfinkel got into a slanging match with Sadowski which, by bringing the disharmony to a head, appeared to dispel it. When the playoffs came around, set to commence in Chicago, it seemed a tonic had been administered to the ball club. They had a deep liking for my father, there was no question of that, and it showed in the way they were to play a stronger Chicago club even.

Though they didn't actually *go* to Chicago. For in the NBA's western division there had been a three-way tie for second, and by the time extra games could decide who was to play whom in the east, the Chicago Stadium was booked and unable to accommodate its home team. Consequently the Stags had to come to the Boston Arena for the three-game playoff.

Because the first game of the series was played on a weekend, I hitchhiked over from college to see it. Boston lost.

This made the mid-week telephone call that would be coming in, down the hall in the dorm where I lived, the crucial one of all the calls my family waited up for, together or scattered as we might have been during those two Celtics years. We hung by the phone on game nights because you couldn't ever be sure NBA scores would come over on the late news. So my father always called; and this week it was clear his job was on the line. It wasn't that losing the job meant catastrophe; only that, successful as he had been at college, we knew how much he loved coaching in the pro game. He had quit playing himself only two years before. Now he was, as he always said, in on the ground floor of something that was no longer makeshift. Though the NBA had been in jeopardy, it showed signs in this second season of having dug in to survive; still this Boston franchise needed playoff wins to produce crowd interest. If the team didn't come through in the playoffs, there would be a coaching change. All this was understood in my family — even by my twelve-year-old sister. Telephone calls from Boston were always tense — a win of course the big thing, but crowd size important too. If we were together and my mother was taking the call, she would pass the game's result to us before saying anything back to my father at the other end. When it was bad news she would say "They lost." My father's words, invariably though, would have been different: "We got beat."

These were the words to be feared that night over the line. But he didn't have to say them: he'd beaten Chicago in the second game, so there was another to go, on the weekend: a reprieve, though short-lived.

Prior to the finale a Boston reporter had written that the Celtics were "doing a good turn for their adversaries" by giving Stags' guard Andy Phillip heat treatment for his injured left leg. How much of a good turn, considering what Andy Phillip had done in the opening game, can hardly be overstated. Phillip in college had been the most famous of the Illinois "Whiz Kids." He was so well respected — and precocious — that by the age of forty he was in the Hall of Fame, the second youngest man ever elected. Not spectacular as a pro, he was the kind of expressionless, rise-to-the-occasion ball player right after my father's heart. This esteem, though, Phillip had had to earn. Ehlers and Stump, from the same section of the country, were wild about him, but rookies' opinions didn't count for much. My father was dubious about players bearing tags like "Whiz Kids" — particularly when they came from the west. But a couple of looks at Phillip in the regular season had made him a convert. So much so, that what he tried to do about Phillip in the first playoff game at Boston tells a great deal about his perceptions as a coach. For one of the hardest things about coaching is to know why you are winning or losing, that is, consistently know, almost second by second. You may be unable to do anything about losing, but the measures you take will be in the direction of this dead-certain knowledge. My father's ex-players had almost a kind of awe about the grasp he had of court action, and his ability to make adjustments — or at least give cautions, since adjustments in sports cannot of course always be carried out. Near the end of this opening playoff game, he was ahead and had things going pretty much his way. That was how it looked to me, sitting alongside him, figuring him calm as ever, knowing how to hold the lead he'd created. And it wasn't the case at all. (By the third game, the entire public could anticipate what only he had understood, for 44 nerve-wracking minutes on the night the first game was played.)

On the Stags' bench, Phillip had remained a spectator, nursing his leg injury. As a first-year player, he was frequently used as sixth man. A playmaker mainly, he had extraordinary court sense, and was more dangerous as a scorer when crucial points were needed. Just inside the last four minutes, a Chicago regular committed a foul. I felt good about that, more so when the Stags' coach Harold Olsen only a scorer's table away was up on his feet protesting. But then I saw my father throw his hands to his head as in despair. It was difficult to take in the sequence of all that followed. The scorers were indicating this was the player's disqualifying foul. But Olsen in no time was at the table maintaining his player had another foul coming. With five fingers thrust out in front of him, he fumed that this wasn't the sixth. Behind him Andy Phillip was getting up off the bench and stripping off his jacket to come into the game. All of a sudden my father reached past me and grabbed the equipment manager's clipboard from him. Then with an intensely sober look on his face he joined Mr. Olsen in front of the official scorer. The manager followed him to the table, but was met with a stiff arm from my father. And now, to my amazement, here was my own father backing up the argument of a visitor. He was confirming that by Boston's own figures, Olsen was right and the Chicago player could stay in the game.

The equipment manager came down along the sidelines in an injured way and sat down next to me. "Your father's screwed it all up," he said. "We've got it down as the sixth foul. What the hell is he telling them five for?" I didn't know, but he was certainly being a good sport, and seemed in fact to have moderated the situation. He and Olsen were talking like a couple of friendly doormen, only it looked like Olsen's turn had come to be accommodating. Now, *he* was willing to concede. What the official scorer had said would have to stand. This was the view taken by the referees, who were in the middle of it by now. Nonetheless my father kept insisting that, since his and Olsen's tabulations agreed, the scorer must have been at fault and the player need not come out.

Meanwhile, at the referees' direction, out came the offending player and in came sixth-man Phillip. A time-out was called, my father's bearing changed. In the huddle he was all business again about what was coming up next. The magnanimous interlude, or whatever it may have been, was over, and I was left at a loss.

The score was 66-61 Boston. When our man missed the foul shot we had coming, Chicago came up the court and scored —

*Phillip* scored — and on the next transition Phillip intercepted a pass and scored again. In a matter of minutes it was 71-66 Chicago. All ten of those turnaround points were scored by Phillip. They meant the ball game. The margin of the final score, 79-72, had been dictated by his stepping onto the court.

In the wake of that exploit, it *was* sporting of the Boston trainers to supply Andy Phillip with whirlpool treatments. As for the discussion at the scorer's table which I hadn't been able to fathom — my father said to some well-wishers later that night, "I saw the whole ball game going out the window when Phillip got up off the bench. It looked like we had it, but only if Olsen wouldn't think about going to the guy with that bum leg of his." Then, as he saw Phillip getting his sweatclothes off — the one thing he'd been dreading — he grasped that Olsen was protesting the foul count. His chance came to him in a flash. That was when he went over to put on his good-sport act. I still see him with the clipboard under his arm, palms down on the scoring table, telling the scorer how he shared Olsen's view.

When the substitution was made he dealt with the team as was required, with an eye still to winning. Andy Phillip would need some luck — but somehow would force the breaks that bring it, or so my father must have thought as he saw his clairvoyance pan out, and had to watch that first playoff contest slip away.

Boston won the second game, 81-78. (Phillip hardly played.) On the day of the third, a local writer asked: "Are the Celtics showing that old college try against the Chicago Stags in a desperate effort to save Honey Russell's job?" It was a relevant question. They had the lead at the half, 40-37. But Phillip came in as a starter for the second half. He turned this game around too, scoring most of his 15 points that third quarter. Here was one game which writers, spectators, everybody must have felt was decided once that clutch performer got into it, and my father's major league coaching career with it. Later that night my father was affably fired by Walter Brown. Both understood

*The Second Boston Celtics.* Photographed before the Chicago playoff series, 1948. Front row, from left: Stan Noszka, Mike Bloom, Ed Sadowski, Art Spector, Gene Stump; back row, team trainer, Dutch Garfinkel, George Munroe, Mel Riebe, Saul Mariaschin, HR. Mike Bloom's shoes show he was a late acquisition. (Ed Ehlers, not in picture, was injured and missed the series; Cecil Hankins had gone in a trade for Noszka.)

*Illinois Collegians.* Left, the DePaul team of 1945, George Mikan at top, Gene Stump next down. Others: Ed Kachan, Jack Allen, Ernie DiBenedetto. Right, Andy Phillip of Illinois: the opponent most responsible for HR's loss of the job at Boston.

the necessity. He would be paid next season for the last year of his three-year contract, and he and Brown continued on as close friends.

In later years, my father tended to fuse the first and third games of his watershed series with the Stags into "that time when Miasek fouled out and Olsen had to put Phillip into the game." It was as though, for the whole series, a function of his coaching was to send telepathic beams over to the other man's bench, to try to keep that one player on it.

That he'd remember the name of the man who fouled out — Stan Miasek, only marginally figuring in the episode — was also characteristic of my father, whose recountings from the past were always accurate, at least with respect to proper names. I only know of one instance to the contrary. It had to do with a different watershed situation — not his own this time. The coaching job at Boston was in fact the only position he ever lost. He'd changed managing jobs pretty regularly in the years before, but mainly because the American League franchises were so uncertain. We even had whole sets of spare uniforms in our basement, mostly reds and yellows as I recall (yellow useful at home or on the road), in the event some eastern town wanted to fill in for a failed AL franchise part-way through a season.

The flagrant situation my father used to recall, in which he got a name wrong, had to do with Kevin Connors breaking into the American League. (The wartime one: the original American League of my father's peak years was a truly major league of NBA caliber.) As I said before, managers couldn't be sure of their rosters in those lean times. Players were not on contract ordinarily, and during the war years — when my father coached clubs variously located in Camden, Brooklyn, and Trenton — availability of players sometimes depended on their military situation. In the case of Connors, who had gone into the army from Seton Hall and was stationed as a tank instructor at West Point, the Brooklyn Indians in 1943 could get his services for weekend games.

My father did not play him in the opening half the first night he reported, but being the club's tallest man, he was told to keep an eye on the opposing center from Trenton. This was Mike Bloom, the league standout whom I mentioned before as a latecomer to the Celtics. Bloom, though 6'6", rarely played the pivot. Instead, he would maneuver from the corner to the top of the circle, from where he could make over-the-head two-hand set shots. Play him close and he would drive by you. My father figured Connors would not be able to handle Bloom.

There was an expedient open to him, considering that Bloom was a slick rather than tough offensive player. Connors at Seton Hall had been a scrupulously clean player. My father decided to overlook this: he would take advantage of Kevin's first pro appearance and send out a tiger. (A watershed occasion all right: Bloom to weep the tears.)

It was after the between-halves talk was over that my father took Connors aside and told him he'd be starting the second half at center. "You've been watching Bloom all along, right?"

"Right."

"Stick everything you've seen up your ass." Connors did a double-take. He might have run into a tank trap. My father had cleared the ground for unexpected instructions.

He told Connors to wallop Bloom at the opening center tap. Connors said, "What?" "Hit him. I want you to belt him. Don't bother about the tap, you can't outjump him. When the ball goes up sock him on the jaw."

Connors told my father he had never hit anyone like that, and my father said something to the effect of, "Kevin, if you don't do it you won't be back with this club next week."

The idea of course was to get Bloom worried. Bloom didn't know Connors and would presume he had a madman on his hands. In theory Connors should be able to threaten him for the rest of the game, get him thinking about defending himself rather than into the rhythm of play.

Connors wanted to play more than a single professional game. So he did it. Bloom went down. From the floor he had an incredulous, indignant look on his face. He whined all the way to the foul line (the foul of course conceded). Not only did the strategy work, but Connors utterly seemed to find himself in that game. It was like coming through a baptism. A die was cast, a mould taken that looked to be permanent. Connors' own words about the incident were, "I did exactly what Honey said and for the next couple of years Mike Bloom was my patsy except for a couple of games." I particularly like "except for a couple of games." Those instructions had given Kevin an edge, but it was not one that could be counted on *every* time the two paired off.

My father loved to tell this yarn. He always followed it up with a sequel, a mixture of truth and invention. It was his one story to my knowledge where the name of the main actor wasn't right. ("I don't even remember Herlihy," Connors was to reply about this, "but do remind you that like all ex-jocks, your father would pad a story for after dinner speeches and as time passed the exaggerations would become facts in his mind.") The following week, supposedly, Brooklyn was playing a team whose center was Pat Herlihy. As my father told the story, "Herlihy was no threat. He was in there to get them the tap. Once they had the ball he stayed out of the way. He was not the kind of guy you wanted to wake up." (All this was true of the original Herlihy, a rebounder for the old Kate Smith Celtics, who had, so far as I can gather, retired just the season before this. He had the perfect bouncer's name, plus the right build for this story.)

The new-found Connors came down the next week from West Point, walked confidently out to the center circle where he met Herlihy, up went the ball, and — to my father's amazement — Connors belted Herlihy.

My father would always pause at this juncture in the story. Then, in unvarying words, he would turn it all bleak with

"Herlihy didn't go down." Everybody listening would know what Connors would be in for. If anything it was re-baptism. Herlihy's surprise was followed by his methodical righting of the wrong. At the half Connors came off the floor a beaten man. "What in the name of God," said my father in the locker room, "possessed you to hit *him*?"

"You told me to, Honey."

"Christ, Kevin," my father said, "that was last week."

Possibly because of some bygone event involving Pat Herlihy, my father imported his name to this story, but the incident wasn't entirely apocryphal. Exactly a week after the Trenton-Brooklyn game, Connors did hit a hatchet man. It was Irv Torgoff of Philadelphia. His name too would have made the story go — perhaps with a Russian flavor — he too was "no threat," but my father didn't have the foresight to see that he'd better warn Connors which opponents not to slug once he'd got him started down that path. In any case he'd sent out a tiger unbeknownst this second time, and had a tale of assault and battery to tell as a result, right name or wrong.

That Connors was not permanently deflated by his going-over could be proved by any number of his antics in his year with the Celtics — his breaking of the backboard on opening night warmup in the Boston Arena, for instance. He was showboating and smacked the glass on one of his layups, smashing it. "It went all milky," my father said, "and fell out in a thousand pieces." A replacement had to be sent for at the Boston Garden where there was a rodeo going on. The Garden backboards were stored behind the Brahma bull pens, and a whole lot of cattle had to be moved before they could be reached. (Speaking of cattle — when the Celtics were changing trains at Buffalo one day, Connors whiled away the time by climbing onto the bronze bison in Buffalo station and breaking its tail off. My father, traveling by a later train, was met by the team and told he'd have to go and get Connors out of the lockup.) Times were different in 1946 when Kevin smashed the backboard — he didn't get a standing ovation as he would today. The capacity house at the Arena had dwindled to almost nothing when the game was finally played — against Chicago of all teams — and lost by two points. A bad omen unquestionably. Every ball player has probably at some point cost his team a game — not many could match Connors in costing a new franchise its opening-night audience.

It would not do to overstate the flagrant nature of play in the earlier pro leagues. To be told to start out with a punch might sooner or later have become obligatory, in the fashion of Connors the Rifleman being required to throw punches. (A similar instruction had once been given to my father when he was starting out, as I'll mention later.) Meanwhile, grudges and vendettas would hardly be the end result of a planned aberration like this. That would be especially true of those wartime days, when team rivalries and league standings were hardly ever of great import. It was showing up and getting bread-and-butter money for individual games that mattered. Players were paid off right after their showers in dollar bills, and rosters shifted so frequently that there was hardly any occasion for really heated personal rivalries to develop. Effects of foul play tended to wear off — it wasn't all that "foul," perhaps even having a ceremonial quality to it, indicating seniority or "territorial rights." If a newcomer tried to take a certain spot on the floor, say, he might get the kind of shove that wouldn't be in order for some other place. In the Mike Bloom incident, my father was just trying to rush Connors' education a little, figuring he could steal a win maybe that one time.

By the arrival of these mid-war years my father had put in seven years at Seton Hall, and he was partial to his former players, who after all had been drilled to be pretty much professional types. He would often be after Sadowski and Connors (the two biggest men he had yet recruited), so that one even replaced the other as center for the Celtics. Ordinarily, the presence of Sadowski meant wins, that of Connors, losses. Quite apart from the problem of players moving around in the armed services, over the years 1939-1946 there was one other phenomenon in pro basketball that made for all the roster-shuffling that went on. This was the post-season tournament to determine a professional world's champion. It was held in late March in Chicago; but once it had caught on, other cities would sometimes sponsor a tournament before Chicago, billed likewise as the world championship. This went down fine for players and coaches, naturally eager for the extra prize money. The Chicago promoters didn't really disapprove of their rivals' gun-jumping — they could publicize their own tournament with the help of any that cared to run before it, just as in college the NCAA tourney obligingly followed the NIT, neither claiming it had corralled the nation's best. There was no unnatural frenzy about being "number one."

The rationale for a late-season pro competition was the glut of teams and leagues around the country. The National League had been established in 1938, the year before the first Chicago tourney; it in the west and the American League in the east contended for talent, but there were others too, soon augmented by the service leagues themselves. Then there were some strong teams sponsored by companies, plus the ever-active independent Negro teams. (Of these, the Renaissance, the Globe Trotters, and the Washington Bears were winners of three of the eight Chicago tourneys.)

In one way or another, my father participated in these post-season competitions — once even as a referee! The peculiar thing was, he would most often be taking an assemblage to Chicago that had had no actual status up to the time of the tournament. For example, "Honey Russell's New York Yankees" entered the first one, in 1939 — but there was no such team — they were an amalgam from the American League. They kicked off the whole thing, in fact. The *Sunday Tribune* announced, "The first annual $10,000 world championship professional basketball tournament opens this afternoon ... with John (Honey) Russell's New York Yankees playing the

bearded House of David five in the first game starting at 2 p.m."
His team got past the House of David, only to lose in the next
round to the Renaissance, the eventual champions. It was the
second time the "Yankees" had to play that day, which might
have hurt.

The only tournament of that sort which my father won was
held in Worcester in 1943, a couple of weeks before the Chicago
event. The team was billed as the Wilmington Clippers but
made up mostly of my father's Brooklyn Indians who had
finished their American League season. This Worcester
championship was a bonafide one, with my father having to
beat the Detroit Eagles and the Renaissance to capture it. The
prize money was the same as in Chicago. "We — my
Wilmington Clippers and I — we beat the Rens in the final game
by four points and they get $800 and we got $1,500." So my
father told a reporter in a joking interview when he got home.
"Me, I got a kid named Sadowski, and a kid named Mac
Kinsbrunner" — the reason he's calling these veterans kids is
that the reporter has been needling him about playing himself at
age 40 in this young man's sport. But as a Worcester paper said,
he did lead the team, "from the bench, and on the court too."
Meanwhile the columnist home in Brooklyn made stock out of
my father's story of the Worcester stands falling down. He took
down the following dialogue:

"Just about this time the stands collapse," Russell laughs, "and 10,
12 people are hurt — "

I tell him not to laugh, that it is hard luck for the promoter, with
law suits and all —

"That shows how little you know," Honey says. "The story of the
seats collapsing hits the front page of the Worcester papers that first
day, and it attracts so much attention the place is jammed for the rest of
the tournament, and the promoter makes a hatful of dough!"

Maybe he sounds too light-hearted here, but in those days a
guarantee wasn't always a guarantee. This time the winners
were paid in full. A local paper recorded the key play in the final

game: "Ed Sadowski, Wilmington's big center, tapped in a basket in the early minutes of the second half that put the Clippers out in front by 22-21 and ended 25 minutes of struggle in which the lead changed hands with each succeeding goal." From there on the small lead held up, enabling the aging player-coach and his crew to collect their double money.

Two years later, the beginning of my father's grumpiness over his meal-ticket center can be spotted. For once again he thought he had Sadowski sewn up to an agreement. This was for an entry in the Chicago tourney that was to go by the queer name of Newark C-O-Two. First prize had been upped to $2,000 by now, and, raiding the eastern teams he had just finished coaching against, my father thought he had put together a winner for the 1945 tournament. He even brought my mother and me out to Chicago for this one.

To say he "raided" his own league is putting it mildly, since in forming his team he had to interrupt the American League's 1945 playoff series. "I just borrowed a few guys" — these being the mainstays of the Trenton Tigers smack in the middle of their playoff with Baltimore. But Chicago meant opportunity, worth causing other people's schedulings to be tampered with. Underneath, there was a sort of Big East mentality to this. My father figured to win this tournament with the help of the Trenton players, whom he'd just had suits made for by a carbon dioxide company. No matter if Baltimore had to wait for its shanghaied opponents to return. Eastern prestige was the reason the *Sun* wasn't peeved over a playoff cancelled in its backyard. The Baltimore paper wished the Trenton players well: "Playing as the C-O-Two team from Newark, the Tigers will represent the American League against 14 of the best pro quintets in the nation."

I remember the train we rode out to Chicago: the *Trail Blazer*. In those days trains had a mystique about them, and on the *Trail Blazer's* seats there were little booklets describing its speed, the new-model reclining seats, and the menu. Talk about

*Kevin Connors,* 1945. Before the Chicago Tribune pro tournament of 1945. Kevin replaced Ed Sadowski in the center slot for the Newark C-O-Twos.

*With Gene Autry.* On the eve of the Celtics' opening game, November 1946. Autry was not yet the backer of pro sports he would later become. He was in Boston for the rodeo, at the time when the spare basket had to be got from the Brahma bull pens, after Connors had wrecked the Boston Arena backboard.

traveling on a mealticket — we were anything but rich and I wasn't used to lavishness. I was sixteen and maybe most excited because of returning to the city where I was born. But also, in a time of war rations, I ate my first shrimp cocktail on that ride and got sick after a dozen such consumed during the stay in Chicago. Nor were they spread over any time to speak of, since my father's script went badly wrong. His C-O-Two team didn't blaze anything like the trail expected of them, and we were shortly headed back on a different train. There was a personnel shake-up responsible for this — a late roster change. (Besides, CO2 is known for putting blazes out.)

C-O-Two was a company, much expanded in wartime, which had hired my father for morale purposes, to help combat absenteeism — a normal war job for an athlete. He persuaded them to promote this entry for the tournament — it would give the company good publicity — and stocked it mainly with these Trenton players. The Chicago *Herald American* gave the club an excellent chance — "eastern basketball will offer its strongest bid for world supremacy," it said, "through the medium of a newcomer to the great cage show — the Newark C-O-Twos." But there was an ominous note. Coach Honey Russell, the paper went on, had expected an ex-product of his to join the squad: that old stand-in for the Swedish Angel, Ed Sadowski. "But Sadowski joined the reigning champion Fort Wayne Zollners."

Who won the '45 title? The Fort Wayne Zollners. Who was the tournament's top player? Sadowski. With whom did my father replace him on the C-O-Two roster? With Kevin Connors of Wilmington. How far did the C-O-Twos progress? Not past the first round, bumped out by the Pittsburgh Raiders. So much for war-work, my father might have said.

How much of an albatross was Chuck Connors, really? I've exaggerated that side of him because my father always throve on the magnified view. ("I made a millionaire out of him," he told one newspaperman, "and he made a pauper out of me.") When the war ended and the next season rolled around — with plans for a new major league already in the wind — my father had a chance to take a kind of Ancient Mariner's final bow. For once the albatross didn't prove lethal.

He was now coach at Manhattan College, but as usual had by October brought together a group for what would be his last American League season — at this point they were called the Jersey Reds. (They had red uniforms, but no particular town to sponsor them; when none was forthcoming, he wound up coaching the Trenton Tigers.) This was to be his 28th and last year as a pro player. Once the season had begun in earnest, and he was dividing his time between Trenton and Manhattan — with so much practice time consumed by the latter job — he seldom put himself into a lineup, unless the team was short-handed. But in October, when he was getting his not-to-be-launched Jersey Reds into being, he happened to play his final memorable game. I had the good luck to be there.

This was the one full-scale game I saw my father play when old enough myself (a high-school senior) to know the sport well. I'd seen him scrimmage, or put himself in as a substitute, any number of times, and of course had been taken to games when I was a boy and he was in his prime. But then I didn't understand what was going on. (I can remember my mother screaming "Underneath!" because my father as a cutter was getting free and nobody was getting him the ball — that kind of thing.) But in this October 1945 game, which he played in the backcourt just about the whole way, I knew what I was watching, and it was edifying.

It took place at Saugerties — the Jersey Reds against the Brooklyn Visitations — an exhibition game, scheduled to test whether American League ball might "take" again in the Kingston area (once a hotbed of basketball, where my father had played many games when he was starting out).

This Saturday, having only a six-man squad, he put himself in early: hit the first shot he took: and remained in the rest of the way. The game was played in the old-pro style dominant even up to that year — the ball moved a lot, without a great number of shots taken. What surprised me was how much my father's movements on offense set the tempo of action for his side, even though he rarely moved further in than the foul circle. Reading of his early days in my mother's scrapbook, I knew he'd excelled as a cutter and driver, but had never caught an inkling that he was such a superb backcourt player. I was sitting in the row behind the empty bench. There was only one other person in that row — the attendance was a sparse 300 or so — and the stranger soon shifted a seat or two over. He had evidently noticed my enthusiasm when my father sank that first shot, taken so surprisingly early. Given unexpected room, he'd immediately thrown up the standard two-handed shot guards used those days, serving notice he couldn't be played loosely: that dictated how he'd be able to function from then on. Played closely now, once he had the ball he'd be able to get rid of it quickly, make plays because he'd proved right off he was a scoring threat.

The stranger in my row said to me, "That's a helluva ball player you're looking at." I said I could see that. He said, "You should have seen him twenty years ago."

"He's my father," I almost said, but didn't, I'm not sure why. This enabled him to keep the information coming — "he would have been on the other end of a play like that in the old days." This man was a genuine admirer who was relishing my father's court presence perhaps even more than myself. Not intending to be elusive, I told him who I was before the half — which made him even more well disposed to things, so much so that during the intermission he came back to our seats with a bottle of soda apiece for us. He'd kept me there talking after the first half ended, because my father had just thrown up one more long shot and hit it; and really, it was almost like responding to a hockey or soccer score for this man: he couldn't praise the perfect shooting enough, because these long arching shots were something new to him, not part of a repertoire he'd known from the past.

Perhaps the vividness of my father's performance, engraved on my mind through all these years, owed much to this older man, and the liking he and the rest of the crowd were showing for an old favorite. Before the ball was thrown up for the next half — since my father now started himself — you could hear a handful of "more-of-the-same's" — "show 'em another one, Honey," and so on. Such calls came from seats around the arena.

For me, though, appreciating the way my father threw passes in traffic was the lesson to savor. Five hundred times I must have heard him belittle "telegraphed" passes, especially chest passes, and now he was bearing out his philosophy as he went on with what he'd started in the first half. He was like a mecca out there for his players: they'd keep looking to get the ball to him, and no sooner would he have it than it would be gone. His basic pass — delivered when he'd have looked a quarter turn of the head from the target — was a neat one-handed baseball zip to a corner or pivot man, or a cutter going "back door" (as they say now) toward the goal. I can't exaggerate the finesse of this feeding, because the marksmanship was again 1.000. He never threw the ball away. Naturally a lot of this ball-handling involved shuttling with another guard, turning the ball over beneath an arm and setting a screen — they weren't always working directly toward a score. If my father ever dribbled, it was usually for not more than a single positioning bounce, so as to get a passing angle or give a receiver an instant to come to meet the ball. Where another backcourt playmaker would have resorted to bounce passes to prevent interference, my father didn't have to use them — his release was that quick. I remember telling him admiringly when we were on the way home, "I didn't know you were such a great passer."

And twice in the game he fed Kevin Connors for goals: once on a lob pass laid up almost alongside the basket rim. A year later almost to the week Connors would be up that high and smashing the Boston backboard; but not this time, as he laid the ball in. Kevin had sneaked behind the 6'8" Don Kotter, no less.

The newspaper account the next day spoke of my father's scoring: two for two from the foul line and four for four from the floor. "Veteran 'Honey' Russell Leads Scoring Attack" went the caption; followed by "Pro Sport Fails to Click" (a reference to that meagre 300). In the account proper: "Russell, a veteran of the professional sport, put on a scoring drive that made Father Time run for cover and amazed basketball lovers of this area with whom he was a favorite for years when American League games were promoted in Kingston." I don't think the writer could have known my father was pushing 44. The ten points scored were modest enough; still, a real night's work by 1945 standards: the final game score was only 34-26.

After he'd hit one more long shot, my father's last basket came on a solo cut, made straight from the backcourt when the ball was on the opposite side of the court and the man guarding him got "nose trouble" (my father's phrase for anyone who turned his head on defense). He was over the foul line in a flash and docking in a layup. "We set him up," my father said later. "I knew he'd turn his head." This he confided in the train on the way home.

At the time itself, his single blast to the basket brought the slim house down. The man next to me punched my arm and said, "*There* it is, *that* was the play he'd go in ten times on, *that's* what I was telling you about, your dad was a *cutter.*"

When the game ended and the team straggled over to collect jackets, the man was up on his feet talking across the chair-back to my not-too-winded father, pointing to me and saying what a treat the whole thing must have been. My father recognized him, and brightened up in that way after a win when you're ready to hear any good thing — then broke into a real grin when the man referred to that basket underneath. "Hey, but Honey," he said, "where do you come up with these heaves from way the

Christ in the backcourt. I'm telling your son here that's not you. I thought I'm never gonna see you make that drive till it's too late. I've got my hat and coat on, I'm saying to myself, hey, you don't pull that out and the boy here can't say he saw Honey Russell play."

My father grinned back knowingly. He gave a little matador's flick with his red jacket, toward the basket where he'd scored, and said to the man, "I made my annual cut."

# Jersey Reds Dump Vissies In Saugerties by 34-26

### Jersey Reds (34)

|  | FG | FP | TP |
|---|---|---|---|
| Allie Shuckman, f | 1 | 0 | 2 |
| Bob Tough, f | 4 | 0 | 8 |
| Kevin Connors, c | 2 | 0 | 4 |
| Hagan Anderson, g | 3 | 2 | 8 |
| J. Garfinkle, g | 1 | 0 | 2 |
| Honey Russell, g | 4 | 2 | 10 |
|  | 15 | 4 | 34 |

### Visitations (26)

|  | FG | FP | TP |
|---|---|---|---|
| Tony Bodego, f | 6 | 0 | 12 |
| Pete Caruso, f | 1 | 0 | 2 |
| Don Kotter, c | 1 | 0 | 2 |
| George Slott, g | 1 | 0 | 2 |
| Ed Conaty, g | 2 | 0 | 4 |
| Dan Christie, g | 2 | 0 | 4 |
|  | 13 | 0 | 26 |

Score at end of periods:
Jersey Reds ..... 6  8 11  9—34
Visitations ...... 8 10  6  2—26

Fouls committed: Jersey Reds, 6; Visitations, 10. Referee—Bob Cullum, Kingston.

*Veteran 'Honey' Russell Leads Scoring Attack; Pro Sport Fails to Click*

*Swansong Season.* Box score of exhibition game at Saugerties in which Dutch Garfinkel (note misspelling) hit HR for what might have been the last cutting goal of his career. *My Father and Myself.* February 1944. My second year of high school, his 26th as a pro with two more playing years to go.

*Pals At Home.* Peggy Russell with her brother Honey, Brooklyn, 1910. *First Meeting.* HR with Charlotte Graf the year they met, Brooklyn, 1920. They married when he went to Cleveland, the "fifth city," to play for the Rosenblums. *Joining the Ranks of the Benedicts.* That's what the *Plain Dealer* caption said of the upcoming marriage of the Rosenblum guard.

# Fifth City — Monsters of the Midway

◆

It was in November of 1918, the month of his father's death, that my father began playing professional ball. He was sixteen then, and had played for Alexander Hamilton High before this. Sometimes he would say he began playing for money at fifteen. However, my father, always accurate about places and 99% accurate with names, was not reliable about figures. He indulged all kinds of misrecollections in this regard. For example, he estimated he had played 3200 games, figuring nearly 120 games a year for 28 years; but such an annual figure, while a possibility in a peak year, could not have been anything like an average over that long time. Why he used to say he began playing at fifteen was that, with an athlete's eye to longevity, he had lopped a year off his age somewhere along the line. He gave out he was born in 1903 — actually believed this late in life — and that would have made him fifteen when he started playing. He was born May 31, 1902, as my mother proves very well, since she and my father's sister are identical ages and both were 1903 babies while my father was a year older than his sister.

The family lived on Baltic Street — they numbered five, since his favorite Aunt Eliza lived with them. With her brother-in-law ill, she was the family provider — she worked as a bookbinder, and every week gave her check to her sister, by means of which that household survived. My aunt remembers the little lane at the back of the house which led to a saloon, and her brother in knee britches going for the traditional can of beer for their father each evening. That was when things were amicable, before the son showed his bent for sports and before my grandfather had to go away, to live for several years in a sanatorium near Paterson.

Once he returned, he took against my father, especially against the idea of his becoming an athlete. He had been one himself in his youth, but had contracted a tubercular leg (as then diagnosed) which became incurable. This caused him to lose all his good prospects in the pharmacy supply business; the sanatorium proved the final step in his decline, and he was an invalid on his return. But late in his life, living again at home, he was hale enough to swing his crutch at my father for getting in late after high school games. Their amicability was gone. His death on Armistice Day forced my father into a breadwinner's role; it also cleared the way for him in his vocation.

So in 1918 he began playing for the first of many Brooklyn organizations, the St. Mary's Triangles. Teams were distinguished in those days as "lightweight" and "heavyweight" — thus a scrapbook item from 1920 reports him on his next team, the Prospect Big Five: "Russell is playing a wonderful game in the fast company this season. Coming out of the lightweight ranks he is rapidly making a name for himself as a centre of sterling ability." He was light and rangy then, a "centre" for one team or guard for another; in that same 1920-21 season the late Ed Sullivan, then a young sports writer, recorded a scoring feat of my father's that made up for a dearth of other news. —Thinking of Ed Sullivan's debut makes me connect up some other names from show-business who'd be encountered fairly often. Bob Hope started on the stage in Cleveland in 1924 when my father was there with the Rosenblums; a few years later, when he was with Chicago, he and my mother and many others witnessed a gangland murder in a ballroom where another sportsman-acquaintance, Guy Lombardo, was playing. In the early thirties, in Easton, Pa., his team followed a midnight Abbot-and-Costello act onto the stage — the theatre having first to be cleared, though: "it must have been the latest game ever played." It was natural to be acquainted with such performers, the reason being, of course, that these particular ones were sports backers for most of their careers, and even participants. I mention them mainly to give a sense of contemporaneity, and to remark the distribution factor: they weren't concentrated in New York and Hollywood as they tend to be now.

What Ed Sullivan was reporting was a record my father set in his first season of major competition. "The metropolitan district record, for total baskets scored in a heavyweight professional game, went by the boards over at Prospect Hall, Brooklyn, last night in the game between the Brooklyn Dodgers and the Paterson Crescents, when 'Honey' Russell of the home team caged thirteen two-pointers for an aggregate twenty-six points....It would have been a drab week-end indeed had not Russell come through with his great performance against the six-foot Jersey team. The week-end was death on basketball news."

While he played for the Dodgers that night with such fellow Brooklynites as Joe Brennan and Red Conaty, the breaking in for which my father gave most credit took place on the teams that had Barney Sedran and Marty Friedman on them. These included the Prospect Big Five, but also groups that played out of the city (he belonged to a couple of Brooklyn clubs and to teams far afield as well — that was how these players got in 100-plus games in a season). It was either on the Easthampton (Mass.) club in the Interstate League or the Albany Senators of the New York State League, both the best in their circuits in the years he played for them (1920-23) and both having Sedran and Friedman on them, that my father got a directive somewhat like the one he gave Chuck Connors at Trenton.

Sedran and Friedman were disliked because they were Jewish. Coffins and hangman's nooses would sometimes be painted on a hometeam floor to mark their spots, and in one hall the team was greeted with signs around the balconies saying "KILL THE CHRIST-KILLERS." In those provinces the rough going of pro basketball was "twice as tough," in my father's words. "The Jew-baiters got there early — they'd have stones inside snowballs and it was hell getting into the hall much less play the game." And fans like these had no trouble inciting their favorites down on the floor when the Sedran-Friedman teams came visiting. My father at the age of eighteen in 1920 got caught in the vortex. Whichever it was — a New York State or Interstate game in which the event occurred — in either case the first half had been mayhem and for his part he had been badly pushed around by the opposing center. At the half, in that enemy hall, the bruised playing-manager Friedman told my father he would have to slug the center at the second half tap. My father said he was afraid to do it — got the ultimatum — did it: changed the direction of intimidation for himself in those opening days of stardom — and was to follow and admire Friedman for the rest of his life.

He followed him to Cleveland, where Max Rosenblum had formed the Cleveland Rosenblums. This was the most famous team my father played for, although in the first two years (1923-25) no regular league play was involved. Max Rosenblum's aim was to field a team the equal of the original Celtics, and a November 1923 headline in the *Plain Dealer* summed up this aim, as it announced what the owner of Cleveland's biggest department store had done:

> ROSIES LOAD UP FOR BIGGER GAME
> ... To place such a team on the floor to represent the Fifth City, Rosenblum has signed three of the best players he could find in New York City. They are Ray Kennedy, forward, and Honey Russell and Marty Friedman, guards.

Ray Kennedy was picked for an interesting reason: he'd played for a club that had beaten the Celtics the year before. Friedman

*Away From Home.* HR with the Albany and Easthampton clubs, 1921-22, both of which he joined when he was eighteen.

*Cleveland Rosenblums*, 1926. The first professional league champions. From left: Marty Friedman, Len Sheppard, Carl Husta, HR, Nat Hickey, Dave Kerr, Rich Deighan.

was to be the Rosies' manager. Of my father, who was the least experienced of the three, the item went on to say, "He is only 21, but is a wonder at his position," mentioning the championship season he'd just had with Friedman at Albany.

The Rosenblums of that period took on all and sundry, so that one might encounter such a description (from a Buffalo paper in 1925) as this: "Entering the small Saint Ann hall, the Rosenblum players, only five in all, appeared somewhat astonished at the lack of floor space but without a murmur made the best of the situation." Some of the sports lingo from those days was extremely winning. Here is the conclusion of the Buffalo journalist's writeup:

> The visiting aggregation's chief asset was the scientific execution of the block play, as all spectators at the Saint Ann struggle will agree. Through the successful working of the block play, Friedman and others were afforded set throws from quarter court, without interference from the opposition.
>
> In the second period, very few long attempts were made by the Rosenblums. They resorted to another style of attack with Russell as the chief offender .... In the goodnight session of the Saint Ann struggle, Russell was about the only one to move down the floor and uncovered a very good liking for the net.

It is hard to think of a nicer metaphor for a second half than "the goodnight session of the struggle." In fact the whole article is courteous. Goodnight sessions in truth they had to be, for barnstorming road trips like that one had to be run on tight timetables. Here is the conclusion of that particular trip as reported by a correspondent traveling with the team:

### ROSIES ANNEX SIXTH IN ROW

*Conquer Kane (Pa.) Five on Latter's Floor*
(Plain Dealer Special)
KANE, Pa., Jan. 22 [1925]. — Rosenblum basketball team of Cleveland recorded its sixth victory in as many

nights by subduing the Kane Independents here tonight, 40 to 21. The same five Rosenblum players have participated in every minute of every one of the half dozen contests, not a substitution being made.

Honey Russell again was the star, leading the scoring with five field goals and three free throws. Kelly McBride also placed in five tries from the floor.

The Rosies left for home late tonight and will play Pulaski Post of Detroit in Cleveland Saturday.

| **Rosenblums — 40** | | | | **Kane — 21** | | | |
|---|---|---|---|---|---|---|---|
| | G. | F. | T. | | G. | F. | T. |
| Friedman, lf | 4 | 0 | 8 | Thompson, lf | 2 | 0 | 4 |
| Schwab, rf | 2 | 0 | 4 | McCoy, rf | 1 | 1 | 3 |
| McBride, c | 5 | 0 | 10 | Lewis, c | 0 | 2 | 2 |
| Sheppard, lg | 2 | 1 | 5 | McNulty, lg | 3 | 0 | 6 |
| Russell, rg | 5 | 3 | 13 | Engstrom, rg | 3 | 0 | 6 |

Up through the 1925 season, although there were some bonafide eastern leagues, there was no way of deciding an outright basketball champion. Yet teams with formidable independent records, like killer chestnuts, could get together to prove a mythical title claim. Max Rosenblum had all along been pointing for such a contest — when he got it in '25 he had to settle for an overtime loss. So a Cleveland headline late that season reads, "CELTS END ROSIES' DREAM AS CHAMPS," followed by this leader: "The dream of the Rosenblums as rulers of the professional basketball world vanished Friday night in the great open spaces of Public Hall when the green-clad Celtics of New York triumphed, 25 to 23, in a weird over-time contest." This was one of the games in which my father was pitted against Nat Holman, who collected one point. The writeup indicated that Holman had got fuming because he'd been shackled, with the result that he committed a whole flurry of fouls. So my father wound up as the game's high scorer, thanks to seven foul shots along with his one field goal. "But we came out here and beat you," Holman could have said. Twelve thousand Cleveland partisans had to go home disappointed: they may not have felt like fifth city but neither did they wind up first.

Nat Holman was one of the two great offensive players of the time, the other being Benny Borgmann. These two, who with my father are among the first five Naismith Hall of Famers, were the men beyond all others responsible for his reputation, for there was invariably a build-up of expectations as to how these scorers would do when they came up against him. There were many standoffs, and some occasions when they outplayed him, but ultimately he seems to have had their number. Elmer Ripley, another Hall of Famer, once told a newsman of the complaint Benny Borgmann used to make about my father. "'All Honey has to do is throw his shoes into the cage, and I'm finished.' That's how well Russell covered him."

He had other special assignments too, guarding local pointmaking favorites in various towns — like Snooks Dowd of Springfield, whose mother used to sit at courtside and jab her son's opponents with a hatpin. The story, well authenticated, was that Dowd would maneuver his guard to where the mother sat, then make his cut at precisely the time she was making her jab. My father said he grew accustomed to it; did not look forward to playing there, however. Even less inviting were the coal towns where miners came to the games with nails which they heated on their head lamps, then flipped at visiting players. "Puffs of steam would rise from a player's back"; that's how you could tell you'd hit your mark. The cages went out in the early twenties — metal or rope, they protected players from the crowd and vice versa; one hopes the miners with their lamps went out with them, the temptation no longer present for flipping nails through reticulations — visiting stars like my father too often the target.

He was rated the best defensive player in the game. The dedication with which he approached defense is possibly best attested by what he once said of his teammates when a switch was in progress: "They knew they had picked up my man and they bore down hard on him." Later as a coach, in his first tenure at Seton Hall while he was still young, he always scrimmaged with his teams and never relaxed on defense: not only because he was trying to instill it in them: it was simply native to him.

The last pre-war freshman team he brought to Seton Hall, which did not play as a varsity unit because of the war, was the best defensive group he ever coached. For that very reason, five of them went to the pros, the only time an entire college freshman team ever moved into the NBA. (Tommy Byrnes and Bob Fitzgerald, the Knickerbockers; Whitey Macknowsky, Syracuse; Mike McCarron, Toronto; Bob Wanzer, Rochester.) They of course were good offensive players when they entered college — pretty cocky, too, and my father used to say he "had to sell them a bill of goods" about playing defense. Pep Saul, on the Seton Hall Prep team then (later a teammate of Mikan's on three straight NBA champions), once told me a story about a huddle he was in, when my father wanted to make a point about defense to the prep group. "We were playing the freshmen," Saul said, "and your father told us, 'I'm going to overplay Macknowsky.' He said if we watched him after Whitey gave up the ball, he'd prevent him from cutting by stepping out ahead of him to the weak side, and then make him go parallel the other way. I'm talking about pretty far back near the half-court line. He had Whitey looping back there for about five minutes. Every time Whitey reversed, Honey would have anticipated him, and in the end it looked like they were playing their own game, racing for one sideline and then the other, no matter what side of the court the ball was on." This sounds a bit of a mean stunt to have pulled at the start of the year on a freshman, but before selling bills of goods I suppose the goods need demonstrating. Anyway Macknowsky, by way of his teammate Bob Wanzer, got revenge later in the year. Wanzer was the real cut-up of this outfit, and he'd arranged a standing bet with my father that sooner or later he'd get by him for a score. He meant of course a layup — a cripple — my father would never have paid him for some heave that went in by luck.

The freshmen had the ball on the day they played this trick against the coach; he was guarding Wanzer, who took him over to the side of the court. From fairly deep in the backcourt Macknowsky took one of his patented set shots, which my father could see of course from the corner of his eye. Naturally he would not turn his head to see the result; but a second later, Wanzer and Whitey both clapped their hands to indicate it had gone in — nice shot — and began backpedalling on defense. My father turned now to go back to take the in-bounds pass, only to feel Wanzer go by him and see that the whole episode had been faked. Someone else had caught the ball on the downflight near the goal — the whole crowd of them howling one can be sure — as Wanzer received the pass to score his only cutting goal ever on my father, and collect his bet. The money was paid a day later; Wanzer knew enough to keep running, right out of the gym.

To return to Cleveland in 1925 and special guarding assignments: it was in a walkover game that season that my father met George Halas, playing for a club calling themselves the Chicago Bruins — most of them ex-Illinois football players. In mid-game my father made as determined a defensive switch as he ever can have made, because of a play that, as it turned out, was to change his career.

Halas had a slight cast in one of his eyes. He was not playing my father, but at one point — the game was already out of contention — my father broke free for a goal and just as he laid the ball up was knocked barreling into the crowd, from the blind side. As he told it, he climbed back all in one piece to the floor and in the time-out that had been taken asked one of his teammates, "Was it that wall-eyed bastard?" That indeed was who it was. Halas — tough then as ever, but my father was furiously sore, and he said in the time-out, "Who has him?" The answer came, and he said, "You have [whoever] now, I have him."

He proceeded to go after Halas to the final whistle. He admitted Halas, expressionless the whole time, gave as well as he took. Two years later, when the new American Basketball League was a year and a half old, and my father's Rosenblums the first title-holding World Champions, he found himself purchased in mid-season from Cleveland by Chicago. Halas was owner of the Bruins' entry in the league. Garry Schmeelk was manager. Halas told my father he had bought him with the intention of making him playing manager the following season. He reminded my father of the 1925 game, telling him that he had made up his mind that when the chance came, he wanted him playing for the Bruins.

The new American League of 1925-26 had a schedule of 30 games and concluded its play with Cleveland as champion, the other franchises being Chicago, Fort Wayne, and Detroit in the west, and Brooklyn, Washington, Rochester, and Buffalo in the east. My father was the league's leading scorer with 221 points — this was fairly phenomenal for a guard, and he also set the league record for points in a game when he scored 22 at Detroit. Rusty Saunders, who played in 34 games because of having moved from Brooklyn to Washington, finished with 241 points, but my father's average was higher over the regulation 30 games he'd played. In the next two years, with the league increasing its teams and the number of games scheduled, he would finish ninth and then fifth in scoring. And that inaugural season he made the first of four consecutive all-league teams.

I summarize these facts because 1926 was the peak year of his career. "The game they really had to win that year was with Washington," I remember my mother saying. This was around the time of my father's death; she could recall such a long-ago game because it meant for her a free trip home to Brooklyn — wives allowed to travel with the team for the playoffs. The way the schedule was organized, the first-half winners, Brooklyn, figured to meet Cleveland at the end, but Washington stood in the way. With two second-half losses, they could still tie Cleveland on the last day. In my mother's scrapbook — she was a new bride that winter — there is a full account of the Rosenblum games of that time: these clippings I'd seen when a boy, though without appreciating all the season-ending drama. What I did remember, though — hearing my mother say "they had to beat Washington" — was a certain vivid cartoon, of George Washington being poled across the Delaware, and meeting, in a block of ice, the figure of my father in a basketball suit.

It was in disconnected flashes like that that the scrapbook often came back to me, but a re-check proved the cartoon did herald this game. Its caption made a play on the small audience for the original Delaware crossing, compared with the expected turnout when the Washington team came to challenge Cleveland:

> Can the crossers get past Honey Russell and his pennant-pointed mates? That's the question due to "pack 'em in." See that fellow in the ice, just ahead of the boat? That's Honey — sure enough.

A crowd of 8500 came to Public Hall to see Cleveland clinch the pennant, and the Rosenblums outperformed themselves — holding Washington scoreless from the field the entire second half. Since the reporters had monickers for all the league entries (Chicago always called Second City, Fort Wayne the Hoosier City, and so on), I expected to see "capital city falls," or maybe, "there went the goodnight session for capital city." But it didn't happen. Their nickname was undemocratic: they were the Washington Palaces. So the department-store team had gotten its pennant for Max Rosenblum — at palatial expense. And my mother could relish her first trip home to Brooklyn, compliments of the store

Surprisingly, on the eve of their match with Washington the Rosenblums had padded their schedule with an exhibition swing through four Ohio towns. The very thing you'd have thought they would have avoided happened: they came up with an injury list. Now the American League teams all had seven- or eight-man rosters, depending on whether the coach played, so with two men temporarily lost to him Marty Friedman added an extra player for insurance, Gil Ely of Detroit. Ely played against Washington, and the league permitted Cleveland to keep him for the playoff against Brooklyn, giving Friedman the unheard-of number of nine players for the championship.

The series, moving its site to Brooklyn after two games, might well have gone five. But it only went three; and in beating Brooklyn on three consecutive nights, Friedman did something to show how he regarded my father as the glue of his team. The first game had been close, Cleveland coming from behind to win 36-33. But on the next night they shot out into a lead and sat on it, "saving some of the energy for what is expected to be the final game tonight in New York," as the newspaper account put it. And since Friedman had nine men, "In the last few minutes the regular line-up with the exception of Honey Russell was taken out." I don't know if my father would have been proud of that line, but he had a right to be. He was the only one to play every minute of the series. The next day the Rosenblums swept it, keeping the regulars in the whole way; they took this game by only one point. Who knows but what the breather Marty Friedman was able to give four of them, 24 hours before, might have paid off in that finale.

So my father had spearheaded a team to a world championship, the first formal one on basketball's calendar. Though he led them to the first-half title the next season, he would not be there to help them after that. "We were just as good till Max traded me," I heard him say once, referring to the rumor that when the famous Celtics joined the league for 1927, they so outclassed the opposition that their New York club had to be broken up. Not true: Cleveland took the first-half title, and it wasn't till Max Rosenblum had broken up *his* club that the Celtics came on to win — after my father had been traded to Chicago.

It was a much weaker team he was headed for (he argued he was sent to lend more balance to the league, but George Halas doled out a hatful of money for him); and the Celtics went on to sweep things in the second half. Nat Holman was the New Yorkers' star, but as for *their* "glue," that had to be Dutch Dehnert. Thus the compilers of the 1927 all-league team had to make a choice at guard between Russell and Dehnert, and they made it this way:

> We believe these are the five best men who could be selected for their positions. Note we do not say they are necessarily the five who have been most valuable to their teams. Take the case of "Dutch" Dehnert, for instance. Take him out of the lineup and the Celts would not be nearly so formidable, even with the great Nat Holman left. But individually, for speed, passing and goal shooting we believe that "Honey" Russell — the Russell of the first-half championship Cleveland team — deserves a place on a collection of all-stars ahead of the big Celt guard.

As this passage implies, the Chicago years would turn out leaner for him, though rewarding in their own way, and certainly productive of the most robust experiences of his life.

It was because the American League had been formed, with its players bound over to contracts, that my mother married my father in January 1926 and went out to live with him in Cleveland. She had met him six years earlier (February 19, 1920 — she remembers the date because it was her first in the office, and he told her afterward he knew she was for him when he saw her come through the door) — this was at the Intertype Corporation, a printing firm on Court Street in Brooklyn. My father was working for Intertype also, and she remembers the company picnic to which he took her on their first outing together that June, when he won a medal in a footrace.

Everyone who knew him then called him Honey, a name his aunt who lived with him always called him, disliking the name

John. (To my father this aunt Eliza Keyes, his mother's sister, was a paragon. If you wanted to predict his answer, the easiest question you could ask him would be to name the finest person he had known: he would answer Auntie.) But my mother was too skittish to call him Honey. She lived with her mother and two older sisters in the then remote farm-gardens of Flatbush — she never saw her own father, who died before she was born — and she and they, in that atmosphere of correct Catholic femininity, called him Jack. By my two cousins on my mother's side he was in later life called Uncle Jack; but to his sister's son, he was Uncle Honey.

The older Graf girls (my mother's name) may have been particularly austere about this; my mother, called "Babe" to underline her status as youngest, was only sixteen when she presented to the ménage at home this young man whom everyone called by such an intimate name. My mother remembers going speechless once when, my father having come to call, someone flushed the upstairs toilet and the sound carried downstairs. This was the house in which my family were to live while I grew up from one to twenty-two. My mother's mother and elder sister lived there too; and with my two younger sisters, the house never lost its feminine ambience; though there was nothing squeamish about toilet flushing in after years. It was remarkable for my father to have lived there with his in-laws all that time, both women calling him Jack, the pair of them lording it over my mother — except of course he was always on the road, so that his married life resembled a sort of fitted-in ongoing honeymoon.

My grandmother's house was a small two-storied duplex; we lived in the lefthand side, she rented the other side. Once you entered you could ascend straight to the bedroom area; the hall up there led along the inboard side of the house, the four bedrooms in a line to the outboard side — my parents' being the only sizable one, spanning the whole width of the house at the front. My grandmother's room was at the back.

My father's mother also lived in Brooklyn, but a long trolley-ride plus a transfer away from our house. She didn't begrudge my other grandmother this domain, but did harbor the fantasy that there was space for her there too, and resented not being able to live with us, or at least next door. So the fact of the whole family packing in with one grandmother (not to mention our aunt) did rankle her, and made for bitterness she didn't hesitate to direct toward her son. It came mostly through looks — if animated, her face would drop when he came in a room. I remember distinctly how, when she didn't open Christmas presents we'd brought to her house (she was in the care of a practical nurse that winter), my father walked across the room and picked up a day-old paper — and flipped from its back pages to read results of games he'd already read about the previous day. He wasn't long-suffering toward her; she had a knack of making him more silent — though he wouldn't have intended silence to start with — than anyone else could ever do. To him, she was a dampener.

With my other grandmother he got along banteringly — in the way some men, used to being served by women, can keep the kidding going while accepting late-hour snacks for their card game, or, let's say, repairs to a baseball glove or new lining sewn into basketball kneeguards. He'd call her "Jenny," now and then "Road-apple Jenny" to embarrass her. Fat and short as she was, she had to hear how some garment under the tree at Christmastime was ordered from Omar the tentmaker's; another time it might have come from a parachute company. She never minded his teasing and, though she was the disciplinarian in that household (to us children, "Never say can't" was her catchword), him she catered to. One woman who wouldn't serve him, though, was my Aunt Mae. They were moderately friendly — all the singing done at parties was to her accompaniment on the piano — there she was gifted, and he, in turn, at singing harmony. He'd start off with a melody, just the slightest hoarseness in the opening note, she'd be into the song that quickly, and from there on his voice dropped to harmony — and I'm sure that whole predilection of his for team play, subordination, was at the source of this.

But why she wouldn't attend any of his whims was because of the way he dressed in the morning, summer or winter. He'd be down reading the paper in his undershorts, maybe an undershirt. He never noticed that a woman in her forties was coming through the room — my every-day-offended aunt. One morning she daringly paraded before him in her slip — into the living room, out, back in — trying to shame him, but he noticed absolutely nothing. If she'd been Sally Rand and fanless he'd have missed it all. And so there was a coolness — not an enmity — but enough to let him know not to seek domestic services from that quarter. Mae, I heard him tell my mother any number of times, was the most self-interested person he'd ever seen.

To go back to my parents' "ongoing honeymoon," and their courtship leading up to it — not untypically, my mother and he had no sooner got engaged (April 1925) than he was off, to Maine this time for baseball. She was able to visit him once, at Old Orchard Beach. Soon after that the baseball season in Maine produced a story, strangely apocryphal-sounding to me, which nonetheless did reach print. The man who ran the Portland baseball team, he told the columnist Willie Klein, committed suicide on a day the players were supposed to get paid.

> "Every Saturday night we lined up at the owner's door to be paid. The fellows would start shoving and this night the line was so unruly a few of the fellows pushed right through the door and hit off the owner's body hanging from a rafter.
> 
> "Well, that was the brokenest club you every saw," Honey continued. "Some of the fellows didn't have a cent to their name.
> 
> "I heard about a team in Bangor that needed an outfielder. So I wired that outfielder Russell was ready to report. The answer came back 'no outfielder needed.' This didn't stop me. I wired back 'pitcher Goodwin available for work.' The answer was 'pitching staff filled.' I needed a job

so I tried once more, wiring 'catcher Woodhouse ready to report.' That did it. I was ordered to come in. But wouldn't you know. I didn't have a catcher's mitt.

"Anyway," Russell continued, "I got to Bangor around 2 a.m. and in a cafeteria I heard about a kid in town who had a mitt. I got to his house, woke up the old man and made a deal for $10. In my room I kept writing the name Woodhouse so I'd remember who I was supposed to be. Later when I reported someone in the dressing room hollered, 'Hey, Russell, what are you doing here?'

"I looked around and it was Dolly Stark, with whom I played a lot of pro basketball and who later became a big league umpire. I raced over and explained the Woodhouse gag but everybody on the club called me Russell. They thought Dolly used my first name. I had to make Stark practice calling me Woodhouse so he wouldn't queer me with the manager.

"That's not all the story," Russell grinned. "I couldn't use the glove that I went out of the way to buy. It was brand new and the pitches kept popping out. I looked like I'd lose the job but the catcher on the other side let me use his mitt that day and later I picked up a used job for $1.50."

Now my father was not all that poor, though the really big basketball money would not commence for him till the next season, as he knew. But however much those impetuous telegrams seem straight out of folklore — and no matter how he grinned across the table to Willie Klein — there's a kind of dolor in this story, and I get the thought of weight descending ("I looked like I'd lose the job") on the man traveling incognito just after having become engaged.

He was obviously not trying to get back home! And he also gives the sense, "going out of his way" to buy the glove, of how responsibility can push you and have you end up worse.

Maybe I'm at fault for making this lighthearted story sound heavy. The earlier courtship years make him seem more boyish by comparison. In February 1920, when my mother met him, he was playing in the "lightweight" basketball circuit and was drawing a salary at Intertype. He wouldn't leave Intertype until the next season, for leagues in the higher bracket, upstate and in Massachusetts. That first year, my mother remembers an advertisement she saw — a horse-drawn wagon came through the streets with big posters on it, announcing a game for the St. Mary's Triangles, with "HONEY RUSSELL" featured in large capitals, and herself reflecting, "That's Jack Russell at the office."

In the summer of 1921, my mother played an angel-of-mercy role which shows what a boy my father was after all, hardworking athlete though he may have become. His best friend, John Lanheady, was out of work that summer, while my father and some other Brooklyn basketball players were playing baseball out in Southampton, Long Island. They played for the town team and were hired for various evening jobs, like watchman and policeman, by the community. Lanheady was no baseball player (he had played some basketball; he was about 5'10", but jumped center because he had long arms). One thing special about him was his cooking. Since he was out of work and my father, along with Rody Cooney and Joe Brennan, had rented a bungalow out there, they hired John to come out and cook for them — at no salary, just "found."

But since all these players had access to the kitchens of Southampton mansions, there was never any occasion for them to eat at home. They merely slept at the cottage, and would return at night to a grousing Lanheady, to whom they had brought no food. The place was "at the back of the beyond" (as I heard it described), and he had no transportation, no money, and nothing but some cans of coffee in his larder.

It all seemed pretty humorous to them, so that when my mother went out for a visit she was brought by the sleeping shack to pay a call on the grouse. She found him, faint from malnutrition, handcuffed to his bed. He'd been complaining he would leave, and they'd made that the excuse for a roughhouse. My father's policeman's handcuffs were spotted by Rody Cooney, and brought into the gag as an afterthought. How long

Lanheady had been kept in that condition was hard to say. My mother, seventeen, insisted they go off and bring back bread and some vegetables for soup, and cooked for the ailing cook and tended to him. He got well (but my mother remembers a rash he contracted, which lingered). John oddly never resented the whole impractical joke.

In due course John Lanheady became my godfather, and was an exalting man to be around, because of the strange jobs he was always holding. He was a private detective, also for a long time a Pinkerton agent. He had a classic Irish face of the almost hairless type, a deadpan no matter what monkeyshines he might be up to. His long arms gave him extraordinary leverage, like a chimpanzee's, so that he could bring off what seemed to me were amazing feats of strength. For instance, he could take your hand between his thumb and forefinger, and applying the tiniest effort — not even holding tight with those two fingers — rotate your wrist so that you knelt right down on the ground, nothing you could do about it. He also did tricks with coins. As a guard at the Brooklyn Navy Yard, he was able to get me in to witness the launching of the battleship *North Carolina*. What do I remember most about it? That's easy. First I was disappointed because the *North Carolina* carried no gun turrets: only the barbettes showed above the hull. But to replace the fascination of big guns there was, at keel line, an enormous amount of grease — a literal wall of fat — which John showed me lining the ways, and which got burnt clean away as the ship slid down. This was in June 1940, the month of Dunkirk and the fall of France. I realize now, and maybe even did a bit then, how momentous was the launching of a super-battleship, but none of that (if the expression can be used) could hold a candle to the wall of fat.

John was also supposed to have saved my father's life. It was in a fracas which broke out after a game they played for a church team as boys — an away game "at an Italian parish." The players were caught in a pocket, a knife was drawn behind my father's back, but John saw it in time to intervene. This was a story both of them told and without variation, although how really dangerous the situation might have grown is hard to say. Priests broke the mêlée up, and the visitors got away with torn uniforms, probably well bruised up. It is the kind of story that sounds clichéd — knife, fist, deliverer — hard to judge as to the factual. I have not belittled it though, because one thing is certain: John *would* have saved my father's life, if it was in his means to do so, at whatever hazard. Not only did he always come to my father's defense, but, like any squire to a knight, he was faithful in the most ordinary circumstances. Whenever my father came east to play in New York, if the two hadn't already met, Lanheady would naturally appear at the arena at gametime, ready to carry his bag in.

It was on a January weekend when Cleveland played at Brooklyn that my parents were married. John was best man; my mother's sister Mae was maid of honor. There were efforts to bring these two together, but neither ever married. Thus my aunt stayed on with her mother and sister and what turned out to be the rest of us, and John, after his parents died, lived with an unmarried brother and their spinster sister, and cooked over thirty years for that household of three.

My father's baseball career had become checkered rather early. He said he was signed in 1919 by Wilbur Robinson of the Dodgers, but released that same spring for failing to report to spring training (basketball remained too lucrative in March). For a couple of summers he went to Southampton; then in the early twenties he was signed again, this time by Reading of the International League. But again he put himself on bad terms with the management by reporting late, and ultimately this practice of his — due to his basketball commitments — resulted in his being barred from organized ball. So in the later twenties he was usually to be found playing in one of the outlaw leagues in Pennsylvania, while in the thirties, having come east for good once the depression caused the American Basketball

League to fold, he played regularly for semi-pro teams around New York.

At the end of his career he was a pitcher, but that was not how he started. Originally he'd been a catcher ("catcher Woodhouse reporting"), the position he liked best. However, a basketball crony talked him out of catching, on the theory that all that squatting was bound to cost him some speed, and worse yet take years off his basketball career. This may have been good advice, but my father maintained that after he became an outfielder he never again hit the way he did as a catcher. "You're in the game more, there's that part of it; but the big thing for me was, I used to sweat more, and I didn't feel the same up at bat unless I was sweating."

Nevertheless he was an outfielder by the time of his marriage, and he and my mother spent the summers before I was born in Pennsylvania and Maryland, where he was playing in the Blue Ridge League. A 1927 game he played there may seem to rebut his theory that he couldn't hit well after standing around in the outfield. My mother must not have been at this game, because she certainly would have made a story of it — since my father was arrested that day.

What happened was that his Hagerstown team and their opponents were all herded into a caravan of black Marias for breaking a Pennsylvania blue law by playing on Sunday. The mass arrest, however, was simply a matter of authorities doing some mock enforcing. The fans themselves stayed at the field and picnicked, knowing the teams would be back; bail was posted for each player as he signed in at the magistrate's, and ultimately, now all cooled off and stiff — so the newspaper account runs — the players arrived back at the field and resumed the game. They were literally "outlaws" in this case. My father's team was at bat, he was the first man up, and he proceeded to hit a home run. The reporter who covered the whole sequence made much of this, how it was that "Russell" stepped out of a car, walked up to the plate, and ripped the first pitch thrown at him out of the park. Still I'm not sure my father would have given ground on his conviction that he "couldn't hit when he wasn't sweating." Supposing he was asked about this, I can imagine what his answer would have been: "The pitcher was colder than I was." But it was a story I found in a newspaper while checking the Blue Ridge League, not one of his own.

One other factor was involved, in my father's move from catcher to outfielder. He threw what players call a heavy ball. As a catcher he was always knocking the hands off infielders, throwing a sinkerball to get runners out. This couldn't be modified; but the heavy ball would serve him well in his later years when he took his turn as a pitcher.

In some of the outlaw baseball my father played in Pennsylvania, he was in games against stars like Shoeless Joe Jackson and Happy Felsch, both banned from the majors for their part in the Black Sox scandal. But there were plenty of others in Judge Landis's bad book for lesser offenses. Baseball certainly didn't control its stock of talent as it was later to do, and independent players on the way up did not have to go through the organized minors. In my father's first year in the Blue Ridge League (1926, right after the Rosenblums had won their championship), Hack Wilson had just left the Frederick team for the majors, and Rollie Hemsley, later to star for Cleveland, was about to end his hold-out and join that same Frederick club. (Had Hemsley balked further about his pay my father would have been spared a signal event in his life, as I'll explain, but the point is that Hemsley was holding out in an outlaw league as a *rookie*.) Not only were famous names like "Shoeless Joe" symbolic of anarchy — men difficult to deal with — but so were the less well-known, for instance a player like Seafoam Reynolds of Hagerstown. In 1926 one could read this account of a man who would surely not stay put for long.

> Hagerstown will probably have Seafoam Reynolds in the outfield this year. The dizzy outfielder has seen service with a number of clubs in the league and is expected to

> stick with the Hubs. He is a pretty fair hitter and covers a lot of ground. He is one of the players, however, that are hard to manage and causes a lot of turmoil on any club.

My father, not hard to manage once you had him, would replace Seafoam, or at least play his position the next year at Hagerstown. His own Blue Ridge team that first summer was Waynesboro. And in a game Waynesboro played at Frederick, he went through what might have been the watershed experience for him in baseball. At the very least, a ball that Rollie Hemsley hit that day was to have a considerable effect on my father's life.

Years later, in 1945, my family were approaching Frederick on a motor trip south, when my father suddenly slowed down. He had remembered from twenty years back a spot in the road where there was a bad bump. To us children this was a prodigious feat; however, he did have that kind of memory, a sort of docketing capacity which owed nothing to sentiment. I mention sentiment because this happened outside of Frederick. In the car he had referred to the incident of the fly ball hit by Rollie Hemsley, but this could have had nothing to do with his feat of memory. I am sure the bad spot in the road came back as a geographical not psychological bump.

My mother saw it happen — they'd been married barely six months. Hemsley's ball was hit to shallow left-center so that my father from left field and the shortstop (my mother cannot remember his name) were converging. They collided at full speed, it was clear that they would do so, and knocked each other out. The shortstop was smaller than my father, so that his forehead caught him on the mouth, and my father's two front teeth were knocked out. One had been taken clear off, the other was dangling, as my mother saw when he looked up at her from the stretcher. "It was a terrible day," my mother said. "It took something away from him, that collision." She remembers him sitting at home at Waynesboro that night, arms hung between his legs, and she says she could see an imponderable effect taking shape, a sort of despondency that, she felt, he never quite shook off. But it was not a carryover that had to do with basketball, she would add, only in some way with baseball. He returned to the Blue Ridge League for another season. After that, and a couple of more winters at Chicago, he would become an easterner for good, and after 1930 play baseball and basketball, or coach these sports, for teams no further west than West New York.

In the middle of the 1926-27 season, when George Halas purchased my father for his Bruins, my mother returned to Brooklyn rather than move to Chicago for three months. Thus my father made the move from Cleveland on his own. His first day in Chicago he checked into a hotel — it was the day of a game — and found a message telling him to meet Garry Schmeelk at the Congress Hotel. He went over there carrying his basketball bag, and noticed as he came out of the elevator alcove that several doors along the corridor were open. He saw some heads look out at him as he passed along — paid little attention, kept to his business of looking for the number he was after — then all in one sensation felt the presence of someone behind him and of something prodded into his back. He was told to drop his bag. There were two men. What was he doing there, one wanted to know, while the other was stooping for the bag — what was he carrying in there? "I'm a basketball player," he said. "I'm looking for Garry Schmeelk." Kneeguards on the top of his gear verified what he said, and relaxed them a bit as did the mention of Schmeelk, upon which they escorted him some rooms further down where after a knock Garry Schmeelk opened the door. He took in what had happened and had an uproarious laugh for himself. The others had become completely easy, though not my father. In fact it turned out later that, while not having planned the reception, Schmeelk could have expected my father's appearance on that floor to have precipitated this shakedown. The hotel was one of the headquarters of the North Side Moran gang, toward whose members it turned out that Schmeelk was friendly. He was after all their neighbor.

Vincent Drucci, coequal with Bugs Moran in that group, which was operating in its heyday (it was two years before the St. Valentine's Day massacre), lived in the Congress Hotel and played in a daily card game with a set of cohorts which included Schmeelk as the only non-mobster. My father was invited to join in. They played for modest stakes and the game was uncantankerous and aboveboard. The players frequently displayed weapons, more for the reason that they were "on call" than anything else; and my father was present more than once when "calls" came.

Drucci was quiet but the commander of this portion of the Moran retinue. If he went out the other players (supposing they remained) would indicate that some particularly formidable assignment needed handling. Recalling Drucci, my father would say that he had the coldest, least humanly responsive eyes he had ever seen — that he was more or less affable, easy come easy go (despite his missions), and inspired no particular trepidation, except for the chilling eyes. Drucci, who might have been a stand-in for either of Hemingway's killers, always wore a derby, and returned to one of the card games once with two holes through it. That mattered neither more nor less than the usual spruceness with which he rejoined a game after effecting his business. Not that my father was all that conversant with such goings-on. It was not as though these card players were forever slipping into overcoats and ducking out — just that a stack of chips in front of an empty seat could keep registering on an outsider, when no reference was made to when their owner might be back.

One afternoon while playing cards with Drucci's men my father and Schmeelk were discussing an upcoming home game they were worried about. As my father told the story, he and Schmeelk kept coming back to the fact that Chuck Solodare was to referee it. Of all the referees my father ever passed an opinion on, he never rated anyone higher than Solodare. (A couple of seasons after this one, the two of them would be involved in a play, a center tap after a basket, in which several players crashed to midcourt when the ball was tossed up, caught Solodare in a wedge, upended him and caused him to suffer a broken neck. But by season's end he had come back to referee some games in a neck cast.) Solodare was so respected because he was fair, almost to the point of delinquency, to visiting teams. That was the trouble. Schmeelk and my father knew that Chicago playing at home would get no breaks from him. Evidently they laundered this subject for the better part of that afternoon's poker game.

On the night of the game the two teams were warming up (I forget the opponents) and at game-time no referee came out on the court. The Chicago players knew Solodare was in the building because someone had brought the game ball to him in the dressing room. Often enough there would be only one official in those days, as was the case that night. Finally after a long delay someone was sent to find him and he answered, from behind his locked door, that he would be out in a minute. When he came onto the court with the ball under his arm he was white faced and looked ill and had a strip of tape over one cheek.

He went straight to the center jump circle, saying nothing to anybody. The players were ready enough and came right out on the floor. Solodare threw up the first ball and when it came down called a foul on the visiting team. There had been nothing like a foul, but this was to set the pattern of the game. Solodare kept calling homer fouls throughout. He virtually handed the game to Chicago. When there was beefing he stood and looked glassy-eyed. Ordinarily Solodare, right or wrong on a call, was ebullient and colorful, so when he took the beefing stonily, the players gathered that he was sick — my father said this seemed obvious and so play staggered on to the finish. When the game was over, with Chicago the victor, Solodare deposited the ball on the clock table, marched to his dressing room, put on his coat and hat over his referee's costume, must have thrown his street clothes into his bag, and marched straight out of the arena (the

Broadway Armory).

A few days later, whenever the next card game was, one of the Moran group asked in a by-the-way tone how that game the Bruins were so worried about had come out. Schmeelk and my father said they'd won it and it wasn't mentioned further.

Working for Seton Hall in later years, my father had many occasions to bring in Solodare as referee. That Chicago evening marked the only anomaly he had ever witnessed. Solodare had kept his reputation for fairness, and my father tried to get him for important games simply because of his great experience and the fact that he bore down all the time. For a long time coaches used to take care of their own home-game scheduling of officials, and the long-standing friendship between Solodare and my father made it possible to get him to come to the South Orange gymnasium rather frequently. Something that only half-perplexed my father, game after game, was that crucial calls had a knack of going against his interests — but he chalked this up to Chuck's bending over backwards, since after all he had hired him. He never connected Solodare's behavior on the Seton Hall floor with the 1927 incident in Chicago. The two of them had always been on good terms, in fact their friendship seemed bonded by the circumstance that my father had been one of the participants in the neck-fracturing episode — that was a great highlight to recall, testifying to the ruggedness of the old days.

One evening however at an Old Timers' dinner, after Solodare had retired, he alluded to the night in Chicago. My father had to be re-apprised of it. Solodare seemed taken aback somewhat. He had supposed my father and some of his teammates, if not beforehand, had become parties to the incident after the fact. What incident, my father wanted to be told. Upon which the whole situation crystallized. While he was dressing before the game, Solodare's door had been opened and two men walked in. The one in advance had an automatic by its muzzle and without a word had come straight up to

Solodare and clouted him with the butt, knocking him down. Then the other had spoken: this was in earnest, something they were prepared to carry through. He hadn't made any mistakes yet. He was to see that in the next hour the Bruins did not lose. If the Bruins lost that night the other end of the gun would be turned on him. It was that cut and dried, as to how he was to regard his life.

How, one wonders, could Solodare have been a friend to my father if he had suspected even the slightest complicity among the Bruins? Imagine him all those years, thinking the men whose games he refereed had let him be roughed up like that. Perhaps he felt the players themselves had been intimidated into going along, or that they had only a general sense of how he had been approached. He had had adhesive tape in his bag and had covered up the contusion. But he must have been ashamed, too, of being brought so low. He could never afterwards ask about the thing, could not be certain who knew of it, could not confide: and when it blew over with no repercussions he put it away.

The context of the times ought to be remembered. While mobsters did not traffic in basketball fixes, wild things were apt to happen in public places like the large indoor arenas. One clipping from the 1928 season involving the referee Lou Sugarman gives an overtone of the atmosphere in which an exposed official might well become gun-shy. The Bruins were playing the Philadelphia Warriors this night when, late in the first half, a cameraman took a flash picture. "Sugarman, who had coasted along fairly well to that point, stepped into the spotlight, which he never relinquished for the remainder of the evening. The photographer's flashlight boomed so loudly that the startled Lou blew his whistle and ducked, *mindful, perhaps, of bomb outrages*. In the mêlée Johnny Beckman tossed a one hand shot from the corner and Manager Halas and Honey Russell won the five minute debate. The score counted."

Once, after hearing my father tell the story of the dressing-room threat against Solodare, I asked whether the hoods bet on the game. "Not a dime," he said.

If the Moran people had taken any more than a passing fancy to the concern of their card-playing friends — if there were collected bets to be boasted about, or family jokes about what they'd done — my father and Schmeelk would have had to catch on. But there was a sheer lack of interest in the whole event. The pair who muscled Solodare had perhaps been taken a couple of blocks out of their way. Beyond this they didn't care, and this seems evidence of the contempt they must have had, to a man, for just about everybody, including the ball players with whom they shuffled and cut and exchanged meaningless winnings and losings on those regular afternoons.

My father was twenty-four years old then and may seem to have been a little naive. To judge him as culpable would be a mistake. In his essence he was above all a concentrator. (Even at cards.) Threats and bribes did not occur to him. He was not beguiled by the card players and their affiliations: when at home, ball players have open afternoons; he simply whiled time among them.

An ironic instance of his failure to be up on things occurred a year and a half after the Solodare episode, in the summer of 1928. That year my mother was pregnant, they were living in Chicago, and for the only summer during those years he was not playing baseball. Instead he was, of all things, attempting to sell real estate around Chicago and in particular in Cicero. Halas, who was a real estate man, had put him on to this, though as my mother recalls he didn't make a single sale, at least none of any substance. "We'll be rich if only I sell a house a week." This was the optimism of that hottest summer of her memory, when they lived in an apartment that had a Murphy bed. When they let it down it was aimed straight at the door, and many of the nights were so stifling that they had to leave the door open. Thus they could be looked in on, sleeping, as though on a public slab, by anyone walking by.

There was a week that summer when my father's business in Cicero drew him to the most dangerous spot in the midwest, Al Capone's fortified headquarters at the Hawthorne Inn — my mother was visiting the Halas family at their vacation home in Antioch. Walking up to this mantrap like Childe Roland, my father would not face his moment of glory, though my mother was to face hers in saving the two Halas children, Virginia and Muggsy, certainly from serious injury if not from death. Gazing from the front room where she was chatting with Mrs. Halas, my mother reacted to what happened just barely in time. The children were playing in the family car, parked in front of the summer house, on a slope that ended in a precipice. My mother saw the car start rolling—Virginia had released the brake—rushed out to cut it off, jumped on the running board, banged her head wildly but was able to pull up the emergency brake. Tops of trees were facing the radiator where the car came to a halt, on the verge of the dropoff. My mother was well along in her pregnancy — some might call it a pre-natal experience for me. She was already friends with Min Halas but they became fast friends after that. (To this day she carries in her wallet the memorial notice of Min Halas's death.) Bonds forged like this might have made it harder, in view of a certain overnight transaction by George Halas, for her to learn she'd be parting that winter on very short notice from her friend.

Why my father was at the Hawthorne Inn I've never been able to find out. While it had to do with real estate, he had no notion of the sort of place he'd walked into, no more than when he approached the northside Congress Hotel. Once inside, he was surprised to see hardfaced men posted all over the lobby, and even more surprised to notice that all the windows had been fitted out with steel shutters. As he was getting his bearings a group of men came around a corner and with the central figure among these he had a flash of mutual recognition. The man greeted him and leaving his entourage came over: it was Capone. My father of course had heard of Capone but up till then had not realized he *knew* him whereas Capone knew *him*. They had been boys together in school in Brooklyn, on Butler Street. Capone was three years older, but began school late and was left back once, and my father used to recall having been in a class with him. But he had not associated that Caponi (as the name was pronounced) with the midwest ganglord. What speaks so much of my father is his having walked nonchalantly into the Hawthorne Inn, which after all was a famous headquarters, without the slightest knowledge of where he was — he an erstwhile "member" of the Moran gang!

Capone knew he played for the Bruins — their short talk was confined to that. Just suppose my father had suddenly thought — but he didn't know about this — of the day two years earlier (September 20, 1926) when Drucci and his boss Bugs Moran led a caravan of cars past the Hawthorne, "and at high noon . . . with blazing machine guns . . . riddled the place with more than a thousand bullets." A short time before, according to J.R. Nash in *Bloodletters and Badmen*, a Capone lieutenant had tried to kill Drucci at the Congress Hotel; this retaliation (the Hawthorne was almost bulletproof) got one victim: Louis Barko, the man who'd been sent to get Drucci. The first half of a basketball season prevented my father's learning any of this; he had been in Cleveland in September 1926; and there were still three months before he'd be going to the Congress Hotel and its wintertime card games.

At the beginning of April, 1927, with that basketball season over, my father and Garry Schmeelk (also a Brooklynite) had engaged a sleeper that would be leaving Chicago for the east in the early morning. They had a drawing room on the train. Vincent Drucci, with a basket of liquor for them, came to see them off. The three of them, perhaps one or two others, drank till the small hours while the train remained in the station. My father and Schmeelk turned in before it left, after waving goodbye to Drucci on the platform. When they arrived in New York some twenty hours later, they read in an evening paper that Drucci was dead. He had been picked up by the police for some rowdiness having to do with the mayoral campaign of Big Bill Thompson, and in the squad car had become angered and tried to wrest a detective's gun from him. The detective managed to retain the gun and shot Drucci dead in the car. Garry Schmeelk did not return to Chicago the next year; my father did, as playing manager according to Halas's plan, and brought my mother with him. That marked the end of my father's association with gangsters.

The years with Halas didn't produce any pennants, any more than they produced real-estate sales, but that didn't mean my father's court value had diminished. He'd been bought, so the Chicago program said on his arrival there, "for the highest price ever paid for a basketball player," and in that category he wasn't slipping. When as a boy I saw the orange program in my mother's scrapbook, other items caught my attention; it would have been better had the high price tag made a sharper dent on my mind. I'd have been spared a shock, the result of a recent flip-through of the scrapbook's last pages. A clipping from the 1928-29 season gave me the first of two surprises. It recorded a Bruins' win away from home, and — something I don't remember reading as a boy — the fact that I myself had been born that December 12th. "He got the news about you just as a game was starting." So my mother had once informed me. Now I read: "Shortly before game time the Bruin leader received word that [a baby boy] had been added to the family circle. Russell has always dominated the play of the Bruins but never more so than last night."

Fair enough; who wouldn't play elatedly at such a time, so I felt, turning the page, to face an entry I had no idea was waiting:

RUSSELL, BRUINS' CAPTAIN, SOLD TO ROCHESTER

Below the six-word headline was my father's picture; below that, a terse column significantly omitting the name "Honey":

> John Russell, captain and coach of the Chicago Bruins professional basketball team, has been sold to Rochester, N.Y., it was announced last night by George Halas, Bruins' owner. The sale involved no other players . . . Rochester is leading the American league in the second half schedule.

What ought to have run through my head, given the "second half schedule," was that there'd been a time lapse here. But turning the page from the birth announcement to this notice astonished me. I had a single thought: "My God! He went and used me as an excuse — he's held up Halas for more dough!"

That was instantly plain, and so was Halas's reaction: "John Russell sold. . . ." (Friendship, my mother's saving of the two Halas kids, none of that entered my mind. It was blocked from all coherence by a page turn.)

Of course I'd got it all wrong. My birth came along during the first half — it wasn't till February that the "second half schedule" for 1929 even began. My father hadn't gone to Halas dangling baby booties and demanding more cash. It was simply that my mother's bookkeeping had become sloppy. With a baby on the scene the neat succession of pasted-in articles broke down. There were even some December 1928 scores in the book after the "notice of sale," and, two months out of order, they'd helped me mis-date the Halas decision to unload his star who'd tried to pull the newborn infant routine.

As it turned out, it was in March that my mother packed off with me by train to her mother's in Brooklyn. But if she was forced to interrupt her friendship with Min Halas, it was only that Chicago had failed to become a second-half contender. Whereas Rochester was, and my father, bought by Halas in '27, could just as rightfully be sold off by him to some high-roller elsewhere in the league — "overnight conversion of a liquid asset."

From the disordered last pages of the scrapbook, it emerged that Rochester had four games remaining when they made the deal with Halas — for pennant insurance. One of those games was to be played at Chicago. My mother was now in Brooklyn; someone sent her the Chicago *Tribune* (Min Halas?) — for there was a flurry of expectation about the game; the Bruins could be spoilers, and meanwhile my father was returning to his stamping grounds at the Midway. Here is the last basketball entry in my mother's collection:

> Paramount in interest is the return to Chicago of John ("Honey") Russell . . . . Local fans have designated the occasion as "Honey Russell night," and they plan to honor him in a fitting manner. Russell was one of the most popular players that ever wore the colors of the Chicago five and fans have started a petition to bring him back . . . .

Chicago beat their old captain and his new club, the loss costing Rochester its pennant chances. Ironically this may have helped bring him back, for he'd be playing for the Bruins in 1929-30. Or could it have been a form of lend-lease Halas had arranged with Rochester? In either case, assets began to lose value now; 1929-30 was the beginning of the end for the league, as the first ball thrown up that season was preceded a few days by the financial collapse on Wall Street.

George Halas's sports empire is known today not for his short-lived Bruins but longer-lived Bears. Another reason the page from the orange program has remained in my mind's eye is that, first seeing it as a boy, I was arrested by the heading: "John 'Honey' Russell — New Chicago Bear." At first I thought the reference was to the football team. On further reading, "Bear" turned out to be just a normal synonym for "Bruin." Actually, though, my father, who sometimes said football was the sport he loved best, did become for a time a member of the Chicago Bears, which Halas had formed only a few years before. The problem was, Halas half let and half refused to let my father play on the team.

At the start of the 1928 season he was with them, since he

*Arrival at Chicago.* HR posing at Chicago Stadium after joining George Halas's Bruins, January 1927.

*Rivals.* Nat Holman, top left.; Benny Borgmann, bottom right; Dutch Dehnert, bottom left. Pictured in Chicago Bruins' program of 1929-30, HR's last year with the club. These Hall of Famers were his three most persistent rivals.

had remained that summer in Illinois. The account for the Bears' opening game against the Cardinals, on September 23, has "Russell" substituting for Ted Drews at right end, and that looks like him — unless the Bears had another Russell, though I could not find the name again in accounts of that fall. In any case he was a squad member in 1928 and '29 and played at least in pre-season scrimmages and exhibitions. These were the teams of the Red Grange era. Grange was hurt in 1928, but it was he who would lead the Bears and professional football to begin their climb — the sport was junior to basketball and not yet flourishing. My father was not the only Bruin on the club. Tillie Voss, who was his pivotman in the winter, was the Bears' regular left end; nor was it all that unusual to find this doubling up in professional sports. George Trafton — who later became a wrestler, played a bit of basketball and once fought Primo Carnera — was the center on the team. "Me though — a sure bet for the taxi squad"; for once the fall had really rolled around, Halas became gingerly about my father's putting on a football uniform. His fear: injury to his "highest price ever" basketball guard.

All through the years we lived in Brooklyn, though, he kept up his connection with Halas and the Bears, and when they would come east for games with the Giants and Dodgers at the Polo Grounds or Ebbets Field, the two of us would invariably go. By the time I was old enough to be brought, my father's best friends on the team were Joe Stydahar and Danny Fortmann. They were the co-captains, the perennial all-league left tackle and left guard, and roommates as well. Like my father, they both would have their front teeth out when suited up for a game. To me this annual visit of the Chicago Bears, which came before Christmas, was better by far, since we'd be in the dressing room beforehand, watch the game from the bench, hear the halftime adjustments and dressing downs (if any) given by Halas — it was to be treated like a prince. I used to hold Stydahar's teeth. I'd have a Bear blanket over me if it was cold. I couldn't have missed a year, from the time that I was ten to let's say fifteen.

Of the two games I'd call unforgettable, the earlier (and murkier — not just on account of my youth) ended on a great play. This was a George McAfee run, in an exhibition game in Ebbets Field his second year with the team. I remember him traveling to his left through mist; it was one of the early NFL games played under the lights. He was bringing back a punt with time about gone on the clock, crossing the field from the right sidelines (the Bears had sent everyone to rush the punter), with his number 5 getting markedly distinct as he neared the Chicago bench, tacklers missing him one after the other. Almost out of bounds at his own sidelines, he made a last cut and went the final 30 yards for the score. Chicago won, 13-10. From out of the pretty bad light from the other direction, down where McAfee had run past the goal post, my father materialized — I'd totally forgotten about him. What had he done, run down there? Here he came charging toward where the Bears were, arm-slapping his way past players till he reached Stydahar, to whom he shouted, "Did you ever see a block like that one Danny threw?" The others as well as Stydahar had seen it. Someone like myself fixed on the running McAfee would miss it, though, and I had missed it. Fortmann had come across from where the line of scrimmage was, about the 10-yard-line where he'd tried to block the punt, and leveled two Dodgers on account of the exact timing of McAfee's cut. There were the Dodgers, standing up now with helmets off, but of course not jumping up and down. Exhibition game or no, they'd never beaten the Chicago Bears (Brooklyn never did beat them), and by inches and seconds had just missed this time. Why my father had heaved up out of the mist like that I'll explain in a minute — it makes me think of the game that was the best one of them all.

This one I place probably in 1942 when I was thirteen. It had to be after the Bears had beaten the Redskins in 1940 by 73-0, because I remember being told by Danny Fortmann that this was a run-up score in retribution for bad sportsmanship on the

Redskins' part in their 7-3 victory over the Bears earlier that season. That was a game in which McAfee (just short this time) had been piled on and knocked out after taking the ball to within a foot of the Redskins' goal. The Bears had to suffer a delay-of-game penalty; losing that yardage forced them to go to a pass play, and the receiver had been held arms pinned in the end zone as the game ended. That at least is how I remember Fortmann telling it. I also remember that Hugh Gallarneau was with the Bears by then. He had played in the 1941 Rose Bowl with Stanford, and afterwards on the Bears ran tandem with McAfee at right halfback. It was my father who explained, before I heard it elsewhere, that most backs (being right-handed) ran better to their right, and that teams which could secure backs who could go to their left were fortunate. The Bears had two in McAfee and Gallarneau.

Stydahar, Fortmann, almost everyone on the Bears would say that McAfee was the most spectacularly gifted of football players; there was nothing he could not do brilliantly. In fact McAfee is a legend because he could not pile up records of any sort — he was injured a lot — yet is remembered as a quintessential star. I liked him and everyone else on the Bears, but I secretly revered Gallarneau because of his name. I thought "Gallarneau" was the perfect name for a running back. Coming over a booming, yet still somehow curt stadium loudspeaker, the syllables of "Gallarneau carried" resonated like no other I have ever heard.

So Gallarneau was relatively new on that team, and I remember being introduced to him in the locker room. I wonder, now that I think of his name, about how often names suit men, because never were there so many intriguing ones for football players as that team had. Plasman, an end who didn't wear a helmet; Artoe, a tackle who was a great kicker; Fortmann, only one of a stable of strong guards (Bray, Forte, Musso); Turner, who turned the ball over at center to Luckman, the "fortunate" quarterback; Maniaci, a maniac of a running back; Swisher, a swivel-hipped one; Standlee, a fullback who was hard to knock off his feet....

Why this was the best of all Chicago Bears games was that my father didn't take me to it. He arranged that Stydahar and Fortmann should bring me over to the Polo Grounds with them, since he'd be arriving from somewhere else. One thing that tells something about my age was that, on the Saturday before, when the Bears had got into town, my father called up Stydahar's room while I was sitting by the dining-room table, eavesdropping on the arrangements. He must have been answered by a husky or poorly comprehending voice, because he laughed and said, "What're you doing, Joe, corking off?" But I didn't know what the phrase meant. My mind started swimming with inchoate semi-lurid conjectures — it could have been my father's chuckle that did it. Anyway, arrangements were made for the next day. I went up from Brooklyn to the President Hotel, and met the two of them up at their room. The team did not leave all together but rather in small groups. I went with Stydahar and Fortmann and Al Baisi, Fortmann's substitute — on the subway, which turned into an El on the way to the Polo Grounds. We went in one of the train doors and some other Bears who happened to be on the platform walked in through the others on the same car. It was a soaring feeling to see all the Sunday travelers' faces look up and try to take in what this polite soft-stepping invasion of their space was. Newspapers that a few of the players carried with them, with sporting sections face up, were displaying some of their very pictures, although I judged that most in the car could not, even though interested, go from newsprint to three dimensions and make the precise connection. "Princely" again about describes the feeling.

Since my father pretty certainly got to that game late, I have a tendency to superimpose him on it in an erroneous way. That is, I remember him mainly as handling one of the yard-marker sticks. It used to be a practice for the visiting team to supply someone to help the head linesman with those first-down

*Left Tackle, Left Guard.* Hall of Famers Joe Stydahar and Danny Fortmann of the Chicago Bears. *Monsters of the Midway!* Joe and Danny again, now with shoulderpads on. Much more formidable.

*Bear Braintrust.* George Halas with quarterback Sid Luckman in the Bears-Redskin championship game of 1940. Their faces reflect the blueprint that led to the NFL's most famous score, 73-0.

markers, and in retrospect I can't remember my father ever sitting with me on the bench, though he must have done so after he got there that day. Instead I can only recall him running up and down with the head linesman's crew; and that is the way that whole series of games jelled for me, with him, insofar as he was part of it, coming in and out of one's preoccupied field of vision like that. Thus he'd surprised me by coming out of the mist on the night of McAfee's touchdown run. He'd been handling the chains down towards the Brooklyn goal, from where the punt had been boomed to McAfee, and had had to stand by them through the whole play, in case an offside or some other infraction had been called. None of that struck me that murky night — it was just time to stick by him now, they were putting out the lights — but in later games I more or less got used to it.

With the war full on Joe Stydahar went into the navy, and for a time was commander of a gun crew on a merchantman. He came for a visit to our house in Brooklyn one evening. The way he filled the doorway in his lieutenant's uniform staggered my mother and aunt, though they were used to big men. This fact sticks in the memory twice over because of something having to do with his jacket. It must have had plackets let into it to accommodate his bulk. I remember my aunt pointing out some such odd fact about the coat. (Not to him of course — to my mother or grandmother out in the hall, when she was hanging it up.)

When Stydahar was coaching for the Los Angeles Rams (whom he took to their first NFL championship, in 1951), he put my father on the Rams' staff as a pass defense consultant and as his game scout for eastern opponents. My father knew a great deal about pass defense, his preference being man-to-man coverage, because receivers could then be handled by moves basic to basketball defense. He argued that zone coverage too often made for ambiguity. There was almost a morality to this. Most of all maybe a tremendously quick eye for *where* a breakdown had just occurred. I've seen him watch a game start and say, of the defensive team after the first play from scrimmage, "Number 55 isn't hitting anybody." In fact, he did this at the stadium of the college where I teach; simply announced, to a colleague of mine sitting with us, number 55's delinquency after the first snap of the game. It caused my colleague to watch this linebacker for a series of plays while the offense marched down the field. My friend told me, at the hotdog stand at the half, that my father must have been a wizard. "How could he tell that fast? I thought 'this old guy's crazy' and so I watched 55, and you know what, he didn't do one single thing for ten plays. And he's backing up the line for God's sake. It was like your father'd spooked him. Six points it cost us before they get him out of there." Myself, I'd watched too, after overhearing my father say that — by then his eye for what was wrong didn't surprise me too much. In fact, back when he worked for Stydahar, I'd gone with him to the Polo Grounds when he was scouting Rams' opponents, and in one respect had my own small assignment.

As late as the 1950s, game films were not heavily utilized for scouting — most professional games were not recorded at all on film, and certainly there was no machinery for distributing copies around the league so that opponents' plays could be analyzed all week long. Each Sunday my father would be deputed to go to the Polo Grounds or Shibe Park in Philadelphia, to scout the Giants or Eagles or whoever they were playing.

By that time most teams used the T-formation, though a few were still single-wing clubs. But the Giants, under Steve Owen, had their own offense, run from what they called the A-formation. This looked a little like a short punt formation, with the line unbalanced to the right. Radio announcers used to say, "Line right, backs left." Where the tailback and fullback were behind the center as in a single-wing lineup, the quarterback and wingback were behind left guard and outside left end, on the weak side. Owen had also devised splits along the offensive line — he was the first coach to do this. There were many reverses run by the wingback to the strong side of this formation, while the counters and spinner plays were run to the weak side by the tailback, who carried the brunt of the offense. The quarterback was a blocker.

To scout the Giants my father had had sheets of mimeograph run off of the A-formation. He would sketch in the defense as the game started, and draw the plays from up in the stands. Movement of backs was necessarily different from what the other formations offered. Thus on days when available I came in for a small role, that of watching number 21 on every offensive play.

This was the blocking quarterback. I can't remember his name, but he led almost every play, and so if my father got caught behindhand (trying to diagram the line blocking) the direction of the play — at least of the blocking back — could be recorded. I had my own set of circles on a page and watched him go, while my father next to me had the tenfold duty of trying to focus the others. The system to some degree worked — we (or he) had of course the advantage of getting to see the Giants almost every other week. On reflection, I believe I had to watch number 21 on defense too — he backed up the line — but I can see where this might have just been a sop to me. Naturally he met plays coming his way. No shades of our friend 55, who'd be spotted so quickly years later for not doing his job. Otherwise, though, there wasn't too much to bring to Joe Stydahar's attention from what he did there.

# Depression Schemes — The Son Also Rises

My becoming a sidekick of my father's was naturally a very gradual process; I was not so precocious as to be interested in his activities when I was a little boy during the depression. Then he was still in his playing prime, so that our family wasn't affected too much at the start of the slump. But basketball was to take a much more serious nosedive than baseball in the thirties, and my father got affiliated with more odd schemes in that decade — motorcycle races, baseball pools, basketball played on stages — than at any other time. He also returned to his schooling, by re-enrolling at the Savage School for Physical Education in 1934, which he'd left one year short of a degree when he'd gone to Cleveland for the 1924 season. Savage's had a three-year program, and after a gap of ten years my father was back there to complete his work leading to a certificate for teaching in New York.

Savage's was a well-known school, serious about grounding its students in anatomy, kinesiology and the like, all of which would be of value to my father in the coaching years that were now to come up. The college's motto was the not too original *mens sana in corpore sano*, which struck a lighter note when I learned that Henry Miller had attended the place — *the* Henry Miller, who could have learned some interior geography there, though the latitudes of Capricorn and Cancer wouldn't have been treated in the curriculum.

Uncharacteristically for my father, a yearbook from Savage's exists among his effects. In the "Class of 1934 Celebrities" page, it is nice to see his name down the column as "Most Respected." Of course he was older than the others, working hard in the outside world, but it is also apparent that he fit in with the ordinary doings at the school (he's photographed with the Newman Club, for instance). For a reason to be explained shortly, I find it intriguing that whoever wrote his class's "Last Will and Testament" started out with "Honey Russell — leaves his teeth to Abe Galinsky." The bequest was not unprophetic of a direction once taken by my father's dentures.

For him to go back to school at age 31 was a sign that the depression had bitten in, but my father originally left Chicago, before the 1930-31 season, largely because the older of my two sisters was due to be born. That autumn my mother had held out against spending any more winters in the midwest. Five were enough. My father therefore got his release from George Halas and came home, to sign on with the league's Paterson club. This turned out to be the sixth and last year for the American League. Early in the season, the Chicago *Tribune* reported how attendances had fallen tenfold: crowds once numbering seven or eight thousand had dropped down to the hundreds. The end had been foreshadowed the previous year, when the Rosenblum franchise folded. The league was down to six teams in 1931, and had no choice but to disband after that season.

What happened in towns that had supported franchises down to the end? Some inevitably futile alignments were attempted. In December 1931 two ex-American League teams, Syracuse and Rochester, were described as getting underway in their quest for "the professional championship of Central and Western New York." Barnstorming was the only answer, and it came back in. In my mother's scrapbook there is a poster for

Lincoln's Birthday, 1932, announcing a game at Pittsburgh between "Rosenblum's Celtics" and "Benny Borgmann's Brooklyn Americans." The "Celtics" have four members of that old team (Barry, Banks, Dehnert, and Lapchick) along with two of the earlier Rosenblums — accounting for their portmanteau designation. They are pictured in little rosettes. On the handbill's opposite side, standing one behind the other in a line are my father and four others said to be ready to play for Borgmann's "Brooklyn Americans." They are wearing *White Plains* uniforms! Thus had pro basketball reverted to its old quick-change act, now that the Wall Street crash had put a finish to the solid half-dozen years of the American League.

All the same, despite the number of jerseys my father might be able to pull out of a suitcase, he got affiliated in league ball again, for within two years the second American League had come into being. This happened essentially because of two teams. One was the famous St. John's Wonder Five, who after graduation in 1931 had formed the New York Jewels and caught hold of the metropolitan fans' interest. It was the first time an ex-college team had done something like this. The other was the Trenton Moose, formed in 1932 to compete in the Eastern League — the teams all based around Philadelphia.

The Trenton *State Gazette* of October 26, 1932, reports the signing of my father for this new club. Their manager Ted Kearns (recalling Max Rosenblum taking long aim at the Celtics) wanted to upend the Philadelphia Sphas, who'd for years done a land-office business in that small league. The *Gazette* followed its new team more quietly than say the Cleveland *Plain Dealer* (no cartoonists keeping the sports pages jumping: depression-time cartoons were long-faced anyhow — like those of Hitler and Mussolini found elsewhere in the paper). But despite their lacking the ethos of a big-city club, it took but one addition to make everything click for the Trenton Moose, after which they would make their move against the Sphas.

The acronym Spha stood for South Philadelphia Hebrew Association; today at the Hall of Fame an exhibit testifies to the prowess of this team on up to the mid-1940s. With competitive interest stirred up in 1932 by the Moose and the Jewels — both teams with *followings* — eight clubs along the eastern seaboard were formed into a new American League in 1933-34.

I said the start was quiet in 1932 — there is no Moose legend. But by way of my father's sister, a timely fifty-year update arrived in my mailbox not long ago — a page from the *Sunday Trentonian*, May 9, 1982. It was a commemoration of the Moose a half-century back, offering the only picture I've ever seen of them, a group in fairly disposable-looking uniforms, with a caption beginning "Here is the team acknowledged as best in the world in the 1932-33 season."

One may ask how far chauvinism can be carried — "best in the world" were they, and by what criterion? But weirdly enough the *Trentonian* was not trumping up some far-fetched outerbridge claim. No team this good ever represented a Jersey town; accomplishments could be cited outside of league play as well as in it.

My father leading their scorers, the Trenton Moose beat the Sphas in the 1933 Eastern League playoffs, and also took the first-half championship of the new American League the next season (repeating the pattern of the original Rosenblums). The Sphas then returned the favor and beat them in the 1934 playoffs. For that year and a half, Trenton could claim it had the best basketball team in America, and this was the second time my father would head up such a group. But more than that, he always called the Moose the best club he ever played for. He had reached and passed age thirty in those two seasons. It would start to get downhill from here (he re-entered school that same 1934 Trenton year). With diploma in hand the next year, he'd begun coaching football in Newark (Kearney High School), and thus was moved to organize the Newark Mules for the next pro season, taking some Moose with him and breaking up the combination. Mules and moose were good designations for those veterans, as the picture of the 1935 team shows.

I do not think nostalgia — in that these were his last starring seasons — had much to do with his nominating the Trenton teams as the best of his experience. To him, balance was the bread-and-butter word for winning consistently in basketball, and "The long and the short of it is, that's what we had." Winning the Eastern League's second half they were 14-1, and they would handle the Sphas 3-1 in the 1933 playoffs. On top of that they won three specially arranged "challenge" games. That two-month, 20-2 achievement was as good a stretch of basketball as my father was ever engaged in. Yarns from the old days are one thing. Against them might be weighed the feeling you sometimes get when you hear athletes talk, that for once exaggeration doesn't come into it. I always had that feeling when I overheard talk about the Moose. No wonder my aunt's surprise message was so welcome — somebody remembered them.

The forwards on the team were George Glasco and Rusty Saunders, natives of the town, who'd recently been with western teams of the *kaput* major league — they may have given Kearns the idea of going after my father. Howie Bollerman at 6'6" was center, replaced the following year by Tiny Hearn, the tallest player in the country at 6'9". The key late acquisition, though, was Lou Spindell, who came to Trenton by way of City College (where Nat Holman had begun to coach): he gave dazzle to the lineup — the one extra cutter they needed. The hub of their offense (where cutters wound up scoring) was the pivot play, and "there were only two great pivot players" — here was another fiat I heard plenty of old timers lay down. One was Dutch Dehnert of the Celtics, and the other Rusty Saunders now of Trenton. The game still included the center tap after each score, and a disciplined team always had to have smart big men to get them the ball back after scoring. This, Bollerman and afterwards Hearn could do — it meant even more than rebounding (not much scoring was asked from big men). So over that

20-2 stretch, standard accounts would crop up in the *Gazette*, like this: "With Glasco, Spindell and Saunders rushing in to take the ball when it was not back-tapped to Russell, the Moose were in almost constant possession of the leather."

Thus the Trenton team had its balance, its speed ("Spindell had a Ford motor in his rear end," my father said), and its all-important ball control off the tap — "we'd come up in spades with special plays late in a game." (It wouldn't be long though before the center jump had gone.)

Hard to beat the combination: for while a pivot offense was geared to scoring underneath, on those small courts of the old days — the ballroom of the Philadelphia Broadwood Hotel for instance — there was no better end-of-game strategy than to hit the pivotman and cut *without* going through and trying to score. George Glasco, who still lives in Trenton, told me at my father's funeral, "The game's changed, okay, but that team was the sharpest I've ever seen. I mean in the one special way of all the players knowing what the others were going to do. This meant off the tap — when the other clubs knew we had it — and off the pivot play. Right, we could take the air out of the ball [he meant hold it], and when we moved it it didn't hit the floor. But the big thing was, in real close games we did everything the same, I mean we went to the trickiest plays, like the pivotman batting the ball to the cutters, because the whole thing was routine to us, standard, it wasn't gambling." Nor was it hard to see why my father had been sold on that team forty years back from when I heard Glasco describe them. The part about the ball not hitting the floor was a giveaway. If there was one facet of basketball for which my father had almost no respect — with exceptions made for certain players like Kinsbrunner, Cousy, Bob Davies — it was dribbling. Controlling the ball meant keeping it moving, and his view was that a dribbler "froze" his teammates. The four-corner stall offense used in college today acknowledges the point: the "others" go to the four corners and stand. He saw that strategy come in and while he admitted some dribblers could control play, "not on the old ballroom floors they wouldn't." (Any sort of showboating, it goes without saying, left him cold. With his old-timer's respect for two points, he'd have fined any player who took off for a 360-dunk. On a topic like that, he'd have said, "Why not hit a home run and handspring around the bases?")

In the series in which Trenton beat Philadelphia, Cy Kaselman, the league's best shooter, led the Sphas. Kaselman's 17 points in the final game set a record, but my father got 15 in that game and Trenton won, 34-28. The newspaper account gives some flavor of the times in reporting the team's enthusiasm. "The Moose were nearly delirious after the successful completion of their climb.... Manager Kearns was so jubilant that he let the players keep their suits."

But then came a hint of further heights for the scaling: "It could not be ascertained immediately whether the Moose would play any more games this season. That will be doped out after the celebrating is over."

In mid-season of 1933 the Moose had scheduled and beaten the Jewels. They now had come so far that they agreed in late March to play the Celtics and the Renaissance, at Trenton and Philadelphia, and beat them both before large crowds. The magnitude of the feat may be better understood in that these were two of only three pro teams to have been voted into the Hall of Fame *as teams*. The Negro Renaissance were at their zenith; the Celtics barely below theirs, having regrouped just after the folding of the American League, and missing only Nat Holman who had retired. They too had managed to beat the Rens that year: when the Moose beat both of them, on the heels of their series with Philadelphia, they could claim what amounted to national honors. Against the Celtics, Holman's protégé Spindell went on a 21-point tear and the game wasn't close. Near the end of the Renaissance game, after Spindell had broken a 32-32 tie with a foul shot, my father provided the clincher on two of his patented cutting plays. "Honey Russell put the game on ice by registering two straight field goals on accurate pivot play passes from Saunders and Spindell." There was the season, the one he always remembered as his best one, wrapped up.

The Trenton title was mythical, of course, and I don't think number one status made my father fond of those years, so much as something else: Trenton was the only outstanding team, besides Cleveland, on which he performed purely as a player. Not having to coach — just being out there helping put game after blue-plate game on ice at age thirty — it must have been delicious, depression days or no.

One man unaccustomed to losing, who took it all very well, was Eddie Gottlieb. In 1918, Gottlieb had helped the South Philadelphia Hebrew Association launch its team, and had been with them ever since. His career ran parallel to my father's — for 28 years they were competitors in the same world, right up to the establishment of the NBA, though Gottlieb played only a few years, and was manager the bulk of that time, while my father kept playing. Losing the 1933 playoffs did not ruffle Gottlieb's equanimity. "Gotty was far from being down hearted," so one account reads, and "was the first to congratulate the new champions." He would retaliate the next year and defeat Trenton, and cop half of the remaining twelve American League titles. Parallels between him and my father do not stop there, for when Boston went into the NBA under my father in 1946, Gottlieb took the Philadelphia entry into the same division and had the honor of winning the first NBA championship. It was he who brought Joe Fulks into the league, so he also had a hand in turning the game of basketball around, because of Fulks's success as a jump shooter.

My father never played a minute for a Gottlieb team, always against them. Opponents always, different kinds of men entirely, but each imbued in the world of sport as long as the other — I think it not overstatement to say that my father loved Gottlieb. There was a steadfastness about him that could be

*Breaking up a Winner.* The powerful Trenton Moose were broken up when HR put together this entry for the 1935 season of the new American League. Here are his Newark Mules, in a picture notable for its rogues' gallery highlights. Front row, from left: Lefty Kintzing, Red Conaty, Fred Romp, Benny Borgmann, HR; back row, Lou Spindell, Tiny Hearn, Gaza Chizmadia. My father had taken Spindell and Hearn from Trenton with him.

*New York Jewels*, 1937. The core of this team, the St. John's Wonder Five, are identified in italics. From left: *Allie Schuckman, Mac Kinsbrunner, Rip Gerson*, George Slott, *Mack Posnak*, Jack Poliskin, HR, *Matty Bergovich*.

counted on. The highest praise my father could bestow on a person was that he or she was "always the same" — you would know what to expect. People who rose out of doldrums and then plunged back into them never engaged my father's interest. Continuity of personality did.

Among the flowers arriving to the undertakers at the wake held for my father — I cite a couple like "Red Holzman and the New York Knicks," "Red Auerbach and the Boston Celtics," because they are there in my mind's eye in proximity to this one other — was a basket with a small white sheet pinned to some leaves, and handwritten on it, "Eddie Gottlieb."

Late in a game at Philadelphia in the 1934 season, my father got his front teeth knocked out for the second time. He had retained the roots of the original teeth, on the bases of which he had had pivot teeth installed; these were knocked out and the roots themselves broken this time. Doc Sugarman (the Lou Sugarman of the Chicago game mentioned some pages back) was the referee this night and a practicing dentist in Philadelphia. He took my father to his office after the game and, in a session that lasted until two or three in the morning, probed for the broken roots, a terrific ordeal for my father to undergo. It was probably not as traumatic an event as the baseball collision — he had not been knocked out — but he said it was the most painful thing he'd ever had to go through.

There is a kind of winsomeness about having a referee be the one to take you back and treat you professionally after an injury. I say this conscious of having come a great remove from the event itself. At first thought one might have supposed the thing unrivalled in a sense — who ever had such an experience in precisely those terms: the ref stopping the play and (to telescope it a bit) reaching into his bag and producing the equipment for handling the casualty? But on second thought one suspects that Doc Sugarman probably had a number of such cases. On the matter of dental injuries, I am reminded that my father had a friend, a sometime ball player named Marty Kaufman, from whom we three children received free dental care in those prewar years. This was on account not only of friendship but also of the stream of athletic injuries my father referred to Marty Kaufman. (My father was the "referee" in those cases.) I used to hate having to go to that office, with the ordinary child's antipathy to dentists, but also with an aversion for the ultra-Jewish bowery locale where Dr. Kaufman had his practice. We lived in a Jewish neighborhood in Brooklyn, true enough, but this East Broadway area, with carts on every corner, unfamilar smells from half the doorways, and extraordinary numbers of old people, was another world.

Forming his Newark club for 1934-35, my father scheduled some exhibition games for the American Legion hall at Kingston. An October news clipping reports the Newark team's visit and their manager's planned return trip: "Next week Russell will return to Kingston with the New York Rollers, to see if he can give the Legionnaires a worse trimming than he was able to with his Newark five last night." The article looks forward to the "bill of fare": preliminary game, feature game, and maybe best of all, "Two hours of dancing after the contests with music by a Kingston orchestra."

Mid-depression was on the country by that time, and all kinds of booking schemes were practiced by ball players like my father and sports promoters in general. Thus the name "Rollers" mentioned above refers to a team playing out of the Brooklyn Roller Rink on Empire Boulevard, which featured post-game roller skating for the crowd. The fact that he played for the Rollers, plus his decision to wear a dental plate now that he'd lost his teeth again, led to a bizarre incident in my father's life. It was one more example of a concatenation of circumstances that always seemed to make his life adventuresome.

At the Empire rink, the promoters had brought in an old-time skating performer for an exhibition before the basketball game. This old campaigner happened to be deaf and dumb. He dressed in the same dressing room as the two ball clubs, and my father and the other players saw him in there when they came in as he was ready to go out. It was apparent that he could not speak, and they exchanged makeshift salutes as he passed them by on his wheels.

Dressing for the game, my father as was his custom took out his upper front teeth and dropped the plate into the side pocket of his suit jacket. The game was played. Between halves the skater gave another demonstration, but left after that, since when the game was over the crowd would be taking to the floor.

When he was dressed for the street after the ball game my father reached in his pocket to retrieve his teeth. They weren't there. He searched about but only for a minute, because he remembered having seen another blue suit on the clothes pole in the dressing room, next to which he had hung his own. The former was now gone. He reasoned that it had to belong to the old skater, and that the teeth were in it.

My mother was waiting outside — they and the Conatys and another couple (my mother forgets whom) were going out that evening, which made it imperative that my father have his teeth. Red Conaty was an outstanding Brooklyn ball player, oldest of three brothers who all played pro basketball, and the Conaty children were the only near neighbors of my youth whose father also was an athlete. My parents saw a great deal of them. My mother thinks the third couple that evening might have been the O'Tooles. Frank O'Toole, a small, wiry man, my father's insurance agent, was a great pinochle crony of Red Conaty and my father and a follower of their sports doings. Where Red's son and I, both the same age, were less than enthralled about accompanying our fathers to workouts at the St. George's Hotel — when we were in our teens — Frank O'Toole's son Tommy, a year younger, used to welcome the chance to go. He became the best basketball player of the three of us; was my own closest friend in Brooklyn days; and later captained the Boston College team of 1952, whose 22 wins held up as a record for thirty years. Of Frank O'Toole, who was a self-endearing man but who could be aggravating to his friends, my father used to say — referring to Frank's turn for buying a round of drinks — "O'Toole's a guy with fishhooks in his pockets."

So it was my mother and Ann Conaty and Celestine O'Toole who were waiting in the roller rink seats when my father emerged pointing to his vacant space and saying they'd have to hunt up the skater who unknowingly possessed his teeth. (I have another reason for hoping the O'Tooles were along. My father once took Celestine for a spin on a dance floor, after yet another of those "mixer" events of ball-game-and-dance-on-premises that have gone out of modern life. They whirled into another couple and Celestine's shoe caught in the other lady's, sending her down. Whereupon her wig rolled off and she was revealed to be skin bald. This was a woman they had all seen before, though they did not know her — after she rushed from the floor that night, cramming her poor hair on, they never saw her again.)

It was not difficult to obtain the deaf skater's address, which happened to be a boarding house not far away on Eastern Parkway. All six people in the car were giddy from the start at the thought of how my father was going to go about explaining the problem of his missing dentures to a deaf man. When they reached the house, the landlady obligingly told my father which room the skater occupied, but it was two flights up and she declined to accompany him.

He reported that it was a dimly lit hall up there. He of course knocked, knowing the uselessness. He waited, then tried the knob, and the door gave way to a black room. He went in and felt along the wall — the light from the corridor offered no help — he was hoping he would encounter a clothes rack or closet with his hand, had no such luck, penetrated a few steps with hand sweeping in front — and touched what he recognized as the hanging lightcord. The skater was breathing fitfully in sleep. My father decided to pull the lightcord. He did it and as the light came on saw on a chair across the room the blue jacket he sought. He heard the old man turn over but did not look back at him till he'd found the teeth; then turned round with them held up in the air, toward the now absolutely awakened face that had come up off the pillow. Nothing but fear registered as my father in his overcoat went through a dumbshow: shook the teeth, pointed to the jacket, pointed to his own mouth trying to give a revealing grin that would be conciliatory at the same time. He then put the teeth in, still trying to communicate the essence of the event to the man on the bed, saw it was no use, reached up for the lightswitch (at which the man flinched, cringing back), so that my father made it apparent he was striding toward the door as he pulled the cord angularly, to show that he was on the way out. The six in his party were stricken with laughter for the rest of the night, my mother says, as they kept re-conjuring the scene. All through the years my father would maintain that the roller skater could only assume that he'd been the victim of a dream.

When I saw the Savage's yearbook of 1934 with the memo, "Honey Russell's teeth to Abe Galinsky," I thought that might have been the old skater's name, but later on pieced together that the roller rink episode could only have dated from the following season.

The years from the middle-to-late thirties were years of a couple of memorable automobiles for our family: a secondhand Pierce Arrow — its headlights grew out of the front fenders — and after it an even older Franklin with giant elliptical headlamps. Both had been in service as limousines and were consumptive gas eaters. My father bought the first because he had signed on in 1935 to manage a team in Utica. The seven-passenger Pierce Arrow could carry a whole ball club plus basketballs up and back from Brooklyn. What our neighbors might have thought, to see such an uneconomical long car outside our two-family house on East 37th Street, it never occurred to us children to wonder. With its jump seats, it was a good car to play in: in fact its back was like a whole room, especially fine to be in on rainy days.

My father got into some small trouble with this car as the result of a tragic accident for which, thankfully, he bore no responsibility. He and his players were driving back one night from a game upstate, when they felt the car receive an odd bump from the rear on a stretch of road that showed nothing to be behind them. They stopped the Pierce Arrow and walked back some ways with a flashlight until they came on a motorcycle in the road, the cyclist dead. I'm not sure how quickly the police became involved — that is, I don't remember hearing that the next car to come along was a police car — but it happened that the young man killed was running from the police, had left his headlamp off, and must have been looking back when he came full tilt into the rear of my father's car — even though it was the lightest of bumps.

My father was free and clear but the dead man's parents were distraught enough to threaten to bring charges against him. He went to Frank O'Toole since he was insured by Frank's company, and received a four-word instruction: "Get out of town." O'Toole was insistent on this, so my father called up his Aunt Lil in Ridgewood and went over to stay with her the next week. That made him unavailable for the first inquiry. His leaving town convinced the victim's parents of his guilt, although a clear lack of evidence forestalled the manslaughter charges they wanted to bring. When he did meet these people, they vilified him and even the police thought he'd done a cowardly thing in leaving — the parents in fact presented him with a bill for their son's funeral and in a shrill scene (so my mother attests) demanded that he pay for this — which of course he did not do.

The whole thing shows a naive, unquestioning, almost quiescent side to my father, as far as practical matters, the seeking of advice and so forth, were concerned, at least while he was a comparatively young man. The humiliation he underwent made him seek out O'Toole to discover why he had given such advice. He never forgave him when he heard the answer: Frank simply hadn't believed his story.

The one vivid thing I can recall about seven-passenger-car II, the Franklin, was that it had a thick glass window you could roll up between the chauffer's compartment and the rear seat. I not only left this window rolled up one day, but left both rear doors in the locked position, so that none of us could get in the back seat again. It was springtime. The car wasn't needed for basketball trips then, and so for a few weeks before my father decided what to do, our family when taken for a ride would all have to jam together up in front — another sight, and this one we *were* conscious of, for neighborhood speculation, given all that wasted room behind the invisible glass. A trip to Coney Island, however, brought things to a head, though why the solution didn't occur to him before I don't know. My father hadn't got short-tempered with us children, but having to ride all the way back like sardines, the three of us weren't as happy as Coney Island usually made us. Reluctance to break any auto glass had all along kept him at bay. Now at last, provoked by our squabbling so my sister declared, he had a garage friend dismount one of the heavy rear doors, and the Franklin was brought back to roadworthiness.

Roadworthy enough it was, but the Franklin did have one odd feature. Its floor shift would unaccountably keep jumping out of third gear. When we drove up to Lake Champlain in 1939, and on trips from our cottage I made that summer with my father, who had begun umpiring in the Northern League, I used to hold the Franklin in gear. My father could steady the gearshift with his knee by extending his leg unnaturally outward, which he did when no one else was along. But starting that summer I traveled with him increasingly more often. My memory tends to convince me it was when I had the job of holding the stick in gear that the "sidekick" bonds began to form. He'd have more to say on the way up to a game (I might have been sleepy on the longer trips); I'd be the talkative one on the way back, details of the game and so on.

It was on one of those trips that I saw him injured. A foul ball caught him on the inside of the ankle, just where the shinguard flap left off. It was an ugly purple by the time he could look at it, in the umpires' dressing room; he could get into a moccasin okay (that's what he drove in), so he decided not to shower and to start straight home in his umpire's suit. There were no questions from me that day; he couldn't come back with anything. I'd glance at his face, see it was still set the same, he was hurting. It was his driving foot, too; I just held onto the gearshift and kept quiet.

That injury laid him up for a week, the ankle all enlarged and blackened, my mother completely upset by its color though he could tell it wasn't broken or chipped.

What made me talkative, on return trips other than that one, was my having been alone through the nine innings. There was I at ten, the one person in the stands as partial to how the umpires were faring as to what was happening on the field. If I heard "Go on home, ump," I'd say to myself, "he's not an 'ump.'" But not look around of course. You knew enough to swallow your emotions, always had to keep mum, if you were kin to an umpire.

But I've gotten ahead of myself and wanted to speak about basketball bookings in the thirties. The St. John's Wonder Five, as I mentioned, had become by 1933 the New York Jewels of the American League. Two of them, Mack Posnak and Allie Schuckman, my father had brought onto the Utica team in 1935-36, and that season he became the playing coach of the Jewels. The other three members of the Wonder Five were Mac Kinsbrunner, Rip Gerson, and Matty Begovich. Four Jews and a Russian representing a Vincentian college were wondrous enough, but this group earned its name through exploits on the court.

When my father coached them he generally played as sixth

*Ready to Sparkle.* Joe DiMaggio, before exhibition game in which he was slated to play for HR's Jewels, 1937.

*Borrowing More Ringers.* The West New York baseball club added some heft after the major league season ended. Here, flanking Mayor Effert, are Ruth and Gehrig, who helped the club beat the Bushwicks, October 13, 1930. At right front, HR, wearing glove.

man, and could substitute equally well at forward, guard, or center. Trying to attract customers in lean attendance years led to many schemes, such as, for an exhibition game in October 1937, signing Joe DiMaggio to play. DiMaggio had just completed his second year with the Yankees and was a torrid athletic property. He worked out with the team, but on the night of the game before a full house at Arcadia Hall DiMaggio was introduced at courtside in his street clothes. At the last minute the Yankees had reneged on their permission to let him play. Such was his popularity that, when he went out to throw up the first ball, the fans were so carried away in their ovation that they were genuinely appeased though having been deprived of the chance to see him play. There were no repercussions, no sour grapes or claims for ticket refunds. (I think they were sophisticated enough fans — at Arcadia Hall, that is, not at the Roller Rink — to realize DiMaggio would have only made a token appearance in the ball game anyhow.)

Apropos of the celebrity status of major league stars in those days, my mother has a large photograph of my father with his West New York baseball teammates pictured together with Ruth and Gehrig in Yankee road uniforms. The picture is captioned "Ruth and Gehrig playing with the West New Yorks vs. the Bushwicks winning score 8 to 5 at Dexter Park, Oct. 13th 1930." My father barnstormed more than once at season's end with Ruth-and-Gehrig assemblages, and always told one story about the two men. "Ruth would usually throw away his white baseball stockings after a ball game. Gehrig washed his own out, and when he would see Ruth throw his away, he'd go get them and wash them out too, and come away with two pairs." How apocryphal this story may be I have no way of judging. I am inclined to think he saw this happen at least once.

Gehrig of course overlapped with DiMaggio (Ruth did not) and I remember seeing the two in action at Yankee Stadium — an indelible moment with Gehrig at bat (he hit after DiMaggio) in a game against the White Sox. Why the moment comes back is that it connects with a baseball-pool scheme my father was involved in. He and Eddie Wilde, the Jewels' general manager, had started a sports booking agency and as a sideline distributed printed-up cards which I used to see but didn't understand. These listed the American and National League teams and had the numbers 1 through 9 next to each name: I now think people circled names and/or numbers for varieties of betting combinations. One payoff the agency had to make was for "runs for the week," but, as I vaguely understand it, there were also prizes for such things as "best inning" on a given day, based on a multiple of the total runs scored by a team in that inning.

Here, then, was Gehrig batting against the White Sox when, just as the pitcher was about to deliver, my father jumped from his seat. He wasn't the only one: there was a general roar, against which could be heard the crack of a bat. On the scoreboard a 16 had been slipped into some late-inning slot of a game being played elsewhere. Gehrig had connected with a line drive which, with everybody up pointing at the scoreboard, I missed seeing — also the catch Mike Kreevich made of this blast. My father'd seen both those astonishing things, but the paramount murmur-roar was "sixteen runs in one inning" and somehow (belatedly) I gathered his firm would be having to make a huge payoff. Initially I thought it was the figure 16 itself which had wowed the still buzzing fans; and meanwhile had to rely on my father's report of what happened after Gehrig swung and connected, and I felt cheated at missing the Kreevich catch. Of course it was Gehrig who had a right to feel cheated.

In the same year he toyed with DiMaggio playing for the Jewels, Eddie Wilde got up the idea of staging a few games — literally staging them — at theatres like the Brooklyn Paramount between showings of a feature film. In contrast to the fellow-feeling I described as starting at age ten, I distinctly remember the exciting thing about the Jewels' games at the Paramount (when I would have been eight) was to be able to see the movie — at night no less. I can remember the games all right: the brightness of the lighting, the fact that the players were all a bit above eye level from where my mother and I sat. The Jewels wore gold pants and white shirts with a gold "J" on them, and I do remember my father, fairly bald by then and dark jowled, and the fun of seeing him come onto the stage, picking him out from the rest during the warmup — this was the first year they had begun taking me to games. The court I know was very small and the games slow-paced, anything but free-wheeling. (Only a clown would let himself get near falling off the stage.) But those facts don't stand forward in memory at all. What registers with great vividness is that on the two nights I was allowed to go to the Paramount, "The Plainsman" and "Charge of the Light Brigade" were the features. And on both occasions there was this to relish about seeing them: my mother and I first saw the movie; next watched the game; and afterwards saw the movie *all the way through again*, my father joining us part way along in the second showing. And on top of that the tickets were free.

The Jewels played in some theatres on the road too. My father's way of recalling one such game was preserved by the columnist Murray Robinson in the New York *Journal-American* of September 5, 1964:

> Possibly the strangest basketball game of all time was played on the stage of the State Theatre in Easton, Pa., between the Brooklyn Jewels and a local club starting at 2:30 a.m. on May 9, 1937.
> 
> "We started that late," Honey Russell, the basketball Hall of Famer and Milwaukee baseball scout recalled recently, "because we had to wait until the burlesque show was over to set up the court.
> 
> "We brought two heavy glass backboards down from New York, and then we found we'd forgotten to bring the posts to set them on. So the stagehands hung them from the flies at the end of long ropes.
> 
> "The game was a fast one from the start, but we began noticing something peculiar as it went on. The baskets

seemed to get easier to reach, like they were getting closer to the floor. By half-time, the points were a cinch. We hardly had to jump at all to score.

"And then it dawned on us what was happening. The weight of the heavy glass backboards were stretching the ropes, and the baskets were dropping closer to the floor all the time. There was no time to rehang them, so we kept on playing. Toward the end of the game, the taller guys could look down into the baskets instead of up at them. If we'd gone into overtime, the backboards would have rested on the floor."

No question but Murray Robinson has got my father's authentic accents here. The exaggeration in the last two sentences is a hallmark. It suits the remove in time — 1937 to 1964. The May 9 date is somewhat astonishing, given my father's unreliability with figures, but there is little reason to demur on that score and meanwhile we can be sure of the place. The one time I heard my father tell the story, Abbot and Costello were part of the stage act the Jewels followed; but in that retelling, his point was that it became *harder* to score once the baskets had sunk lower. In neither case did his listeners come up with any rebuttals. (But how far can ropes stretch?) There always seemed to exist, between him and his audience, a tacit acceptance that a fundamental crazy situation was being passed along, and that some of the incidentals need not be overscrutinized. That it was a "fast game from the start" is very possible, since my own eight-year-old's memory of a gingerly played game on the Paramount stage could be suspect, and I never would have queried my father on a crux of that kind.

For real speed in those days, the motorcycle races at the Bay Ridge Raceway, which my father, a partner in National Sports Enterprises, helped inaugurate were unrivalled. They were held at night on a black cinder track, from which spectators were separated by a board fence; the lighting was dim and on the far side of the oval the huddled cyclists became indistinguishable from one another; then they would swirl by in front of you with flour-sack-like numbers on their chests and backs, each rider braced on an inside metal shoe that shot showers of copper sparks all over. Cinders flew toward the stands too, when a bike made too wide a bend I suppose, and a woman was once struck in the eye by one, for which my father and his partners were liable. Then as always this was a dangerous sport. I know there was a grandstand but can never remember being seated at these races. I seem to recall whoever I'd be with being stationed some ways along the fence, away from the stands and not far from the pits: possibly because of communications going on between the promoters and the riders and their mechanics. I have a sort of "paddock" remembrance of the thing. I would start with my father, who always on the move would leave me in custody of someone else, Frank O'Toole for instance, who sold tickets there and would be free to stand by the rail once the races had begun.

There were some deaths during the two years we were involved in the Bay Ridge Races. I do not know if the main backer of the event, Tommy Lynam, buried the competitors who were killed: Lynam was an undertaker. He was the target of banter on this subject, so I learned from some surviving partners of the National Sports Enterprises days. I wouldn't have known what an undertaker was then, so do not associate that calling with the memory I have of Lynam, that he was the thinnest and sallowest person I had ever seen. Cheerful and crisp enough for all that, but he makes an unerasable picture when his name is recalled. My father spoke of him as looking like "an advance man for a famine."

That particular tag was one my father would make use of every so often, one of a store of expressions he had which singled out physical shortcomings. Thus someone with a large nose would "have to use a bedsheet for a handkerchief," or else was able to "smoke a cigar and take a shower at the same time." Anybody bowlegged either had "cruller legs" or "couldn't stop a pig in an alley." If the problem was buck teeth, the person endowed could "eat an ear of corn through a picket fence." (The one everybody used, "a taxicab with the doors open" for outstanding ears, was too commonplace for my father to resort to.)

Women came in for a few of these barbs, less often for physical shortcomings, though. Maybe twice, I heard my father say something savage about women over-fond of their looks — once it was a primper on a television quiz show, who caused him to say, "God gave her a skull and flung some meat at it." Much more likely, he'd saddle women who talked too much with labels like "Pathé news." My sister Dotty sometimes had to bear the brunt of that one. We three children laughed, I guess from the time we could talk, on account of his jingle made up especially for us, about a little man named Bill, "who lived in a can on a garbage hill / never took a bath and he never will / AH CHOO! dirty old Bill." The rhyme sequence is the oldest of any I can recall. A stuffed shirt, in my father's jargon — he'd have us children giggling once we caught on to this — was "a big shot not spelled with an o."

His generation had a real penchant for stand-bys like these. Far from suggesting callousness, they show a ripeness for invention that characterized him and many of his companions. A kind of running hyperbole contest went on within their circles and seemed second nature to them. Certainly to him, at all events. He had a whole Sears' catalogue of "gamesman's" language — of little routines like "Tell your story moving," which used to dampen his grandchildren's ardor; or just plain nonsense litanies like "Friends to the end/Lend me five/This is the end" — but it was all in a manner of chiming in, in that dry voice he had, and not really seeking the last word.

It would be wrong to exaggerate this playfulness — it's perhaps better described as a *readiness* for playfulness, for those were years of effort, and the returns were more often than not unrewarding. "Lend me five/this is the end": still, plenty of fives had literally to be borrowed. In 1938 when my father took up umpiring, in sandlots for teams like the Brooklyn Union Gas

Company, he would for such work earn five dollars, a figure my mother remembers with conviction. Yet like as not returning from one of those games — they were out at the end of the trolley line, I'd take lump sugar along because there were goats out on those lots — we would be nearing our house when he would say, "Fox in the bush! One up!" and start knocking me on the arm till I put up a finger. Then you had to put one finger up or be thumped in penalty, because he had seen a rabbi before you had — or an old-clothes man, or anyone else with a beard who qualified as a fox in the bush.

Foxes in bushes on East 37th Street and goats on the flatlands of East Flatbush — how rural Brooklyn could seem. I remember seeing a fox in the bush the Saturday I earned my first fifty cents. I'd usually wander away from the Gas Company game I'd been brought to, but this day the batboy who worked for the teams hadn't shown up. "How about *him*?" my father'd asked the coach — then stood by encouragingly as the batboy's routine was explained. I was nine and a little nervous about taking on this chore, but since I'd been butted the week before, I didn't mind staying put this week. Anyway, the half-a-dollar I earned came in that form: not a quarter from each team, and this impressed me. Just as we got off the trolley, I dug in my pocket where the sugar cubes still were to get the coin out, and my father nudged me and I saw the fox in the bush. I came out with the words as fast as he did so there was no winner. It was a peddler with a sack, and the fifty cents in my hand made me think he'd be lucky to have that much on him. It wasn't compassion — what I felt was the half dollar was a *lot* of *money*. (One-tenth, it amounted to, of what the umpiring had just earned for our family: something I didn't realize.)

Most of my father's tag-lines were obviously overheard. Yet the ready service he found for them, and the improvements he made, marked a faculty that brought him maybe a stage beyond the ordinary quipster. The last evening we were together, when he seemed to be making a comeback against prostatic cancer, we were watching the New York Mets on television and a relief pitcher fresh in the game kept kicking a lot of dirt around on the front of the mound. My father always disliked pitchers who stalled, and of this one he said, "They must have picked this guy up out of some arboretum."

My father's degree at Savage's had opened the way to some high school teaching as well as coaching, and his job in Kearney High School led in turn to his being hired by Seton Hall in 1936, to coach the college basketball squad and to teach at Seton Hall Prep as well. If the salary was low, he had the benefit of being able to pursue his bachelor's degree too, which he received from Seton Hall in 1939; he followed this with an M.A. at NYU in 1941.

Though he'd had the Pierce Arrow and was later to have the Franklin, we were mostly "between cars" in the later thirties, and my father commuted by subway, ferry, and rail to Seton Hall. Of course he was coaching the Jewels then in Brooklyn too. The Seton Hall job became solid after the second season, which was a winning one, with Sadowski on the team and assurances of winning thereafter. At this point my father probably should have moved us all to New Jersey; but my mother's allegiance to my grandmother proved too strong. It was not till I was out of college, when he had his championship team of 1953, that they moved to East Orange, and a little after that to Livingston. All the time before then he managed that hard commuting — which even extended to those two Boston years with the Celtics and before that, the wartime commuting to the C-O-Two Fire Equipment Company.

My father's subway riding was always against the grain. Even on teaching days he did not have to be at Seton Hall until the afternoon: on "practice-only" days he'd be riding trains during late rush hour though the cars he rode would be empty. This was true, too, when he coached up at Manhattan in 1945-46 — the daily trip there encompassed the entire span of the IRT line from Flatbush to the upper Bronx. He was not teaching at Manhattan and always left about the time other Brooklynites were getting ready to come down out of the city, and passed the lot of them in those clangorous tunnels as though traveling on a one-way street. I don't know if that lightened the trip at all.

The great break my father got at Seton Hall, so extraordinary that it also would affect his second tenure there, occurred in the fall of 1938 when Bob Davies walked onto the court to try out for the freshman team. My father hadn't recruited Davies. He was a Harrisburg boy who had come to the college on a baseball scholarship.

Near the end of his playing career, Bob Davies took up golf, and it wasn't long before he was playing in the low seventies. (Someone recently wrote in *Sports Illustrated* about what a good *tennis* player he is, in his sixties.) He had been a four-sport athlete in high school, and looked destined for the major leagues — playing in the Red Sox system, Davies in the estimation of many scouts could have moved straight onto the parent club if only he moderated his swing, for he was an unmatched fielder at second base.

It was my father's contention that Davies was the best natural athlete he ever saw. Since he went so far in basketball — All-American, named to the Silver Anniversary team of the NBA, and inducted into the Hall of Fame — his other athletic abilities have tended to become eclipsed. But all this may give an idea of the windfall that came my father's way when Davies appeared among his tryouts.

The Seton Hall varsity won its last four games that season, with Sadowski a junior. Then Davies moved onto the team and over the next two years they won 39 straight games: the total string tied the national record at 43. On defense Davies was a gambler — a diver, as my father called it, and as a coach he relished coming up against divers. He used to set up the "muff" play against them — a faked chest pass that guaranteed two easy back-door points if the defender overcomittted to the "muff."

But Davies for all that was permitted to dive: my father did not try to make an orthodox defensive player out of him (in fact he couldn't), and used to say that Davies' reflexes were so good that he could not only get away with gambling but recover when he was fooled and not cost the defense that much.

Davies was a spectacular dribbler, the only ball player my father ever coached whom he encouraged to put the ball on the floor, because off the dribble Davies made great passing plays in the front court. He was first to perfect the behind-the-back dribble, though I think he was ordered to keep wraps on this — after all, it was a backcourt maneuver not likely to lead to a score. A leaper gifted with split-vision, Davies would hang in the air and pass behind his neck to unseen cutters coming out of the blue; his teammates got used to this and they became a whirlwind group to watch.

The team became so popular in his sophomore year, playing mostly at the Orange Armory, that Seton Hall's present gymnasium, far in advance of its time and second only to Yale's then, got built virtually overnight to accommodate them. Their schedule began there in Davies' junior year, and when fans came in they saw a mural on one side of the lobby, still there, of my father and the first five. On the other side the fencing team had a mural — they were better than the basketballers, and *never* lost while my father was at the Hall. The gym is now called Walsh Auditorium, after the old Archbishop of Newark, who used to sit in a balcony seat at midcourt behind the clock — almost as though presiding. During one game that year, when my father had used a flock of substitutes in the first half because he was trying to keep the score down, Archbishop Walsh sent down a pencilled note at halftime which read, "YOU DID NOT USE STRATEGY IN THAT HALF." In his small handwriting my father wrote back to him, "He wasn't dressed."

The most publicized game Seton Hall played that year was for its 43rd victory, against Rhode Island State to open the 1941 Invitation Tournament. But it was followed by a solid trouncing from LIU (defending their own hold on the 43-game record, which they'd set), a loss which dimmed my father's team just when the whole Garden had gotten intoxicated by them.

A cheering priest had actually died of a heart attack in the grandstand during the victory over Rhode Island. Newspapers had picked this up, but didn't tend to see anything hubristic in all the fanfare that was surging around this team. The *Daily News* pictured them on its back page, above the caption "UNBEATABLE?" At twelve, I wasn't surprised at the word, only at the question mark. When it came to LIU's "strategy," Clair Bee didn't need an archbishop to prod him: "hold down the star" was Bee's philosophy, and he decided to double-team Davies. The plan worked, mainly because, though Davies was a great passer, his teammates came up with iron hands that game, and either dropped his passes or muffed the shots he'd set them up for. There weren't any alibis, even though Davies was heartbroken — Bee and LIU simply owned that game.

Two nights later at the NIT finals, my mother asked me to go down and catch hold of my father at halftime and ask him if we'd be leaving before the tournament awards were passed out. There I was, rooting for Ohio University, who were doing surprisingly well against LIU: I was holding a grudge against Bee's goony team. He had two big awkward centers, goons was what I thought they were, Beenders and Holub, who had rebounded all those missed shots off Davies' passes the other night. Working my way down to ground level, I reached the underpass to the floor seats as the half ended. There was my father, standing in his usual station, with a tide of people coming past him, including LIU players on their way to the dressing room. As I reached him so did Clair Bee, who paused and said to him, "What do you think, Honey?"

My father said something about the middle being blocked up, and I felt myself stiffen angrily — what in the world was he doing, did he want Bee to win?

"They're quicker than I thought," said Bee. "They're picking off some of our stuff."

"Maybe if you break Beenders in and out of the pivot, instead of having him stay in there and cause traffic...."

"That's a point. You think we can give-and-go on them?"

"If you open the middle I'm not too sure you can't, but it means busting the big guy out of there."

I could hardly stand this talk and walked off a few yards but that was about the end of it. Whether or not Bee took the advice is hard to say, since my interest flagged once Ohio began to look outclassed in the second half. We beat the rush to the subway; awards didn't matter, but what had halted me was any conversation at all between the torpedoer and the one torpedoed.

Different from the team's rise-and-fall contests in the NIT was the one that closed out the season in the new gym, for the 42nd win. This was against the University of Baltimore, an experienced team which had won every game but one (and that loss to LIU). It featured a great dive by Davies. Near the end of the game Seton Hall was losing by a point. My father sent Al Negratti (later to coach at Portland) over to the scorer's table in case a jump ball situation arose, for in those days you could substitute for the jumper and Negratti was a good tap-getter. People were thronging the court behind the basket where the scorer's table was, and when a whistle stopped play Negratti thought a jump ball had been called. He reported for the teammate he thought involved. But he reported to the scorer, not the timer, and in the press of bodies down by the table the scorer couldn't get the timer's attention. Meanwhile the play was ruled out-of-bounds, Baltimore. From mid-court, the Baltimore player threw the ball in. Davies had lain back, anticipated the throw-in, and in the gamble of the year intercepted it. He was past mid-court when the timer's horn blew (not a buzzer those days), ending the game he thought. But he drove into the basket, laying the ball up. The game was won. There were still over ten seconds on the clock. The timer had only just been apprised of the attempted substitution, was blocked from seeing play resume, and had blown the horn after the throw-in. Of course he could not stop the action then.

The uproar can be imagined. The referee's decision to allow the goal was the only one left open to him, but that was not what Baltimore's coach thought, and he threatened to remove his team from the court in protest. He was prevailed upon to continue — took Seton Hall off his schedule thereafter — but his team could not pull the game out in the several seconds remaining.

What Bob Davies did not do was the mark of the performer he was. To give a name to the instinct involved is impossible. Something checked him from a false reaction to that horn, and his perfect form on the lay-up bore out the instinct. A year later on the same court, this time *in* a jump ball situation, a senior on the Davies team wound up with the ball and the same kind of room, the same vanishing seconds left. It was against Dartmouth. Again there was a one-point deficit, with a chance to drive in and win, but my father's player shot this time from about the place where Davies was when that last-year's horn went off. The ball cleared not only the backboard but the balcony rail above it, by yards, ending up in a row halfway to the roof. Talk about adrenalin. It took more time to get the ball down than it did for the rest of the game to be played and for Dartmouth to make off elatedly to its dressing room.

During the winning streak my father had no coaching problems, but in the team's senior year, when their record was 16-3, he did have some. I was not aware of this then, but evidently he had to confront his ball players about their jealousy of Davies. Davies should have inspired little of that — he made other ball players look good — yet it may have been inevitable. Still, Tim Cohane, a New York writer who had my father's confidence, was able to report in February 1942 that all appeared "serene once again with the Seton Hall basketball team." Mentioning how "some of the veterans were resenting the publicity being accorded Bob Davies," Cohane went on:

>Russell proved himself an adept psychologist when he called the team together before the St. Peter's game a couple of weeks ago. Instead of commiserating with the complaining seniors, he rightfully defended the even-tempered Davies, who never has found trouble finding a hat to fit him.
>
>"You other fellows might as well realize," pointed out Russell, "that without Davies, you wouldn't have gone any place. You never would have gone through last year undefeated; never would have made Madison Square Garden. You're just ordinary ballplayers, who have hooked up with one great player to make a pretty fair team. You can go along being a pretty fair team, only if you cut out this jealousy business."

The quoted words are undoubtedly very close to the ones my father used, though they are different from the kind he might resort to at a halftime, when agitated over mental mistakes. Because he sounded much tougher than this when being constructive. He must have been extraordinarily angry to tell his seniors, "You're just ordinary ballplayers. . . ." For one thing, he didn't believe it; they weren't. One of the seniors, Bobby Holm, would become a solid guard for many years in the National League. Another, John Ruthenberg, could not have missed as a professional player but was killed in the war. A third, Ben Scharnus, played for Cleveland in the first year of the NBA. They were all good.

The keenest point of all, concerning what Cohane reported of my father's words, is that they have no heat in them. They seem, and I am sure were uttered this way, off-hand. I put that down to deep personal anger. The one thing my father had no sympathy for was the resentment that grows out of envy. There was a fund of gratefulness that went into his makeup, which precluded his condoling with athletes who could feel short-changed over a teammate's success. His defense of Davies, when that did happen among some of the others, was total in the very indifference with which he put the case. "Tacitly,"

*Seton Hall Mealticket, Pre-war.* Bob Davies, who led the college team to 43 game win streak, broken in March 1941 in the NIT. Davies also coached a year at the Hall, and was responsible for bringing in HR's post-war mealticket, seven foot Walter Dukes. *Streak Broken.* John Ruthenberg (13) rebounding against Hank Beenders of LIU in the game that cost Seton Hall its 44th win and a record. John Ruthenberg wore a tragic number. A bomber pilot afterward, he was the only varsity athlete at the Hall to be killed in the war.

*Blindsided.* Walter Dukes playing against Louisville, March 1953, in the game after the Hall's other great win streak had been snapped. It might well have been Dukes's neck, from the way Al Russak came after him here.

Cohane went on to say, "the Setonians agreed that Russell was right."

My father never minded having either of his winning streaks broken, in the sense that they were numerical achievements. Yet besides the 43-game record, he did hold for a time the record for a single season, 27, set by his 1953 team. (In 1956 San Francisco broke both these at once, their star being "the other Russell" — as my father laughingly referred to Bill, who'd prove so much more important to the Celtics than their first Russell.) Surprisingly, Bob Davies had a hand in this second record as well. For in 1947, while playing for the Rochester Royals, Davies coached at Seton Hall. His 24-3 team was made up mostly of my father's veterans returning from service. But the strain of the National League schedule became too great and after a year Bob had to give up coaching. In Rochester, meanwhile, he had discovered an amazing prospect, and secured him for the future at Seton Hall Prep. So in the year my father returned to the Hall, he found waiting for him on his freshman list a seven-foot center who could also run the quarter-mile with the best in the country, Walter Dukes. My father's own new recruits, Mickey Hannon and Richie Regan, were to blend in beautifully with Dukes, who became the mainstay of three increasingly potent teams. Among other things, Dukes set the record for hauling in rebounds in a college season, and the figure has no chance of being broken — 734. That was in 1953, when NIT and coach-of-the-year honors came my father's way, and a ride off the court on everyone's shoulders at the end.

There was a particular reason why Dukes, who'd been an All-American in 1952, had his rebounding total rise up to that spectacular 22-per-game average in 1953. On the '52 team were two strong rebounding seniors who complemented Dukes in the frontcourt, Roy Belliveau and John Ligos. They were due to be replaced by sophomores Arnie Ring and Ronnie Nathanic the next year, but Ring, the rebounder of that pair, was declared scholastically ineligible for the first half of the season. The backup man at 6'4" was Henry Cooper, who because of my father's finagling became the reason Dukes went into the record books.

Of course there was no plan to set any records. Cooper, who could not jump the way Ring could, had a knack for playing big men in front — when a shot went up he'd either bump the post man under the goal, or else roll inside him if he'd moved out, his first job being to deny any lane to the boards. "Keep your can on him, Henry," my father would bellow out to Cooper. He was anything but a fair-haired boy, and loved the trouble he caused centers on the opposition. Invariably they'd be surprised, starting off a game, to find *Cooper* in front of them all the time. Dukes would then float from the weaker shooting of the opponent's forwards, to prevent lob passses from being thrown to Cooper's man. Assured that Cooper would block out the center, whoever he was and no matter how mad he got, Dukes was in a spot to sweep the boards clean, and sweep them he did. One sop my father threw to the hard-working Cooper. He always said, "Henry, get in there in that first minute and throw up that junk shot of yours, I don't care where you take it from. If you make it you can take another."

All this amounted to an unorthodox adjustment, occasioned by the loss of a proven rebounder for half a season. While Ring was out the team never did lose, and its final record was 31-2.

The '52 team, never ranked first in the polls like its successor, was a club with more depth and down the line the best he ever coached, according to my father. Its season record was 25-2. Along with an early loss, there came, after 22 wins, a rather baffling one to Loyola, in the Chicago Stadium that had jinxed my father's pro years. Both were by three points. But only three other games that year were close: a road win at Villanova, and home-and-home victories over Louisville, each taken by two points.

The win at Louisville broke a home-victory string — Louisville had never lost in its Armory — and brought in its wake, when the Seton Hall seniors returned the following year, a riot. *Life* magazine carried the story with some full-page pictures; it was an event so serious that the schools severed relations afterwards. The riot was fomented by members of Louisville's football team deployed behind Seton Hall's bench — one of them got in a shot at the back of my father's head, but that was minor compared to the battering his team took — in a jammed building to which not one policeman had been assigned. Photographs show Dukes being head-hunted all through the game; guard Harry Brooks having to get fifty stitches in his face; guard Mickey Hannon coldcocked on the Louisville Armory floor.

It was because my father felt the building up behind his bench that he would accept no apologies from Louisville's coach Hickman "in the corridor outside the dressing room last night," as the Louisville *Times* reported. "Hickman said, 'I'm awfully sorry about this, Honey,' extending his hand. Russell took Hickman's hand without looking at him and without making any comment."

He'd been in the mêlée but (as at the time he bawled out Bob Davies' teammates) he didn't show heat. I think his deepest bitterness was always tinged by this dry-iciness: certainly long afterward you could detect it in his voice, dismissive, no yarn to be got out of this event from him.

And as it happened that was Seton Hall's second and last loss in 1953; their 27-game streak had been broken the night before, in a game at Dayton. There was no occasion for rancor then (Dayton writers praised the team for their demeanor after the perfect season had been scotched). When I asked Arnie Ring about the riot in Louisville, he said yes, the riot was bad, a lot worse to the players than either loss, though some had been banking on a 30-0 season by then. (At home earlier they'd beaten Dayton as well as Louisville.) But he said on that weekend he'd learned something about my father that never left him.

It had to do with a train.

Leaving Dayton, the team found they had a Pullman reserved for them, though the trip was short. The car was to be attached to a late train going through — Ring and the others were asleep when this took place. He'd woken, he said, with his face against the cold window, at a stop where mail was being taken on, and looking out onto the platform saw my father standing there in his suit, talking with a station attendant. It was five a.m. What was obvious to Ring was that the two men knew one another. Ring had no idea what town they'd reached — Cincinnati, was it? — he could hear nothing as the train clanked in place but watched the men's breaths in the air as they talked. What must have made my father get out, or so it struck him, was just plain interest; and it dawned upon him, he'd had almost no thoughts about the man except as his coach before, what interest he took in people (to say nothing of recognizing old faces); how *normal* it was to see him there, odd flakes of snow being blown about, sacks of mail being wheeled past the two speakers, both seeming warm because steam seemed coming from their breaths as well as rolling out from under the train. I don't think for a minute (neither did Ring) that my father was suffering from insomnia due to the loss. He didn't suffer from insomnia. As for Ring, the cold window made it easy to drop back to sleep.

He was in for another surprise on arrival at Louisville — the managers were coming through saying the players didn't have to get up. Their sleeping car was being uncoupled, and would soon be switched over to a siding for that day. They were then informed ("the number one team in the country," Ring said the thought had flashed through his mind) that they were not booked into a Louisville hotel, and would be sleeping in the railway car that night after the game. No hint of this disposition had been given earlier. But the team managers knew and the reason was soon enough explained. The Seton Hall-Louisville series had, up till the previous year, been played in South Orange. Starting in 1952, Louisville had secured a home-and-home arrangement. That was how come my father's junior team had knocked off Louisville twice in 1952.

I told Ring I knew that — we were talking at an awards dinner where we chanced to meet a few years ago.

"Everybody had forgotten something," he told me. "When we came in there the year before it was the Hall's first game in the south with Dukes on the team. They wouldn't let him register in the hotel we were staying in. They'd already, the management in the hotel, got a place for Walter way the hell and gone over in the colored section. He was almost late for the game — turned out your father found out Walter hadn't eaten either. He gave the manager hell: the one he sent to take care of Walter before the game because he wasn't allowed to go to the restaurant in the main part of town with us either."

Ring said none of that last year's business was brought up, only the fact that the train would be where they'd stay for the '53 game. Where they ate (I asked him) he didn't remember. Box lunches? He didn't think so. There wasn't any particular fuss beyond the flat no-hotel announcement. They'd lost one — Louisville, wanting revenge, would do anything to pin a second loss on them, they were ready for a game nearly like the one they got — but for the fifty-to-one roughhousing, no, that was another matter. The loss, the dropping out from "number one" position, they would come back from such downspins and win the national tournament soon to be played (Louisville was in it too, but erased early so there was no rematch). My father, Ring said, had decided he wasn't going to be surprised twice by segregated accommodations for visiting teams coming into Kentucky. (It caused me to wonder whether there might have been any extra lift to the win he got, in 1952, via Harry Brooks's last-second foul shots.) So it was to the train on its siding afterwards that the battered players returned to sleep, a kind of meagre oasis conjured up (at least Ring conjured it up to me) as the story ended.

The 1952 season came to a halt with a 4-point loss in the NIT to the eventual winner, LaSalle. This was no fluke loss, but an inspired game. A LaSalle freshman, Tom Gola, playing for the first time in Madison Square Garden, outplayed Dukes, who took the blame for not laying off Gola as he'd been ordered. It was in that tourney that Gola, recently voted into the Hall of Fame, had the beginnings of his reputation made.

The most rankling fact of all was that the 25-2 Seton Hall team did not receive an NCAA bid. This was the last year in which schools could participate in both national tournaments, and Seton Hall's not receiving an at-large bid caused my father, when he had the number-one ranked team the next year, to spurn the NCAA when its bid did come. LaSalle also, ranked second or third the whole 1953 season, elected the NIT over the NCAA. The tournament bracketing separated Seton Hall and LaSalle as the top seeds, but now it was LaSalle's turn to be upset early, and so the Gola and Dukes teams did not meet for their rematch. Instead it was St. John's that the Hall beat for the NIT crown.

When my father returned in the fall of 1949 to Seton Hall and lined up a 40-game schedule for his freshmen, he was at the same time returning to an intact varsity. He knew he would face an embarrassment of riches when Dukes and the others turned sophomores. One of the upperclassmen he inherited that first year somewhat resembled Davies.

To make Davies sound less like a home-town version of the fair-haired athlete, it's worth mentioning that opponents saw him in the same light as partisans. The man who dealt the roughest blow to Bob's career was Clair Bee. Bee combined coaching with writing, as many know, and two years before he died, he revealed that his character Chip Hilton, the children's-book hero he strung so many plot around, had as a real-life counterpart Bob Davies. This "charisma" was evident in the 1940s, when Bob was called Abner after the Al Capp character by his classmates. Along with their heroics went their unspoiled world view. Likewise, some people used to refer to Sam Lackaye as L'il Abner. It was not a nickname with him as it was with Bob: they had somewhat the same Welsh good looks, but Sam was much more powerfully built, more of a driver than Bob, less of a playmaker. He'd been the best prep player in New Jersey in 1947, when he went to Carteret School — then moved on to Villanova where he and Sherman White starred on an outstanding freshman team. But both transferred — Sam to Seton Hall, and Sherman White to LIU. They played against each other in 1951, when once again Bee beat my father; but the aftermath of this win was tragic. It was the last game played by White and LIU that year; just afterwards, the 1951 betting scandals broke. White was implicated, his career ruined.

The year before, Sam Lackaye was the scoring leader on the losing team my father coached (11-15) before he could bring his freshmen into action. In a way Sam carried that group; he had stamina and flair and a faculty for being in the middle of nearly everything important on the court. He was a crowd-pleaser like Davies, but his style of play only half-pleased my father, who would be thrown too often into near-pantomimes of despair because of some chance Sam (like L'il Abner) might have taken on the court.

Returning as co-captain the next year, Sam was not sure of a starting position, and as it turned out he didn't play a great deal. For me, what complicated this situation was that I had become a close friend of Sam's. It was Sam's girl Carole (now his wife) who was sitting in the Garden green seats with my girl friend that night of the consolation game I spoke of at the beginning. That previous summer, Sam and I had worked as beach cops on the Jersey shore, where our job was to keep invaders off our town's unguarded beaches. These were miles apart at the town's extremities, whereas the beachfront hotels were centrally situated. Sam knew waitresses at each hotel and we'd meet at lunchtime to cadge meals from these places. At the start I told him I was too far north to make it to the hotels for lunch; his reply was, "Stop a car."

"What do you mean, stop a car?"

"Step out into the road and hold your hand out. They'll be glad to take you down."

He was right. A sudden hand sticking out of a uniform made the startled driver think he'd done some misdemeanor; his relief to learn you only wanted a lift made for the most amiable ride each day to and from the hotels. Our access to their kitchens made me realize what Southampton must have once offered, and why my poor godfather John Lanheady never had the chance to show off his cuisine. At the boundary beaches we looked after, on which fishing alone was permitted, the rules were largely known, trespassers could be shown a posted sign, and neither Sam nor I ever made an arrest. In that we probably matched my father's record when he was a summer policeman at Southampton.

When my family drove down to visit us that summer of 1950 (in a Buick, the first new car we'd ever owned), my father brought his mother along. She was not ill at the time — but she died suddenly the following February, from complications attending a broken hip. Toward her my father was a dutiful son, though, in her last years, constantly annoyed by her. He would now only grudgingly visit her, because she had magnified her habit when in his presence of pulling long faces and bemoaning things. She was lonely, and she was sharp enough to go along with being teased by her grandchildren, playing up to us, making believe the things we'd exaggerate to her were being taken literally. But any eagerness would stop when my father stepped into the room. Silence would then prevail.

In the bathroom of the cottage Sam Lackaye and I rented, the valve in the water tank leaked, so that there was a constant inflow of water to the toilet. On the day of her visit my grandmother said, just as we were all in the car to go to dinner, that she needed to use the bathroom. She was gone a long time, so I was told to find out what the matter was. To make short work of that, I called into the house, "Hey, Sam, ask my grandmother if she's all right." There was a pause, then he came to the door and said, "She says she's pretty sure she's all right." This was followed by another interval. At last she appeared and Sam walked out with her to the car. She explained, clearly on stage-center: "I thought I was finished but something kept tinkling, and I thought it was me and I was afraid to get up." We all laughed, in fact it set my sisters giggling for the rest of the evening — except my father, whose face kept the fixed look it had taken when she went into the cottage. I have seldom seen him wooden-faced during hilarity. He may not have thought she was being droll at all.

I think of Sam's presence then because — though the events are not comparable — I once saw him turn grim-lipped over quirky behavior on the part of his own mother. In fact I was the cause of it. Sam was the only boy and youngest in his family — his father had died when he was small. His mother, whom I hadn't met, idolized him and followed his athletic career devotedly. The winter of his senior year she was infuriated that Sam was playing so little, even though he was a captain of the team. He brought me home to stay over one night, after a game in the Christmas vacation, but he'd forgotten to tell her I was to be staying. These games were televised, so she must have seen that her "Sonny" had again played only briefly. When he went upstairs to tell her we were home, there was a pause up there, something you could feel tangibly downstairs. Then her voice came down distinct. "You let that person into the house, you bring him to your house after what his father ——" Then something from him: then "I don't want him here, I don't want him under the roof, do you hear?" She did not hold on like that very long, else I would have had to sleep in the car; neither did she come down. Next morning she made breakfast but was uncivil for as long as she was in sight. Sam as I say was grim-lipped in her presence. It was no laughing matter, and about the only time in my life I felt unwelcome because of whose son I was.

As a friend of Sam Lackaye I didn't exactly get critical of my father. It was a situation that could have made for mixed loyalty, except that Sam was fairly equable about it. "Honey's a good defensive coach," he would say. He would always say "Honey" when we talked things over; not by design, it was merely the way he looked at things. "But he doesn't tell us a lot on offense." "He figures you can do that already. He's got smart free-lance ball players, Regan and the others, what are you going to tell them?" "Maybe, but you can feel lost out there. He puts a lot of pressure on you, because the five guys, they know they're supposed to know what he wants, but it all depends on the score. I mean he doesn't give us many sets, and the whole bunch sometimes don't know one minute to the next what the hell he expects them to do." "But I would have thought if anything he overcoaches." "Honey doesn't overcoach, though sometimes maybe in a game he does, because he's liable to yell three things at you while you've got the ball and make you think you're doing every damned thing wrong. He gets you thinking so hard it ends up you've stopped running."

Lackaye meant that, toward late stages of games, especially, my father always knew *proportionately* what kind of moves his players ought to be making while they had the ball and a lead, and he expected them to know the same things too, and they *knew* he expected them to know. This weighed on many of them — when to make the other team come out after you, when to pass up an otherwise sound percentage shot. Some ball players with instinctive gifts, like Sam, could not play as well in the end for my father as they could starting out, because his presence and their growing sense of his expectations ungalvanized them. To give him credit, he knew this after the fact now and then — one time, after a late-season loss in 1958, his worst season. He caused this loss by calling his point guard Paul

Szczech over to the bench for instructions while Szczech dribbled the ball and listened to him. It was brain-boggling, the frustration he caused: Szczech was called for not getting across the ten-second line while standing inches from it, virtually held there by the jersey as my father talked on. The referee was standing right there, his arm coming down in repeated strokes as though he was counting a fighter out. My father paid no attention. The other club was awarded the ball and broke the tie on the next play to take the game away. No question where the fault lay, the coach was to blame.

A whole paradigm connecting sport to life suggests itself to me when that referee's counting arm comes into mind. What could my father have expected — that on the last stroke Szczech would hop the line and preserve the game? Nothing like this at all, obviously — it was more like being tranced into thinking time could be coped with. When there is no time, the oddest achievements can take place — Al McGuire salvaging a game by putting up a T as he toppled out of bounds. The antithesis had hit my father, urgently laying down law as he held Szczech on a spot. Instants resolve everything, replacing what seemed to be swatches of time. Andy Phillip standing up to get his jacket off: just one other flashbulb going off to frustrate all best-laid plans.

One person Sam Lackaye and I met the summer we were boardwalk policemen was the man who placed off-track bets for Greentree Stables in our South Jersey area. The next summer we were not rehired but were back at the shore anyhow — from where I commuted to work on the night shift at Ballantine's, Newark. We sometimes encountered the Greentree man, who never bet his own money but did give us leads quite often, culminating in one which he said was the best he would ever be able to tout to anyone. Greentree had a two-year-old colt which they knew was outstanding, but which had begun to turn in workouts that summer of 1951 surpassing their expectations. What was more, for the best of these works the clocker had misrecognized the horse and recorded the time against the name of an older animal. Greentree would be running the colt in New York soon, and when we saw his name we could be certain an enormous amount of stable money would be placed on him. All this came true as predicted, except that the horse, none other than Tom Fool, was scratched on the morning of his first entry, so it wasn't until August that we saw him entered in an overnight race at Saratoga. Watching for his name had been such an obsession for us that, instead of betting through bookmakers, we decided, five of us, to start out for the track at midnight. This would mean the loss of my job at Ballantine's, a job my father had as usual got for me: he didn't realize my failure to report would mean being laid off, although I did — but it was the kind of thing to put behind oneself in the excitement. (Our family had a rented cottage at Point Pleasant that summer, and this was how come we were all together discussing the trip on the night we were about to take it.)

We carried a chunk of my father's money up with us to Saratoga, also the bets of a few other friends, and all told had something approaching $1,000, which would have seemed an enormous figure to us under other circumstances. In the present one, it could have come short of that or gone well over it and not affected our exhilaration.

We arrived far too early in the day to gain entrance to the track, waited till we could get in, meanwhile made a pact not to let any of our money filter out in any small bets before the fifth race; so we sat out all the preliminaries in the paddock, which at Saratoga consisted of conveniently separated trees around each of which a horse would be walked.

After the fourth race was over we wandered in under the stands and, having consigned all the betting money to Sam, disposed ourselves about to watch him place the money down at a $10 window. There weren't many bettors at the selling windows that early, yet we were covertly watching for any effect Sam might cause as the man in front of him punched out nearly a hundred tickets. The seller had remained bland, but when Sam gave a large bright laugh saying so long to him he did smile back, shaking his head.

We divided up the tickets which we expected to be cashing separately afterward, and started back to the paddock. The morning line on Tom Fool was 8-1: good but not marvelous workouts were under his name in the *Telegraph*, and some such comment as "promising colt" in the handicapper's column. In my father's best years for George Halas he had been paid about $8,000; his Boston Celtics contract had been $7,500, and he was working for about that now at Seton Hall. I mention these figures as having been standard, perhaps a bit above average, for the late 1920s and 1940s. They would of course have meant opulence in the '30s; and here we were, in still-moderate 1951, with Tom Fool going off at 8-1, about to realize an amount which equalled an athlete's whole season's earnings.

When we got to the paddock we walked to the nearest horse being exercised around a tree, looking for Tom Fool's number. The first one wasn't him, and we swung over to the next nearest: not him either, and it was the same story with the other numbers; none were his. "Where the hell is he?" I was taken with a sudden idea and ran for the projection of grandstand which hid from view the infield odds board, expecting to find Tom Fool had been scratched. This was insane, for an announcement would have had to accompany a late scratch. There was his number with a golden 6 next to it; the morning line had changed and his odds were 6-1. Now I ran back toward the others, whose backs were toward me; they were striding toward what had now become a bent wall of people over at a far reach of the paddock, and inside that circular wall, walking round his tree, was Tom Fool. The paddock odds board changed about that time, and he was 5-1. "Riders up" had not been called. This was a weekday; these spectators had simply materialized. All five of us realized the secret was out, and we looked past hats and over shoulders at Tom Fool who seemed like a mirage, then back to watch the odds fall further. By the time he was out on the track they read 9-5.

It was still the same sum of our own money that had been risked — but Tom Fool came down the stretch all by himself, lengths ahead after 5 furlongs, with the odds having stablized at 2-1. He paid $6.00. He was ridden back into the paddock area where people were milling, and Ted Atkinson got off him. Waiting there was Lackaye, and from behind he picked Atkinson straight up into the air. No matter what they have to hear, jockeys never get manhandled at race tracks, and absolute alarm went across Atkinson's features. But in a second he realized he'd been hoisted out of sheer gratitude, and walked off composedly when put down. We watched Tom Fool's handlers lead him off, and Atkinson make his way through the crowd with that knit but remote facial look jockeys have before and after they ride.

I have indexed Tom Fool in this book, as my family would understand, just above Fortmann, Danny. From that summer onward my father, who loved racing, followed Tom Fool's career. He saw many of his handicap victories in New York, where Tom Fool was equally well liked for his ability to carry weight over distance and his unruffled temperament. My father never would have connected, though, the three-year pattern of Tom Fool's racing which ran concurrent with his own Seton Hall team's showing. For his sophomores had been just about as promising as the colt in his two-year-old year. Then in 1952 came the might-have-been's: Tom Fool was sick during the time of the classic races for his age, and Tom Gola in a thoroughbred performance stopped my father's gifted juniors short. It would take another year, 1953, for Tom Fool at four to be voted horse of the year, and for my father at fifty, on the strength of his seniors, to receive the same honor as coach.

Not all the repercussions of our betting trip to Saratoga had cause to be celebrated. I was fired from Ballantine's. As far as work was concerned — I was a college graduate now — this was only the most recent of several abortive summers. I did not realize what a backlog I'd built up of potential grievances, that caused my family to worry about my seriousness. Our Point Pleasant cottage had become a meeting-house for friends of mine, and I perhaps should have realized that my living the summer out on Saratoga winnings might have begun to irk my parents — but I didn't take this in. Then one weekend the two of them were going off to some friends' place in Pennsylvania, and they brought my aunt down from Brooklyn to chaperone the girls in the cottage while they were away. These were my two sisters, Dotty, who was 20, and Peggy, 15, along with a couple of Peggy's friends. On the Saturday night some of my friends dropped in — an impromptu party started up — all was innocuous except that I stirred up some drinking games, my aunt became angry and stalked off to bed, and the one who consumed drink the most conspicuously from start to finish was myself. Later on I became convinced that I was fascinating my younger sister's friends. There was an old fraternity pitch that the male kneecap was a different structure from the female. I had a beer balanced on my knee, while sitting on my spine in a wicker chair (the glass I was tolerably sure of keeping stable). I'd put my wrist under the knee of a girl friend of Peggy's, who was on her back next to the chair. I kept trying to show her that her knee was too rounded for the beer can to remain on it, which beer can she kept adjusting with light taps, but to no avail: she could not get it to stay there unsupported. She of course had short shorts on; it was hot.

Into this innocent, insipid really, scenario my parents walked, back a day early from their supposed Poconos weekend.

My own friends made a quick collective exit. They were glad to have an excuse to go, they'd become so bored. It was that contrast more than anything else which had its impact on my parents, my mother especially. I was the single one, in room-center, out of line and of coherence.

An admonishment from my father came next day, in a sort of sandbox back yard behind that house. "I don't know what to make of you, Mick," he started out by saying. He didn't look straight at me after that — turned so that our shoulders were in line, and the two of us were looking back at the house. Only another street beyond it was the ocean, but it and any other vistas were cut off from where we stood. "To see you the direction you've been going these last couple of years has made your mother and I pretty disheartened." He stopped for a minute and I came up with something like, "I didn't realize I'd been doing anything that was so displeasing. . . ." I was stunned. The degree I must have been indulged was taking shape with suddenness because I hadn't known I'd ever been out of favor at all.

"We're worried that you don't seem to have any interest except clowning around with those goms who show up around here, and as far as your mother's concerned you seem to take it for granted that we're running a place for these crumb buns to free load any time you've had a losing day at the track. You're going to have to begin to straighten yourself out, and I'll tell you one thing, if you could have seen what you looked like to your mother and I when we came in last night, you'd have been embarrassed for the whole lot of us and that includes your aunt and your sisters."

He was still facing away when he paused.

"'Why does he have to be the only one that's drunk,' your mother said to me. You weren't rolling in the gutter, I realize that, but here you are glassy-eyed with a bunch of young dames around you, how do you think it must have been like to walk in and say 'that's my son' to yourself?"

"I don't know, I can't say," I said.

"We may have been concerned a bit before, so I suppose I should have said something to you, but I didn't think either that I'd walk in somewhere and because of a way I'd see you my heart would fall."

"I guess I understand," I said.

He literally meant that last portion, as was most clear to me, and though I may not have the exact dialogue, the words are close enough. If his heart hadn't dropped he most likely would have avoided walking out in the backyard to have a talk with me. In fact I record the incident because it was the only one of its kind ever to take place — not only between him and myself, but between him and my sisters as well, who never gave cause for his heart to drop. They corroborate a point that may seem incredibly naive for me to try to make. Literally the strongest words of disapprobation he ever directed at my sisters were "*Straighten up*" — referring to their posture. He was open to their friends and mine, generous enough also to these friends — it was a principled generosity, but ample and natural enough for all that. Yet my father — why should he, I suppose? — did not show unremitting warmth toward our friends and could quickly enough demote them to "clowns."

Standing there in the sand behind the house, I pictured Sam Lackaye and my other friends making their exit the night before. I'd gone and strangulated that party. I didn't blame them for slipping out, but — because it had only happened the winter before — as I heard my father dismiss them (he used the Irish word "goms" — *gawms* it is, in the only spelling I've ever seen: it means, roughly, hamburgers, down-and-outs) — as I heard him categorize me and them, I thought of Sam Lackaye's mother. I knew she was a nice woman, but her son, he was the one she segregated — through him she could be hurt, and when it came to that pain, well then, friends, overnight-stayers could be ruled to the outer darkness. So it was with my father. In a totally different way from Sam, whose mother was wrenched because of the fewness of minutes he was playing on a basketball floor, I had wrenched my father — because of a few minutes, but they'd culminated in a pattern I didn't know was even being formed, on a cottage floor with my hand under a girl's knee. Blotto of course. The similarity hit me about parent-love. Sam's mother wanted the rodent out of her house, the contaminator. My father, never anything but hospitable — I'd had half a dozen college friends walk into an away game once and he put them up in his players' rooms, had cots brought in for them — my father had shown another side because of pain delivered in an unexpected way. It might be true to say he was not natively charitable, in that the distinction he made between his family and the rest of the world was grained in, below the depths of consciousness and choice. . . .

It was a good thing I didn't play under my father, considering what an extremely ordinary athlete I was at best. But one summer, the summer of 1946 when I had just graduated from high school, circumstances fell out in such a way that I did end up playing baseball for him. And from the day I put on the uniform — well before the time I was to get into some games — I was subject to some pretty unremittant razzing from one of his ball players whose name happened to be Bob Pelka.

This was in Rutland, where he had taken the Northern League managing job. It was a league sanctioned by the NCAA, college players getting fairly decent salaries which did not affect their amateur status. To go back a little, I should mention that my father stopped playing baseball around 1938. He was a semi-pro pitcher when he wound up his playing days, so he'd come the route, having started out catching as I've said, and then played the outfield in the relatively long interim.

His connections with the Northern League stemmed from the umpiring he did up there in the summers of 1939-41; with Rutland itself, from our having moved in the third of those summers from Lake Champlain to the smaller Lake Bomoseen outside of Rutland. The league disbanded during the war but was reorganized in 1946, almost exclusively in Vermont, and now my father came up to manage.

Before coming to the Rutland ball club, Bob Pelka had played for my father at Manhattan that spring of 1946. He was a left-handed-hitting catcher, grim and petulant on the field, waking up his infielders, jabbering at his pitcher. He had a flat Pennsylvania accent, and talked from lips that were close together, the corners of his mouth stretched sidewards as though wiredrawn. A good catcher's snarl. He was only medium-sized, but aggressive; also he played in a lot of hard luck.

Though Pelka respected my father he landed in arguments with him often, because of being argumentative in the first place, but also because my father was a taskmaster about signs. Pelka would be always mixing a few of these up (while catching) and also missed some others (while hitting). To me he took instantaneous dislike, and we were thrown together often, inasmuch as I pitched batting practice for the team and mostly he had to catch it. He was nominally the second-string catcher though he did play about half the time.

Warming up he jeered me about my fast ball, something I didn't have much of. Whenever I got into any semblance of a wild streak in batting practice, he would step out with his mask off and shake his head, looking down first and muttering, then say something like "Jesus Christ, Jack, throw the ball in underhand. It's all garbage anyway, get the ball in for Christ's sake." Or, if he was batting, "One of these, you better be ready for it, Jack, it's coming right back through your belly button." I was seventeen and feeling perpetually stung or about to be stung by Pelka. And while my father had brought up mostly metropolitan college players to Rutland, he did try out one high school pitcher from Glens Falls when we got up there, and here came up with the sensation of the league. This was a boy of sixteen, Dean Currier — he was only about 5'9" but powerful and had unquestionably the best fast ball in that league. Robin Roberts was at Michigan State and pitched for Montpelier that summer, but though he was fast Dean was faster. Dean got hurt towards the end of the summer and left the team, by which time I'd become good friends with him, being the only one anywhere near his age. He didn't become the major leaguer that everyone figured he'd have to be — the following year he hurt his arm, while still in high school, and that was it for him

Having Dean on the team did me no good at all, because

Pelka could and did make comparisons that finished me off age-wise. Insipid or pampered or just a bloody tag-along, whatever image it was he had of me was certainly connected with my father, and I suppose it wasn't unnatural for at least someone to resent my presence like that. One thing comes to mind, on looking back, that could have been a factor — I always had good equipment: a good glove, good spikes. There was a good leather toeplate on my right shoe, to prevent the shoe from wearing out — pretty conspicuous for someone to see who might be dressing next to you. And one thing that might have galled Pelka no end — something I never thought of then — was my sliding pads. They'd been a gift from my father a Christmas before. I wore them every day. Sliding pads are of a light-quilted material that protect your hips and thighs. For somebody not even on the *roster* of a team, let alone a pitcher who wouldn't have been encouraged to run the bases hard if he did get on, to wear sliding pads must have seemed the pinnacle of affectation to a mind like Pelka's. But I wore them because of the wool of the Rutland uniforms. I didn't like the itchiness.

In the Rutland dugout and on the team bus I sat as far away as possible from my father, who also wore a uniform, and coached from the first base coaching box when Rutland was at bat. A feature of the Rutland dugout might have had some bearing on Bob Pelka's hostility. It can be approached through a description of my father's behavior on the coaching line. For now and then early in the season he might be gazing abstractedly at the crowd, when suddenly he would draw himself up and fold his arms across his chest and put an idiotic smile on his face. The first time he did this I was sitting near two of the older pitchers, Ed Malone and Tom Gorman, and they both burst out laughing, before Malone called out to him, "Hey, Honey, are you gettin' your picture taken?" It was something out of the grasp of the others on the bench, all unused to the ways of pro ball, but it was soon made clear what was going on. In fact as soon as Malone called out to him my father broke his pose and gave a saluting tug to his cap, grinning over at the bench before turning to the serious business of coaching.

A woman in the stands had evidently let her knees come apart, that was all. It was an old stagers' routine. Later on, at family parties for instance, my father might sit up and mock-straighten his tie if say his niece happened to be "caught bending" in his direction, but this was the first time I'd seen him try that particular sight-gag, and he only dared try it a time or two more in front of the home Rutland crowd.

In the Rutland dugout, however, were certain slats, right at eye level if you turned your head around, and through these, from the safety of the shade inside, those on the bench could look into the crowd and see up and under dresses as much as they liked. Pitchers would be lounging on the bench four days out of five, and Pelka as reserve catcher was often there too, for the duration of whole games, and of course I was there. When our team was in the field my father sat at the lefthandmost corner of the dugout, from where he could call out best to his catcher; I originally stayed over to the far right. With the team in the field and only a handful of players on the bench, nobody did any turning around to look through the slats. But when the team came in and my father got up to coach, on certain days half the bench might be seen writhing in torsion to take in what was behind them as opposed to what was out on the field in front.

Better or worse yet, from the far righthand corner of the dugout the first base coach could not be seen, nor could my father see into that nook from the coach's box. Thus Pelka and some of the others made that their favorite haunt.

I felt in a considerable predicament. I wanted to look through the slats, but I had to figure my father knew what was going on, so I made a point to move over to the middle of the bench where I could be in full view of him. In point of fact he did not know all that was going on — neither that the watchers had made such a science of their game, nor that there were these perpetual watchers in the first place. And one day while we were hitting, and some hitter or runner missed a sign that provoked him beyond measure, he came storming off his coaching lines to the dugout to bawl out the whole team on the matter of alertness, and came on five or six of them, including Pelka, with their eyes glued to the almost invisible slits in the far right corner, utterly absorbed.

"What the hell is this, a baseball team?" he roared in at them, and in a minute they'd become "goddam great lovers" who would be turning in their suits and given opera glasses and return tickets back to New York in the shortest possible time. But the people up at the north end of the bench were by and large exempt from the brunt of this, and of them I was one by necessity. I could see how Pelka might have held this against me too. The worst blow to him in this instance was that he was a conscientious ball player.

Errors of omission like missed signs were bad enough for Pelka to have to fret about, but the kind of hard luck he played in extended beyond even errors of commission, like trying for a pickoff play when the situation didn't warrant it and having it backfire to the team's detriment. He was simply plagued with misadventures. The turning point of the summer involved him. The team had gotten off well, in first place for the first couple of weeks, had gradually begun to slide toward the second division, and then just past midseason in a game at Keene had a late-inning comeback in the making, one that had a "feel" about it that made everyone regard the outcome as crucial. It was the eighth inning, we were a run down, Pelka was on third base and there was one out. The pitcher uncorked a wild pitch — so wild that it went high over catcher's and umpire's heads and Pelka, often a hazard as a baserunner, had no problem here. He came smoking home, but the ball, carrying all the way to the distant backscreen, hit a horizontal support pipe and caromed straight back to the catcher, again on the fly as though thrown. He put the ball down on the sliding Pelka, finished the rally, and — if ever one play could have done it — the ball club for the year.

Only a short time later, we lost another road game in Brattleboro, with Pelka having another rough episode on the bases, just as hard to live down, according to his lights anyhow. I ought to mention that we often sang in the back of the ridiculous bus the Rutland franchise had procured for us. Sporadic and uncouth songs, for the most part, and they probably began because we had got in the habit of cheering our bus driver Shorty towards the end of a trip — indeed so much so that as the season progressed we got to cheering him earlier and earlier on the road home. All this was in anticipation of the bus not being able to make it back, because it was terribly antiquated, Shorty was a dangerous driver (he often peered from *under* the rim of the oversized steering wheel, and my father sat in the righthand front seat nearest him anticipating for Shorty, and having to bark signals at him), and besides, returning from southeastern trips like Brattleboro and Keene there was a sizable hill near Rutland which the bus almost literally seemed to need to be rooted over by cheers. So, even after losses, late on into the evening after supper, some impromptu songs might get started up punctuated by the yells, single or in concert, sent up toward Shorty.

In the game at Brattleboro Pelka had got on first leading off an inning, and was followed at bat by Danny Perlmutter. Perlmutter might have been the best hitter — a City College player — in the whole metropolitan conference, but he used to fall asleep in the outfield thinking about hitting. He lived only for hitting, legged out everything, wanting extra bases, a perpetual digger but only in the offensive phase of the game. Pelka or whoever else might be catching would always have to be yelling out to him to get repositioned for this or that hitter coming up, and Perlmutter took all this verbiage so blandly that he had received, nor did he mind it at all, the nickname of "the Rock." He certainly caused my father more nightmares than Pelka did because he was only "present" in half of any game.

This day he hit a high fly to right-center field. Pelka started toward second base, watching to see if the ball was caught. Perlmutter, very fast, streaking with his head down from the time he'd hit the ball, rounded first without even a look at my father who was trying to slow him down, and when the ball did drop between the outfielders, and Pelka started to make speed now for second, he was passed by Perlmutter who pulled up there ahead of him. Just before the ball got relayed in, with the two of them standing on the base, Perlmutter could be seen saying something to Pelka. Then Perlmutter turned and started running back to first. The ball had now reached the shortstop, who tagged Pelka standing on the base. The umpire was yelling something, pointing back at a space between second and first and indicating an out had been made. Pelka stepped off second in bewilderment and the shortstop tagged him again. My father had come across the infield calling for time out to the base umpire but the home-plate umpire had also come out and now made a powerful out sign at Pelka, erasing him in this bizarre double play. Perlmutter was already out for passing the runner. My father obviously did not blame Pelka, not even for stepping off the base. The thing had been too confusing. The season was long lost anyhow. My father told Perlmutter what he'd done but barely griped at him. When Pelka came in to put his catcher's equipment on, fuming, somebody asked him what had Danny said. Pelka, kneeling while buckling on a shinguard, looked in at all the people on the bench and said loud enough for everyone to hear, "He said, 'You stay here, I'll go back.'"

That night on the way home on the bus some wizard (not me: I wouldn't have dreamed of it) began a chant which got picked up by everyone in the back. It went to the tune of "Barnacle Bill the Sailor," truncated at the end:

> You stay here, and I'll go back,
> You stay here, and I'll go back —
> You stay here, and I'll go back,
> Said the Rock.

To this song Perlmutter was as impassive as Shorty the bus driver was to all the cheers and imprecations sent his way. But Pelka didn't even like to hear it hummed.

Shorty on these trips used to park the bus, in most cases, somewhere along the ball park's fence paralleling one foul line or the other. If the game could be viewed from that position, though remote, he would watch it from there rather than from a seat inside the ball park, leaned against the fence at times, out to pasture as it were. His answers to any greetings or questions were inaudible. Once I said hello to him from the bull pen, and he nodded back his peaked hat. He would say a few words in confirmation of anything asked, but you couldn't understand the words, spoken as though short cylindrical objects were in his mouth. He was punctual and by game's end would have driven the bus up to the nearest gate from which the players would be emerging; as they climbed aboard he would look dead ahead, perhaps to discourage comments to which he'd have to give his indecipherable reply. Certainly he made no comments, win or lose or be rained out.

When a game was over Shorty didn't have to get down from his seat, the bus being so old that it had no equipment lockers underneath it, so that everything had to be carried aboard and stowed among the seats. Thinking back, it seems that something was the matter with the door, which swung to by means of one of those pivoting bars. I seem to remember my father having to hold it, from that front right seat; this could be a misrecollection, even a superimposing of that whole business of the Franklin's floor shift, which had to be held on trips. The sensation is strong in retrospect, though, that he did have to tend that door — maybe it would be on taking lefthand curves.

In the closing weeks of the season, with the team now planted in the second division, and with several injuries having been incurred (including one to Dean Currier), my father put me on the active roster. I had by then pitched a couple of games for the Whitehall semipro team, just across the New York border, as well as throwing all that batting practice, so it wasn't too bad a thing for him to do — in fact it was economical since Rutland was paying me all along, $100 a month. I suppose to Pelka it looked like a gesture of throwing in the towel. He was catching almost all the games now. And he knew by this time that my father wouldn't be returning to Manhattan (though he himself would), for as I said at the start this was the season which my father decided to finish out with the Rutland team, even though he had agreed in early August to sign on to coach the Celtics. Not for any game though was my father ever one to contemplate in advance throwing in a towel. When he indicated that I would be starting a game in Keene, Pelka grumbled fairly openly — certainly said within earshot of me, if not of my father, that did we know my God who was pitching — what kind of a joke trip was this going to be, and so on.

I was pretty rattled starting off that game, which had to be hard for my father to take; I got scored on in the first inning, and had given up five or six runs by the time he decided I was finished in the fourth or fifth: he had one of the recent starters relieve me, with Pelka's prognostics borne out. One more pitcher of ours then dropped off with a sore arm and my father, who had been doing the batting practice, put *himself* on the active roster. On our final trip north to St. Albans, he put me in in a late inning when nobody was left and I was as wild as though I was throwing in an airplane. He had to put himself in. We were well behind, had lost the game, but he pitched a couple of commendable innings and got everyone out. He also came up to bat. I had never seen him in a baseball game, and he had never hit in batting practice — why should he have? Fungoes and infield practice were enough to occupy his time day in day out. But at 44 he got up to bat, fouled off a pitch (he always disliked hitters who took strikes — though he pretty religiously gave the take sign when a team of his was behind), and hit the second pitch on a nice well-met fly which the right fielder caught. (He once told me that when he was a catcher and outfielder his power was to right-center.)

On the last day of the season Rutland was to play a home-and-home doubleheader with its "companion" team Bennington, who had won the league championship. Ed Ehlers, the best player in the league, had left them by then to get back to Purdue for football; the team remained otherwise undepleted. Bennington won the morning game at Rutland; both teams then traveled over to Bennington, Pelka due to catch the gloomiest mismatch of a game of his life seeing that I was due to start it. He must have figured he'd be catching my father again a little bit along, a more palatable charade than the other at least.

I won the game, though, and went nine innings to do it, 5-3. Technically speaking, I could get my curve ball over when behind hitters. From the time my father had begun grooming me around the age of twelve in our Brooklyn driveway, he had insisted on my being able to throw a curve that was a strike. I always could, and could at Keene, but happened to have it get hit that day. (At St. Albans, no, different hands, different head, relief jitters.) At Bennington, to Pelka's amazement, hitters were hitting the curve ball, especially when they were ahead on the count and laying back to swing, into the ground and being thrown out. Behind in the eighth inning 2-1, our team with Pelka getting one of the hits got four runs and so we won.

My father didn't say a word to me during the game, neither of encouragement nor of anything else. He went about his managerial sign-giving, and called to Pelka a few times when we were in the field. I'm sure he congratulated me after the game but don't remember it or anything particular about coming off the field except that I was very tired, so tired that I was the slowest dressing and the last out of the dressing room. Everything was gone from it including the bats, which it was my job to put onto the bus — we didn't have batboys traveling with clubs in that league — someone had put them on the bus. As I came up the steps with my bag I of course saw Shorty first, looking straight ahead from under his cloth cap, worn low on his head so that his ears were pushed out, and saw the big hoop with the keys in the ignition. A cheer went up in the bus, then everybody clapped, a happy affectionate sound, and my father, whom I looked at, was sitting in the first righthand seat, in an open shirt with the straw hat I'd given him for Father's Day slightly tilted back toward his nape. He was very proud, that was easy to see. He of course didn't clap. Perhaps at theatres after shows he clapped, but at no sports event, either during or after, did he ever applaud. The others kept the little flourish going, Pelka too, seated about halfway back, probably the second most tired. I made it back to the rear, they gave Shorty the sendoff cheer, and later that night the raspberry cheer to hoist the bus up the southern grade to Rutland for the last time.

# WITH HIS GUARD DOWN

In that Rutland summer when we were staying in a cottage on Lake Bomoseen, our next-door neighbors were a family from Wollaston, Massachusetts, George and Dot Cole and their daughters Barbara (my age) and Susan (younger). The two sets of parents got on well together, liked drinking of an evening, and since the Coles lived outside of Boston, they were delighted to know of my father's upcoming job with the Celtics in the winter. This family became my parents' one set of close friends during the two years at Boston.

Dot Cole liked him a good deal — many women did — which did not prevent my mother and her from being good friends themselves. There was no reason to be suspicious. Whenever our family went to Boston we would all stay at the Coles'. I was eighteen then and liked Barbara, though in a standoffish way, thus looked forward to our visits to Wollaston.

On a night during one of our stays, the Coles and my parents went out to a neighbor's party. To my annoyance, Barbara's sister Susan stayed up just as long as Barbara, and only went off to bed when Barbara did, to the room they shared. I was to sleep in a room downstairs, George's study, so off to that makeshift bed I went, but couldn't sleep and was still lying there looking at the ceiling on the other side of which was Barbara, when the four party-goers returned. It was very late, and coming through the front door they were in the middle of a lot of laughter.

They made for the den, and possibly because they'd been opening and closing doors, Dot Cole made some remark about my father needing elevator service for that little room he lived in at the top of the Boston Arena — at which my mother burst out with "Over my dead body," which sent them into louder laughter: but entering the den they shushed themselves, and George said he'd go off to the kitchen to get drinks. Soon the laughter began to pick up again, over what appeared to be a running riposte between Dot Cole and my mother. I heard George come back in and caught the word "elevator" again a couple of times, which seemed to be the trigger for their laughter. Then a clear pair of phrases — "that elevator was still going up" — "All the way?" — from my mother and Dot made everything clear. It was a whole farrago of doubletalk they were up to, over which they'd grown hilarious, the two of them half-stifling themselves trying to keep the pitch low so as not to awaken me in the next room. It was all about the attractiveness, and the measures they took to ensure it, that these wives of twenty years' standing still had for their mates.

I was a lot more awake now than I thought I'd been a half hour before. For my mother to reveal such knowledgeability (in the bits and patches that got through to my room) was a wonder. She always had a wide-eyed quizzical innocence about her, which was in force right up to my father's last days. He used to take a short walk after breakfast, and one morning before he started off she unloaded some mystifying facts on him about a couple of women who were neighbors of theirs. He gave an incisive opinion about them. No sooner was he out the door than she was on the telephone to my sister, to ask her what a "thespian" was.

As it turned out, when Dot and my mother opened up about what was what in their lives, their skirmish took a new direction. Dot began on the theme of my mother keeping herself down in Brooklyn as a great boon to that long honeymoon marriage. Upon which she commenced to rag my father, whose voice had a non-admissive, playing-the-innocent ring to it, as he came back with "Not on your life's" and parries of that sort. Then something he said which I didn't hear sent her into a fit of laughter. No sooner did she regain her voice than she said she'd have to go to the bathroom or wet the place if she laughed again. My father said, "Don't go, Dot, just tie your shoelaces tighter and stick around with the rest of us." Her "I — don't — HAVE — ANY" hit two different registers and she may have actually wet — at least they simmered down now, and I was no longer able to pick up much after that. Except for one more time, when their talk reached a pause after taking on a matter-of-fact tone. In the lull Dot came out with something she may have thought would knock my parents off their chairs. She named that well-known naughty number in the high sixties. I thought — my God is she going to explain that. It became an altogether different level of eavesdropping. But before it could grow into something really *in extremis*, my father said back to her, "Sixty-eight, Dot." "Sixty-*eight*!" she shrieked. No way he could have made a more glorious blunder: you could hear in her voice a wild delighted certainty that she'd make him pay for it. But he'd set it up. He had a tag line. "You lead off Dot," he said, "and I'll owe you one."

It was a capper of a curtain line. Rising to the bawdy occasion was something he was well up to doing. Provided the occasion was silly (though this one had gone pretty far), he could come out with stoppers like that one. But the memory really serves as a counter to an opposite quality in him, for he was an embarrassable man.

Not that he ever took pains to shield me, as a child, from grosser allusions to sexual matters. To be let into earshot of someone like Rip Gerson, the St. John's Wonder Fiver who played on the Jewels, when I was nine or ten, was a sort of baptism into blasphemy that keeps it wondrousness even to this day. Gerson ran together strings of the most unmentionable nouns and participles, clowning in the dressing room before a game, or in indignation after one, in a manner I've never heard equalled. And there would be my father, present in the very greatest immediacy, showing no sign of flinching, either on my behalf or on his own. Gerson could see a child was there. The first time or two it was withering to hear him. At the same time Gerson (whose nickname Rip never seemed puzzling for a moment) would have his other teammates in such a perpetual state of laughter that the presence of a possibly red-eared nine-year-old could not remotely have entered their minds, and so I was pretty well spared.

So much for places my father would have felt were sanctioned. As to any obligations to me about the facts of life, he never felt it incumbent to speak with me and no word passed between us to indicate we were both aware that generation was the fundamental principle of life. Perhaps I need to take that back: one Christmas before coming up for a visit (I was teaching at South Carolina, and would travel up with my wife and two sons at least once a year), he insisted the best show in New York that season was *Who's Afraid of Virginia Woolf?* He'd gone to see it on his own — the only time I ever heard of him going to a play by himself, and considering its length and his own restless nature it surprised me to hear he'd stayed the distance. But the point is that he had taken the trouble to go see that play, and for him to imply it had an impact on him (he never recommended a play in such terms before) was revelatory. For in that piece of information — each year he offered to get us theatre tickets, since he'd once got the son of a ticket-agency manager into Seton Hall on a scholarship, and thereby had one of his typical entrées of that sort — he was clearly endorsing all the unfiltered sexual contretemps the Albee play contains. This was the closest he ever came to an admission of the force of sex, although he once attended a class of mine, the opening day of a seminar as it happened, when I quoted some lines from Faulkner's *Pylon* which were sexual in subject matter. The passage, ending in a pure pentameter (this was the reason for quoting it: the course was on prose style) described a stunt-flyer, just abandoned by his leading-lady parachutist, regarding his own phallus. What he looked down to contemplate was

> the bereaved, the upthrust, the stalk: the annealed rapacious heartshaped crimson bud.

And following on this was a quotation from *Ulysses*, with what is known as a "cursus" forming its conclusion:

> He kissed the plump mellow yellow smellow melons of her rump, on each plump melonous hemisphere, in their mellow yellow furrow, with obscure, prolonged, provocative melonsmellonous osculation.

There was reason enough to have chosen some passages like these to help drive home some early points about prose being written at differing zeniths — but I had not counted on my father being there. I could tell while putting those sentences on the board, and afterwards while making exemplars of them, that my father was thinking along in acquiescence: it was an odd communication, given our normal reticence about sexuality.

We were not very close in literary taste. His favorite novel was *Ivanhoe*. A feeling for Conan Doyle we both did have, and he loved one book I gave him: *Donovan of OSS*. Thinking of Conan Doyle, I realize that *The Complete Sherlock Holmes* was the book most read in our house — and (to paraphrase Churchill) it's possible that this one book delivered to my system the "bones of an English sentence." Where did that lead me? To modern British literature. For as long as I can remember, it's been the writing of Englishmen that I've admired most. And since along with that went a craze for animals, my parents would continually be scouting up animal books for me, the best of which (I've still got them) were written in those days by men with F.R.Z.S. after their names. It took me a while to realize this meant Fellow of the Royal Zoological Society, but in the meantime I was being further and further permeated by the sentences of Englishmen.

One other thing comes to mind about literary susceptibility. When on the brink of graduate examinations and having run out of studying time, I farmed out some reading to my father and two sisters — including some poems — and a night or two beforehand they were sitting around a table for a session of priming. I remember my father giving a thumbnail capsulization of MacLeish's "You, Andrew Marvell." He said something like, "This is about the sun traveling through a whole day starting in Asia. There's a fellow who feels how it's gone down back there, now that it's arrived where he is, and in the end he feels how the night will come over him while he's still in the original position, face downward." This was a poem I had actually read and, even knowing "To His Coy Mistress," had not been able to decipher. Fatigue might have had some bearing. But I remember how directly my father went at it. The day-track of the sun, that's what the poem was about. Next case. —There were several next cases. I've still got his one-page summary of *The Secret Sharer*. Now that I think of Conan Doyle, the OSS, plus this handwritten scrawl of my father's, I seem to spot an affinity in him not for secrecy so much as tacit sharing (Dr. Watson as confidant, for instance, his favorite in the Holmes ménage).

Here are some sentences he wrote me as he tackled Conrad for the sake of my doctoral orals. It was a pure Dr. Watson assignment.

> Story of new captain of a strange ship uncertain of himself and of the opinion his crew had of him ... in a small China harbor discovers a naked swimmer at the foot of the ship's ladder. Invites (what he first thought an apparition) aboard and bringing him to his own cabin heard the man's story....
> 
> The Captain referring to the hidden mate as his second self took a long chance endangering his own ship by bringing it in very close to the China coast [I originally thought my father wrote "hanging it in" which would have been marvelous] in uncharted waters in order to permit his

'secret sharer to escape to the mainland. . . .

In spite of opposition from his crew he brought his ship in under cover of darkness and the chief mate slid into the sea, a free man, a proud swimmer striking out for a new destiny.

The uneasiness of the skipper undertaking his suspect plan, isn't that what's in the report of my own fellow-conspirator?

But to come back to the embarrassable ingredient in his makeup — he could be brought up short by the unforeseen. Usually there would be something about the set of his lips, something parsonic, that would tell you he'd been taken out of his element. He was a polite man, so that, if not made angry, a hesitancy — an irresolution to say something contrary — would come over him, in small matters, say, such as receiving inadequate consideration from a waiter or an usher. Man of the world essentially that he was, he yet lacked the panache to feign annoyance, or become demonstrative in any outré fashion. Thus he sometimes had to swallow some pride, now and then sacrifice some imposingness of manner that he otherwise might have seemed assured of.

In matters of cruder forms of embarrassment he telegraphed the results, couldn't turn the play so to speak. Some of his acquaintances might have been surprised at this sensitivity. At a dinner in his honor, where he was given the "Baseball Scout of the Year" award — it was at Toots Shor's in 1970 — one of the officials of the New York Mets' farm system gave an utterly vile talk just before my father's acceptance speech as guest of honor. (This man moved along from the Mets soon afterward — he's done well since then managing from a dugout, but he delivered a front-office blockbuster that night.) Plenty of liquor had flowed, and he arrived at the podium maudlin. A Mets' executive had just died — he said that getting to his hotel the night before he felt so bad he had his bellhop order a whore for him. "I told him she needed to have a tight twat and big tits. And would you believe, when this broad came to the room, what kind of nerve she had? She wanted to know from me, 'Where's the Johnny with the big mouth and the little cock?'"

Bowie Kuhn, who had given an impeccable and most unbaseballish speech already, and was sitting next to my father, was put so aghast at this almost fescennine exhibition that he had to remove himself physically from the room; but before doing so he whispered into my father's ear that he should "go after that bum." Of course Kuhn's parting directive was an impossible one to leave anyone with. The evening was irreparably marred. So after my father was introduced he made not the slightest allusion to the drunken jabber which was still reeking in the air. No doubt he was right to handle it that way. Nevertheless he was discomposed. "How did I sound?" he asked me afterwards. "Did I carry it off all right?" He wanted to have hit the thing off — he was a good laugh-getter as a speaker, with a neat way of managing wistful-ironic closes to his talks. But next he imparted to me not only what Kuhn had told him, but the fact that he hadn't said any of the things he'd intended in his speech. He'd lost gusto — everyone in the room had, perhaps anyone having to speak in his position would have felt the same — and said he decided to ad-lib his way into the one anecdote he did tell and then sit down.

The one other time I saw him embarrassed like this occurred in East Orange in the mid-fifties. The son of a neighbor used to drop in if he was in town — his name was Irwin, he was about my age and worked in Chicago for a paperback distribution agency. Basketball was one of his passions, and he was a tremendous talker on this and Lord knows what else — a nonstopper in fact, but helping this along was his transparent good nature; and if there had been days my father would have preferred to duck Irwin, I don't know that he ever took steps to do so.

This day in he came all a-talk and I happened to be present, but my mother was not. I went in to get drinks, returning with these to find that Irwin had a paperback book in his hand. There was no chance that this was his reason for coming over — he came to talk basketball, and eventually did. But he happened to have the book on him, evidently one he'd been having good luck distributing. He had it open to page one, and announced to us — my father at one end of the room and me coming in from the other — that this novel had one of the grabbiest beginnings he'd run on to, then quoted the heroine's opening lines. They went, "Darling, your *this* in my *that* feels like a lightning rod," or else it may have been, "When you put your *this* in my *that* it feels like a big neon sign turning on" or what have you. My father turned a tinge of pink and I felt my own collar tighten: Irwin looked around fulfillingly, as though ready to turn a page, but I pressed a drink on him. I could think of no gambit word nor could my father. Our eyes almost met but slid: the rug got some attenion, a hiatus grew. Then Irwin dropped his book back into his pocket, not apparently detecting he'd administered a knockout to his host. The force of the unexpected had struck. A key factor was that my father had no recourse to admonishment, because he would not have wanted to wound someone in Irwin's shoes. His embarrassment was at last dispelled when Irwin moved on to some subject, if not yet basketball, that was less of a conversational land mine.

Irwin, working out of Chicago, was the one who located in a Chicago prep school a ball player who starred for my father's final Seton Hall team, in 1960, Arthur Hicks. It was a good 16-7 year — right around the 70% won-lost average my father compiled in college. His team was near tournament caliber — he would have liked to receive an NIT bid but probably could not have won there — thus was able to walk off a winner of the last game he coached, against his main New Jersey rival, St. Peter's.

Irwin's discovery of Hicks had a sting in its tail. Richie Regan, who had become freshman coach after playing in the NBA for Cincinnati, inherited my father's position, with good material and Hicks and the other leading ball player, Henry Gunter, only juniors. But that first season of Richie's those two got involved in point-shaving charges and were the first cited in the scandals that erupted that year. Nothing more dispiriting could have hit a new coach, though Richie stayed with these players as long as he could, gave them the benefit of the doubt through the original allegations and denials — then had to see them set down, careers as athletes finished.

My father, after eighteen years of coaching at Seton Hall, was just by chance spared being entangled in the exposé of dishonest ball players. Embarrassment by its nature involves, most often, pain felt on behalf of others who have been incriminated. He left coaching one year early enough to be spared that. On Regan's behalf, he felt miserable. One interview he gave the Newark *Star-Ledger* (August 13, 1961) concluded with him "storming," as the interviewer said, against the riggers of these games more so than the players:

> ". . . If these warped minds would only work as hard at being honest as they do being dishonest and looking for the fast buck they'd be geniuses. It must take a lot of planning and sweating to fix the point spread.
> "Something must be done to win back the public. It isn't right for a fan every time he goes to a game to ask himself, 'Is this on the level or am I being a sap for spending hard-earned money to watch a rigged game when I can park in front of my TV or bowl?'
> "I wish the NCAA would start stirring," Russell concluded, his mood such that if he had a fixer in front of him the violence would be worse than anything TV has managed to produce.

As years went on — since he was only 57 when he retired — he was given to saying that he had begun to suspect some of his players, and that this was a factor in his decision to withdraw. I am not so sure. Two years before his last, in 1958, Seton Hall had had a 7-19 record, the only losing season he ever suffered in college except for the opening years of his two tenures of coaching. Despite his six NIT bids in the previous seven years, the poor season landed him a good deal of criticism — covert, rather than direct; all the same, traceable as high as the president's office at the school.

There was an added complication that made my father pretty well peeved and rightly so. Some of the authorities at the university *wanted* him to feel embarrassed about a situation they deemed a conflict of interests — his baseball scouting for Milwaukee — on account of a transaction which found him completely in the clear. His best freshman basketball player in the year the varsity lost 19 games was Hank Fischer, attending Seton Hall because his own father had been an old baseball teammate of my father's. Fischer was one bright spot assured for the '59 team, but meantime my father was also trying to hide him at Seton Hall as a baseball prospect. He had seen him pitch in high school and figured him to be a sure major-leaguer when he matured — but agreed with Fischer's father that the college scholarship should be put first by all means.

When it turned out that the baseball owners that winter instated a rule to curb high bonuses, effective after the 1958 season, a dilemma came up. Fischer pitched for the Seton Hall freshmen and was a sensation. The scouts were immediately onto him. His father, as per their agreement, reported to mine that approaches had been made to Hank in the $50,000 range, and that his son seemed bent on accepting. The elder Fischer didn't welcome this turn of events any more than my father did; but there was no question in my father's mind about the figure. He went up to Yonkers and signed Fischer to a Braves' contract for $55,000.

The rumblings in some quarters at Seton Hall were to the effect that my father valued his Braves' scouting position over his commitment to coaching — he'd put one hat on top of the other and stolen his own scholarship player from himself under his own nose. There is no question but that the 7-19 record had plenty to do with this invidious logic — turn it around and there would have been no grumbling. Nobody at Seton Hall could be made to understand that big bonuses were going out and that

Fischer was determined to sign a contract and leave college. My father was right about his being major league caliber, though Fischer's best record with the Braves was only 11-10. At least one man at Seton Hall put it all in the right perspective, the sports information director Larry Keefe, who said the real problem was that the Hall had fed Fischer too well. In his freshman year he'd grown two inches and picked up 25 pounds and there was no way after that of hiding what had only been a potential major league fastball. Bats were flying out of hitters' hands; there was no mistaking the velocity now.

This climate of unspoken criticism was partially responsible, even though he'd come back in 1959 to a 13-10 record, for my father's announcement that the next season would be his last. Hence a slightly sour flavor attached to his retirement, suggesting to me, maybe wrongly, that only long after the fact did he question his players' performances in 1960. Wasn't there the argument that it would be too precocious of gamblers to try to rig games around a pair of sophomores (Hicks and Gunter), on a team that wouldn't have been picked as a dominant ball club anyway, affording the large spreads within which the fixers liked to work? Nor would Seton Hall then have generated all that betting. This same argument could be brought to bear about the Dukes teams, which lost only five games their last two seasons. For when in retrospect my father — in an ungenerous moment — said he wasn't 100% sure about Dukes and cited seven losses in that team's first year, one could come back and maintain that, Dukes not having played much freshman ball because of an injury, again the gamblers would have had to have amazing foresight to try to fatten their pockets off a sophomore team. That was the year, 1951, that the first college scandals broke, but the proven teams in New York like CCNY and LIU were the ones involved.

There remains the chance that somewhere along the line some ball player or another of my father's was dishonest with him. On a Saturday afternoon in January 1960, I think of my mother describing him standing in a doorway outside a Brooklyn armory where he'd just been beaten by LIU. There was a snowstorm and they were supposed to be going on to another game that night, but he told her to flag a cab, they were going home. He'd deputed her to find the cab because of Jimmy Breslin, who had taken shelter in the same doorway. Breslin had covered the game and my father was unburdening to him a whole raft of suspicions about the way his players had failed to follow orders. He had an arm against a wall, keeping Breslin pinned inside there — my mother, ducking back in from the cold every minute or so, heard him say, "I don't think these two black kids I've got are honest, did you see them out there Jimmy?" The gist of it all was the scouting report. Someone had given him a perfect layout on what to expect from LIU — "we were absolutely ready for what they showed" — and it all ended up (my mother having actually gotten a cab) with "The hell with scouting, the hell with basketball when your kids just hand ball games over like that."

Breslin was released and made a bee-line into the snow, my parents' cab headed in the opposite direction. Scouting, sacred to my father, had been jettisoned there on the spot; my mother said she'd hardly ever seen him so furious about accurate information being sent down the drain. He had been intending to scout his next opponent, St. Francis, that night in Brooklyn. "The hell with scouting" — here he was, in his last year as a coach, she'd never heard him say a thing like that before, or seen him hold a frozen sportswriter prisoner, either.

Maybe my not wanting it to be true that he had dishonest players keeps the jury out for me, despite my mother's story. I admit that, if he had coached another year, what was visited on Richie Regan would have been visited on him. Still, when the truth is out — when you know you've been sold — maybe it becomes an easier matter to put behind you. My father's 16-7 team of 1960 was an average team for him, and in my recollection he didn't go back to losses like the one to LIU and reconstruct them. What he did do after retirement was go back to *earlier* years — to this or that old miscue of the past, causing one to have a glimmer of the impoderable legacy left by those betting fiascos. Mainly, just the possibility of fixed games would in later years feed into my father's propensity for exaggeration. When he had very good teams, he did not believe he should have lost any ball games *at all*. A homecourt loss you'd sometimes hear him rehash as though it were almost an abomination that it should have been incurred — I don't mean in a mood of recrimination (that came in long retrospect, a kind of re-irritated tooth as I've been saying), yet still in a pre-justified way, as though by every right he should have had a win. Coming home after a game, late at night, he would hardly be able to swallow the fact of defeat. Still this was a very private side of him. As the coaching years receded farther and farther, his paranoiac wondering did give rise to some sourness; but none of this ever got magnified into more than a slight tic. You wouldn't find him stopping dead, as some thought hit him from the past to reanimate suspicions about his players, leaving people to fend for themselves, say, on curbs in snowstorms — it never became pronounced enough to be embarrassing.

There were other kinds of embarrassments he was open to because of a normally unsuspecting nature. One transition in his life I've only touched on came in 1943 when Seton Hall dropped its athletic program, and he went to work for the C-O-Two Fire Equipment Company of Newark. That summer he worked for Parkway Baths, a boardwalk bathhouse with its own sunbathing beach, located between Brighton Beach and Coney Island. There were handball courts, a punching-bag pavilion, basketballs and medicine balls for the seasonal or daily customers, beach umbrellas and chaises. First aid was dispensed too — beach-goers picked up splinters by the score. I worked there also — my first summer job, since I'd turned fourteen. My father, besides overseeing what little there was to oversee and playing a lot of handball, would give morning calisthenics lessons to a group of mostly heavy Jewish ladies. Sundays, the most crowded day, he would be off umpiring, to my great consternation; because even though one of the locker-room boys was lent to help, the "field," as our small beach was called, was one hotbed of traffic, confusion, and complaints. A swell day for me to be in charge. I remember my bafflement once, trying to re-fold a stack of chairs while a wizened woman kept saying something across the counter about "hannie, hannie." She wasn't holding a splintered hand toward me, I couldn't understand her and kept turning back to the chair stack while she became more and more vexed. She finally burst out to demand more fully: where was "Hannie, Hannie Russie, the man mit the haxicizes."

But that fall the C-O-Two offer came his way. He was to organize recreation at the plant, get things started like horseback-riding clubs and a company softball team (brought in a ringer from the midwest to pitch one game, so that the company trimmed its big rival Walter Kidde), and especially promote bowling — all of this in turn designed to control absenteeism and heighten plant morale. A company car was sometimes available to him, and as happened with so many other families, this war work marked the beginning of comparative affluence for us.

My father's time was once again his own in this job. He still kept an office over at Seton Hall — continued to recruit athletes there for the Prep teams, his eye on the future. He was not an absentee director of absenteeism, but after days which might keep him twelve or fourteen hours over in New Jersey, he'd now and then take a weekday off to go to the track. Most Saturdays would also find him at Aqueduct or Jamaica or Belmont. My mother was put out by this — it caused the one short spell of discontent between them. "Regular frequentation of the track," I heard her say one time, "that's what the lawyer is going to call it." For her the economic clouds had cleared only to threaten a reswamping with new financial worries. He lost pretty heavily for about a year — the problem was, he had begun by winning — but once the war ended (and the C-O-Two inducements) he got hold of himself and was able to put racing in perspective, keen though he always was on it.

One racetrack episode he liked to repeat on himself. He had become a friend of a Burns guard assigned to the jockey room at the New York tracks, and one day rode out to the races in a hired limousine with this guard along with a jockey (his name is lost) and the jockey's father. On the way out the rider said his card that afternoon figured to be outstanding — he told the passengers to bet him through the day, starting with the daily double. He did win the double, on which all three men collected. Then *his* father suggested that they'd perhaps be pushing their luck to expect the son to take the third race. They got off him and he won it. Now the second-guessing began. They doubletalked themselves off the son's next mount; bad conscience dogged the three of them after that, and they never made it back to the golden goose (the boy won six of six). What a day for the Burns guard, having to keep up pretences in the jockey room after each race. It fell to them as a trio to echo the rider's high spirits all the way back in the traffic, through which their chauffer slowly picked his way. It isn't hard to picture my father's face trying to keep the smile-muscles from flagging — I'm sure with his hat squared on his head — bearing up till he could get into the subway and back with relief to Flatbush.

But what makes me most remember his wartime job, offbeat in so many respects, was a visit he paid to a new friend, an executive of C-O-Two. As would happen when he went to work as a claims agent for the General Adjustment Bureau, in 1951, it was natural for him to be on easy terms with company higher-ups, because of his own place in the athletic world. And at C-O-Two, he naturally got thrown among executives because of the special reason (morale) for which he'd been hired, even though the post was more or less a sinecure.

One thing he was often asked to do, and sometimes proposed himself, was to give acquaintances items of sports equipment from whatever storeroom it was he had current access to. It might astonish some to learn how often a coach or player is asked to supply tickets to friends; but even more so athletic equipment. In the case of the C-O-Two director, my father was bringing him a couple of basketballs. I don't remember why I happened to be along — perhaps Seton Hall Prep was having a practice session to which I'd gone with him. In any event he picked up two basketballs from Seton Hall, and we drove over in the C-O-Two car to the director's house. There was one son in that family, a good bit younger than I — in grade school certainly — who was to get the basketballs. It was early evening, nice weather, when we walked up the drive bordering capacious grounds.

We took off our coats and went into the living room; I sat down, still having one of the basketballs with me, while my father handed the other over to his friend, who called to his son and beamingly passed the other ball on to him. His wife came in — I was introduced — we four sat down and they three began chatting while the boy went off somewhere with his ball. I sat with the other ball on my lap, content to be there rather than asked to join the other boy, since he was really too small for even a short-term acquaintanceship to be pressed on either of us.

Everything went cordially. They included me in the conversation, a relaxed half-hour grew on towards an hour, by which time it dawned on me, quite obviously much earlier on my father, that we had not been offered anything. Rationing did not impose stringent measures in those days, drink at least was not hard to come by — these people drank (in fact my mother complained of the liquor consumption of all the C-O-Two friends my father had made), but evidently not in the afternoon or, failing that, in parlor circumstances. Thus the time drew out a little less seasonably than at the start. Meanwhile, the wife found occasion to leave the room, and perhaps fifteen minutes later called the boy (that is, I heard the remote call), shortly after that speaking to her husband from the adjoining room, in which I had heard her moving around during the last minutes.

There was just a small entryway from the living room to that room: from where my father sat, he could see into the other room, while from where I sat with the basketball, I could not. It turned out that that was their dining room. And the last communication from the now invisible wife turned out to have been a summons. My father's friend stood up and said they were about to have their dinner, but said this unstudiedly: my father shifted on his seat, as though to get up, but the other didn't in the usual way step back and assume that familiar stance of one about to say farewell. He moved off in mid-chat as it were — he was intending to continue the topic he and my father were into, and my father, now half-sat forward, had a strained "held" sort of look on his face, attending to the thread of the talk as the other man (out of my sight now but still evidently in his) took his place at table. In the other room the wife and son were invisibly seated. I could hear their undertone. All became quiet for a brief minute: the father said grace. Then he talked a bit out toward our room, and I could hear forks and knives going and things being passed.

My father when he would re-tell this story over the years — and he did that many times — always maintained it was I who said, "We may as well go." That is not a memory I have. I was fourteen or fifteen, and remember the afternoon much as I have recorded it, but its vividness is conditioned by my having heard my father narrate the episode — not, incidentally, to every comer in the weeks after it happened. He told it more frequently in recent years, and it might be said that its impact, though it had one on the day itself, was curiously muted and grew belatedly. An odd tardiness. There was no breach of friendship, in fact, and although my father in telling the story would end by saying "Jack put down the basketball and the two of us walked out," he still must have said something by way of a goodbye.

It is easier to remember walking back down the drive — for what boy hasn't been a delivery boy? — and the picture had now doubled to the two of us going in, each with a basketball, and here coming out, arms comfortably free-swinging. My father was quiet driving back to Brooklyn. He said something about inhospitality, but I can remember no vehemence of mood — not, truly, in myself either. Possibly the thought came up then which, in any case, is natural to superimpose now: the realization that the humiliation had to do with the quasi-servant's role of all athletes. No slight was meant, no oversight on their part perceived, so it seemed. The family may well have thought they had been gracious.

I wonder whether my father may have been checked that day from an overheated reaction by his original bewilderment, or whether he had made, on the spot, an allowance for the utter curiousness of human behavior that he certainly had the capacity to make. In either case, he might have spared the adults a roasting while I remained with him, only to let out a real bellow about it to my mother when we got home.

An incident I tend to associate with this one comes from when I was smaller, and walked into the backyard of my friend across the street, Raymond Sans, to call for him. His father, who worked for a publishing house in Manhattan, was sitting out there in the sun. Raymond's father had an always-washed Chevrolet which remained parked for entire days in front of his house, since he used the subway like everyone else. Opposite it was our Pierce Arrow or Franklin. Mr. Sans had looked askance at our car many a time before this. He was not an agreeable man — tyrannical to Raymond, his youngest — but on this sunny day, with my own house and our car out of sight, he had a word for me while I waited for Raymond to come out. "What are you going to be when you grow up," he said to me, "a *ball* player like your father?"

In the whole matter of gift-giving, there was something prodigal about my father that was about evenly matched with something conservative. To balance off his generosity he also had a flair for accountability. He had become a baseball scout in 1947, at the end of his first season coaching the Celtics. He signed on with the Braves, still in Boston under the Perinis, and became in due course their head eastern scout while they were at Milwaukee and, later on, Atlanta. After his retirement from Seton Hall in 1960, it was crates of bats and boxes of baseballs that could be found in our basement, along with duffelbags containing batting helmets, catchers' equipment, rosin bags, an assortment of gloves — rather than the sneakers and basketballs and sweatsuits that went with the basketball line. To this day my mother has, besides all this baseball hardware, three regular uniforms of the Braves, Montreal Expos, and Chicago White Sox. For my father moved with several others from the Braves to the new Montreal franchise when John McHale became the Montreal president; then, when at seventy he was retired by the Expos, he signed on for a less demanding scouting job with the White Sox. It was after a trip to their 1973 winter meeting that he died, testing himself after a recovery from a cancer-caused setback, determined to make that week's trip alone to Sarasota, where he would be in harness again as usual.

He kept all that baseball paraphernalia in our basement because he ran frequent trial camps to which he invited high school and other amateur ball players — and the story just now of the two basketballs put me in mind of a time when one of his sub-scouts gave away two baseballs.

In charge of scouting in Pennsylvania, Connecticut, New York, and New Jersey for the Expos, my father had numerous sub-scouts and bird-dogs working for him, along with two men under contract to Montreal, and assigned to him on a regular basis: Artie Sullivan and Jimmy Quigley. Quigley was a friend from back in Savage School days, and Sullivan went back even further, to the time when he and my father played for the St.

Mary's Triangles. Sullivan and Quigley scouted for extra income, but, too, to keep their hands in. There was a sort of rivalry between them. The fact that their trial camp duties were never perfectly defined led to some humorous mix-ups — perhaps not from their point of view — usually traceable to overzealousness.

My father in his parsimony had designated two black satchels to be used for sorting baseballs. One contained recently used ones plus new ones in tissue, and the other, those which had gone somewhat brown with wear. These were thrown out to the ball players for warm-ups and later served for batting and infield practice. One night when the three men were returning from a trial camp to which they'd gone in one car, they stopped for dinner at a roadhouse, where they had one or two cocktails more than usual before ordering. That is, Jimmy Quigley and my father did — Sullivan was fairly abstemious — with the result that their waitress got chummy with them, especially with Quigley, and showed great interest in the fact that they were baseball men. At some point along the way, Quigley asked my father for the keys to the car, went outside, and came back with one brand new baseball and another from the "good" bag that had barely been used. When the waitress served them he gave both of these to her (she evidently had a son), at which she expressed great delight.

But Sullivan had begun to smoulder. He thought this had been derelict of Quigley, and remonstrated with him through the meal. Finally Sullivan reached the breaking point, after the waitress had become almost flirtatiously accommodating to Quigley: he went after her as she was going to get their check and told her his friend had made a mistake, would she please go back to the kitchen and bring those baseballs back, they were not the right ones. She was a bit put out but went as bidden while my father, caught in the middle of an argument now, was asked for the keys again, this time by Sullivan. Artie said he was going to pick two decent balls out of the "old" bag with which to compensate the waitress. He did go out with the keys — they'd finished dinner by this time — and came back in with two scuffed baseballs. At the prospect of accepting these the waitress, who had brought the others back, became crestfallen. Now Quigley began reviling Sullivan in front of the woman, which gave her enough heart to say that these were so *brown*. Sullivan suggested that she take them back to the kitchen, where he would *wash* them for her. And he did just that — with steel wool while the kitchen crew watched, he told the others afterward. The mother was not well pleased, but put the best face on it. She hadn't proved able, any more than my father or Quigley, to put up a better show of rights than Sullivan had done, from whose point of view the correct bag at least had been used, if there had to be these giveaways.

In a way the antics of Quigley and Sullivan represented two halves of my father's own nature, served up in pantomime. In this instance the less usually dominant of the two won out. Still it was part of him, this conservatism, and it may have rubbed off on Sullivan, even though baseballs were expendable by the gross, as far as the Montreal organization was concerned.

My father would never have had a scene stolen from him like this while coaching in a game, or actually conducting one of his trial camps, which were organized right down to the last relay man in the pre-game drills. He was forceful and direct, too, at bargaining tables — for instance, at club meetings during the free-agent drafts. His judgment of ball players' potential almost never proved faulty, and he spoke his mind uncompromisingly — not always to the liking of other scouts or farm directors, since group opinions never meant much to him. As he got older he tended to get more fixed in his judgments, became more convinced of their trustworthiness.

He was not the kind of scout to pride himself on landing high-bonus players; having come up from the hard days, he was generally opposed to handing large sums to unproved talent. All the same, in the cases of both Sandy Koufax and Carl

*Jurisdiction.* Umpiring at the Polo Grounds, July 1943. This picture, in the consensus of my family, shows exactly what HR was like, how he stood, how he looked. He was almost always a calm arbitrator, except on the day when his subscouts upstaged him.

*Talent Scout.* HR in his Braves' unifrom before leaving for a trial camp.

Yastrzemski, Long Island boys whom he wanted to go fairly high for and who were both turned down by the Braves, he would rankle over having been overruled and was not above reverting to that old saw of baseball scouts, "I could have had him for X dollars...." To be in on the ground floor for Hall-of-Fame types is one thing — flattering in retrospect, plenty of room for "if only's" — but it's not what scouting is all about. The first criterion of good scouting is not so much the finding of talent as not being out-found. The cardinal sin is not to have a report on a player signed from your area, especially one signed at a high figure. In this respect, my father's coverage was impeccable. He could not be "out-found" in his four- or six-state area.

Another endowment, less common, that draws a line between competent and very successful scouts, is the ability to foresee that a non-prospect, if shifted to a different position, might have definite major league potential. Here my father's own experience — playing all positions in baseball, playing the other sports as well — helped give him that sense he had of latent assets which could make for intelligent gambles. He made some coups this way. For instance, both Don McMahon and Joe Torre were third basemen when he first saw them in Brooklyn. Joe was a very heavy one and Don a questionable hitting one. My father signed them to contracts, McMahon as a pitcher and Torre as a catcher, before either had really pitched or caught. Though that is putting it too baldly, because one of the side-values of the many trial camps he conducted was that unbeknownst to other scouts he could put a McMahon or a Torre out on the mound or behind the plate and see enough to help confirm his insight.

There was no question in his mind about these two. And he had virtually no competition in signing them. McMahon pitched in the major leagues for 21 years; and Torre, long both the Mets' and Braves' manager (whose brother Frank was another signee), reached the peak of his career not long before my father's death, when he won the 1971 MVP. By coincidence, another of my father's finds, Earl Williams, received rookie-of-the-year honors that year in the National League: a twin killing that was pretty much the envy of the scouting fraternity.

Well-liked as he was among his fellow scouts, I suppose a backlog of incidents, large and small in scale, where he proved right could have caused minor embitterment among his superiors. The Braves' organization valued my father, yet they might have been relieved when after some twenty years he moved over to the Expos. I remember making a trip with him in the spring of 1965 to the Waycross, Georgia, spring training headquarters of the Braves' farm system. This was a trip he made every year, and since I lived in South Carolina, he scheduled a visit that one year to coincide with my spring vacation and we drove down and back together.

The previous summer, I'd accompanied him when he signed a Trenton boy named Dick Hart to a $25,000 contract — the one time I'd happened to be along for such a thing. The probity of that signing had impressed me. Hart had many football scholarship offers, his brother played for Pitt, and thus there was a lot of tension about whether he ought to turn professional. My father said simply that he was going to make one offer. The boy and the family could consider it, weigh all things up, and decide. Before he named the figure, they could take time to discuss the pros and cons: the same held after the sum was named. But he made it clear: there was to be one figure named. If they wanted to broach the possibility of a higher amount, he would thank them for their time and say goodbye. This he meant, I realized. He liked the boy enormously — and during the hour spent there he took a liking to the family, even the would-be hard bargaining brother. But before he named the $25,000 they could see there was to be no jockeying latitude. He simplified their decision by one-third by doing that. They had two choices and need not struggle over some further-bargaining tack. Out of such directness, one could see in turn their own liking for him grow. All of this may or may not have been par for the contractual course. I admired the way it was done nevertheless.

To take a long drive together, spend a few days in Waycross, was an inviting prospect. He drove his car down to Columbia; I drove ours from there. That in itself was vacation-making for my father. His once-a-year ramble to Waycross was something he looked forward to, because this was where the progress of all his signees (except those on the major league roster, for whom "progress" from the scout's point of view was over) could be judged at one time and place. There were several fields and dormitories, a large central dining hall, a building with training and meeting rooms, and a small, better-appointed headquarters building with sleeping quarters for management and guests. The whole atmosphere was mildly military, and this extended to a pass-system for the players for leaving camp. (Hart, incidentally, was unhappy down there — he was either just married or about to be married. Though the hardest hitter in the Braves' farm system, he was discouraged, and discouraging to the coaches, because they were having a hard time with him as a converted outfielder. These were combinations that never got reconciled, and though Hart did get some record-making minor league home-run production he did not stay long in baseball. Earl Williams, who moved into the Braves' catching slot predicted for Hart, was signed by my father for much less, a prospect he knew was good, but whom he had to rate in his own mind behind Hart.)

At the headquarters, the heartiness of the three or four young directors seemed a shade forced. While all the ground rules for non-trainees were gone over — card rooms and pantries and racks for the *Sporting News* pointed out, the arrival of a piano-playing crony made to sound imminent — it was clear that my father's reception had been tepid. It wasn't exactly an atmosphere of sufferance, but one that seemed to have calendar and clock behind it: a kind of scheduled comradeship. The management lived in a sort of bachelordom here. They were all family men; this stint was like going to summer Reserves. It made for a settled context, extending beyond the camp as well. In a word my father seemed to bore these men into whose routine he'd dropped, though they were in way of being friends.

A party at a Waycross civic club was arranged for the second night we were there. But it was one that made for dispersal as soon as it got under way. I had the impression of relays having been set up: someone to drive us out to the place; someone showing up later to drive us back. Such an evening might not seem that much out of the ordinary — it was the daytime shoptalk that set an odd new tone which seemed to edge my father, at sixty-two, out onto the fringe. Much of it had to do with Torre, by then with the parent club, who in 1963 and 1964 had had two bang-up years. Nothing that my father asked about Torre, nothing he said even allusively, as when he compared Dick Hart with Joe, went down with the contingent at Waycross. The uneasiness of mood seemed to mark the unrest of these younger men, in the face of my father's knowledgeability, a side of him that he sometimes let become too expansive. Thus I think they took the tack of being unflattering about Hart and Torre, who were busting the cover off the ball in two different training camps, because they were unconsciously tired of my father and his perennial visit.

In the end we shortened our stay, with the excuse that we had to spend Easter back at Columbia (where my mother had been left off), and made an unprotested exit that Saturday after the workouts on the ball fields were over. We drove back on a rainy night, driving well into the morning: driving was something he liked, at night-time especially, and best of all at night in rain.

Men with families the two of us were, and we were returning from an outstation, one of those communal projects (odd how baseball's own term "farm" suited it) where regimen led to weeding out, to classification. Most of it based on discipline. We were glad enough to get away. Fitting that the piano player had been a no-show. But why should driving at night be so releasing? I'd say there was a Conrad quality to it, as the headlights carved through a defined tunnel made solider by rain. Unguarded talk, with hardly a turning of heads.

With his scheduling trips like this — with the claims of the baseball job vying with those of his insurance work — it can be imagined how some people in the General Adjustment Bureau might get disgruntled with my father, and see to it his desk was piled with loss claims needing attention on his return. As usual, though, he was friends with the powers-that-were. (At one point the G.A.B. president's son, Phil Winchester, was manager of the Seton Hall basketball team.) More importantly, he also got his work done. That vein in him of accountability did prove a kind of minor impediment, causing work backlogs, which he eventually would overcome. To pay on a loss without seeing it — something another adjustor might do as a matter of convenience — he could not do. He didn't grumble much at those who took that route now and then. "Naw, Jimmy didn't even see the loss. What the hell, he's had a seat-belt on his armchair the last ten years. Nothing new there." You'd hardly hear much more than that when he was phoning somebody. It was just that he himself was constitutionally unable to handle a claim without pacing premises and itemizing contents with the insured.

As he was assigned to handle more complicated claims, though — and as larger sums became involved — his incapacity for broad-sweeping accommodations began to nurse in him a grievance. It indicated to what degree he was not a man of this world, after all. The General Adjustment Bureau was an agency retained by big insurance firms and rated by the volume of business turned over to it for settlement. Its agents didn't spend the bureau's money but the client companies'. What really brought a man approbation was a record of many claims settled and worlds of money paid out. To my father's annoyance, his fellow adjustors who spent the highest sums of the G.A.B. clients' money were the ones lauded each year with plaques and dinners and multi-million-dollar-club certificates. So that the inflated claims my father was geared for knocking down, the proofs of value he sought and sometimes challenged, the horn-locking he engaged in with the agents of the insured, all would go, and well he knew it, to his own potential disadvantage. Such factors could postpone settlements even though the home companies were saved money in the process — whereas wholesale success attended the opposite measures of one man in particular, his personal *bête noir* in the insurance business. This was a colleague who settled nearly everything over the telephone with agents with whom he was in league, and whose calendar was rubbed clean week after week while the sums he cost the home companies escalated to his credit.

The philosophy of "window-dressing," a favorite word of my father's, was here of course incarnate. If you paid a $100,000 free-agent bonus, you must shine the brighter among the fraternity of baseball scouts; a $2,000,000 fire loss, and the same would hold for insurance men. If your basketball team showed three warmup suits one under the other as it flashed through its pre-game drills, while you coached from a director's chair flanked by a contingent of assistants, this would increase the success of — if nothing else — your recruiting program. In this well-known world my father to some extent had his being, but in it he did not compete. He could be wry or caustic about some of its flourishes. His favorite story about that G.A.B. colleague, who was after all somewhat of a friend, had to do with the man's game room in his home. For parties of some scale were thrown there — where the man had his own pinball machine. Pinball records were kept from one night to the next, the scores posted; but there was no jackpot. The dimes the guests expended remained in the machine: only Jimmy had access to that little strongbox, and only after his guests had departed was it tapped.

When my father left off coaching at Seton Hall in March

1960, his G.A.B. employers were glad to anticipate that at least all those wintertime interruptions caused by basketball would now be things of the past. No sooner had he retired, though, than he was invited by the U.S. Air Force to visit the USAFE base at Garmisch, Germany, and along with some other coaches and referees, conduct a week-long clinic there for military personnel who were assigned athletic duties at bases in Europe. All accommodation and transportation were to be provided by the military. It meant a trip of some four weeks. His immediate supervisors at G.A.B. frowned, but their supervisors assented, and though he could expect insurance claims like no others he ever had miring his desk when he got back, he set off high-heartedly on his first trip to Europe.

The foursome he traveled with were treated to some touring in Germany before the week in Garmisch. Routines seemed to harden up once they reached the base, and he reported himself in letters home to be having a decreasingly delightful time. The workpace at the clinic was exacting, moreso than he had expected. And though not disappointed by the sights he was able to take in on the Continent, he spoke early on of homesickness. Once the clinic was over, arrangements had been relaxed to let coaches and referees plan their own itineraries. When he began traveling alone — to Rome, Venice, Zurich — even though he would be put up at service-arranged billets, the strain of all the moving about made itself evident in the tone of his letters. At the end of his tour, having always hankered to see Ireland, he scheduled a week's visit to the British Isles.

One enlivening moment came as the result of the flight connection made for him to go to London. "Weather reports had been none too good," he wrote, "so the Air Force people were afraid I would get stuck in Wiesbaden if they didn't get me out in a hurry so I grabbed at the chance." This was a C-47 paratrooper craft which was to be taking some jumpers for a practice drop over Belgium before continuing on over the Channel to England. My father in his overcoat and hat, with one considerable suitcase, was bundled in with the men and sat ranged with them in the craft's storage area — he was rigged up in a parachute as a matter of routine.

These paratroops tried a trick on him which they must traditionally have resorted to whenever a noncombatant hitchhiker like himself had been put among them. When they did it, they were the ones surprised. At some checkoff point, the lieutenant in charge of the jump feigned surprise to see that my father's suitcase had not been attended to. He started issuing orders to have the suitcase fastened to a drop-chute, giving off allusions that my father was the CIA civilian who, as they had been warned, would be trial-jumping with them. My father made half-demurs — probably in just the right spirit. When the hook-up time for the static lines came, he allowed himself to be connected up between two soldiers in the jump line. They were beginning to wonder now, and he said that after the plane banked and returned to the point of the drop, and the jumpers began to go out, he went right to the door, with his hat still on. *They* were the ones who had to say no, wait. The plane had eventually to make another pass, as they got him unharnessed after this upstaging he had managed. Here was one story he could tell that undoubtedly roused his dampened spirits.

Riding out a joke like that of the paratroopers was meat and potatoes to him, for he recognized from the first moment that he could not have been permitted to jump. In such cases he could assume a *faux-naiveté* which was just the opposite of the embarrassment he was sometimes heir to. To give a related example of his stealing a march on a jokester: once I took a college friend to Schenectady where, serving out the third year of his Celtics contract, my father in 1949 was coaching the Schenectady entry in the Eastern League. (Where I became "Mahoney" at another time.) At dinner before the game that night this friend, Bill Stevens, was regaling my father with some stories about our college coach, who for instance in skull practice used to look over the heads of his auditors and say such things as, "The center of gravity — that little point just above the crest of the ilium — you've got to keep that center of gravity low." At moments of intense pitch he might suspend himself between two student desks, exaggerating how impossibly high a stance he had assumed, and say, "You see, I am too high; I have lost contact with the ground; when you have lost contact with the ground, you cannot Go...." He pronounced "Go" with a kind of frenchified aspirate emitted from a narrowed palatal chamber — "you must be able to Geau" — his favorite coaching word.

My father enjoyed Stevens's imitations immensely. Stevens in turn, though, was a lover of inside information, betraying a keenness my father must have detected later on, from the way Stevens hung on his words during the pre-game talk in the dressing room. Hence on the sidelines just before the game, while his starting players were huddled around him for some last word on assignments, he must have detected Stevens craning his neck from a seat nearby, so as to hear the instructions. For he said, "There's one thing about this ball game, fellows. I want you to bear down on this, because it's going to make all the difference. I want you to keep your centers of gravity low." All their heads came up and Stevens simultaneously stumbled right off the edge of his chair, smack onto the jacket pile on the floor. He clutched some jackets to him and spun away like a team manager experiencing an attack of epilepsy, under the noses of the semi-tense ball players and two feet away from a pair of surprised referees who were ready to start the ball game.

In England a couple of days before he went to Ireland, my father was able to tell his parachutist story to the writer Henry Green (Henry Yorke), who himself had recently retired from the directorship of a firm that made and sold distillery equipment. Henry Green was a man three years younger than my father — he died five weeks after him. A friend of the other novelists of his generation, like Waugh, Powell, and Isherwood, Henry differed from them by leading a double life; for as Henry Yorke he remained all through his writing life an industrialist with his hands full. Even in the war he kept up his end in the managing of H. Pontifex and Sons' business, now geared to war contracts, while serving in the Auxiliary Fire Service that together with the R.A.F. had saved London — where my father was now homesick — from destruction.

Only perhaps in their multiple range, the broad-flung scope of their interests, were Henry and my father very much alike. By 1960 Henry, who suffered from dyspepsia and diabetes, was on the way to becoming the confirmed recluse he was to remain over the final ten years of his life. How my father came to have his address was through me. It had been no more than a shot taken in the dark. A book I had written about Henry was scheduled to be published that fall of 1960. So I wrote him to request permission to quote. Because Henry Yorke always kept himself from public attention, he had the reputation of being unapproachable. His letter back to me, in which the opening sentence went, "Of course quote all you want to & gratis," made him sound simply likeable. His telephone number was on the stationery — I gave number and address to my father not especially thinking that he would use them. It was one referent in the city of London — I had no other, and my father had none. If he had a free evening in London, since he knew I'd done the dissertation and had heard me talk about Henry's writing, perhaps he would put through a telephoned hello.

Only just before he flew home from Ireland, I got a letter from him saying that he'd done just that and had met Henry.

What Henry was to say later was that almost from seeing my father in the doorway he had recognized his loneliness. "I thought he was a policeman," he said. "He must have been the broadest man I had ever seen." (My father still wore his parachutist's overcoat.) "He came up for a drink, having telephoned and said that he would be unengaged after dinner — with the Army, was it? Some Americans from your Army over here, who, don't you know, irresponsible men, were criminally prepared to drop somebody whom they'd invited over to this island to do some things for them, but only up till mealtime would they be obliged to him in return. After that what else but to drop this man, someone of importance after all, off on his own into London. It was all written there in your father's face. Their behavior was impermissible."

Dig, Henry's wife, felt Henry exaggerated the orphaned condition of my father in London. She thought he'd been rather jolly the evening he had drinks with them. (He might not have informed them, but did tell us in a letter something that bore Dig out: "Last night the local Air Force athletic director took me on the London subway to Piccadilly Square, Trafalgar Square, Leicester Square and the Haymarket.") He had a raft of ready stories for his hosts; but Henry ranked with or ahead of my father as a teller of tales. My father wrote back about how hospitable the Yorkes had been and how funny Henry's stories were. A chance visit like my father's may have been something of a tonic: it was certainly out-of-the-way enough, and as my father said, "Mr. Yorke is a *rabid* sports fan and while he goes for any and all sports his favorite is boxing. He questioned me closely about every phase of all our U.S. sports and of course I was easily able to give him plenty of highlights."

My father wrote a second letter about Henry. He had stayed late the night of his visit, in the house he described as high and very narrow, like its neighbors off Belgrave Square — just a room wide, with one room set above the other, accommodations that seemed to intrigue him (perhaps because the narrowness was more pronounced than that of the row-houses of Brooklyn, the kind he had been brought up in, which connoted not wealth but poverty). When my father was a boy his mother had always been good at making Yorkshire pudding, and so before leaving the Yorkes' he mentioned this fact to Henry and asked was there a place they might recommend in London that specialized in Yorkshire pudding. After thinking a minute Henry said, "The Normandie Hotel restaurant on Sunday afternoons." Three days later (he had visited the Yorkes on a Thursday evening) my father, booked to fly to Ireland, remembered it was Sunday and recalled the recommendation about the Normandie. His flight was scheduled for late in the day. There were no Air Force encumbrances, he was flying this last leg commercially — so he decided to go over to the Normandie in the early afternoon, taking his bag along with him. From there he would take a taxi, with the Yorkshire pudding under his belt, and arrive early at the airport.

At the Normandie, Henry and Dig were waiting for him. No sooner was he seated at a table than he was handed a message asking if he would join Mr. Yorke at his table. It was a rosy afternoon for him to recall — the Yorkshire pudding was only fair — but he had an easy flight to Ireland, a country he knew he would like; and he could not have been made to feel more at home, or more kindly thought of, than by this gesture of Henry Green and his wife. When I met Henry and Dig in 1963 it was only natural for Henry to say right off, "And how is your dear father?" I've often wondered whether Henry's detection of my father's loneliness might have caused that mutual warmth that sprung up between them. They were both yarnspinners, but without that initial openness of Henry's my father would surely have told no yarns. There is no telling what inspirits friendships.

A bemusing fact about their meeting was that, undesignedly, there was my father being a way-paver as of old for me. Here was a world which I was about to enter — not Henry's own world, but the fringe of the world of letters — and here was my vanguard of a father, accidentally reconnoitering that world. All fair was the way I felt. I was unprepared for Henry's second question, though, for with a twinkle he asked, "And how are the Philadelphia Braves?"

It was baseball not basketball Henry connected my father with. A serious fan of cricket, he had once seen a baseball game in the States, and understood the sport to some degree. Thus it was that my father sent the Yorkes a baseball which he'd autographed for them. Dig wrote back to him:

> My dear Mr Russell
> 
> Henry and I were *so* pleased to receive the Baseball ball from you . . . and I can't tell you how honoured we are to have your signature on it as well. I really must apologise a great deal for not having written to you before, but Henry lost your card [his Milwaukee Braves card] for about 10 days! we thought it had gone to the cleaners in his suit pocket! but all was well as it turned up safe & sound in his diary.

Writing to me a bit later, Henry also mentioned my father's gift and its now unfamiliar environs:

> When you write to him tell him we have the baseball he kindly wrote on in an ashtray &, what is delicious, in this back-of-the-woods, *no one* knows what it is! Some really think it's a bit of sculpture.

Readers of Henry Green's novels know that in the tactile worlds he creates there is small ideational content. On their surfaces his books are as secular as works of art can get. When Alan Ross, the editor of the *London Magazine*, once asked him the reason "none of your characters are interested in ideas — political, religious, sociological or any other kind," Henry gave this answer:

> "Why? I'm not! Nor are you, Alan. And it's got nothing to do with loving someone."

His "Nor are you, Alan," put all apologies aside. Henry Green's direct and personal way of looking at everything makes a comment he once made about my father slightly uncharacteristic. It is perhaps irrelevant to quote, lest undue weight be put upon it — yet it possibly evokes a man ringing a stranger's doorbell, who could be induced to trade tales over gin in a drawing room, but who'd come to a foreign place alone and did most things alone, such as entering a hotel dining room for a Sunday afternoon pudding, albeit with good expectations:

> I think often of him, I can't think why, except I believe he is a very *good* man. I mean a sort of saint, which is silly, but I do.

Of course, there are picaresque saints. When my father was questioned about his trip to Europe — perhaps his only interview: he was out of coaching now, and this was for a local weekly near where my parents lived — he emphasized just a couple of things. One was kissing the Blarney Stone, which to him amounted to a "second-story job."

> "Almost broke my back doing it, too," Honey chuckled. "They ought to bring that thing up to the level, so tourists wouldn't have to bend over backwards and hang down into a hole to reach it."

> Honey toured the continent for several weeks and couldn't find any sauerbraten in Germany or spaghetti in Italy.

> On the train between Germany and Italy, rolling through the Brenner pass, Russell ran into another problem:

> "Every passenger who came in to share my compartment had a salami and wine — and I had to join them, they were so friendly. By the time I got to Italy, I was pie-eyed in the interests of international good-will."

> Russell visited with novelist Henry Green in England — and discussed sports, not literature.

> "During the war in England, firemen were permitted free entry to every home in order to make fire-fighting more effective, Green told me. So all the burglars and thieves in London joined the fire volunteers, and gave the police plenty of trouble."

To Henry he might for a moment have passed for a policeman, but it is the burglars who in the end "go it alone" and catch people's fancy. While I pressed him for stories from London, wanting to know what Henry talked about, I never asked him in those days what it was he might have told Henry. I wonder whether the story of his breaking and entering the roller-skater's bedroom for his teeth came up, or the one of his trying to burglarize the Chicago Stags by giving their big man an extra illegal foul.

I recently learned of one other "illegality" he practiced. Perhaps it would have bemused Henry Green, since it involved juggling business with art — (in this case, the coaching art). Unlike most others, this occasion required the complicity of a referee, only now what was involved was my father's popcorn machine.

Probably I have made it clear that he got along well with referees. Where I remember them best is in his office in the Seton Hall gym. Ahead of its time though this building was, there'd been an original miscalculation which put the officials' dressing room in between those for the home and visiting teams. This, practice proved, would not do. On the other side of the building my father had been allotted a tiny office. In it were a desk, a cabinet, a row of coat hooks, and a shower stall. It became the referees' dressing room. I remember it best as a coat room, because one of my father's generosities — to all those who asked for tickets from him — was to have their coats stored in his office on a game night. The coat hooks took up most of the referees' gear, so that the desk was always piled high with overcoats, and many an invisible referee can I remember, speaking up as he undressed behind this wall of cloth, to whoever might be listening on the other side.

I mention all this not to recall the spartan tastes of my father — Lord, how he'd have grinned at the approaches to a modern athletic director's sanctum — but to indicate how there had to be compatibility between him and his hired officials, for them to have dreamt of putting up with such accommodations. The place offered no buffering at all in the event post-game tempers became sour. Yet though I saw some arguments, I never heard a referee complain of the hatcheck atmosphere of that room.

In it I met Charley Eckman for the first time, who recently told me the popcorn machine story. It caused me to wonder whether the closeness of those quarters made for natural conspiracy, so that my father might have felt safe in raising the business in the first place.

Eckman, who was later chief of the NBA officials, was considered by my father to be the best of the modern-day referees, ranking with Chuck Solodare from the early days. No one could ever upstage Eckman — it's hard enough just to get an answer out of him. In fact it's possible Eckman never had a conversation with anyone, for he would never permit control of a situation to be wrested from him. My wife remembers a meeting between him and my father at a racetrack. On sighting him, my father began to pull out some clipping he wanted to show Eckman, but Charley was too fast for him — he'd already got out a newspaper featuring some exploit of his own, and was brandishing it as they came together. Not only that, but his first words were, "Buy me a drink — you might die soon." (Neither piece of paper had anything to do with racing. But Charley could combine many elements, and all those sporting elements took notice of him in turn. Two racehorses campaigning in Maryland have even borne his name: Charley Eckman and Motormouth Eckman. I once saw one of these on the same program with Restless Honey.)

Despite all this, it was with Eckman that my father struck up an arrangement about the popcorn: probably Eckman alone: other referees might not have been as open to the idea. The machine my father had acquired went back to some connection in his C-O-Two days — some businessman who wanted to make him an entrepreneur in turn. He didn't have it in Boston, though, and must have begun leasing it when he came back to

New Jersey in the early fifties. It was a Manley popcorn popper — the brand name I remember, though I never saw the infernal thing. (It always struck me that way because more than once he suggested that I operate it. I wanted nothing to do with it.) During basketball season my father had the machine placed in the lounge near the bowling alleys in the Seton Hall gym — downstairs where, between the halves, the crowd would go for refreshments. And Eckman says that one of the ball club's managers either ran the concession or (more probably) came up to signal when the popcorn buying had stopped. This then was the arrangement — Eckman would delay the start of a half until receiving the all-clear popcorn signal from my father. I am aware of how preposterous this sounds, what with rules requiring a fixed time between halves of a game; Eckman nevertheless goes on to say that one time Joe Lapchick had his club there and had got infuriated at whatever it was Eckman was doing — bouncing the ball over by the entranceway, hobnobbing with the ushers — as though giving the home players a longer between-halves period than was allowed. There they all were still shooting out on the floor while Lapchick had finished briefing his team, who were now sitting on the bench ready to go. Lapchick, after some irate beckoning, finally got Eckman to stroll to within listening distance.

"What the hell's the delay, Charley, get the game started for Christ's sake. What's going on anyhow?"

"It's Honey," Charley replied as he came over, whereupon Lapchick's face suddenly changed as he apparently thought something was wrong with my father. He looked downcourt at the opposing bench, to see my father directing a look back his way. My father now leaned over and began nodding constrainedly at Eckman.

"Is he sick? What's the matter with him?"

And then Eckman told Lapchick about how the popcorn had to be all sold, that my father had a machine downstairs, which must have struck a hundred bells at once in Lapchick's head —

an opponent who'd known my father and his ways for more than thirty years. Lapchick was no man of ease on a bench. Basketball had contributed so much to his ulcerous condition that he kept milk at hand, to drink during the games when he was coaching. But Eckman says that far from reaching for his carton, Lapchick threw his hands up with an "Oh my God" and went into a peal of laughter. It was the one time Eckman ever saw Joe unsoured on a bench.

I only saw Lapchick in the Seton Hall gym once. Long drink of water that he was, he was haunting the area down by the visitors' bench, near the exit arcade. I watched him standing with a downcast look, completely abstracted, like a stake in the flow of crowd going past him to the lobby. He was scouting the Hall's opponents, and it's possible that was the case on the popcorn night Eckman told about. I can't place a time he was coaching there, though I've told the story the way Eckman did. Eckman could have been approached just as impatiently by Joe for keeping him stuck in the building on a scouting night. One can imagine Eckman turning his back as only a referee can do it, and Lapchick building up to a rage as the delay was spun out till the crowd had got back to their seats.

Lapchick and my father were hardly friends. There was a bit too much rivalry between them (though their college teams seldom played one another; for just when my father was winding up with the Celtics, Lapchick was starting off as coach of the Knickerbockers). Essentially, even though Lapchick was a winning college coach, my father remained a little rankled by the fact that Lapchick, in his opinion, had never been a smart ball player as a member of the Original Celtics. He hardly needed to be, one might add. Dehnert, Barry, Banks — not to mention Nat Holman — were all court strategists, and Lapchick was their tap-getter: younger than the others, too, and required to play a steady game at center rather than lead the team. All this is to put a very fine line upon it. But my father slightly begrudged Joe's sometimes laconic, sometimes frenzied behavior on a

*Delay of Game.* Are they waiting for the popcorn signal? It looks as though HR is rushing Dick Gaines into action in a game. But could he be delaying the start of a half, as referee Charley Eckman said he always did, till the popcorn buying had stopped? (Dick Gaines was the star of HR's last trio of tournament teams, the Seton Hall squads of 1955-57, which compiled a 54-24 record; Gaines was a 20 point scorer on those clubs.)

*At the Hall of Fame.* The basketball dinner of 1968, where Adolph Rupp was guest speaker. The foursome who met in the cocktail lounge are identified in italics. Sitting, from left: Erich Illidge, *Honey Russell*, Hank Iba, Dutch Dehnert, *Adolph Rupp*, Chuck Taylor, *Nat Holman*. Standing, from left: John Bunn, Branch McCracken, Bill Mokray, Bob Kurland, Benny Borgmann, Willie Smith, *Joe Lapchick*, Bob Douglas, John Roosma, Howard Hobson.

bench, and when seeing him caught in either of those attitudes, would put it down to his not knowing what coaching moves to make next.

Lapchick, Holman and my father had the good fortune to be inducted in the Hall of Fame around the same time, not as coaches but as players. All were regular in their attendance at functions up at Springfield, the latter two having for instance attended Lapchick's induction in 1966. In 1968, when the first annual banquet to honor new inductees was held, the three were present. If my father unwittingly had had a small triumph at Lapchick's expense, with regard to the halftime popcorn, an evening-up of the account came about on the night of this banquet.

Adolph Rupp was slated as guest speaker for the dinner honoring the '67 inductees, and Rupp would be voted to the Hall that same year, 1968. My father had met him but didn't really know him. Although Seton Hall regularly scheduled both Western and Eastern Kentucky, along with Louisville, they had never played Kentucky nor even been on a doubleheader bill with a team of Rupp's. Holman, and more particularly Lapchick, had of course had several important games with Kentucky in the past. On the other hand, for a number of years after his NIT win in 1953 my father had coached a college all-star team that toured the country with the Harlem Globe-Trotters. As a result, he got to direct some ex-Kentucky players. "They were well coached," I've heard him say, "but I could always show them a few things about defense." They appreciated that, like other seasoned players who might be exposed to his coaching for the first time.

This information has bearing on what follows. Adolph Rupp, with his 800-plus victories and his .800 victory percentage, had amassed the greatest coaching record in basketball history. He customarily took a back seat to no one. He had always enjoyed the imposture (he was a very rich man) of bringing himself and his poor Kentuckians to New York, where he would administer annual upsets to the big-city coaches, presumably surprising himself. This "country-boy" guise was tolerated all through the basketball world, and while Rupp could not have been endearing to his competitors — certainly not when they went down to Kentucky to play him — he was clearly the mogul of the college game. Everyone respected him, for all his persiflage.

After the 1968 investiture banquet, he happened to be in a cocktail bar with three of the big-city coaches, my father, Holman, and Lapchick. It was an occasion for expansiveness on all sides — after all, Rupp was guest of honor and his greatness was due to be honored that year at Springfield, and the others were men who had refined the game as players before Rupp's rise began. Of them, Holman with 421 coaching victories was a distant second to Rupp, with Lapchick and my father comparative babies at 335 and 309 wins apiece.

My father, who said he'd been enjoying their set-to round the table, was not prepared for the moment that capped the evening and caused faces to fall in a way he relished recalling. Rupp had led up to this by saying something like, "Here we are, four pretty successful fellows, do you agree with me?"

No one could quarrel with that.

"Now do you want to know which one of our group at this table is the best basketball coach? I'm talking about the four of us."

My father and Lapchick and Holman looked at him.

"Honey here," he said.

There was a distinct pause as my father took this tribute. Those were the last words the others were expecting, since they knew my father'd never had any competitive experience against Rupp.

"This man Russell," he repeated, "has always been the best coach of the lot of us."

My father didn't feel a lightning stroke had hit him, or even assume the source of Rupp's information might have been some old Kentucky players he'd impressed. In fact he wasn't flabbergasted at all, and felt delighted at seeing his old Brooklyn rivals' faces fall, men he'd known since they'd all been boys. He felt Rupp meant it, the accolade; he gave Rupp credit for having come to that conclusion on his own — out of long acquaintance with the game, and probably by keen observation, such as my father would never have known he was under. After all, there'd been hardly a year since the pre-depression days with Halas's Bruins that he hadn't managed some ball club or other. Rupp had had ample opportunity to spot the coaching soundness.

Probably no moment had ever been more gratifying to my father at Springfield than this one — including, I would guess, his own indoctrination four years previously.

The bar bill came around soon after that. Anyone who knew my father will testify to what a bill-picker-upper he was. (I only remember him angered a single time on the occasion of his reaching for a check. It was when his great friend Rick Telfair had fallen asleep into a plate of spaghetti, at a dinner to which my parents had been asked as last-minute fill-ins. The dinner was given by Rick for some out-of-towners not one of whom my father knew. Yet the whole contingent — plus their wives — permitted him to handle the tab and afterwards the somnolent Telfair.) He characteristically had brought out his wallet and was about to commandeer the bill when Rupp, also flourishing a billcase, began insisting he must assume the charges. There is no protocol to go by at a time of high honors. Having delivered the banquet address, Rupp may very well have felt that the largesse devolved on him; whereas in ordinary celebrations it would be normal to treat the guest of honor. Rupp took the scoresheet from the waitress. My father felt the pressure of Lapchick's foot next to his own under the table. He ignored this, whatever it meant, and catching hold of Rupp's wrist, succeeded in plucking the bill away from him. He now insisted that the girl accept his twenty. At this point Lapchick gave him a terrific, hurting kick under the table. How many times had they probably hit one another aboveboard? — but Lapchick was not contending for the bill. He was shooting a grim look at my father like a man furious over a misdeal. Nor had Holman any money out. My father succeeded in paying.

As they left the bar for their hats, Lapchick, always a man of pained expression, now detained my father. He was shaking and shaking his head. My father, who could easily be brought into a stew by such behavior, wanted to know what had led Joe to kick him in the ankle like that. "Didn't you see he meant to pay the damn bill," Lapchick said. "Don't you know about him?"

"No."

"It must be a dozen times I've been with the guy, and he's never made a move for his wallet before. Nobody's ever seen him break his money out. Here he comes up with his one and only and you break his arm, Honey."

My father hadn't had anything to go by. Maybe he'd been in the presence of superior benchmanship on his one night of rivalry with Rupp. Maybe, too, things evened out as they do in life: who knows but what the popcorn profits of a single prolonged halftime might not have covered that bill.

Well, my father had paid. At least on that score there was no cause for disembarrassment.

# CONCLUDING

◆

"He was the only man who called me Irving."

The late Dr. Irving Bayer, who had been senior specialist in tumors at New York's Hospital for Joint Diseases, said this often about my father in the few years he knew him; he was overheard saying it again at my father's wake. The two men had met through Clair Bee up at Kutsher's, the summer basketball camp which Bee operated in the Catskills. It was years since Bee's rivalry with my father had come to a bittersweet conclusion. His final college victory came against Seton Hall — but the '51 scandal broke in a matter of days, poisoning Clair's last season (the win over my father, however, not one of the tainted ones in which his LIU players confessed to shaving points: the heat was full on them by then).

Bee never returned to the college game. In later years my father kept contact with him through baseball. Once or twice a summer he would run a trial camp at Kutsher's, bringing up with him some baseball figure like Eddie Lopat or Gil MacDougald — the reason for the visit being to vary the pace for Bee's campers, who were overfed on basketball. The boys, often enough their visiting parents too, came out happily to see some baseball aspirants competing: after all, it was the right time of the year. My father would mostly invite players from his list of Westchester County prospects, whom he would thus get an extra chance to see. Bee paid him well for this. It was Dr. Bayer, whose son went to the camp and who had some arrangement with Clair whereby he was physician on call, who was the keenest advocate of these visits. He had become friendly with my father by way of them.

Bayer and his wife and son were as knowledgeable about sports as any people my father ever met. He became a kind of mentor to them — nothing officious implied in the term — it was just that they had an analytic interest in the details of any game they might be going to see, and when my father was along he would, like any good retired competitor, call the shots and turn out so often right that it went as an engaging sort of edification for them.

The esteem was mutual, though, because medicine had a fascination for my father. Not that he was a hypochondriac; nor was he a lay student of medicine. But he had been well grounded in physiology at Savage's, and when it happened that a physician friend broached some subject — a treatment, a surgical complication — he could follow along with some of the acumen that the Bayers, for instance, could display vis-à-vis his own expertise in sports.

Dr. Bayer was instrumental in having him treated by an ophthalmologist once, who sealed a hemorrhage behind my father's retina with a laser beam. The miniscule calibration utterly intrigued my father, whose admiration for this specialist was unbounded. There was an element of reciprocation here, though. The man evidently made a perfect hit with his laser. It became one of those occasions where the patient shines out in his own right, having afforded the doer the gratification of achieving the optimum result. The point was, my father could relish the good fortune from both directions. He was glad to have his complaint cured, but also — disinterestedly, so I think — able to empathize with the other man's high spirits on account of this small-scale triumph.

When, in August 1971, my father had a lymph node removed which revealed cancer, it was Dr. Bayer who undertook the future treatment. My father lived for more than two years after this: initially made desolate; but after the tumor was located as prostatic, recognizing there was a chance to fight the disease, so that the daily round to which he returned did become the familiar and full round. He could even show the old faculty for intriguement the day Dr. Bayer sat him down amidst a ring of specialists at the New York hospital, to discuss the best prospects for arrest.

The treatment they said they'd choose — had they been in my father's shoes — was hormonal, and they said this would be most effective if he underwent castration. He was sixty-nine. They discussed other alternatives, about which they could be reasonably sanguine, but couldn't recommend, for arrest of the cancer and probable prolongation of life, anything where his chances might be so good. Just his way of describing the consultation makes me see him as a man who could hold things away from him, I mean under stress, as he could in sports. He seemed able to have got into their minds — able, that is, to perceive in these unafflicted men how they had ranged over to his mind and condition. He didn't feel in the middle so much as among them. It became a problem, a problem to them all, and a disinterested as well as interested judgment was being called for on both sides. To be able to reflect back to that ring of men — the day he made the decision — might have been the one thing to forestall the whipcordings of doubt that could otherwise have come along afterwards. Again I think of my father as a concentrator. He had in his life engaged in his share of self-pity, but not in respect to this matter. I think the doctors' and his thoughts had merged so well that misgivings and second-guesses were just not going to make any headway with him, whatever happened. He did in fact face a downhill road, which was to take a steep dive a year or so after this operation — but he'd become engrossed in the physiological problem itself, almost as if it were not his own, and this marked one of the special saving qualities in him. The decision and the ramifications were all very *interesting*. He made a good recovery from the surgery (though it was more than bargained for, since hernia was discovered and repaired at the same time). He did not go blabbering that he was testicle-less, naturally enough, but his way of discussing the decision later, to a friend or two, to me and my brothers-in-law, was calm, no meritoriousness suggested. He didn't allude to any sense of bereftness he might have felt beforehand, or of having to steel his will or anything like that.

When at my father's death Dr. Bayer put a personal announcement in the *Times* — which appeared next to the obituary written about him there — one of our acquaintances read a misprint into the notice and thought that his longtime friend Mac Baker had sent it in. Mac Baker, who had retired the previous winter, had been chief surgeon of Irvington General Hospital for many years, and the friendship dated back to early Seton Hall days. Mac had been a star NYU athlete — I remember his anger when NYU also came out unclean in the '51 scandals. Residing in South Orange, he had virtually donated his services to the Seton Hall teams from the 1930s on.

Mac always came across as a powerfully opinionated, generous, potentially fractious man — certainly fractious when it came to referees — and he was the one who excised the lump above my father's collarbone, which would indicate a malignancy. Baker had to dissemble somewhat after that. Only recently, talking over the telephone to my mother, he admitted how cast down he was after seeing the results of that biopsy. He could not let my father know how bad he felt, but neither could he summon the detachment needed to continue on the case. This too he belatedly revealed to my mother. Thus it was that he called in Dr. Bayer, and thus it was that the diagnostic and early treatment sessions were held as far away as uptown New York.

Just after the confirmation of the malignancy I drove up to see my father. It was August 1971 and my family had been planning a trip with him to Saratoga (a place I'd never returned to since Tom Fool had run there). On one of the days of my visit he was scheduled to have the stitches removed that Mac Baker had used to close the incision. I drove him over to Irvington: the idea in his mind, with nothing yet known about the origin of this cancer, was that he was dying. At the hospital there was some consternation at the information booth — a message for us that we were to go up to Dr. Baker's office and wait because Mac was in surgery, but a big to-do being made, because that floor was not one an out-patient could go on or walk through. The issue was resolved by an official downstairs, who said he would call the nurse superintendent on Mac's floor and give us permission to wait by the desk up there — only a step or two from the elevator, as it turned out. Up we went, and on emerging were met by an unwelcome gaze from the nurse on duty. She had received the permissions message and stationed us by that counter while she went off to see if Mac had yet returned to his office. (Perhaps Mac's impending retirement had some bearing on that nurse's air of ill-will. Like many another chief in a hospital, he did not abide by rules affecting the average staff-member, but as was true of my father, his own heyday was waning; at least it seemed his summoning us to that floor had made for unusual grumpiness.)

Something bad happened then, for while we were standing looking down the vacant corridor, from a door just a yard away came a man's voice which said without inflection, "Oh what pain I got." My father threw me a look. It was like an announcement of his whole future. Too much was too clear — anyone at the desk would have heard, but would have also heard that this was not a plea. The moment seemed unmerciful: the proximity of the door to the desk, with all its bottles and their tabs of paper attached, was altogether the worst part of it. After an interval again the statement came, physically sited low, horizontal or cantilevered is the only way I can think of it as it came from the door, and, not asking. My father shook his head and turned away from looking at me. Only fifteen minutes before, as I was turning his car into the hospital parking area, he had said look at him, here it was now, what he'd come to, his entire life had been for nothing. Useless, all the work — no value, worthless. I'd told him, parking the car, that any number of people might have done this world a favor by not having been born, but that he was not one of them. That he was wrong to demean and undersell his life. That he had given something to the world, not taken or hurt things in it, and would be remembered. I'd told him then that I meant to write about him. This particular promise didn't mean much to him on hearing it, but probably words in a stream, contravening what he'd said as that building and its driving entrances came up in front of us, did check or help to neutralize his mood. If so, what of those other words up on that floor? So unexpected, they may, as his look seemed to say, have thrown him back. Whether or not they did, he was a man of sympathy. It was not, I am convinced, all terror that they engendered. (This suffering was not, in the end, to be his lot.) But it was helpless and hopeless, hearing the voice. Not only projection on his part, though that had to enter; also compassion, but one was stock-still in a hallway. At least this can be said: that two years later, when having to check into a hospital — down in weight, appetiteless — he was introduced to a roommate who could only wave, a man not in pain but with a purple-marked jaw indicating radiation treatment, he was able to say to me while getting into pajamas, "What a smalltime man I am, Mick. Can you believe it, I go around thinking it's me alone who has worries" — with a hitch of his head toward the man watching television from his pillows — "look at the way I've thought only about myself."

Eventually we were ushered along to Baker's office on that ward. Here all changed and my father became like his mother. He went from way down to bright. He meant to accommodate — if this meant dissembling his low spirits, all right. Baker was still in his green gown. "We'll give it a battle," he said to me in greeting, while going up to my father and taking him by the arm just below where his short sleeve ended. It was one of those mock-wrestler's holds which made my father butt him back with a shoulder, whereon both began laughing. "Take your shirt off Honey and we'll have a look at what kind of a heal we've had there."

The rest of it went like that. It was a clean small linear wound. Baker asked me about the south as he took out the sutures. (I'd recently moved from South Carolina to Maryland.) Always partial to the south, he had his Florida residence set up, where he meant to retire. He'd by now sold his house in South Orange and was camping that last summer in an Irvington apartment.

The South Orange house I remembered well. It was a Tudor manor, hewn beams set in stucco over stone, where I'd stayed one weekend around my thirteenth birthday (about the time of Pearl Harbor). This house had something never seen in those days — what all of America has since taken for granted — a basketball backboard hung up over the garage, along with a paved forecourt more than ample for pickup games of three-on-three.

They played for hours on end there: the two boys about my age in the Baker family, plus neighborhood friends, and on this occasion myself their guest. Mac had married Polly Terrill, and these were his stepsons, Chick and Lee Terrill. Mac's affiliations with the south, I think, began when Lee Terrill attended North Carolina State. I don't know whether Mac donated physician's services to the State basketball team, but he did become fast friends with Everett Case down there. I'm reminded of Bayer as medical consultant to Clair Bee — what Bee and his LIU teams did for basketball at the Garden in the 1930s, Case would do for the mid-Atlantic area later. It was he who got fans clamoring down there — the holiday-time Dixie Classic was his innovation; the Atlantic Coast Conference and its tournament ultimate legacies. Imitators came in flocks after he'd set a pace. A friend of mine once spoke of his ball players as "Case-hardened, every one of them." Mac Baker was a fantastic fan of his.

The strongest team Everett Case put together, the only one to win thirty games (a mark equalled by the David Thompson championship team) — his 1951 group which included Sam Ranzino — had as their captain-elect Lee Terrill. This team was after national honors as an entry in the NCAA tournament while also being seeded second in the NIT. And what should happen — putting some strain on Mac Baker's loyalties — but that State should come up against Seton Hall in its opening NIT game at the Garden. This was my father's young team that was to lose to Brigham Young, but it had to get by Everett Case's club to do that, and it got by them with room to spare, 71-59. It was a terrific loss to Case, who mumbled to a reporter in the locker room, "You can't figure Honey holds us under sixty." His State team had just finished leading the country in scoring.

Following N.C. State all year, Mac Baker had always sat on the bench next to Everett; but that was also true of the Seton Hall games, which would find him next to my father. (Both coaches had to get him to move back a row or clear out altogether, when heat over referees' decisions almost caused technical fouls to be assessed against Mac.) The double pull on his loyalty came from the fact that Chick Terrill played for Seton Hall. He was a junior, a year younger than Lee — very talented, but not a scorer — a reserve on the sophomore dominated team.

My father did a nice thing the night his game came up against State. Mac Baker sequestered himself off somewhere that night — in spirit halfway between both benches, I imagine. He expressed his thanks to my father many times after it, though — for his decision, which he hadn't told anyone about beforehand, to start Chick Terrill so that he could line up against his brother Lee. In those days when players were introduced they ran out to take their spots on the court, so that — I forget the order — the last player introduced was a Terrill and he ran over and shook hands with the other Terrill and that was the way the game started.

Chick played a good part of the first half, creditably too: came back in for a stint in the second: Dukes's play that night swept the whole thing Seton Hall's way, and overnight — as years before when Davies had done the same thing against Rhode Island — they were Garden and New York favorites: to be knocked back two evenings later by Brigham Young.

As fate would have it, this was the last basketball game Chick Terrill played. He did not get into either of the team's losses against Brigham Young and St. John's, and just before his senior season he contracted polio. It was not a disastrous form of the disease, but disastrous enough for his playing career.

Not ever knowing him well, I'd always been fond of Mac Baker because of that weekend's generosity back in the past: it had simply been a spontaneous idea he'd had, seeing me at one of the Seton Hall practices, and saying to my father, why not let me come home with him and play some ball in the yard over the weekend with his sons. I'm sure Mac forgot I'd ever been there, and am certain my father forgot it too. That time was already a good ten years in the past when my father, out of friendship to Mac and Polly, started one boy of theirs knowing Everett Case would be starting the other. The day in the hospital, another twenty years on, was not cause for remembering the nice coaching gesture at all. However, for one moment I did think of Chick getting polio. The reason was that in Irvington General Hospital that August day in 1971, a Notre Dame ball player, a freshman the year before and a New Jersey boy, was laid up, resting in traction with a broken leg he'd gotten on a playground. He was going to get better all right, but Mac said he was fretting about his chances now of playing that year, and Mac had accidentally learned of his presence in the place. After taking out my father's stitches, Mac suggested we drop by this boy's room. He introduced my father to him, and the two of them spent a bantering ten minutes with him. My father asked him how he thought the competition looked at Notre Dame — they weren't usually overstocked there were they? That got a laugh, and for what it was worth the pair of them cheered up this strapping invalid a little bit.

My father's third great medical friend (I thought of starting off, "Honey always called me Justin") was Justin McNutt of Bloomington, Illinois. But so far as I know, no friend of Mac's ever called him Justin. Mac Baker was a Jewish Mac: McNutt a protestant one. But they differed much more than as to origins. The surgeon from Bloomington (I fancied him as my father's tie to the midwest) had no interest whatsoever in sports.

He might have heard of the Chicago Bears or the Cleveland Rosenblums. He did once introduce Henry Aaron to the Bloomington Rotarians (my father had brought Henry out there: Aaron has a famous bad back, and by some peculiar sympathy my father, for the only time in his life, suffered on the day of Aaron's visit from back spasms, and had to be slid out of McNutt's car by Aaron and McNutt, straight as a railroad tie — this being doubly piquant since Mac though an orthopedist could do nothing to ease his problem; my father then committed the heinous sin of consulting a chiropractor out there). But famous sports figures were neither here nor there to McNutt, who raised Shetland ponies, collected African art (got it from the source, so to speak, for he donated his services several different years to clinics and tour-doctoring in Africa), built pianos, fixed engines on ships (if a freighter he was on happened to have a breakdown, as once occurred), and from my father's point of view understood everything there was to understand in this sublunary world. Except that sports did not invade his consciousness.

Another fanciful reason for supposing McNutt to represent the midwest in my father's career is that the McNutts lived next door to us in Brooklyn. That is how we got to know them.

They lived on the other side of the wall, since ours was a semi-detached house and they rented the upstairs of the other side. This was just after the war. My mother and Lucille McNutt were always rapping out signals to one another through the wall. Rap sessions didn't stop there — from my parents' bedroom you could come out onto our porch roof, then enter the McNutts' front room via a similar window. That was a standard way for getting home after parties, when my father, as he once proved to a small crowd on the roof, could roll straight into bed — the McNutts being exhaustless entertainers.

Mac, who had landed in Normandy on D-Day (and characteristically said that no beginning surgeon could have had a greater windfall than to be in the First Army that summer), began serving his residency in orthopedics at Kings County Hospital in 1945. We were always told this was the world's biggest hospital — its grounds began a couple of blocks from our house. One Saturday night — I think while my father was still coaching at Manhattan — he and Mac sat up drinking and got to discussing knee injuries. This night my father's penchant for showing he could keep abreast of medical explanations put him into some hot water. For McNutt told him he could bring together some knees that the two of them might inspect over at Kings County. When my father showed interest, McNutt, not one for delaying, said the morgue was open for research on Sunday mornings, so why not make a morning of it the next day. My father might have perceived where this had got him, but he couldn't very well withdraw. Especially not with McNutt, whose whole ethos did not lead to mincing matters of this sort. (McNutt for example liked lobsters. If somebody told him you could order a barrel of lobsters packed in watercress from Maine and that a telephone call would get you a catered feast, air shipment, backyard delivery and all the rest of it, he would say, "All right; let's call up." He'd expect you to produce the number.)

Besides, the two of them were far into their cups. Again this meant nothing to McNutt. He got my father's consent for an 8 a.m. trek to the morgue.

Raps on the wall woke my mother next morning — this was Mac rapping, not Lucille, to pass the news that coffee was ready over there and it was time to get started. Bufferin not coffee had to make do for my father's breakfast. "I was hoping he'd forget," he would say whenever he told the story. Anyone knowing McNutt would recognize the forlornness of the hope. The walk down to the hospital woke him up a bit. Once there, "McNutt picks out a couple of gowns he says we'll need to put on. I can hardly hold my arms up for mine, which he ties around in the back. The one thing I figure is the only way to get through this is to go one step at a time.

"Now we go into a colder room with cabinets in it with steel drawers, great big drawers on sliders. McNutt rolls one of them out and there must be a hundred legs in it. I don't want to look at any of them. He begins sizing this one up and that one up and asking me what I think. I don't hear him too good, his voice is a mile away. The next thing you'd think he's a grocery clerk handing them over to me, and out we go carrying three or four legs under our arms.

"I'm only hoping we don't meet anybody. Mac says we're a little late starting but we'll try this one room anyhow and when we go inside there's a row of slabs, each one with a stiff on it and doctors in gowns standing around. No more than I'm thanking Almighty God we can't use this place than Mac spots the last slab in the corner is empty. The other guys are all turning around to wave hello, nice morning, and we go past nodding with our arms full.

"Now the one thing I hope I can do is just stand there like a wooden Indian. Mac's all absorbed and I open my eyes once in a while to see he's still doing something. I'm about up to here with the smell, which is coming across but good.

"Then what happens, one of the other doctors calls the whole bunch of us over to the stiff he's working on. He asks *me* to hold the head. He draws a line across the top of the forehead with his knife. The dead guy's supposed to have kicked off because he was a hell of a drinker. I'm still holding the head and he gives a rip — pulls the face right down. The sweat comes right out all over me, but thank God this guy doesn't need me any more and McNutt takes hold of me and walks me back over to our slab. The only thing good is it's all gone a little back down from the top of my throat when we get away from there. The others go on jabbering and I'm wondering is the Christawful morning going to end? I almost feel I better tell Mac I've had it, but he's got the legs into a bundle and maybe that's it. But now the guy at the other slab is calling for everybody to look, only Mac and I don't have to go over now. He's wringing out the brain into a jar like a sponge, which gives up maybe a half a pint of alcohol in front of us. It's not funny, this is the time to call it quits, which McNutt sees. We manage to go and put the knees back in the drawers, and dump the gowns and that's it, we're out of there."

That was, I confess, a less than adequate attempt to give the way my father told the story. I miss more than anything the sense of shared enormity his yarns could bring — words passing through the alembic of his dry voice, and helped by his expressive long face. He didn't overtell the stories. His transitions, too, I can't work in — his "B' Jesus," his "N' more than [this] . . . but [that]," his swift evocations of setting. These have gone.

The stint in the morgue with Dr. McNutt does not really grade as an embarrassment. He gave the morning too much of a battle. That phrase, "give something a battle," was a characteristic one of his. He might use it for facing up to an operation one of his children had to go through, or maybe for mustering the will power to walk his twenty snail-paced laps around the dining-room table, as he would do in the last stages of his illness. Such determination meant conquering embarrassment, and proclaims a quality, perhaps *the* quality, that carries an athlete through. In some ways his grip on himself could become exasperating. Not the fight itself, but some offshoots of it: for example, feigning he was all right or even cheerful — as he did on the ward in Irvington that day with Baker, or as he would with Bayer when pain and depression caused him to put in a call to New York, after which, reaching his friend on the phone, he would say incomprehensibly that he felt fine — at which my mother would clench her fists and make as if to wrest the phone away from him to explain the grounds of the call — though she never did. In the morgue, some overchivalric sense kept him from giving McNutt away (nonmedical men weren't supposed to be in the dissection room). You can almost see him, like an umpire battling sunstroke, forcing his physique to stand the gaff, almost as if to keep a bet going. He'd started out that way by letting McNutt roust him from bed in the first place. (Please the doctor before all else.) But laughter rather than applause had to be the reward for carrying the day this time, it was all so nonsensical.

It is fun to think of laughable occasions when, nothing so rigorous being called from him, that free spirit of his got doused. There were some memorable come-uppences, as when, dismounting once from a jitney bus from Disneyland, which was shuttling him and my mother and the Rick Telfairs back to a motel, he got a blowsy young woman's bare behind flashed in his face. It was a humid day, she was getting up just in front of him. Her dress had been annealed to her back by the leather seat, so that as he leaned forward getting out of his seat, her behind (she had on no underclothes) came panning almost flush against his nose. My mother had to hold herself against a lamppost after she got out of the bus: the Telfairs, who saw it all in technicolor and who were probably the laughingest of all my parents' friends, almost went out of their minds at this bonanza: and my father's dignity was never retrieved for those particular three, who had each had a ripe look at his face. Whether the sweat popped out on it is anybody's guess.

It would have been fun to be present, too, at Cameron Field, the public recreation park in South Orange, on Labor Day in 1957 — though I had not earned the right to be there. There was my father in his car — one projects oneself into the back seat to watch him arguing with my mother — thoroughly outfaced by a duck. That morning, down in New Brunswick where I was living, he had staged a baseball trial camp at which I had helped him out. The Easter before, my younger sister had given me a duckling which had now grown into a duck. This animal, Gregory as we called him, was a loud disturber of neighbors' sleep, and had been going around of late destroying tomato plants in the veterans' village where we lived, across the river from Rutgers. My father and my mother, who had made the Labor Day trip down with him, had volunteered that evening to take Gregory over to Cameron Field, which they passed on their way home, and where there was a large pond full of white ducks like himself. Being a pet, he usually behaved himself all right in a box and didn't mind car rides; also, my father knew the director of the field, Mr. Farrell, who lived on the grounds, so that they anticipated no problem in jettisoning Gregory.

What they had not reckoned with was that, this being Labor Day, the park was thronged with people. My father drove in and decided to back down along a path leading to the pond, past many picnickers. He was wearing his Milwaukee Braves uniform. Even having gotten fairly close to the water's edge, he realized he would be a sight getting out of the car — a fifty-five-year-old man in a baseball suit and moccasins, carrying a duck. So when he stopped he told my mother he wasn't going to get out in front of all those people, and she would have to take the duck down to the water. But she hates animals. She fears them in almost every variety. She said she wouldn't do it, so they'd better drive right on back to New Brunswick and give the animal back to me.

That was of course not feasible. Which of them held out longer? My father in his baseball togs. He refused to get out of the car. People were already looking at them and could see the top of the Braves' gray traveling suit — he was not going to expose more. My mother, who is heavy, got reluctantly out, opened the back door, and reached into the back seat, gingerly pushing Gregory's wings together from the top and grabbing him that way. Even that was all right. He was used to being handled. She carried him down and with a kind of underhanded flip lobbed him out into the water. My father, they told me, watched through the rearview mirror. Then the unforeseen happened. Gregory ruddered around and started back in, quacking. Up he came onto the verge, now to make a bee line for the car, trailing my mother. She broke into a run. My father got the engine going, and my mother reached the open back door ahead of the waddling Gregory. Upon which she was driven off like a bandit's moll, leaving the duck squawking and abandoned among the holiday makers.

We never heard a repercussion about it from Mr. Farrell, who perhaps wasn't on the premises that day.

Fifteen years later, almost to the day, on a morning in late August 1972, I was riding behind my father, who was wearing this time his Montreal baseball suit, as we drove toward the Catskills. It was his reprieve year, the one that saw his health hold up because of the success of the testicular operation. In August 1971, as I mentioned, a trip we'd planned in that direction came a cropper because of that bad biopsy result; in August 1973, a family get-together for a week in Southampton, to celebrate my mother's seventieth birthday, was also aborted when a sudden decline in my father's condition forced him to have to return to New Jersey. My mother the chauffer, he'd ridden all the way to the end of Long Island only to tell her she'd have to turn the car around. (Before going back, sick at heart, he foisted a packet of twenty-dollar bills off on my brother-in-law: he'd meant to do the treating that week, especially to duck dinners at John Duck, Jr.'s. The proprietor of that restaurant, who took over from his own father, had been the batboy for the old

Southampton team my father had played for in the days of his courting my mother. To dine at John Duck's was to have been the highlight of my mother's birthday. A thought, if only a pennyweight thought, for Gregory touched our family — my sister who had given him to us was there — when that dinner did come off, minus the two who had planned it.) But from these dates one can see that my father had a year to go before the final setback, and he was hale enough on the 1972 afternoon to be ready to conduct what was to be his last trial camp at Kutsher's.

Why he was driving and not myself was that we had planned to stagger the driving. From Kutsher's, while he was superintending the baseball tryouts, I was going to drive my mother and wife and son up to the Catskill Game Farm. This was a lot farther away than it looked on the map. I remember, when the afternoon got compressed, leaving the others on a bench and actually trotting around the game farm so as to take in as much of the hoofed stock as possible. All this because, to my mother, the key event of the day was to get back at the specified time to Kutsher's — where my father, so she expected, would be well tired out: but this was the pattern of life with him anyway — he the worker around whom timetables were organized, the rest of us a pack of flyabout freebooters.

That morning when we arrived at Kutsher's, an hour before the scheduled time for the workouts, I'd gone with him to learn from Clair Bee where to pick up the bases and who would be helping down at the field and so on. The name of Mac Kinsbrunner came up between them. I'd remembered my father often bawling Kinny out between halves when they were on the Jewels — my father in charge as player-coach. It was always for dribbling too much (Mac was a great dribbler). That day I'd learned that Kinsbrunner had died. Clair and my father, both older, both looking fit, shook their heads — the thing was, Kinny'd been known to have a bad heart, but over the last years had come close to being a millionaire, managing as he did the

Concord Hotel, among the best of the Catskill spas, right up there in Clair Bee country. This nipping of a run of good luck, I think, was moot in the air as they spoke of his sudden death. Bee I could see was a sensitive man — I'd only met him once before, in 1941 when I was twelve, at the Garden after he'd broken my father's winning streak — I didn't want to shake hands with him back then but of course had to. Some newspaper had caught a picture of me crying. Of my father then I remember the withheld, self-punishing anger, after a game in which he hadn't brought his players into contention — so different from the constructive anger sent those times at Kinsbrunner in the locker room. Now here they were, two friends, "Bee and Honey" (as Neil Isaacs called them in an apt chapter on them in *All the Moves*), lamenting a younger third one who'd got so far and then been checked in the prime of life.

It was time to get moving; I had to handle the preliminary baseball arrangements. From his office window Bee pointed out the route to the ball field, set deep in across the road from the main house at Kutsher's. Driving there to drop off my father's equipment, I passed some of the outdoor basketball courts over which the Kutsher's campers were deployed. A day of baseball would be a change of pace for them. So I thought, driving in along a cinder running track, until I saw a group of young campers resting on seats next to this track, who were of all things decked out in football equipment. They were evidently taking a break, at this basketball camp, with a baseball interlude scheduled to come up for them, from a morning *football* session. Helmets, many with the emblems of professional football teams on them, were lying about on the benches or the ground. It was then then the idea was driven home to me, an idea that had become everyone else's byword, as to how America's sports priorities had changed.

We left my father, but were on time getting back, even though this meant pushing pretty well from the time we left the game farm. We needn't have hurried so hard. There he was, behind the backstop on his campstool — campers and adults were scattered along the small grandstand — I heard him call out to someone warming someone up way down the line, "Last pitcher." So they evidently were to have a last inning coming up. The football platoon of Kutsher's campers was gone.

I drove home that evening, but as I say, I sat in the back during the drive up. I hadn't known that, over the course of those past few summers, my parents, sometimes with friends from the baseball scouts' group, had taken to staying overnight at the Concord Hotel on days after trial camps at Kutsher's. Mac Kinsbrunner would invariably roll out the red carpet for them ("It was plush," said my mother) — no wonder this had become a semi-regular thing. I had never been to this place, nor, naturally, were we to go there that summer day. Over the past couple of years, though, my father had told me that he was trying to get Kinsbrunner into the Hall of Fame. He had nominated him a couple of years running.

There may have been something adventitious in this. By which I mean that, notwithstanding how good a ball player Kinsbrunner was, the fact of his summertime role of magnanimous host must have had something to do with my father's championing of him. Had he not run into Mac again, it would have been unlikely to occur to him to promote his name before the Hall of Fame committee. And Mac's success, in the kind of exclusive castle-keep the Concord had become, must have played its part as well.

So on that morning going up to the Catskills, with my mother in the front seat and the rest of us in the back, and my father driving against winding mountains, the hotel itself got somehow mentioned — the fact that if we'd gone to Saratoga last year, we'd have probably stayed one night in Kinny's place, or that very night itself, if he'd been alive. I asked my father was he making any headway these days with his effort to get Kinny into the Hall of Fame: how was all that working out. We must have hit a straight stretch of road about then, for my father turned his head half round, the number on his baseball shirt shifting as he answered, with that kind of rearward lean you sometimes see when a person in a front seat speaks to someone behind. He said with that taken-for-granted rasp in his voice, "How the hell are you gonna shill for a guy that's dead?"

*Heritage.* Not Bob Wanzer of the Rochester Royals, but Ryan Russell, HR's grandson, playing in his first game for the University of Rochester, December 1977.

# Chronology

*1902:* May 31, in Brooklyn, John David Russell born; father John Campbell Russell, mother Helen Keyes Russell

*1903:* August, sister Margaret Russell and future wife Charlotte Graf born

*1918:* November, death of father; begins pro basketball career with St. Mary's Triangles

*1919:* Graduates from Alexander Hamilton High School, Brooklyn

*1920-23:* Plays for Albany (New York State League) and Easthampton, Mass. (Interstate League) with Barney Sedran and Marty Friedman

*1923-25:* With Cleveland Rosenblums, managed by Marty Friedman

*1926:* January, marries Charlotte Graf; April, leads Rosenblums to championship of the new American Basketball League; named to first of four consecutive all-league teams

*1927:* January, bought by George Halas to play for ABL Chicago Bruins: will be playing-manager over the three seasons to follow (and a Chicago Bear for two of them)

*1928:* December, son John born, Chicago

*1929:* March, traded to Rochester Centrals for "pennant insurance"; October, returns to play and manage a last year for Halas's Bruins

*1930:* Returns east to join Paterson Crescents for ABL's final season

*1931:* March, daughter Dotty born, Brooklyn, where family have settled in; ABL forced to disband on account of the depression

*1932:* Joins Trenton Moose of the Eastern League, the club HR named the best of all he played for

*1933:* March-April, Trenton Moose win Eastern League playoffs over Philadelphia, plus special series vs. Celtics and Renaissance, to earn honors as nation's top professional team

*1934:* March, new American League underway, and the Moose beaten in playoffs by Philadelphia; June, graduates from Savage School for Physical Education; September, begins teaching at Kearney High School, and joins Newark Mules for the American League's second season; will also play out of a Brooklyn roller rink this year, for the American Rollers

*1935:* December, daughter Peggy born; by now, playing for the New York Jewels, featuring St. John's Wonder Five, whom HR will manage for four American League seasons; association with owner Eddie Wilde leads to *National Sports Enterprises*, essentially a booking agency lasting till the war, it will involve HR in motorcycle racing and the operation of a baseball pool

*1936:* Signs with Seton Hall College, for first tenure there of seven years, during which HR will win 100 games and lose 33; will also instruct there and pursue bachelor's degree

*1939:* June, receives B. S. degree from Seton Hall; later in the year leaves the Jewels to begin three-year stint as player-coach for Wilkes-Barre Barons' American League franchise

*1940:* Seton Hall squad, led by Bob Davies and Ed Sadowski, post a perfect record, 19-0, but receive no tournament invitations

*1941:* March, Seton Hall ties national college record of 43 straight wins; streak broken by LIU, co-holders of the record, in NIT semifinals; June, completes M. A. degree at NYU

*1943-1945:* With Seton Hall's sports program discontinued during war, accepts job as director in C-O-Two Fire Equipment Company — duties are plant morale and prevention of absenteeism; continues as American League player-coach with Camden and Brooklyn Indians, New York Gothams — and even forms a C-O-Two team for the annual pro basketball tournament held in Chicago; at war's end, August, signs to coach baseball and basketball at Manhattan College

*1945:* HR's 28th and last season as a player, managing Trenton Tigers; Manhattan College basketball record, 15-8; in July, while managing Rutland baseball club, receives Walter Brown's offer to coach Boston Celtics in new major league

*1947:* While coaching Celtics, accepts Boston Braves' scouting job which will keep HR in the organization 21 years, during which time team franchise will shift to Milwaukee and Atlanta

*1948:* With Celtics' defeat by Chicago in April playoffs, suffers loss of basketball job; honoring contract, Celtics have HR manage its Eastern League club, Schenectedy, in November

*1949:* Signs on for second (eleven year) tenure at Seton Hall, where HR will compile 194 wins vs. 97 losses; begins three-year association with Cleveland — Los Angeles Rams, as pass-defense consultant and game scout; also begins job as insurance adjustor for General Adjustment Bureau, Newark

*1950-53:* Seton Hall teams headed by Walter Dukes and Richie Regan compile three-year record of 80-12; in senior year win the NIT with record 27-game win-streak, leading to Coach of the Year honors from N. Y. writers association

*1954-1957:* Final triad of tournament teams at Seton Hall, Dick Gaines and Charley Lorenzo the quarterbacks

*1960:* Retires after 19th season of college coaching, record, 309-138; September-October, on invitation of U. S. Air Force, travels in Europe to give basketball clinics at U. S. service bases

*1962:* Elected to Helms Foundation Hall of Fame as college coach

*1964:* Elected to Basketball Hall of Fame in Springfield as a professional player

*1967:* Retires at 65 from 19 years of service with General Adjustment Bureau

*1968:* Leaves Atlanta Braves and becomes head eastern scout for Montreal Expos, for whom HR will work four years

*1970:* Honored with Scout of the Year award by N. Y. writers and the Hot Stove League (organization of professional baseball scouts)

*1971:* Signees, Joe Torre (Cardinals) and Earl Williams (Braves), named as the National League MVP and Rookie of the Year, respectively

*1972:* At age 70, retires from Expos, signs with Chicago White Sox as scout

*1973:* November 15, dies; gravestone in Totowa, N. J., inscribed, John "Honey" Russell, 1902-1973

# Index

Aaron, Henry, 202
Abbot, Bud, 51
Albee, Edward, 152
Angel, Swedish, 23, 43
Artoe, Lee, 85
Atkinson, Ted, 134
Auerbach, Red, 6, 99

Baisi, Al, 86
Baker, Mac, 196-202, 206
Baker, Polly, 199, 201
Banks, Davey, 93, 188
Barko, Louis, 79
Barry, Pete, 93, 188
Bayer, Irving, 193-196, 199, 206
Beckman, Johnny, 76
Bee, Clair, 117-118, 126-127, 193, 199, 209-210
Beenders, Hank, 117-118
Begovich, Matty, 106
Belliveau, Roy, 121
Bird, Larry, 15
Bloom, Mike, 14, 36-37, 39
Bollerman, Howie, 95
Borgmann, Benny, 5-6, 55, 93
Bray, Ray, 85
Brennan, Joe, 51, 66
Breslin, Jimmy, 161
Brooks, Harry, 123, 125
Brown, Walter, 5, 10, 34-35
Byrnes, Tommy, 56

Cann, Howard, 13
Capone, Al, 78-79
Capp, Al, 127
Carnera, Primo, 83
Case, Everett, 199-201
Churchill, Winston, 153
Cohane, Tim, 119-121

Cole, Dot, 149-151
Cole, George, 149-150
Conaty, Ann, 102
Conaty, Red, 51, 101
Connors, Chuck, 15-16, 35-39, 43, 46-47, 51
Conrad, Joseph, 154, 175
Cooney, Rody, 56
Cooper, Henry, 122
Costello, Lou, 51
Cousy, Bob, 96
Currier, Dean, 135, 145

Davies, Bob, 96, 115-121, 123, 126-127, 201
Dehnert, Dutch, 61, 93, 95, 188
DiMaggio, Joe, 107-108
Donovan, Wild Bill, 153
Dowd, Snooks, 55
Doyle, Arthur Conan, 153-154
Drews, Ted, 83
Drucci, Vincent, 73, 79-80
Duck, John, 208-209
Dukes, Walter, 15, 17, 121-126, 160, 201

Eckman, Charley, 186-188
Eckman, Motormouth (horse), 186
Ehlers, Ed, 23-28, 32, 147
Ely, Gil, 60

Faulkner, William, 152
Felsch, Happy, 70
Fischer, Hank, 159-160
Fitzgerald, Bob, 56
Fortmann, Danny, 83-86, 134
Fool, Tom (horse), 132-134, 197
Friedman, Marty, 51-53, 60
Fulks, Joe, 98

Galinsky, Abe, 92, 103
Gallarneau, Hugh, 85
Garfinkel, Dutch, 24, 28-30
Gehrig, Lou, 107-108
Gerson, Rip, 106, 151-152
Glasco, George, 95-96
Gola, Tom, 126, 134
Gorman, Tom, 140
Gottlieb, Eddie, 98-99
Grange, Red, 83
Green, Henry, see Yorke, Henry
Gunter, Henry, 157, 160
Gunther, Coulby, 3

Halas, George, 9, 57-58, 61, 72, 76-78, 80-83, 92, 133
Halas, Min, 78, 81-82
Hankins, Cecil, 26-27
Hannon, Mickey, 121, 123
Hart, Dick, 172-174
Hearn, Tiny, 95
Hemingway, Ernest, 73
Hemsley, Rollie, 70-71
Herlihy, Pat, 37-38
Hickman, Peck, 123
Hicks, Arthur, 157, 160
Hitler, Adolf, 93
Hollander, Zander, 25
Holm, Bobby, 120
Holman, Nat, 5-6, 13-14, 54-55, 61, 95, 97, 188-192
Honey, Restless (horse), 186.
Hope, Bob, 50
Hutchins, Mel, 19

Isherwood, Christopher, 179
Isaacs, Neil, 210

Jackson, Shoeless Joe, 70
Julian, Doggie, 6, 30

Kaselman, Cy, 97
Kaufman, Marty, 99-100
Kearns, Ted, 93, 95, 97
Keefe, Larry, 160
Kennedy, Ray, 52
Keyes, Eliza, 62
Kinsbrunner, Mac, 4, 41, 96, 106, 209-211

Klein, Willie, 64-65
Kotter, Don, 47
Koufax, Sandy, 170
Kreevich, Mike, 108
Kuhn, Bowie, 156
Kurland, Bob, 12, 22, 27

Lackaye, Carole, 127
Lackaye, Sam, 127-134, 137
Landis, Kenesaw Mountain, 70
Lanheady, John, 66-68, 128
Lapchick, Joe, 93, 187-192
Ligos, John, 121
Lombardo, Guy, 50
Lopat, Eddie, 193
Luckman, Sid, 85
Lynch, Danny, 13
Lynam, Tommy, 111

MacDougald, Gil, 193
MacGilvray, Ronnie, 17-19
Macknowsky, Whitey, 56-57
MacLeish, Archibald, 154
Malone, Ed, 140
Maniaci, Joe, 85
Marvell, Andrew, 154
McAfee, George, 84-85, 87
McBride, Kelly, 54
McCarron, Mike, 23, 56
McGuire, Al, 16, 131
McGuire, Frank, 15-16
McHale, John, 168
McMahon, Don, 171
McNutt, Justin, 202-206
McNutt, Lucille, 203-204
Meyer, Ray, 12
Miasek, Stan, 35
Mikan, George, 12, 22-23, 26, 56
Miller, Henry, 91
Moran, Bugs, 73, 79
Munroe, George, 26-29
Musso, George, 85
Mussolini, Benito, 93

Nash, J. R., 79
Nathanic, Ron, 121
Negratti, Al, 118
Norton, Ken, 13

218

O'Hare, Joe, 17-18
Olsen, Harold, 2, 32-35
O'Toole, Celestine, 102
O'Toole, Frank, 101-102, 104-105, 111
O'Toole, Tommy, 101

Pelka, Bob, 138-148
Perlmutter, Danny, 143-145
Phillip, Andy, 31-35, 131
Plasman, Dick, 85
Posnak, Mack, 4, 106
Powell, Anthony, 179

Quigley, Jimmy, 168-170

Rand, Sally, 64
Ranzino, Sam, 200
Regan, Richie, 15, 17, 121, 130, 157-158, 161
Reynolds, Seafoam, 70-71
Riebe, Mel, 24
Ring, Arnie, 121-126
Ripley, Elmer, 55
Roberts, Robin, 139
Robinson, Jackie, 25
Robinson, Murray, 109-110
Robinson Wilbur, 68
Rosenblum, Max, 52, 54, 59-60, 93
Ross, Alan, 123
Rupp, Adolph, 189-192
Russell, Bill, 6, 121
Ruth, Babe, 107
Ruthenberg, John, 120

Sadowski, Ed, 22-25, 28-30, 39, 41-43, 114-115
Saul, Pep, 56
Saunders, Rusty, 58, 95-96, 98
Scharnus, Ben, 120
Schmeelk, Garry, 58, 72-77, 79-80
Schuckman, Allie, 106
Sedran, Barney, 51-52
Shakespeare, William, 25
Shor, Toots, 155
Smith, Kate, 37

Solodare, Chuck, 73-77
Spindell, Lou, 95-98
Spock, Benjamin, 25
Standlee, Norm, 86
Stark, Dolly, 65
Stevens, Bill, 178-179
Stump, Gene, 26-29, 32
Stydahar, Joe, 83-89
Sugarman, Lou, 76, 99
Sullivan, Artie, 168-170
Sullivan, Ed, 50-51
Swisher, Bob, 86
Szczech, Paul, 131

Telfair, Rick, 191, 206
Terrill, Chick, 199-201
Terrill, Lee, 199-201
Thompson, Big Bill, 80
Thompson, David, 200
Torgoff, Irv, 38
Torre, Frank, 171
Torre, Joe, 171, 174
Trafton, George, 83
Turner, Bulldog, 85

Voss, Tillie, 83

Walsh, Archbishop James, 116
Wanzer, Bob, 20, 56-57
Washington, George, 59
Waugh, Evelyn, 179
West, Jerry, 20
White, Sherman, 127
White, Whizzer, 25
Wilde, Eddie, 108
Williams, Earl, 172-173
Wilson, Hack, 70
Winchester, Phil, 175

Yastrzemski, Carl, 171
Yeats, John Butler, 10
Yeats, William Butler, 10
Yorke, Dig, 181-183
Yorke, Henry, 179-185

Zawoluk, Bob, 15, 17

John Russell's previous books have been about British writers, including *Henry Green: Nine Novels and an Unpacked Bag,* *Anthony Powell: A Quintet, Sextet and War,* and most recently, *Style in Modern British Fiction.*

*Honey Russell: Between Games, Between Halves* was designed by Mark Esterman and Merrill Leffler and typeset in 10 on 13 Trump on a Mergenthaler Linotron. Cover design is by Sandy Harpe. Text is printed on Warren Olde Style, a neutral pH paper, by Edwards Brothers and smythe-sewn in both the paperbound and clothbound editions.